THE
FLIGHT
OF THE
EAGLE

• THE • FLIGHT OF THE EAGLE

• PER OLOF • SUNDMAN

TRANSLATED FROM THE SWEDISH
BY MARY SANDBACH

PANTHEON BOOKS, NEW YORK

Library of Congress Cataloging in Publication Data

Sundman, Per Olof, 1922–
    The flight of the Eagle.

    Translation of: Ingenjör Andrées luftfärd.
    Reprint. Originally published: 1st American ed.
New York: Pantheon Books, 1970.
    1. Andrée, Salomon August, 1854–1897—
Fiction. I. Title.
PT9876.29.U51513 1983   839.7′374   83-3968
ISBN 0-394-71594-2

CONTENTS

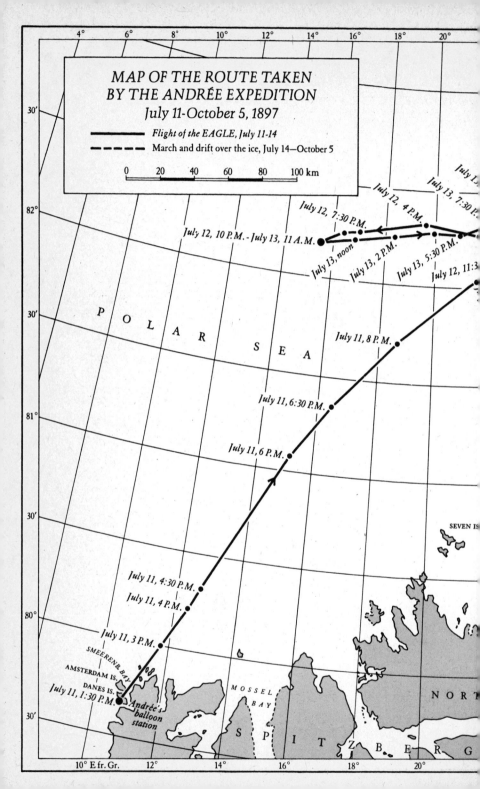

MAP OF THE ROUTE TAKEN
BY THE ANDRÉE EXPEDITION
July 11-October 5, 1897

Flight of the EAGLE, July 11-14
March and drift over the ice, July 14—October 5

0   20   40   60   80   100 km

P O L A R   S E A

July 12, 7:30 P.M.   July 12, 4 P.M.   July 13, 7:30

July 12, 10 P.M. - July 13, 11 A.M.

July 13, noon   July 13, 2 P.M.   July 13, 5:30 P.M.

July 12, 11:3

July 11, 8 P.M.

July 11, 6:30 P.M.

July 11, 6 P.M.

SEVEN IS

July 11, 4:30 P.M.

July 11, 4 P.M.

July 11, 3 P.M.

SMEERENB. BAY

AMSTERDAM IS.

DANES IS.

July 11, 1:30 P.M.

Andrée's
balloon
station

MOSSEL
BAY

S   P   I   T   Z   B   E   R   G

NOR

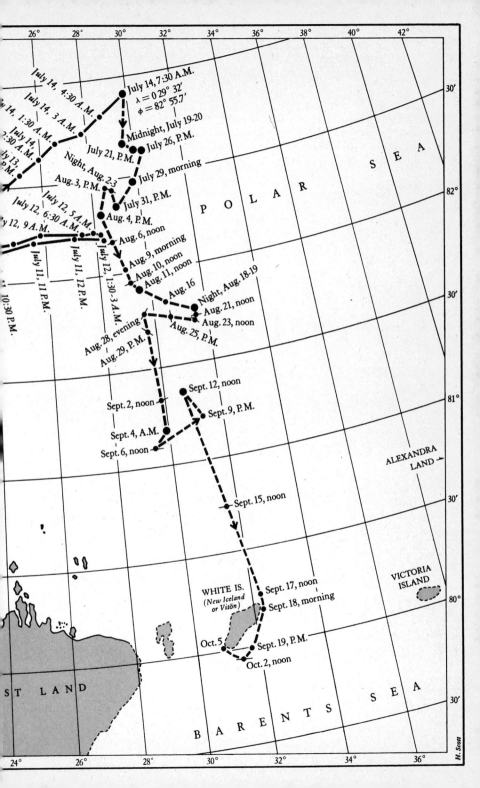

INTRODUCTION

On Sunday, July 11th, 1897, at 13.33 G.M.T. the balloon the *Eagle* took off from Danes Island, Spitzbergen. In the car were Salomon August Andrée, the chief engineer from the Patent Office in Stockholm, and his two young companions, Nils Strindberg, an assistant lecturer at the Technical College, and Knut Fraenkel, a civil engineer.

The object of their journey was, if possible, to reach the North Pole. A strong southerly wind carried the *Eagle* off in the right direction, and it disappeared.

On July 15th a carrier-pigeon was shot by the skipper of the Norwegian fishing-vessel *Alken*. It carried a letter dated July 13th, 12.30 p.m. Two floating buoys with communications from Andrée were found, one in May 1899, the other in August 1900. Their brief messages sounded optimistic. 'Weather delightful.' 'All well on board.' 'In excellent spirits.'

During the next few years relief expeditions were sent out, but no further trace of the *Eagle* or of the three men was found.

In due course the governing body of the Association of Swedish Inventors chose a new member in place of the absent Andrée.

Thirty-three years later, in the summer of 1930, a small Norwegian scientific expedition was in the Arctic Ocean east of Spitzbergen. The leader of the expedition was the geologist Dr Gunnar Horn. He had chartered the little whaling-vessel *Bratvaag,* the crew of which during the voyage was to engage in its usual occupation of sealing. The skipper's name was Peder Eliassen.

On August 5th they reached the island which the Norwegians call Kvitøya or Hvitøya, and the Swedes Vitön. On some charts it is also called Giles Land, White Island or New Iceland.

Vitön, which lies just north of the 80th parallel, is an inaccessible island, with no bays or natural harbours. Very few people—perhaps no more than a hundred to date—have ever had any excuse for landing on it. Usually it is almost entirely covered by ice for the whole year. Only in warm summers is anything more than the extreme edge of its shore of rocks, stones and gravel exposed. The summer of 1897 was a warm summer.

The summer of 1930 was also a warm summer. Peder Eliassen dropped anchor just before midnight. A herd of walrus were sighted, and the following morning two parties were sent out in small boats to hunt them.

Gunnar Horn tells us that when one party went ashore to collect two walrus that had been shot, two young men—named Olaf Salen and Karl Tusvik—went farther inland to look for drinking-water and in their search saw a tiny stream.

When they reached it they saw a dark object close beside a snow-drift. They immediately went up to it and saw that it was a boat protruding through the snow. In the boat they saw the tip of a boat-hook, on which words were engraved.

These words were: 'Andrées polarexp. 1896'.*
They had found Andrée's last camp.

The whole of the *Bratvaag's* crew of seventeen men went ashore. 'It was with very strange emotions that we stood upon the shore where, thirty years ago, the brave Andrée and his companions had reached the end of their last journey. In deep silence we approached the spot where they had camped. There lay their boat, half buried in snow, its stern pointing inland. Beside it lay a sledge—and be-yond it, under a wall of rock, Andrée himself. The Lapp moccasins on his feet were much worn, but otherwise his clothing was in good condition. Beside him lay a gun and a primus stove. There was still paraffin in the tank, and when we pumped, a.fine jet spouted from the burner.'

Andrée and his companions were probably the first people who had ever gone ashore on Vitön.

Everything that could be hacked out of the snow and ice was

---

* Andrée had planned to make his expedition in 1896. He had gone to Danes Island, built the big balloon-house, and filled the *Eagle* with hydrogen gas. But he had waited in vain for southerly winds. He had been forced to give up and return home. The following year he had been able to start. Most of his equipment was marked: 'Aées pol. exp. 1896'.

taken on board the *Bratvaag*. But Gunnar Horn underestimated the interest the world would take in the find he had made. Instead of turning back to Norway he continued on his way to Franz Josef Land. Two days later they met another whaling-vessel, *Terningen*, which was on her way home. And so it was that two days later still, Jensen, the skipper of *Terningen*, was able to report in Tromsö that the last camp of the three balloonists had been found on Vitön.

Both the preparations for and the start of Andrée's expedition had attracted an enormous amount of attention all over the world. It seems that the find on Vitön was an even greater sensation. In no time at all an invasion of journalists from all over the world descended upon the little north Norwegian town of Tromsö. Only Jensen was there to be interviewed. The *Bratvaag* was puffing about somewhere in the Arctic Ocean.

It was not until August 30th, a good three weeks after the landing on Vitön, that Gunnar Horn happened to hear a faint, crackling order from the *Bratvaag*'s wireless, telling him to return immediately to a Norwegian port.

There are well-informed, sensible people who assert that the find on Vitön marks a turning-point in the history of journalism, and that present-day newspaper reportage—hectic, excitable and with a thirst for illustrations—was born in Tromsö in August and September 1930.

All whaling-vessels available in Tromsö were chartered by different newspapers so that they could put to sea in search of the *Bratvaag. Stockholms Tidning* and the *New York Herald* joined forces in one boat, *Dagens Nyheter* (Stockholm) and King Features Syndicate in another. Three aeroplanes were held in readiness to fly photographs back to Stockholm, and while they waited made reconnaissance flights to find the *Bratvaag*.

In 1897 James Gordon Bennett (of Stanley and Livingston fame), the editor of the *New York Herald*, had been prepared to pay Andrée 100,000 Swedish crowns* for permission to send one of his reporters in the *Eagle*'s car. Andrée had refused with thanks. In the autumn of 1930 Gunnar Horn was paid 40,000 crowns* merely for the world copyright of a story of 3,000 words about how the camp on Vitön had been found.

* The value of the Swedish crown in 1897 was about $.27. In 1930 it was equal to about $.26.

Fabulous sums were offered for the rights of first publication of Andrée's diary. The first offer was half a million Swedish crowns. According to newspaper reports this rose later to seven-and-a-half million crowns.

But neither the diary nor the other finds on Vitön were for sale. A Swedish-Norwegian Government Commission had been set up to deal with the matter. It was to be treated seriously and with dignity. Financial speculation was unthinkable.

Vitön was a Norwegian island. The camp had been discovered by Norwegians. All the same the Norwegian Government generously announced that they would present the whole find to Sweden. Swedish newspapers eulogised Norwegian magnanimity in high-flown language.

While journalists from all over the world were jostling one another in Tromsö, a Canadian aviator and a certain Major Burwash found two camp-sites on King William's Land, Greenland. They had belonged to the British polar explorer Sir John Franklin's unlucky expedition of 1845. What had been known as the "Franklin Riddle" was thereby solved once and for all. But no journalists invaded King William's Land. They stayed in Tromsö.

Franklin's expedition cost 129 human lives.

On Andrée's polar journey only three men died.

H.M.S. *Svensksund*, the gun-boat that had taken Andrée and his companions to Danes Island in 1897, was refitted and sent to north Norway to bring home the remains of the three men.

Her southward voyage along the Norwegian coast was one long triumphal procession, albeit a somewhat stormy one. The three coffins, securely lashed to the after-deck, were smothered in flowers.

At Gothenburg they were welcomed home to Swedish soil. The *Svensksund* was escorted into harbour by an enormous fleet of fishing-boats, the church bells tolled, thousands of torches and flares were lit, and 125,000 people lined the quays. A wreath of ivy was presented on behalf of the British Fleet by Captain Nelson.

In Öresund the vessel was met by two Danish men-of-war. The Danish Prime Minister, the Minister for Defence and the Commander-in-Chief of the Danish Navy were on board one of them. Once again the church bells tolled—in Hälsingborg on the Swedish shore, in Helsingør on the Danish. Seven planes from the Danish Air

4

Force circled over the *Svensksund* and threw down wreaths and flowers. Salutes in honour of the dead were fired from the ancient Danish fortress of Kronborg, one a minute for as long as the *Svensksund* was in sight.

Through the Stockholm archipelago the *Svensksund* was accompanied by two destroyers with an admiral, the Commander-in-Chief of the Coastal Fleet, in command.

When the cortège passed Vaxholm the town council presented a wreath with the inscription: 'Noble deeds always win a response from Swedish hearts.'

When she entered the Stream in Stockholm the *Svensksund* was enveloped in the dense smoke of saluting batteries. Air Force planes performed daring dives, and once again the church bells thundered.

King Gustaf V spoke: 'They set off and disappeared into the distance. Their fate only augmented the number of riddles. But at last they have returned home!'

Archbishop Nathan Söderblom spoke in Storkyrkan: 'Your lips have been silenced. But you speak through your deeds. Silently but clearly you say to a whole world: "We have struggled and suffered and died as men. We endured to the end. Our expectations were shattered, but we never gave way to passive regret."'

This wave of hero-worship and enthusiasm hit not only Sweden and Scandinavia. All the newspapers of the Western world watched the progress of events and joined in the chorus of homage.

When the greater part of the photographs taken by Strindberg were successfully developed the *Times* wrote: 'No more remarkable photographs can ever have been restored from death to life', and added that they inspired 'awe and fear'.

Later in the autumn the Geographical Society in Stockholm published the book *Med Örnen mot polen* (English translation: *The Andrée Diaries*). This contained most of the documents and photographs found on Vitön, and appeared simultaneously in English, German, French and Italian, as well as in at least half a dozen other languages, including Esperanto. In Sweden 30,000 copies were sold on the day of publication.

When Andrée and his companions disappeared in their balloon, they left Sweden and the world the 'Andrée Riddle'.

Thirty-three years later when the find on Vitön solved the riddle,

5

Andrée's diary and Strindberg's notes and photographs transformed it into an arctic drama.

The 129 victims of the Franklin expedition were too many. When death is multiple it is unreal. Three dead men are tangible, obtrusive, real—almost alive.

The Andrée riddle, transformed into the Andrée drama, soon developed into a new mystery.

After a long and painful journey the three men had gone ashore on Vitön. Shortly afterwards all three had died. Why? How?

Strindberg had died first. That was indisputable; he had been crudely buried in a cleft in the rock. Andrée and Fraenkel had clearly died lying side by side in the tent, probably within a short time of each other, as neither of them had tried to remove or bury the other's body.

Andrée had shoes on his feet, Fraenkel only socks. But Fraenkel had put on a black mourning-ribbon.

The crew of the *Bratvaag* had a simple explanation: the men had frozen to death. Not in itself impossible. They were fairly lightly clad. But they had plenty of warm clothing lying unused in the boat. It seemed hardly possible that they had frozen to death.

Had they died of starvation? They had quantities of bear meat and seal meat as well as quite a few other provisions.

Another guess was that they might have died from food-poisoning, that their tinned foods were contaminated. There is nothing to suggest that this is plausible.

Others maintained that Strindberg died as a result of an accident, and that the other two died from lack of oxygen in the tent, which falls of snow had sealed too effectively. This theory must be rejected, among other reasons because at the time in question the tent was far too worn and tattered.

The majority of reference books and newspaper articles have accepted the explanation that Andrée and Fraenkel died of carbon monoxide poisoning, caused by incomplete combustion in the primus stove. This is credible, even if the tent was worn and leaky, but it also presupposes that the stove was burning when they died. However, when Gunnar Horn found it in 1930 the stove contained three quarters of a litre of paraffin. A simple theoretical argument—

though a little too complicated to reproduce here—shows that the stove must have been turned off in October 1897; otherwise it could not have contained any paraffin. Andrée and Fraenkel cannot have died of carbon monoxide poisoning.

The question of how the three men had died, especially Andrée and Fraenkel, was discussed in detail in a number of books and newspaper articles throughout the thirties and later.

One thing was clear. The parts of their bodies that had been recovered bore no trace of external injury. They had not been attacked.

In 1952, a Danish doctor, E. A. Tryde, published a book on the Andrée expedition, *The Dead Men on White Island*.

Tryde had read Andrée's diary with the greatest attention, and had taken notes of all the conscious or unconscious references to the symptoms of an illness from which the three men had suffered. He discovered that quite early on in their journey across the ice they had suffered from fever, cramps, diarrhoea, trouble with their eyes (snowblindness), stomach pains, muscular pains, rashes, and small boils.

The combination of these symptoms indicated that their illness was trichinosis, contracted by eating infected bear meat. In the Andrée Museum at Gränna, Sweden, Tryde discovered remnants of two polar bears shot during their journey across the ice. These were subjected to microscopic examination, which revealed that both bears had been infected with trichinae. According to Andrée's notes they had eaten at least twenty meals from these bears. There was good reason to believe that at least some of the bears they had shot earlier on were also infected.

I find Tryde's argument convincing.

If he is right, hundreds of millions of trichinae must have invaded the bodies of the three men shortly after they landed.

Trichinae seek out transverse muscles. The heart has a musculature of this kind, but the trichinae do not like the pulsating contractions of the heart and they move on through the chest. Their passage through the heart leaves a network of tiny pin-point scars.

How many tens of thousands of trichinae passed through the hearts of Andrée and his companions?

A man suffering from severe trichinosis usually dies from general prostration, or from pneumonia, or from sudden heart failure brought on by great exertion.

My novel about Andrée's polar journey of 1897 is a documentary novel founded upon historical facts. All the persons mentioned by name really existed. I have tried to fit them into the historical events with the literary additions that were necessary to make the book a novel.

The book is to a great extent a work of imagination, but my ambition has been to ensure that nothing in it that is imagined should conflict with the known historical facts.

Andrée's diaries are preserved, likewise Strindberg's observation books, his photographs and notes. Knut Fraenkel left us only his brief meteorological notes. It was obvious to me that my novel must take the form of Fraenkel's story.

His story, as I have told it, is apparently objective, but only apparently. In his fictitious account Fraenkel gives *his* version. He arranges his facts. He omits what he wants to omit. Sometimes he lies.

All the same he may possibly graze 'the truth'.

Andrée was a wise and practical technologist, a capable Swedish civil servant. He made only one unwise decision in the whole of his life: the decision to try to reach the North Pole in a hydrogen gas balloon. His expedition, unlike Franklin's, was doomed from the very beginning. And Andrée must have realised it long before the start.

What can have given wings to such a piece of folly? Why did it arouse such boundless enthusiasm? What made these three men— in their own time, and in the thirties—the great heroes they became?

Translated by Mary Sandbach   PER OLOF SUNDMAN

PART ONE

STOCKHOLM
AUTUMN 1896

I

I slept badly on the night preceding that momentous November day, not because I was nervous or uneasy, but because, absurdly enough, I had broken some bone or other in the little toe of my right foot the evening before.

The pain was noticeable when I went to bed and it increased as the night wore on. True, it was not bad enough to prevent me from dozing off, but I awoke every time I moved in my sleep.

On two or three of these occasions I occupied myself by dipping into and reading bits of Flammarion's *Urania* and *The End of the World*, after first trying to make myself as nearly comfortable as I could by humping up the pillows under my shoulders and the back of my head.

At six o'clock in the morning I drew back the curtains from my windows. The winter darkness was still deep. The nearest gas-lamp was a bright blotch that glittered and glimmered in a complicated pattern of ice-crystals on the outer window-pane.

The tiled stove was hot, and a layer of faintly glowing birch-wood cinders several inches thick lay in the fire-box.

I limped as I walked across the floor.

2

A small group of us had met the previous evening for a simple but prolonged supper. Our conversation had circled round authors like von Heidenstam, Levertin and Strindberg, the prosecution of Gustaf Fröding, strayed over to Bjørnson and Ibsen, from them to Nansen, and from him, naturally enough, to Andrée.

The great Norwegian polar expedition had finished on 21 August. For three years the *Fram* had lain frozen fast in the drift-ice. But at last she had dropped anchor in Tromsö harbour, and on that day of 21 August, after the fifteen months that he and Lieutenant Johansen had spent journeying across or wintering on the ice, Fridtjof Nansen had once more set foot on her deck.

On 24 August, a few minutes after twelve o'clock, yet another vessel had dropped anchor at Tromsö. She was the *Virgo* from Gothenburg, and on board her were Andrée, Strindberg and Ekholm, with their balloon dissected and packed away. They had been obliged to leave their base at Danes Island, Spitzbergen, four days earlier.

"Nansen was hailed as a hero by all the newspapers in the world," I said. "His arctic expedition is the most remarkable and the most successful ever carried out—second to Nordenskiöld's North-East Passage. The students in Christiania were as drunk as lords for three days. They processed through the streets singing patriotic songs, and demanding that the Union with Sweden should be dissolved, but only after King Oscar had conferred a title on Nansen, made him a baron or an earl.

"It's not been like that for Andrée," I said. "He planned and started the most daring arctic expedition of all: to fly to the North Pole in a balloon. The Stockholmers hailed him as a hero when he left for Gothenburg by the night train. The Gothenburgers hailed him as a hero when he left the port on the morning of 7 July to sail to Spitzbergen.

"On Danes Island he had the balloon-house erected, the balloon filled with hydrogen gas, and then waited for the necessary southerly winds. The balloon was the most perfect that had ever been constructed, everything had been planned and prepared down to the last detail. The whole world waited expectantly. German, Norwegian, and English vessels had made their way to Spitzbergen and Danes Island in order to give the tourists they carried a chance to witness his departure.

"But it was all in vain," I said.

"Even an engineer who's a genius can't persuade the winds of the heavens to blow in the right direction. The arctic summer is short. In addition the *Virgo*'s insurance policies were so framed that she was obliged to leave Spitzbergen on 20 August at the latest.

"As we know, on Monday, 24 August, 1896, the Norwegian Nansen and the Swede Andrée met at Tromsö, in northernmost Norway.

"Nansen had succeeded," I said. "The whole world now knows who Nansen is.

"The whole world, the whole of the civilized world knew Andrée's name, knew what he'd planned to do in his balloon. It had been discussed not only in Sweden, but also in Berlin, in Vienna, in Rome, in America, in Paris, and in London. But he'd never had a chance to cut the mooring-ropes of his balloon. He'd failed.

"No one knows what those two remarkable men talked about, the man who was famous for what he'd done, and the man who was famous for what he'd intended to do."

My friends condemned what Nils Ekholm had said and done in violent terms. By this time we had reached the coffee and punch stage.

"Coming back to Sweden must have been difficult and bitter," said one of those present, a civil engineer. "To leave a country that is wild with enthusiasm, only to return to a vacuum of disappointed hopes and expectations. He needed support, above all from his two comrades and companions. Strindberg gave him that support, but Doctor Ekholm turned traitor."

I tried to defend Ekholm, or at least to modify this categorical condemnation.

At Danes Island it had become apparent that the balloon was not as impermeable as Andrée had asserted, and that consequently it would not be able to remain afloat as long as had been expected.

It had also become apparent that the friction of the guide-ropes on ice and water was considerably greater than Andrée had calculated, and that the balloon would therefore travel more slowly, which meant that it would need to remain afloat considerably longer than had been estimated in the original calculations.

This was the outcome of the investigations carried out by Doctor Ekholm with the help of Strindberg, Professor Arrhenius, and Stake, the engineer in charge of the apparatus for generating and pumping the hydrogen gas.

"The margins of safety allowed in the matter of time are so generous," said my friend from the ranks of the civil engineers, "that Ekholm's objections are of no consequence, and are in actual fact naïve.

"What's the point," he said, "of the balloon being capable of remaining afloat for a hundred days or even fifty, when you can be sure that it will reach the mainland of North America or Siberia a week after it leaves Spitzbergen?"

He then proceeded to give us a long lecture about the margins of safety that had to be observed when building railway bridges.

"What right," he asked, "has Doctor Ekholm to demand a greater margin of safety in the case of a balloon voyage than he would observe when building a bridge over a river?"

I pointed out that Ekholm had not demanded that the balloon should be able to remain afloat as long as fifty or a hundred days. The others would not listen to me.

"I can accept and forgive the fact that he grew frightened during the time they spent on Danes Island," said one member of our party. "That he was frightened when he saw the balloon lying at anchor in the balloon-house, that he was frightened when he saw the fragile car, when he felt the icy cold polar winds whistling round his cheeks and the back of his neck, when he became aware of the fiendish immensity of the distances, when he suddenly realized that the ice-fields were pitiless and that he hadn't previously had any idea of what he now found himself about to embark upon."

"Go on," I said.

"He could have withdrawn quietly, simply told the press that he didn't intend to volunteer next summer. Then we should all have known that he was a coward. We should have forgiven him and forgotten him."

"But?" I asked.

"He felt he had to defend himself, to justify his fear. And he chose to attack Andrée. That's what we can't forgive and accept.

14

He accused Andrée of incompetence and carelessness over their equipment. Ekholm didn't retire quietly. In the midst of all his fears the thing he feared most was the judgment of posterity. He turned traitor. He wrote insidious letters to the people financing the expedition, Alfred Nobel and Oscar Dickson in Gothenburg. He forced on us the entirely meaningless public discussion between himself and Andrée at the Physics Society a couple of months ago."

"On 26 September," I said.

"On that day," said my friend from the ranks of the civil engineers, raising his glass, "a considerable number of Stockholmers had an opportunity of personally inspecting two totally different human beings: a very great man and a very small man."

"It's possible that he also wrote a letter to the third of the chief subscribers," I said. "To the King, I mean.

"Monarchs, however, make it a rule to be discreet and reticent.

"In your condemnation of Doctor Ekholm," I added, "you seem to have forgotten one interesting point.

"His withdrawal means that there is a vacancy, that Andrée will have to find a successor, a new third man who is prepared to fall in next summer.

"I can't imagine that there are many people who want to float between the heavens and the ice," I said.

Invigorated by the punch I placed two chairs with their backs together, ripped off my jacket and took a firm hold with my right hand on the two curved pieces of wood that formed the upper part of the backs.

Then—to the applause of the rest—I assumed the position known among gymnasts as the one arm elbow lever. That is to say: a firm grip round the backs of the chairs, the body horizontal with the chest resting on the upper part of the right arm, legs straight and the left arm stretched forward to maintain balance.

"How long can you keep it up?" someone asked.

"That depends on how much you pay me per minute," I answered, and added: "I'd give five years of my life if I could accompany Andrée on his polar voyage next year."

Someone took off my right shoe and tickled the sole of my foot. I lost my balance and leapt from the backs of the chairs. That was when I broke some bone or other in my little toe against a half-open door.

3

I put some logs into the stove and let them burn up with the door of the fire-box open.

My toe had swollen and looked like a great blue abscess.

Winter seemed to have arrived early. Streets and pavements were white with cold snow that crunched under wheels and runners and the soles of shoes.

The sky was clear, the sun gave no warmth, the smoke from the chimneys rose in pillars above the roof-tops. From the hill up Drottninggatan I could see that they were slaking coke out at the gasworks. The enormous cloud of steam moved slowly upwards.

My foot ached and I walked with difficulty, but I was in no hurry and could treat myself to a short visit to the waxworks in the Panopticon at Kungsträdgårdsgatan.

The waxwork Andrée had always made a strange, almost repellent impression on me, although it was said to be a faithful likeness: well-combed hair with the parting exactly above the left eye, tightly clenched jaws, a moustache that concealed the upper lip and the corners of the mouth, a powerful nose, puckered eyebrows that met in a deep line immediately above the bridge of the nose.

The Andrée panorama in the Panopticon had been arranged three years previously, immediately after his solitary and stormy voyage over the Åland Sea in his balloon, the *Svea*.

The dummy's clothes were authentic. They were those that Andrée had worn during the voyage, and I had heard a rumour that he had sold them to the waxwork cabinet, and that they, and some scientific instruments that had been ruined when he crash-landed, had fetched a sum of more than one thousand crowns.

At this early hour of the afternoon the Panopticon had not many visitors. The young girl at the entrance could safely leave her counter and come to meet me. She gave me a friendly smile. Yes, I had indeed visited the place many times. There was certainly no point in denying it.

"I'm trying to see myself as a waxwork," I said, "captured and crystallized at the moment when I—or the waxwork—am placing a pole bearing the Swedish flag on the northernmost point of the Earth's axis."

She burst out laughing. She then measured me with her eyes and declared that I should be an expensive dummy. "Wax costs a lot of money," she said, "even if it's eked out with tallow and stearin."

Clearly she had no idea of how waxworks were made.

4

The Patent Office, or the Royal Patent and Registration Office, as it has been called since last year, was situated at Brunkebergstorg, in the building sometimes referred to as Folker's House.

The cabbies waiting on the square had begun to build their traditional snow-hut close to the big pump. They had managed to build foundations of a sort out of hard-packed snow, which they were just drenching with water, but they were working without much enthusiasm, well knowing that the first snow would probably soon melt.

A number of the cabbies had got out their sledges and bell-collars the more easily to tempt customers. At the onset of every winter ladies in particular seemed to find riding in a sledge a pleasurable novelty.

At the Patent Office I was met by an assistant engineer called

Kuylenstjerna who asked me to sit down for a moment as Andrée had another visitor.

Kuylenstjerna examined me closely and curiously and, after a couple of introductory remarks, asked if I was applying for some post or appointment.

"In a sense yes," I answered.

"I'm the chief engineer's closest colleague," he said, "and I've not heard anything about any new posts.

"There are nine of us engineers here," he added hastily, and almost apologetically. "And then of course there's Andrée, the secretary, and the registrary, Swalin. But the Count's always on the alert and is full of ideas. He has the right connections and knows what technology and development need."

"Which count?" I asked, though I knew perfectly well to whom he was referring.

"Count Hugo Hamilton," he replied, "the Head of the Office."

Kuylenstjerna gave me a wordy and by no means entirely trustworthy account of Count Hugo's contributions as a Civil Servant, and dwelt particularly on the fact that it was Hamilton who, about ten years previously, and in spite of protests from many quarters, had been responsible for the first purchase of a typewriter by a Government Department. "It was a Bar-Lock machine," he said, "and it still stands on a little table in the Count's office. He uses it occasionally, though perhaps mostly for fun."

He asked if I should like to see the new typewriter belonging to the Patent Office, a modern decidedly more rapid machine made by Underwood.

I politely declined.

5

Kuylenstjerna accompanied me to Andrée's room. He then retreated backwards and shut the door after himself.

"Engineer Knut Fraenkel?" asked Andrée.

"Yes," I answered.

"Please sit down," he said, pointing with his pen to a somewhat worn and shabby armchair in front of his big desk.

I sat down.

"Please excuse me," he said, "but I must make a few notes. It won't take many minutes."

He bent forwards. His pen scratched across the paper.

His resemblance to the waxwork in the Panopticon was certainly very great. Nevertheless there were small but noticeable differences.

The many fine wrinkles under his eyes.

The horizontal furrows on his forehead.

The hint of grey in his hair, especially at the temples

The slightly hollow cheeks.

The curved line of worry and disappointment clearly visible between his mouth and his chin.

And then the expression of incipient weariness, which was quite undeniably there, but which was so difficult to define or describe.

"I have your letter here," he said.

"I have your reply here, Chief Engineer," I answered, and laid my hand over the inner left-hand pocket of my jacket.

A rather long interval of silence followed. Andrée studied me critically, but not at all in the way Kuylenstjerna had done fifteen minutes earlier. He sat quite motionless in his chair. His eyes never left mine. His face was very serious.

"I hesitated for a long time before I wrote," I said.

"Why?"

"I was probably afraid of getting no for an answer."

"You're an engineer?"

"I passed my final examination at the Technical College this spring."

"Why do you want to go with me?"

"I should very much like to be one of the first three people to set foot on the ice of the North Pole."

"No other reason?"

"Yes," I answered, "there is perhaps another reason."

"What is it?"

"In your lecture at the Academy of Science in February last year, Chief Engineer, you put forward the view that the pack ice and pressure ice round the Pole were practically impassable for those travelling on foot. That was why someone ought to make use of a balloon. But supposing that, by reason of some mishap or other, a forced landing on the ice, or in Siberia, or Canada, or Alaska became necessary, I think I could be very useful."

"I've always disliked this damned Swedish and German use of titles," said Andrée. "Herr Chief Engineer, and so forth."

"I grew up in Jämtland," I said. "I'm used to snow and ice and cold, and I've made longer winter journeys above the tree line than Fridtjof Nansen had done before he made his famous journey on skis across the Greenland ice-sheet eight years ago."

Another long period of silence ensued. Andrée kept his eyes fixed seriously on me.

On the wall behind him hung a little picture, behind glass and with a narrow black frame. Masses of people, a balloon, a building with a tower.

"The first ascent in Sweden," he said. "The launching took place from Observatory Hill in September 1784, and the balloon was designed by Baron Silverhielm and Professor Wilcke."

"Gustaf III and the Crown Prince were present," I said, "but it was the Queen who cut the last mooring-rope. The balloon landed somewhere in the archipelago, on Värmdö I believe. The passenger, a cat, made off into the woods, and was never found again."

"I bought the drawing in a little bookshop in Västerlånggatan," said Andrée. "It was a hydrogen balloon."

After hesitating for a moment I said: "It's not a drawing, it's an engraving. Many people think it must be the work of Elias Martin."

Andrée's eyes never left mine.

"Elias Martin was a great artist," I said.

"I'm sure, Chief Engineer, that you know who Elias Martin was.

"It may be," I continued, "that in actual fact the experiment with that balloon in the autumn of 1784 wasn't really the first of its kind in Sweden.

"I'm thinking of the attempt to fly a balloon that Grahn and Geijer had made about nine months earlier," I said.

"Geijer?" said Andrée, and leant across the table still without taking his eyes from me.

"No, not the great Geijer, not the poet, but a member of the same family. All Geijers are related to one another, aren't they?

"And Professor Robertson's ascent at the beginning of this glorious century. And Tardini's and Count Sparre's. Tardini was an Italian. Tardini was a genius. No one now remembers his name. How many forgotten geniuses there must be."

"You appear to have studied the history of ballooning," said Andrée.

"Take the ascent made by Sparre and Tardini. That was quite certainly the first time in Sweden that a balloon went up with human beings as passengers. It's said that they had a reindeer with them in the car, as if they had expected to drift very far towards the north. In fact they came down on Värmdö, just like the cat from Observatory Hill.

"After that there were all those foreign balloonists: Sivel, Blanchard, Viktor Rolla, drowned and dead after his ascent from Mosebacke five or six years ago, and ladies, Fanny Godard, Poitevin, and Cordula Alfonso; Eugen Pascal (another man with a name more famous than he was himself!), the corpulent Feller who, according to report, smashed himself to bits against the earth in the neighbourhood of Vienna, just as Tardini, whom I mentioned just now, in his day, smashed himself to bits against the primary rock of Sweden."

Andrée had sat listening to me, silently, observantly.

"Of course they were balloonists," he said, "but they weren't *aeronauts*, merely a variety of light-hearted showmen.

"And," he added, "Professor Roberts's title was self-assumed. His name, by the way, was not really Roberts but Robertson, and he came from Belgium. You also forgot to mention the famous Francesco Cetti."

No, I had not forgotten Cetti. It was of course with Cetti, in his balloon the *Christiania*, that Andrée had made his first ascent in the late summer of 1892, just a little over four years ago.

That was the year I had started my studies at the Technical College.

I had with my own eyes seen three balloonists: Rolla, when he made the voyage that was to be his last, the Italian Cetti, and Andrée.

"Cetti was a Norwegian subject," said Andrée.

"Wasn't he also a clever musician?"

"I'm not the right person to express an opinion on that subject, or say whether he was eminent, capable, mediocre or a charlatan," answered Andrée.

"Oddly enough," he went on, "it would appear that listeners who are otherwise exceedingly knowledgeable and critical have a marked tendency to overestimate the musical abilities of a balloonist."

He then smiled for the first time.

"And," he continued, "people are also much disposed to attach particular value to opinions on politics or popular philosophy that emanate from aeronauts.

"Cetti, as it happens, was also famous as a thought-reader."

"You must have many people to choose from now that Doctor Ekholm has retired," I said.

"To tell you the truth," he replied, "there were more applicants last year. Among many others there was an inventor and wood-carver from Småland called Axel Petersson. One of those rural geniuses. Another candidate was a writer and journalist. His name was Pelle Molin, and he was at that time up in Lofoten, in the north of Norway—or was it Bodö? I refused with thanks and he died almost immediately afterwards of consumption, or a disease of the liver."

"Molin was a gifted writer," I said. "I know that Gustaf Geijerstam is busy making a collection of his short stories which he intends to publish as a book."

"This year," said Andrée, "this autumn, there are considerably fewer candidates."

22

He removed his gaze from my face, opened the left-hand cupboard of his desk, pulled out a drawer, laid a bundle of documents on his desk and ran his eye through them.

"Five Doctors of Philosophy," he said, "plus a professor, that makes six academics. Five officers from various branches of the services, artillerymen, infantrymen, and sailors. Two engineers, three if we include you, Engineer Fraenkel. A captain from the Merchant Navy, and a forestry official.

"In addition," he said, "there are a number of foreigners. But my balloon is after all a Swedish balloon, and it must have a Swedish crew."

"Naturally," I said.

Andrée arranged the letters and documents in a neat bundle and replaced them in a drawer of the left-hand cupboard of his desk.

I was thankful to escape for a while from his scrutinizing and critical gaze.

"You've literary interests?" he asked.

"Unassuming ones," I replied.

"Do you paint?"

"No."

"Make music?"

"Not even for myself."

"I'm a bit afraid of aesthetes," he said. "The Pole is no place for them."

6

We walked in silence to the Opera Cellar where an extremely polite and attentive head waiter took charge of us. "It's cold outside," he said, "but it's arctic in here. Baron Nordenskiöld came in a short time ago, and now, Herr Chief Engineer, you have arrived."

He was right, Adolf Nordenskiöld was indeed dining there with a young lady and an officer.

Nordenskiöld rose. Andrée and he went up to each other and shook hands warmly. They stood together on the floor of the dining-room and conversed for quite a while. The other visitors to the restaurant looked openly or on the sly at the two well-known men. Their conversation was conducted in undertones, but I could hear that Nordenskiöld had a strong Finnish accent, and it reminded me that the man who, in a Swedish vessel and under the Swedish flag had conquered the ice of the North-East Passage, had been born and brought up as a Finnish or a Russian citizen.

The head waiter hesitated for a few moments and then showed me to a table for two. I was wearing rough, everyday clothes, and I had not shaved. This was the first time I had been to the Opera Cellar.

Professor Nordenskiöld returned to his meal and Andrée sat down beside me.

"I told you just now," he said, "that the North Pole was no place for aesthetes. I might have expressed myself more clearly.

"There are those who maintain," he said, "that Andrée is a damned iceberg, a callous engineer and technician. Andrée never reads poetry. Andrée can't endure music. If he ever goes to the Opera it's solely to point out the technical defects of the scene-shifting equipment. If Andrée buys a novel it's because he wants to find new evidence of the way in which industrialism has influenced language. If he goes to the preview of a picture exhibition you can be sure that the gossip columns next day will tell you that Andrée searched in vain for pictures about new milk-separators, turbines, electric motors or geodetic instruments.

"There are those," he said, "who fancy that there is no other form of creative imagination than the one that expresses itself through literature, painting, and music.

"But has there ever been a poet or a painter who has had such a powerful imagination, or dreamt such magnificent dreams as Johannes Kepler, or as Galileo, or Newton, or Polhem, or Pasteur?"

"Or Nordenskiöld," I said.

"There are few people who have made such a difference to my life as Nordenskiöld," answered Andrée. "Without his encouragement and his support in the Academy of Science my expedition would never have come about."

He continued:

"I don't despise poets, or painters, or composers. I don't underrate their importance. But at times—quite often—they seem to me to be engaging in a kind of philately. I don't mean that they collect stamps. I mean that what they do resembles philately. The value of a stamp starts by corresponding to what is calculated to be the average cost of transporting a letter from one place to another. A stamp that has been used and post-marked is valueless. A stamp can only be used once for its original purpose.

"But," said Andrée, "these used stamps suddenly acquire a new value. This has nothing to do with their sensible use—they have already been used—it arises from the fact that a number of persons have begun to *collect* stamps, to stick them into books, to study them under a magnifying-glass, to arrange them according to their value and year, to draw distinctions between qualities of paper and postmarks, to discuss perforations and variations in colour.

"Four years ago," he said, "the British Museum in London received by testamentary gift several kilogrammes of stamps that had been collected by a gentleman by the name of Tapling. The collection was valued at two million Swedish crowns. A false value, a figment of the imagination."

"Supply and demand," I said.

Andrée had ordered lobster, four halves, and soft rye-bread and white wine to go with it. I had not eaten any cooked food all day and I should have preferred to get my teeth into a cutlet, or a substantial piece of beef.

"People succeed in explaining far too much by citing *supply* and *demand*," said Andrée. "There are times when I question the position I myself have adopted as a liberal politician."

"Two million crowns," I said. "If he'd had two million crowns in the bank Nansen would have been able to get together four expeditions to be frozen into the pack ice of the Polar Basin."

I was unaccustomed to eating lobster in public, and I tried to crack the shell, suck it and scrape out the flesh as Andrée did.

We were sitting side by side, not opposite each other.

* * *

Andrée raised his glass.

"Or," he said, "with that sum of money one could equip fifteen balloon expeditions to the North Pole."

"I've never collected stamps," I said.

Andrée smiled for the second time that day. He leant back at an angle and raised his eyebrows. The solemn expression left his cheeks and his mouth, and a drop of wine or saliva hung from his moustache.

"But you understand, Engineer Fraenkel?"

"I'm not sure. Perhaps."

"Try to think," he said. "Can you remember a single artist or poet who has hit on the idea that one might reach the North Pole by means of a hydrogen balloon?"

"No," I answered.

"It takes an engineer to hatch such a splendid idea as that," he said.

"Or a one-time dentist," I said.

Andrée glanced at me in surprise, and then burst out laughing as if at a good joke. I realized that Andrée did not know that twenty years before our time Henry Coxwell, originally an English dentist and later, among other things, an officer in the German Balloon Corps, had written and published detailed plans for polar journeys by balloon.

I did not mention this fact to Andrée.

"Jules Verne wrote a book about a voyage by balloon that lasted for five weeks," said Andrée. "They had it in their library on the *Fram*. Captain Sverdrup told me so when he came ashore at Danes Island this summer and I showed him my balloon.

"That was when we heard that Nansen had left them and was trekking across the ice.

"They'd read Verne's book, and had made up stories during those long winters about a balloon that might suddenly appear and break their isolation.

"They knew nothing about my expedition," said Andrée. "If the winds had been favourable they might really have seen a balloon come floating over the Arctic Ocean."

After our meagre dish of lobster Andrée ordered two large portions of orange cream and a small bottle of sherry, with slices of cream cake, coffee, and brandy to follow.

He seemed to have relaxed and behaved at times as if he had forgotten the reason for our being together.

He told me that the young lady at Nordenskiöld's table must be the latter's daughter-in-law, Anna, who had been a widow for two years, and was the daughter of Consul General J. W. Smitt.

"The lieutenant is serving with the Norrland Artillery Regiment," I said. "I was brought up in Östersund."

"He's probably a relative of Nordenskiöld's," said Andrée. "I've not seen him before. I seldom forget a face."

The lieutenant of artillery had a narrow face, a high forehead, closely cropped hair, low-set ears, an abbreviated chin, an upward turned moustache, alert and slightly protruding eyes under heavy eyelids, a prominent, pointed nose, and withal a voice which, despite its low pitch, was arrogant and very audible, and an extremely self-assured and confident manner.

"I haven't seen him before either," I said. "It's true that I find it hard to remember faces, but there are some faces it's hard to forget."

"I was alone on my many ascents in the *Svea*," said Andrée. "I had no choice. The balloon was quite simply too small for two. I sometimes thought it was too small even for a single individual.

"After my last voyage—it only lasted just over three hours, and covered two hundred and sixty kilometres—the *Svea* was more like a sieve than a balloon. That was in March last year, and there was snow on the ground beneath me.

"Even on my first ascent I found being the only person in the car inconvenient. One balloonist on his own hasn't time to carry out all the scientific observations that are necessary, and which are the only acceptable reason for his being where he is.

"This is particularly the case during his ascents and landings, and is so to an even higher degree if he is using a dirigible balloon that has guide-ropes and a sail.

"My polar balloon," he said, "is going to have a crew of three. Even after my first ascent in the *Svea*—in the summer of 1893—I realized that to be properly equipped for a voyage a balloon must have three men in the car."

"I know," I said. "I've read the reports in the journals of the Academy of Science. Three men: a navigator, an observer, and a secretary."

Andrée took the glass of brandy between his hands, warmed it, held it under his nose and inhaled the aroma with a few slow, deep breaths.

"I was a novice at that time," he said.

"But I was on the right track. There must be a crew of three on a balloon going to the Pole. They mustn't be mere specialists; one a navigator, one an observer, and one a secretary.

"One of them must be the leader," he said, "and each one of them must have his clearly defined scientific duties. But they must also be able to replace each other, since they cannot all remain awake during a journey which may last for seven, or for thirty days.

"What I need," said Andrée, "is two companions who both know how to manage and navigate a balloon, who are sufficiently critical and knowledgeable to make reliable observations, and who can formulate those observations intelligibly.

"They must also possess determination and courage," he added.

"I've never made any ascents in a balloon," I answered, "but I think I shall be able to learn the essentials pretty quickly. The scientific observations aren't likely to cause me any trouble."

"I'm sure you also possess determination and courage," he said.

I picked up my bulbous glass as Andrée had his, warmed it between the palms of my hands, held it under my nose, and inhaled the aroma with long, deep breaths.

"Now listen, my dear Fraenkel," he said.

"Yes."

"I don't want to *persuade* anyone into coming with me," he said. "I didn't persuade Doctor Ekholm into coming. I invited him and he accepted. There was no ascent this summer. We were forced to come back. After our return he voiced his doubts about the possibility of carrying out the expedition in various ways."

"I know," I said.

Andrée continued.

"I didn't try to persuade him to keep his promise any more than

I had originally tried to persuade him to come with me."

"Everyone knows that," I said.

"The same applies to Nils Strindberg," he said. "I chose him from a large number of candidates. I certainly had no need to make any attempt to persuade him. He put himself voluntarily at my disposal. But he, unlike Ekholm, has declared time after time that he stands by his decision, which holds good for the expedition next summer too. I've no intention of persuading him if he should change his mind during this winter or next spring."

A couple of minutes' silence then ensued, during which Andrée consumed his remaining bit of cake, wiped his mouth, and got the waiter to fill up our coffee cups and our glasses.

"Now listen, my dear Fraenkel," he said once again. "I've read your letter, you've had my brief note in reply, we've met today. I've also obtained various pieces of information about you in a number of different ways."

We were sitting side by side. When Andrée spoke it was to the air in front of him. Sometimes his head was tilted back, sometimes the underside of his chin was pressed against his stiff collar and his necktie. Now and then he scrutinized the other guests in the Opera Cellar through narrowed eyelids.

"I'm willing to accept you in Doctor Ekholm's place," he said, "as the new third man of the expedition."

He did not turn towards me. He moistened his right forefinger and let it glide round and round the rim of his brandy-glass until a faint but piercing note slowly became audible.

"But," he said.

"But what?"

"We won't settle things finally this evening," he replied. "I give you two days in which to make up your mind."

"It's not necessary," I said.

"Yes," he said. "You must have two days in which to think things over again, Engineer Fraenkel. Or three days. You must be quite clear what it is you are embarking upon."

His finger glided quicker and quicker round the rim of the glass. His lips parted in a frank smile.

"You must understand clearly that your *decision* is your *decision*, and not *mine*."

"Of course."

"Think everything over," he said. "Think it over once more, twice, three times. My balloon voyage will be a risky and dangerous voyage. You must make up your own mind."

He raised his hand defensively.

"Come and see me the day after tomorrow, or in three days' time. Meanwhile you can have all the information you require about the balloon and the technical premises for the expedition. You can get it from me, or from my assistant, Strindberg, or from the sceptical Doctor Ekholm. But you must think everything over many times. You must be fully aware of what it is you are embarking upon, and you must be absolutely clear that you are completely free, and that your decision is the decision of a free human being."

"At what time the day after tomorrow?" I asked.

"The *New York Herald*," said Andrée, "the big American newspaper. It's owned by James Gordon Bennet Jnr., the son of James Gordon Bennet Snr."

"Surely it was he," I said, "who sent Stanley into the depths of darkest Africa?"

"He's offered me a hundred thousand Swedish crowns if I will let one of the men from his paper come with me as the third man of the expedition," said Andrée. "A hundred thousand crowns. The total cost of the expedition up to now, including the balloon-house, and the journey to and from Spitzbergen doesn't amount to a hundred and thirty thousand.

"Of course I've nothing against Americans," he continued. "On the contrary, I've a great respect for their drive, and their advanced technique. But a Swedish polar balloon must be manned by Swedish aeronauts. I wrote a friendly letter of refusal to James Gordon Bennet."

After a further interval of silence Andrée said: "When I made my first trip in a balloon with the admirable Italian-Norwegian, Francesco Cetti, I watched myself closely. I hadn't hesitated for an instant before I notified him of my desire to make an ascent. I didn't feel nervous before the start—apart from the normal tension one always experiences when confronted by something new and important. That was why I watched myself. I wanted to find out if I was afraid or not.

"I count that as my first voyage in a balloon. It's true that I'd made an ascent in Brussels, at the time of the exhibition, in Giffard's giant balloon. But that was only a *ballon-captif*, a captive balloon, which was cautiously allowed to go up a short way when it wasn't too windy. The capacity of Giffard's balloon was twenty-five thousand cubic metres of hydrogen. It was five times larger than my polar balloon, and there must have been forty-five people in the car, among them many women.

"So, when I made the ascent with Cetti four years ago I watched myself closely.

"That was in August. There was a light westerly breeze. The balloon was small, hardly five hundred cubic metres. The mooring-ropes were untied, we took off. A great crowd had collected. I remember all those upturned faces and how rapidly they diminished and disappeared beneath us.

"I ransacked myself. I found that I was breathing calmly. My mouth was not dry. My armpits were not sweaty. We rose higher and higher. I leant over the side of the car. Stockholm, with all its streets, squares, houses, islands, bridges, and water lay far beneath us, and I was able to look at it all without the least trace of dizziness. I was not conscious of the slightest feeling of fear.

"All the same, I can't exclude the possibility that I was afraid. You see I'd observed that during the first phase of the ascent my hands had gripped two of the six or eight car-lines, as if I dreaded that they would break and the car crash, while I should save myself from falling by hanging to a rope. My grip on the lines was so fierce that my fingers had gone white. The muscles of my arms were almost convulsively knotted.

"Cetti too was watching me closely.

"When we reached a height of six hundred metres—according to Cetti's by no means trustworthy barometer—he said: 'Herr Chief Engineer, you are ominously calm.'

"He spoke perfect Norwegian if you discount his Italian accent. He'd come to the conclusion that the Herr Chief Engineer was '*uheldig lun*', ominously calm. These balloon showmen, these commercial aeronauts, they count on their passengers to be terrified

I was, outwardly at least, calm and self-possessed. That's to say I was a disappointment to Francesco Cetti.

"A free-sailing balloon moves, as you know, at the same speed as the air," said Andrée. "I knew this beforehand of course, but the complete absence of wind round the car surprised me nevertheless. The flag and the brightly coloured cotton streamers with which the balloon was decorated hung limp and motionless. The balloon rose fairly slowly and at a steady pace. I'd no sensory appreciation whatever either that we were rising, or that we were moving eastwards. I was seized by the strange illusion—which I found it hard to shake off—that the balloon was absolutely stationary, while the earth was sinking away under us and at the same time turning westwards.

"Cetti brought the balloon down on a field close to Bogesund castle.

"Soon after we landed Baron von Höpken came driving up in a pony-trap. He ordered his servants to help us to empty and pack up the balloon and invited us to an excellent meal. In the witty speech that he made when proposing our healths he said that he was sorry he could not offer us any more high-flying bird than a pheasant."

We went on sitting for a long time at the Opera Cellar. Andrée seemed tired and our conversation—it was he who did most of the talking—strayed from one topic to another.

When Professor Nordenskiöld left the dining-room he did not get up, he merely raised his hand by way of farewell.

"I remember when Nordenskiöld's ship the *Vega* came gliding into the Stream at Stockholm," he said. "It was in April, sixteen years ago, the greatest day in the history of our country. The *Vega* had begun her voyage twenty-two months previously. She'd sailed up the Norwegian coast, rounded the North Cape, crossed the Murmansk Sea, passed the northernmost tip of the Taymyr Peninsula, made her way through the whole of the Siberian Arctic Ocean, wintered where the Longa Straits become the Bering Straits, and finally reached Yokohama, on the east coast of Japan. There was a telegraph station there and Nordenskiöld was able to inform the whole world that the North-East Passage was conquered at last."

"I was only a child," I said, "but I remember reading about the *Vega*'s homecoming in the *Östersund Post.*"

"You're twenty-six," said Andrée.

"I shall be twenty-seven in a few months' time," I answered.

"I'm forty-two," he said. "Nordenskiöld was already forty-five when the *Vega* weighed anchor."

He smiled for the third time that day. He signalled to the waiter, asked him to remove the coffee cups and brandy glasses, and ordered a quarter bottle of port wine.

"I'm childishly fond of port wine," he said, and turned towards me, still smiling.

I suddenly noticed something very peculiar about his eyes. They quivered, they moved to and fro laterally with tiny, very rapid oscillations. I had never noticed this before, not even on the occasion of my visit to his office, though we had then sat facing each other.

These vibrating eyes confused me and he turned his face away so hastily that I realized that he, in his turn, had noticed that I had become aware of them.

"In Tokyo Nordenskiöld was received by Mutsuhito, the Mikado," Andrée continued. "His journey home took over half a year and was the longest triumphal journey the world has ever known. In Hongkong he lived in the palace of the English Governor, and was presented with an address of homage signed by four hundred people. In Aden he was greeted by a salute of twenty-one guns, and by naval vessels flying the Swedish flag from their mainmasts. In Cairo balls were arranged and a celebration dinner was given out at the Pyramids.

"In Naples he was welcomed back to Europe by cannon that fired a double Swedish salute, and by Prince Belmonte at the head of the students and an enormous gathering of people. King Umberto gave a banquet for him in Rome. King Ludvig did the same in Lisbon. More homage was paid to him in London; and in Paris there was a week of banquets, the first given by the President, the last by Victor Hugo.

"The circle was closed in Öresund. A vessel had sailed all round

33

the Eurasian Continent for the first time.

"In Copenhagen the Danish Royal family awaited him. Many of the students from Lund were also there, for King Oscar had decreed that Nordenskiöld should first set foot on Swedish soil at the Palace, in Stockholm.

"I'd travelled up to Stockholm from Småland," said Andrée. "It was a cold, grey, drizzly spring day, nevertheless I'd come to a city that was in a state of intoxication. Flags and decorations everywhere, Nordenskiöld's portrait and monogram in the shop windows, flags flying from the mastheads of the ships in Stadsgården, the streets crammed with people, the children given a day off from school, the factories and offices closed. It was almost impossible to force one's way into a restaurant for a bite of food. The special editions of the papers said that the *Vega* had left Dalarö, and was on her way to Vaxholm, escorted by Admiral Lagercrantz, His Majesty the King's representative.

"The King had decreed that the *Vega* should arrive at ten o'clock that evening. By the time I got to Stockholm people had already begun to assemble on the rocky slopes of the southern part of the city, along the quays, at Stadsgården, Slussen, Skeppsbron, Norrbro, Blasieholmen and Skeppsholmen. I succeeded in getting a place on the bridge of Skeppsholmen, right opposite the steps of Logården.

"We waited for several hours, but nobody showed the least sign of impatience. We were cold, but no one seemed to mind, and many employed the well-known and time-honoured method of keeping the cold at bay. It grew dark, but Stockholm was more resplendent with lights than ever before. The darkness deepened, and yet more links, more torches, more gas-jets were lit.

"On the Palace blazed the constellation of Lyra. Vega, the brightest star in the northern hemisphere, belongs to Lyra. On the Palace too, in letters of fire, shone the initials of all the *Vega*'s crew, from Nordenskiöld's and Captain Palander's down to those of the youngest deck-hand.

"At about nine-thirty we heard cannon-fire from the direction of Djurgården. It was the *Vega* announcing her arrival. The crowds responded with cheers and applause. Rockets were let off, occasional cannon-shots were fired, there was fresh cheering, more rockets.

34

"Soon after that we heard the roar of the saluting battery on Kastellholmen, and the *Vega* glided into the Stream, accompanied by hundreds of vessels and steam launches.

"She dropped anchor at precisely ten o'clock. Simultaneously a multitude of searchlights and projectors were lit and directed upon the ship and the flight of steps up to Logården and the Palace. Firework displays, the like of which had never been seen before, burst forth from naval vessels at anchor, from Skeppsholmen, from the heights above Stadsgården, from Djurgården and Danviken's Hill. Bengal lights were aflame at every spot where a Bengal light could possibly be lit.

"The cannonade from Kastellholmen swelled to thunder.

"The lights from the many thousand torches, from the gas-jets, from the searchlights and projectors, from the rockets and the Bengal lights and the flashes from the guns of the saluting battery were caught and reflected back by the water of the Stream, and the low-lying clouds.

"On the steps of Logården Nordenskiöld and Palander were met by the Governor of Stockholm. In the Palace itself the King and Queen awaited them."

"Our balloon may be blown to Japan," I said.

"The probability of that is very slight," he answered.

He smiled again, a fleeting smile.

"My dear Fraenkel," he said, "you're already talking of *our* balloon. You too would like to glide into the Stream at Stockholm late one evening, and be greeted by hundreds of thousands of cheering people, fireworks, and the roar of cannon, wouldn't you?

"You need not answer," he said. "Such dreams are entirely natural in young men.

"They're not unnatural in middle-aged men either."

"If our balloon voyage prospers," he said, "Andrée and his men will be the objects of even greater homage, if that is possible, than the men of the *Vega*."

I nodded.

"Why?" he asked, and raised his glass of port wine.

"Because they will have conquered the North Pole," I answered.

"Only partly for that reason," said Andrée.

"Only partly?"

"Listen," he said. "They will be the greatest heroes of our time not only because they will have crossed the North Pole, but because they will have achieved the unachievable.

"Have I expressed myself clearly enough?" he asked.

"I think you have," I replied.

"I give you two days," he said. "Think everything over thoroughly during those two days."

7

Soon after that we left the Opera Cellar. In the cloakroom I trod askew on my injured foot and fell to my knees. The attendant helped me to my feet and smiled at me as if he thought I was drunk.

8

A night, a day, another night, and finally the better part of a whole day.

I wandered about the streets of Stockholm limping.

I slept badly. I lay in my bed with the lamp lit. The ceiling was white. Black cracks, like the threads of a spider's web, spread from its four corners towards the centre. Near the corners they were clearly visible, and broad enough to have been traced in Indian ink with a ruler. They soon narrowed, split up into even finer lines, then vanished completely and never met in the centre of the ceiling.

I read once again Nansen's book about his journey on skis across the inland ice of Greenland, that splendid account of how to achieve the unachievable.

Right from the beginning Nansen's Greenland expedition was

judged certain to fail: a piece of ill-considered foolhardiness, of wild insanity, bearing the stamp of its originator's total lack of real knowledge of the vast and terrible territory of ice and cold which he was intending to cross.

In spite of earlier journeys by Peary and Nordenskiöld, Greenland was an unknown land until Nansen went there.

Nansen's lack of real knowledge was therefore not really surprising. Who can have real knowledge of an unknown land?

Lack of knowledge was the true reason for the expedition.

Who is willing to risk his life to explore continents already explored?

Nansen achieved the unachievable. What he proposed to do was judged certain to fail.

There were obvious similarities between Nansen and Andrée.

To Andrée the exploration of the polar regions was self-evidently a task for the Swedes.

"The Norwegians," Nansen had written ten years ago in his letter to the Norwegian Government, "have not sent out a single arctic expedition, despite the fact that they are undoubtedly the people best suited for polar research, being pre-eminently qualified to endure the arctic climate."

"The Swedes," Andrée had said in his famous speech to the Academy of Science last year, "are noted for their dauntless courage. They are familiar with long winters and severe cold, and they are better suited than others to solve the riddle of the Polar Basin. We have a *call*," he said. "The world looks to us in obvious expectation. The North Pole is a Swedish affair. We have a duty to perform."

Nansen's journey on skis across the Greenland ice sheet was prejudged certain to fail.

All the same he had many people to choose from when he was selecting the members of the expedition. More than forty men had sent in their names; officers, business men, pharmacists, farmers, students and sailors.

Nansen found himself in the same position as Andrée at a later date. He was able to choose his companions from among many applicants. There are always men who want to pit their strength against the impossible, the unachievable.

Forty applicants. Nansen mentions them at the top of page twelve in his book. Twelve is an easy number to remember. They were not all Norwegians. There were Danes, Dutchmen, Englishmen, and Frenchmen among them.

He doesn't mention that there was also a Swedish applicant.

Perhaps my letter never reached him. Perhaps he thought I was so young that it wasn't worth answering. I was only seventeen.

What Nansen was looking for were companions between thirty and forty, still young men physically, but yet mature enough to possess determination and experience, and to be aware of the necessity of constantly getting the better of themselves.

Otto Sverdrup was thirty.

Lieutenant Olof Dietrichson was thirty-two.

Kristian Kristiansen Trana, a close friend of Sverdrup's, was only twenty-four.

Ole Nielsen Ravna, from Karasjok, owned three hundred reindeer, spoke unintelligible Norwegian, and was probably at least forty-five.

Samuel Balto gave his age as twenty-six. In spite of his origins he was quite without property in the Marxist sense of the word. He had worked as a lumber-jack, a huntsman, a fisherman, and a reindeer herdsman. He was a linguist and spoke Lappish, Norwegian, Finnish, and Swedish, and was an indefatigable skier.

Nansen was only twenty-seven when he started on his journey across the Greenland ice sheet with Sverdrup, Dietrichson, Kristiansen, and the two Lapps, Ralto and Ravna as his companions.

Nordenskiöld was made a baron after his voyage in the *Vega*. Captain Palander was given the title of Palander of the *Vega*. Into the bargain they both received a stipend from the nation of four thousand crowns per annum for life.

In spite of ice and snow Nansen's Greenland expedition was a journey across dry land. The greater part of it however was covered at a height of over two thousand metres, and the highest point reached was two thousand seven hundred metres.

Andrée's balloon voyage to the North Pole would be a comfortable journey at a height of two hundred and fifty metres above sea level.

And anyhow, why, oh why, make long and meaningless journeys through the dead whiteness of the desolate Arctic?

What discoveries could you make in a desert of ice in which man could not live?

And the North Pole? What was the North Pole but a white dot on a white expanse?

There are ways of phrasing a question that are decidedly feminine. *Horror vacui* or, *natura abhorret vacuum*. The horror inspired by a vacuum, the hatred of the unknown, the unexplored, wasn't that a typically masculine characteristic?

I was an engineer and a technologist. My knowledge of Latin was a schoolboy's at best. *Natura abhorret vacuum*. Wasn't that in some way connected with old Aristotle? In spite of the fact that he spoke Greek?

To awaken one winter morning, to be a child. To awaken one winter morning and see newly fallen, untouched snow over fields and lawns.

You dress, you rush out, you want to be the first person to set foot on the ground that has suddenly become virginal and untrodden.

When, four years after the expedition to Greenland, Nansen began his great attempt to reach the North Pole on board the *Fram*, his expedition was a purely Norwegian venture.

The attempt cost four hundred and fifty thousand crowns. Nansen refused to accept the contributions that Oscar Dickson of Gothenburg and his wealthy friends had offered. Dickson you see was a Swede.

Nansen got four hundred pounds from England. That he could accept, and also the thousand roubles contributed by a Norwegian businessman resident in Estonia.

He also accepted the sum of more than a hundred thousand crowns offered by King Oscar.

Of course King Oscar was a Swede. That was undeniable. But as King of the united Scandinavian realm of Norway and Sweden he was also a Norwegian citizen. That too was undeniable.

The *Fram* had a crew of thirteen, including Nansen. All of them were supposed to be Norwegian.

But Nansen had let himself be taken in. The second engineer on board the *Fram* asserted that his name was Pettersen, and that he had been born in Sweden of Norwegian parents. By degrees suspicions were aroused. When beset by questions intended to ensnare him Pettersen was forced to confess that his origins were purely Swedish, and that his right name was Lars Pettersson.

He was a skilful and competent engineer. He was also a highly qualified blacksmith, and into the bargain an enthusiast for the art of cooking.

Of course, the good fortune of having the chance to be the first person to set foot on the North Pole was not in itself a good enough reason.

Exploration and scientific research; as I have said it is hard to tolerate the unexplored. It is not so long since there was controversy as to whether Greenland was an island or part of the American continent. Nordenskiöld believed that there were tree-covered areas in the centre of Greenland. Nansen proved that this was not so. We now know that the Polar Basin really is a basin, an ice-covered sea, and not another Greenland. But there must be thousands of islands to be discovered and described.

But not even scientific research and exploration were good enough reasons.

There must be something else, something that went deeper, that was more inaccessible.

Nordenskiöld has told us of a peculiar incident that happened quite a long time ago, during one of the winters he spent at Spitzbergen.

A carpenter called Snabb suddenly left the camp and began to walk northwards, straight across a frozen bay. He walked briskly, as if he had something urgent and important to do.

They called after him. He did not answer. They fired a rifle into the air. He did not even turn his head, just went on obstinately walking northwards, and when dusk fell they had still not caught up with him. The next day they were able to follow his tracks for a couple of hours. Then a brief storm with heavy snowfall obliterated them.

The carpenter made for the north. He never returned.

That happened in 1872.

It is easy to misunderstand Professor Nordenskiöld's little story about Snabb the carpenter. It is not so much about the man who disappeared as about the cardinal point North.

9

The second day after my meeting with Andrée coincided with cloudy weather, south-westerly winds, rising temperatures and enervating drizzle.

I went for a long walk along the many twisting footpaths of Djurgården. The snow was slushy and wet. The moisture penetrated my shoes and was also sucked up by my trousers in accordance with the elementary laws of physics about capillary attraction.

I met two civilian equestrians, and I was passed by two officers of the mounted Life Guards. That was all. Otherwise Djurgården wore an air of desolation.

I sat on a seat out at Blockhusudden for a long time. It is possible that I dozed for a while. My pocket watch had stopped

I had a simple meal at the inn at Djurgårdsbrunn and dried my clothes by the heat from the log fire that burned on the huge hearth.

The pattering of the volleys of rifle fire from Kaknäs shooting-range did not disturb me.

My left foot ached. I tried to walk without limping.

All the snow and ice had gone from Brunkebergstorg when I crossed the entrance hall of the Patent and Registration Office.

Engineer Kuylenstjerna came to meet me as he had done two days previously, but this time he was less arrogant, and did not ask me any impertinent questions.

He led me into a room with three or four leather armchairs and a leather sofa.

He offered me a Dutch cigar and held out a lighted match.

The room had two windows.

Beside one stood a young man with frank, smiling eyes, a frank, smiling mouth, and a frank, smiling upturned moustache.

His face was the face of a youth: a smooth candid forehead, no lines or wrinkles round his eyes, softly rounded cheeks, his hair neatly parted and well-groomed, small ears, and a strong but not aggressive chin.

His smile was the smile of a very young man.

He came towards me.

I rose to my feet.

"Knut Fraenkel?" he asked, and held out his right hand.

"Yes," I answered.

There was no need for him to tell his name. I recognized his face from hundreds of pictures in papers and periodicals during the past year.

"Assistant Lecturer Nils Strindberg, I presume," I said.

His hand in mine was small and slender.

He bowed deeply.

"I'm delighted to meet you Engineer Fraenkel," he said. "Allow me to quote an Austrian newspaper. *'Jener Mann, der mittels Luftballon zum Nordpol und zurück fahren will, ist einfach ein Narr, ein Schwindler oder ein Schwede.'**"

Kuylenstjerna burst out laughing.

Strindberg drew himself up and brought his heels together with a smart clap, like a Prussian.

"Speak up," he said. "Are you a fool, a knave, or only an ordinary simple Swede?"

"I'm glad to meet you," I said. "Allow me to quote an English newspaper. *'The Swedish people are really becoming too ambitious. A nation which has produced Swedenborgianism and the Gothenburg licensing system can afford to leave the remaining glories of the nineteenth century to some other people even to one less renowned than the sons of Thor and Odin,'* or something in that style."

I was still holding Strindberg's hand in mine.

---

* Any man who intends to fly to the North Pole and back in a balloon is quite simply a fool, a knave, or a Swede.

42

His face could very well be described as one great, childishly open smile.

"Neither a fool nor a knave," I said. "Only an ordinary Swede of Danish origins, possibly simple minded, probably more than ordinarily ambitious."

I was seized by a liking for his smile and his happy expression. His hand was slender. It was lost in mine.

Suddenly Andrée was there standing beside Nils Strindberg. He must have come in by the same door that I had.

He shook hands and asked me at once, though without eagerness, if I had thought the matter over.

"My application still stands," I said.

Andrée nodded. "Excellent," he said.

He then turned to Kuylenstjerna, talked to him in a low voice for quite a while, and gave him a bundle of documents which he had brought in under his arm. They left the room together.

Strindberg had sat down in one of the leather armchairs. He was elegantly, almost fastidiously dressed. He struck a match, I bent over his outstretched hand and lit my Dutch cigar that had gone out.

He wore a heavy gold signet ring on the little finger of his left hand. The pearl in his tie-pin was bigger than a pea, his black shoes were almost entirely hidden by grey cloth spats.

While I was letting him light my cigar with the match he held out the thought crossed my mind that he resembled Oscar Wilde.

"The train to Upsala leaves Stockholm early tomorrow morning," he said. *"Are you coming with me, Fraenkel?* My application still stands. *Excellent, Engineer Fraenkel, excellent!*

"Why should it be more remarkable to sail to the North Pole in a balloon than to travel to Upsala as a railway passenger?"

"A car is more draughty and less well insulated than a railway compartment," I said. "You can easily catch cold."

At that moment Andrée returned.

"The cars of balloons are more comfortable than you would suppose," he said. "At least so long as you remain at a satisfactory height."

He took out his pocket watch.

43

"I knew you would come today, not tomorrow," he said. "That was why I summoned Nils Strindberg. He's not had to wait long, at the most half an hour."

His face was the face of a weary man.

"We really ought to draw up a contract," he said. "But first there is another step to be taken which is at least as important."

"What's that?" I asked.

"We must go down to Runan, drink to our brotherhood, and drop the titles."

10

Doctor Ekholm had put his place in the balloon expedition at Andrée's disposal. I was aware that the question of who was to be the new third man was a matter that concerned not only the man himself, and the two other members of the party, but was also one of considerable general interest. This had been made clear by the widespread tinkering with the subject that had gone on in the press after the schism between Andrée and Ekholm at the end of September.

All the same I had underestimated the extent of public interest.

The news was first published in *Aftonbladet*, a paper with which Andrée was closely connected. I bought two copies of the paper, one for myself, the other for my parents.

I went to see one of my closest friends with this paper, hot from the press, in the inside pocket of my overcoat.

"You're limping," he said.

"I've broken a little toe," I answered.

He then looked at me with obvious concern: "What the devil's happened?"

I asked him if he knew who was to be Andrée's new man.

He shook his head. "Crown Prince Gustaf? Heidenstam? Nietzsche? Released from close confinement for the sake of a good cause? Or is it quite simply Nansen himself?"

I spread *Aftonbladet* out on his table.

"In spite of my broken toe," I said.

I had underestimated the extent of public interest.

The following day I was a famous man.

All the Swedish papers, perhaps all the Scandinavian papers, had my name in their headlines, were able to describe me, say when and where I had been born, give details of my education, and report that I had been brought up in northern Sweden. They published pictures of me, made kind remarks about my person, my character and my powerful physique.

Another day passed and I was known over the whole of the civilized world. Telegrams from papers in Germany, France, Italy, Spain, Russia, America, Brazil and so on, assured me that they were certain Andrée could not have made a better choice, and that they were prepared to offer me generous remuneration for my reports from the expedition, and that their generosity would be exceptionally great if they were given the sole rights in such reports.

To think that one's name should be on all lips, not for what one had done, but for what one was prepared to do.

"You'll get used to it," Nils Strindberg told me. "It was worse this spring and this summer."

The attitude of the world to Andrée's plans had first been doubting and sceptical. But people had allowed themselves to be convinced, and had been seized by enthusiasm and trust which steadily increased.

"We were fêted like heroes when we left Stockholm and then Gothenburg," he said.

"Of course there were still some sceptics.

"There were those who asserted that we should never be able to build the balloon-house on the barren islands of Spitzbergen, half way between the North Cape and the North Pole.

"We got it up in three weeks. It wasn't only the most northerly hangar in the world, it was also the biggest. It was the biggest wooden building I've ever seen, twenty metres from base to crown, taller than a six-storey brick building.

"There were those who asserted that in trying to manufacture the thousands of cubic metres of hydrogen gas we required in Spitz-bergen, we should stumble upon insurmountable practical difficulties.

"Our hydrogen gas apparatus functioned perfectly, and it took us less than four days and four nights to fill the balloon.

"We built the balloon-house, we filled the balloon. The band of sceptics grew smaller. Enthusiasm increased.

"Everything went according to plan.

"Everything that is except the winds, which blew from the north instead of from the south.

"There was one little incident," said Nils Strindberg, "which I remember well, and which I shall never forget.

"It occurred a couple of days after the balloon had been filled and was waiting, ready to start.

"The steamer the *Erling Jarl* had arrived and dropped anchor in our sheltered harbour.

"She had on board fifty-four tourists of the most diverse national-ities: German, English, French, Dutch, Swiss, Belgian, even a couple of Rumanians.

"The tourists came in a compact body to look at the balloon-house. I clearly remember that they numbered fifty-four.

"The sailors from the *Virgo* and the crew of the *Erling Jarl* in their smartest uniforms were drawn up in two lines on either side of the entrance.

"In a short speech in German and English Andrée explained his plans and gave details of the way in which the balloon was fitted out.

"The weather was good, hot sunshine and an icy northerly breeze.

"When Andrée had finished a Frenchman began to speak in English. He spoke very fast, moving his arms excitedly as he did so, and begged those present to join him in giving three fourfold cheers: 'three times three cheers, and one cheer more' for His Majesty King Oscar, for Sweden and Norway, and lastly for us polar voyagers.

"After this a very young girl detached herself from the group of tourists.

"She fastened a blue silk ribbon round Andrée's right arm.

"She then gave him a bottle of red wine, and a cake, made with raisins and orange marmalade, that she herself had baked in the galley of the *Erling Jarl*.

"Finally she gave him a little rose-bush in a brass pot. The rose-bush had four buds.

"The girl was not only young, she was also very beautiful. Her dress fluttered in the breeze like a flag. Her hair wound round her neck. She never uttered a word. She kissed Andrée on the cheek, and then ran back and hid herself among the other tourists.

"There stood Andrée holding the rose-bush with its four buds.

"He had handed the cake to Doctor Ekholm, the bottle of wine to me.

"The Captain of the *Erling Jarl* broke the silence with an improvised and not particularly inspired speech.

" 'The rose-bush has four buds,' he said. 'There will be three of you in the car of the balloon. Each of you must take a rose when the balloon takes off. When you reach the magic and mystical point which you are making such vigorous efforts to reach, let the fourth rose fall down, red as the all-conquering power of man is red. If you never reach your magic and mystical goal, if, that is, you find yourselves in a situation in which you are obliged to give up, to turn south once more, then, in spite of all, let the fourth rose fall upon the ice!

" 'For red is not only the colour of victory, it is also the colour of rejected love.'

"His speech was received with fresh cheers from the crew of the *Virgo*, and these cheers changed to the rhythmic hammer-song that had developed of itself during the erection of the balloon-house:

'That we to the North Pole may go,
To the North Pole may go,
May go, may go, may go,
To the North Pole may go,
May go, may go, may go,'

and so on indefinitely. And from the *Erling Jarl* they fired a salute of twenty-one cannon shots in our honour."

"No, I've no idea what she was called or who she was, that girl

47

with the rose-bush and the four rosebuds," said Nils Strindberg.

"She was very young, and very beautiful.

"I'm not even sure of the name of the Master of the *Erling Jarl*," he said.

"I remember him as Captain Bade from Trondhjem. According to Andrée's notes his name was Lund.

"The arctic summer is short. The winds of the summer of 1896 were obstinately northerly. We were never able to start.

"We were already world famous, not for what we had done, but for what we had set ourselves to do.

"On 15 August Andrée gave orders for the sharpening of the big scissors, with which the balloon would be cut into pieces. Five days later the dismembered balloon was neatly packed away and deposited in the *Virgo*'s hold, along with the car, the guide-ropes, the net, the sail and the belly-band.

"On 20 August we began our ignominious retreat.

"That was the very day on which newspapers and placards the world over were spreading the news that Nansen had returned after his long and successful journey through and over the polar ice.

"We arrived at Tromsö. No one took any notice of us, for Nansen and the *Fram* were there. We steamed south along the Norwegian coast where every town and every little fishing village was waiting impatiently for Nansen. We arrived at Gothenburg where we were greeted by a little group of people. The papers were full of pictures and reports of Nansen's journey.

"The evening before our departure from Stockholm we'd been received in audience by King Oscar. When we returned to Stockholm the King had gone to Christiania to do honour to Nansen and his men.

"Sometimes," said Strindberg, "I think that Andrée hates Nansen —if indeed he's capable of hating anyone. But at that time he had reason to be grateful for our failure was covered up by Nansen's triumph.

"Now a couple of months have passed and the Nansen fever has subsided," said Strindberg.

"Now people have realized that, in spite of everything, the North

48

Pole is still unconquered. And they know that our new attempt next summer is assured of financial support by contributions from Alfred Nobel, Dickson in Gothenburg, and a Director called Burman, whom I don't know.

"The Swedes are once again conscious that we have a chance of succeeding where the Norwegians have failed."

"I shall try to accustom myself to being famous in advance," I said.

I I

Of course we had our opponents. One of them was Georg Lund-ström, known as Jörgen, editor of the newspaper *Figaro*.

One day when Andrée, Strindberg, and I were partaking of an early dinner he approached our table with a glass and a half bottle of punch.

"Fluker Andrée, may I interrupt your meal?" he asked.

"You've already done so," replied Andrée.

Jörgen sank on to a chair that an attentive waiter had brought up.

"I've already interviewed you and Strindberg many times," he said. "The person who interests me now is you, Engineer Fraenkel. I realize that you're just a common or garden Charles-the-Twelfth bumpkin. First the victory at Narva. Then the disastrous defeat at Poltava. You've got to compensate for Poltava by winning a victory over the North Pole."

"We've met before," I said.

"I know," replied Jörgen. "I bought a poem from you. It was published under a pseudonym. You got two crowns for it. You were at school at Palmgren's. The Head Master there asked me who'd written the poem. He was pretty upset. I told him to go to hell, and when he got there to study the Swedish laws governing the freedom of the Press."

Jörgen's quiet and over-refined voice had the effect of highlighting his coarse manner of expressing himself.

49

"Our editor friend Mr Lundström once made an ascent in a balloon," Andrée explained. "He made it with Feller. They crashed. As luck would have it they landed up in Djurgårdsbrunn's bay. He's never been able to endure balloonists since then."

"Wrong," said Jörgen. "Never a cross word about the people who make ascents in balloons for scientific purposes. You, Mr Strindberg, for instance. You're a physicist and a photographer—a first class photographer. You can make a real contribution. I would take my hat off to you if I were not bare-headed. But you, Andrée, you're not an aeronaut, you're a flukemonger. You became a balloonist because you wanted to get into Parliament. You got no further than Stockholm's City Council, and the people there couldn't put up with your mad pranks. The North Pole? D'ye think that's going to get you into the Cabinet? You call yourself a liberal, but you're redder than a socialist, and we don't want any red Cabinet Ministers in this country. Obstinate and possessed by fixed ideas like a Marxist. Flukemongering to the North Pole? No one comes back alive from the North Pole. Red today dead tomorrow. It's a shame all the same about Mr Strindberg. He's gifted."

He raised his glass of punch.

"I'm no teetotaller," he said. "Dogmas and fixed ideas make me sick. But I'm a very moderate drinker. Too bad that I should have to empty one of my rare glassfuls in the company of three madcaps."

"You've brought the situation entirely on yourself," answered Andrée.

"Herr Technologist Engineer Fraenkel," said Jörgen. "You've been trained in the art of blasting tunnels, of building roads and bridges, of busying yourself with this and that on the surface of this good old Earth. What the devil d'ye want with the Air? What the devil d'ye think you're going to do at the North Pole? Erect a statue to Charles the Twelfth?"

"I've had an idea," he said. "This is the first geographical expedition of a purely engineering character. Its inventor and organizer: Chief Engineer at the Patent Office. In the car: his lordship again and also another flukemonger of an engineer. Chief financier: Herr Engineer, Inventor, Chemist, Alfred Nobel, and he's already well used to shooting people into the air. It's a shame all the same about Mr Strindberg. He's a gifted photographer."

"You're a stimulating conversationalist," said Andrée.

"Tell me," said Jörgen. "What do balloonist engineers do if they crash into the sea?"

"They drown," answered Andrée.

"If the sea isn't frozen," I added.

12

A fourth man, Vilhelm Swedenborg, was added to our little group. He was to go with us to Spitzbergen as a reserve, a second string, who would be able to fill the vacant place in the car if Strindberg or I were prevented from going at the last moment.

"Anything may happen," said Andrée. "Fraenkel may fall off a rope ladder and break his other little toe. Strindberg may have to go to bed with a heavy cold on the very day the right wind blows."

Strindberg appeared to be depressed by the introduction of this second string. I asked him if he felt it to be an indication that Andrée distrusted him, but he said no.

All the same Andrée knew as well as I did that pressure to make him withdraw was being exerted upon Strindberg from several quarters. Among the many people who were trying to influence him was not only Doctor Ekholm, but an authority of the standing of Professor Arrhenius. Perhaps the most important of all was Anna Charlier, to whom Strindberg had become engaged a few weeks previously.

"Her name is a good omen," I said to him. "Charlier, have you thought what a Charlier is? The hot-air balloon of the good old days was a Montgolfière, and a Charlier was the name given to the early hydrogen balloons. Charlier after Charles, the man who invented them.

"O yes, I admit that I've Swedified the spelling of Charlière and Frenchified the pronunciation of your fiancée's name.

51

"While you and I are having a friendly chat," I said, "there's something else worth mentioning about Vilhelm Swedenborg, our second string, the phantom fourth member of the expedition. He must be a descendant of the great Emanuel Swedenborg.

"This too is a good omen.

"I don't know much about the New Church and old Swedenborg except that he proclaimed that there was some sort of link between the spiritual and the ordinary, material world, and that every living being here on earth was provided with two guardian angels. It's sometimes quite useful to have two guardian angels at hand, especially when you're floating in the whiteness that lies between the misty heavens and the ice-covered sea."

A few days later I was able to inform Strindberg that Swedenborg was married to a daughter of Nordenskiöld's, and that he had been allowed to join the polar expedition as its reserve man in response to the urgent pleas of his father-in-law.

After that Strindberg's temporary depression seemed to blow over entirely.

Vilhelm Swedenborg was in fact the lieutenant from Norrland's Artillery Regiment who had sat at Nordenskiöld's table at the Opera Cellar on the occasion of my first meeting with Andrée.

His duties obliged him to reside in Östersund.

13

The remaining weeks of 1896 were both uneventful and eventful.

The sudden flare-up of interest in me and my person on the part of the newspapers died down.

Andrée and I twice discussed the contract, the agreement that had to be drawn up. It was to be based upon the written agreement of that year which had been signed by Andrée, Strindberg and Ekholm. This agreement regularized the relations between the members of the expedition, the allocation of duties, the publication of reports and of the scientific results of the expedition, and the way in which any income derived from these was to be shared.

Our conversations were usually very short. Andrée's duties at the Patent Office seemed to weigh heavily on him.

His closest colleague, Engineer Kuylenstjerna, asserted that Andrée was more easily irritated than ever before, and that he often complained of having a headache.

On 27 November Gustaf Fröding was acquitted. The jury had come to the conclusion that he had not "committed an offence against decency" by his poem *A Morning Dream*.

I had come to a decision, and this decision was a turning point in my life.

I wanted to have something specific to do.

Andrée asked me to be patient.

He showed me the piles of applications for patents, and delivered short lectures about the need for a new Patents' Act.

Autumn became winter.

It was cold. It snowed. I was not in the least interested in the need for a new Patents' Act.

One of the chief newspapers in Stockholm had advertised a prize for the most suitable name for Andrée's balloon.

There were many suggestions.

Polhem, in honour of the world's greatest technician.

Castle in the Air, to reduce the project to its right proportions.

Swollen Head, to remind Andrée that in spite of everything he was only an ordinary person.

The Flying Swede, a reminder that there was already a Flying Dutchman.

Policeman, not much thought will be needed to discover the profession of the man who proposed this.

Police champion, probably a bad joke by an athlete.

The South Pole, an allusion, as simple as it is astute, to the interaction of magnetic forces.

14

In December Alfred Nobel died at his home in San Remo.

When this announcement appeared in special editions of the newspapers I hurried round to the Patent Office. Andrée's female clerk, or shorthand typist, Miss Lundgren (who had also, with Count Hugo's special permission, managed the book-keeping and accounts of the balloon expedition since the previous winter), was only able to tell me that he had gone off, obviously in a great hurry. He was not in his room, his coat was not on its hanger, nor his hat on the hat-rack.

At twelve o'clock on the following day I went to his private address in Barnhusgatan. I knocked several times before he gave any sign of life, and he asked who was there before he opened the door and let me in.

He was carelessly dressed in a short dressing-gown, and his trousers were hanging down over his sloppy bed-slippers.

His home consisted of a single room, cluttered with furniture, and with the walls hidden by bookcases. It was the first time I had been there. After a rather long interval of embarrassed silence he asked me to go down to a neighbouring café and fetch coffee and buns.

When I returned he had managed to dress and perform a rapid toilet. He had hidden his unmade bed under a counterpane with a long fringe, and thrown a window wide open.

"What's on your mind?" he asked.

"Nothing in particular, really."

"Nobel sent a remittance for his new contribution to the expedition some weeks ago," said Andrée. "I mention this to set your mind at rest.

"I've a cold," he added. "I've migraine, and probably a slight temperature. It's nothing serious."

"Weren't you and Nobel friends?" I asked.

"We met a couple of times," he answered. "We knew one another. But Nobel had no friends. There's a particular kind of person who has no friends. Great men are always lonely men. Nobel had thousands of ideas. He tried to patent far too many of them, and caused us at the Patent Office a vast amount of work. Ninety out of a hundred of Nobel's whims were pure madness. Eight out of those that remained were far too much before their time, were launched far too early. The remaining two were strokes of genius, and were appropriate enough to create one of the greatest fortunes of our day."

"He staked a large sum on your expedition," I said.

"Yes, but not because he thought it would succeed."

"In that case, why?"

"Because it was something *new*. First attempts regularly fail. They are regularly followed by a second attempt. That too almost always fails. But after that, with the help of the experiences gained by failure, people are able to find their way to the right methods."

"You're saying that Alfred Nobel staked his money on our failure?" I said.

"No, but on something that he believed would fail."

Andrée rose with his coffee cup in his hand.

"I could send a telegram," he said, "but since you're here, perhaps you'd be kind enough to go up to the Patent Office and tell them from me that I've a cold and a temperature, and that it will be a couple of days before I can return to duty?"

"Of course," I answered.

PART TWO

PARIS SPRING · 1897 ·

I

Lieutenant Vilhelm Swedenborg arrived in Stockholm from Östersund and we, he and I, were formally engaged as members of the expedition at a modest daily wage, paid in cash.

"Not for money but for honour," said Swedenborg. "I'm in training; always penniless, always financing my expensive habits with loans and notes of hand. I was an unpaid second lieutenant for a long time, but I never had to tighten my belt. And before that I managed to dodge paying my fees at the Military School at Karlsberg by becoming a page of the chamber to His Majesty the King.

"It's an art, my friend," he said, "living the upper-class life one must live as a representative of the upper classes, while at the same time one lacks the large, remunerative estates which properly belong to the afore-mentioned upper classes. Class consciousness costs the devil of a lot of money."

"Page of the chamber?" I asked.

"A volunteer who ranks as an officer," he answered. "Unfortunately only for a day now and then. A magnificent uniform, a gleaming sword with a golden sword-knot. In the immediate neighbourhood of the King at all the ceremonial openings of Parliament. On guard by the door of the King's audience chamber when newly appointed envoys from foreign and exotic lands come to present their credentials. A sworn liegeman, ever ready to offer his life and blood in the defence of his noble Lord's life and blood—a duty beset with exceptional difficulties, since court etiquette requires that you never turn your back to the King. A page should therefore be equipped with eyes in the back of his head, so that he may discover anarchists, revolutionaries, socialists, and desperate Norwegians and render them harmless in good time.

"I repeat, not for money, but for honour.

"The day before yesterday a page at the King's court. Yesterday a lieutenant in the Norrland Artillery Regiment at Östersund. Today reserve man in Chief Engineer Andrée's polar expedition."

Vilhelm Swedenborg had alert eyes under heavy lids, an elegant and well-trimmed moustache, a narrow face, a high forehead, and a long, rather pointed nose.

As a small boy he had once sat on King Oscar's knee at Sofiero Palace.

He was exceedingly talkative. There were noticeable traces of a Scanian accent in his speech.

He was short; I could see over the crown of his head without stretching. He was thin and he had long arms. His movements were as rapid and as energetic as those of a greyhound.

His talkativeness, his torrential flow of words, sometimes changed when Andrée was present, to something akin to taciturnity.

Swedenborg was married to Nordenskiöld's daughter Anna.

2

Great masses of snow fell on Stockholm, the Mälar valley and the archipelago. This snow-fall was followed by short, midwinter days, with pale sunshine and cloudless skies, and by long midwinter nights, with twinkling stars, cloudless skies, and severe cold.

Swedenborg and I were given lessons in terrestrial and celestial navigation by Doctor Carlheim-Gyllenskiöld at the Observatory in Stockholm.

The sextant, with its mirrors, its darkened sight-filter, its alidade, and its graduated curve, is a mystery only to the uninitiated.

Exact timekeeping is also a problem only for the uninitiated, and for those who have not a reliable chronometer.

With a sextant and a chronometer, and given clear weather and generally favourable circumstances, you can establish your whereabouts on the earth's surface with a margin of error of less than three hundred and fifty metres.

After only a week of cramming at the theory and practice of it Swedenborg and I—each on our own—were able to establish, with the help of our navigational instruments, that the Observatory in Stockholm lay in exactly the latitude and longitude in which it does actually lie.

After that we concentrated on the study of meteorology; wind and weather, high- and low-pressure, cyclones and anticyclones; the movements of cyclones and high-pressure and low-pressure areas from west to east, and the possible but speculative connection between these movements and the rotation of the earth.

"We're not getting any factual knowledge," said Swedenborg, "only hypotheses and theories."

"Had you hoped for something different?" I asked.

"Probably not," he answered.

"The greater our lack of certain knowledge, the greater the daring of our exploit.

"Daring results in honour.

"The less you know the greater the need for daring.

"The greater the need for daring, the greater the honour."

3

Late one evening in February Swedenborg succeeded in tempting me, Nils Strindberg, and nearly a dozen other people to visit Slussen and the Katarina Lift.

"I'm paying for this aerial trip," he said, and held out a fistful of rattling coins.

He gave the lift attendant a cigar and a fifty öre tip.

We paused on the platform round the tower of the lift. The long footbridge over Katarinavägen across to Mosebacke was almost deserted.

A light easterly breeze was blowing.

The air was clear. The streets lay spread out, some deep down beneath us, and some on the slope beneath us.

Swedenborg bent over the balustrade and pointed downwards:

"How high?" he asked, "how high are we above the paving-stones of the street?"

No one knew for certain. Someone thought it might be eighty metres.

"At the most fifty," he said. "On the other hand it doesn't matter whether it's thirty, or three hundred, or three thousand.

"At any rate not to an aeronaut. An aeronaut's first commandment: thou shalt not be afraid of heights!"

He took off his hat and his coat.

"The wind is easterly," he said. "To counterbalance the pressure of that wind I should have to lean inwards on the western balustrade, towards the firm floor of the footbridge. On the eastern balustrade, for the same reason, I should have to lean outwards over the free-fall to the street of something over fifty metres."

"You're sozzled," said Strindberg.

I observed that the rest of the party remained silent and passive. Some of them had turned pale. A lieutenant of the Svea Life-guards left us and walked quickly along the footbridge towards Mosebacke. He was followed by a young man in sports clothes and an English-looking cap. The lieutenant pulled up short, turned round, and came back to us. The sporting type continued towards the houses on the southern heights.

"It's my firm intention to put it to the test," said Vilhelm Swedenborg.

He seated himself astride the eastern rail of the footbridge, bent forwards, heaving himself up by his arms, got the tip of his toes on the top of the rail (I can't remember whether it was made of wood or iron), and rose slowly until he was standing upright with his arms outstretched.

"In the name of Kepler, gravitation, Newton, and Emanuel Swedenborg," he said.

Time stood still while he teetered and wobbled, but managed to keep his balance by waving his arms.

Then he moved forwards, counting each step aloud as he went.

We walked alongside him on the footbridge, a tight group of young men.

When he had taken thirty-three steps he stopped.

"Is that enough?" he asked.

"By God it is!" someone said.

Swedenborg leapt inwards towards the bridge, a long leap, which he completed by supply bending his knees.

He put on his coat, and placed his hat on his head. "A balloonist mustn't be afraid of heights," he said.

The lieutenant from the Svea Life-guards seized my upper arm.

"If he'd fallen," he said. "Outwards I mean, if he'd fallen down to the street?"

"Well?"

"We should have had to pick him up?"

"Yes, of course."

"You see," he said. "I've never actually seen a dead man. I mean, a man who's fallen fifty metres, how does he die? He must be disfigured, flattened. But how much is he flattened? And his blood? Does it spatter all over the place? When he's flattened, I mean?"

4

On 1 March Swedenborg and I travelled to Paris to meet Henri Lachambre, the man who was making the North Pole balloon, and receive from him practical lessons in the noble art of navigating a balloon.

"There are many things I should have liked to discuss with you," I said to Andrée, shortly before we left.

Andrée had lost weight during the winter months. His hair had

63

got thinner, and you could clearly see grey, in places almost white streaks in it. He had let his moustache grow so that it hid not only his upper lip, but his whole mouth.

"I've my work to attend to," he said. "Johan Petter Johansson's application to patent a wrench and an engineer's spanner, and the complications arising therefrom, is worrying me more than the polar expedition at the moment."

"There are a number of details," I said.

"Connected with our journey to the North Pole?"

"I should have liked to discuss them."

"When you get back from France and Paris," he said.

When we, Swedenborg and I, left Stockholm, we each got a similarly worded memorandum from Andrée.

"Representatives of newspapers and other journalists: Observe moderate politeness and the greatest possible caution. Don't refuse interviews. Since the interviewers never know what is already known, run over everything that has been said before again and again. Don't contradict current rumours unless it is absolutely necessary.

"General instructions: When you get to Paris ask about everything that has to do with the navigation of a balloon and the polar regions, not only the things you don't understand, but the things you think you do understand. Asking questions is a splendid way of widening your knowledge. Furthermore, don't rely on your memory, make notes."

5

In Paris we were met by Engineer Nordenfelt, the head of the Nordenfelt Company.

"I wonder what's happened to the red carpet, and the brass band?" said Swedenborg.

It was the first time we had been to Paris.

When we reached La Place de la Concorde Swedenborg told the cabby to stop.

"Gentlemen," he said, taking off his hat, "we're here, and there's spring in the air. I can feel the sap rising. Now for the first time I know that the great adventure has begun."

"Don't rely on your memory," I said. "Take notes."

Nordenfelt took us to a small hotel in a house that almost looked as if it dated from the Dark Ages. The rooms were small and spartanly furnished.

"Andrée is an economical man," said Nordenfelt.

The Nordenfelt Company are artillery designers, and their office was established by the famous engineer Thorsten Nordenfelt, who had once lived in London, and was the uncle of our present host in Paris.

The previous year the Nordenfelt Company had undertaken to supervise the construction of the balloon, and in this work Per Nordenfelt had been assisted by Engineer Noel.

"People have asked me," said Swedenborg, "what business I, an artillery-man, have on board a balloon. But who has been supervising the actual construction of the balloon? Why, none other than an artillery specialist. And who is this artillery expert's chief? Why, none other than Thorsten Nordenfelt, the inventor of the best machine-gun in the world. In a word: the art of aeronautics, of ballooning, is clearly closely allied to ballistics, the science of the passage of projectiles through the air."

* * *

That evening Per Nordenfelt arranged a party for Swedenborg and myself at which a large number of journalists were present. They bombarded us with questions in German and English as well as in French.

The landlady at our hotel behaved very rudely to us when we returned late that night, noisy, laughing, and excited. We needed her help in finding our way to our rooms.

The following morning, when we ate our breakfast in her little dining-room, she was by contrast welcoming and friendly. Her two charming daughters, Jeanne and Louise, were always making excuses to come to our table.

We were no longer simply Swedenborg and Fraenkel, two uninteresting tourists from somewhere in the north.

Our pictures were in all the Paris newspapers. We were not the ordinary run of tourists. We were prominent members of *l'expédition-polaire d'Andrée*.

"The sap is rising, the great adventure has begun," said Swedenborg.

6

Very soon after breakfast Henri Lachambre and his nephew Alexis Machuron came to fetch us.

Lachambre was an elderly gentleman with wise brown eyes, and a perpetually smiling mouth.

Machuron was considerably younger. His carefully dressed hair, which he wore combed back, made his head look fascinatingly square, and its squareness was accentuated by his remarkably long, waxed, and upturned moustache.

Lachambre knew about ten Swedish words—he had been at Spitzbergen for the unsuccessful attempt of 1896. Machuron spoke excellent German.

"The two sides of Machuron's moustache added together must be at least twenty-five centimetres long," said Swedenborg. "He really has two moustaches," he continued, "one on the left, and the other on the right. Now I understand why the noun 'moustache' is sometimes used in the plural: 'a pair of moustaches'."

"Twenty-five centimetres, a quarter of a metre, that isn't enough," I answered. "Straighten them out, stretch them, pull them a bit, and they'll certainly measure nearer thirty centimetres."

We drove this way and that through the central parts of the city. Lachambre narrated and described, pointed and gesticulated. Swedenborg listened attentively. He sat leaning backwards with his hat on the back of his head and one leg across the other, smoking a cigar, and occasionally throwing out a question.

The sun was hot. The trees were showing their first bright green leaves. It was spring.

I sat beside Machuron of the moustaches, opposite Swedenborg and Lachambre.

Machuron translated Lachambre's lecture on Paris into brief German sentences.

"You don't understand French?" he said.

"Not very well," I answered, "and I speak it even worse."

"Engineer Eiffel has been seized by the great iron madness," he said. "It's no good talking to him about Portland cement or concrete. The Eiffel Tower is a monstrosity. Twelve thousand iron beams, joined together by a quarter of a million bolts. The tower has been up for eight years. Seven thousand tons of iron, which is being slowly converted into rust. A monstrosity that will crash to earth in less than twenty years."

"Yes," I said.

"Do you think the tower is beautiful?" he said.

"When it falls," I said, "its fall will be very great."

We arrived at Lachambre's balloon factory. There, on the floor of the largest workshop, lay Andrée's polar balloon, empty of gas, flat, spread out, divided into two halves, the upper half furthest away, then a space of at least five metres, and nearest to us, and to the entrance, the lower half of the balloon.

This was the first time that Swedenborg and I had seen the balloon with our own eyes.

I had imagined that it would be dark, almost black. Instead it was light, a pale orange colour.

"By Jove, it's big," said Swedenborg.

The balloon, ordered by Andrée in the winter of 1895-6, was rather more than twenty metres in diameter, and about four thousand five hundred cubic metres in volume.

Henri Lachambre had been given the task of manufacturing the balloon.

It was composed of a total of three thousand three hundred and sixty pieces of silk, Chinese silk.

The upper part consisted of a quadruple layer of silk, then a triple layer to four metres below the equator of the balloon, after which a double layer of silk was regarded as quite sufficient.

The three thousand three hundred and sixty pieces of silk were sewn together with three rows of stitches, in some places with four.

The total length of these seams equalled fourteen thousand metres, fourteen kilometres.

It was obvious that when varnished the material of the silk itself was, for practical purposes, entirely impermeable by hydrogen; it was the seams that were the problem.

Doctor Ekholm's doubts about the impermeability of the seams were his most important reason for putting his place in the new attempt at Andrée's disposal.

"And that's why we two now find ourselves in Paris," said Swedenborg.

"A doubt measuring fourteen kilometres," I said.

The squares of silk had been joined by laying the edges over each other and glueing them firmly together with strips of material sixteen millimetres wide. These glued strips had then been re-inforced by the aforementioned seams, sewn with silk thread.

Each stitch taken left a hole which was not entirely stopped up by the silk thread.

"The holes are very small," said Machuron.

"How many are there?" I asked.

"At least seven million, at most eight million," he said doubt-fully.

These seams had been caulked by covering them inside and out with silk ribbon, measuring four centimetres, which had been glued on with a vulcanized rubber varnish that Lachambre had invented.

The varnish that had been used for sealing the balloon as a whole was a linseed oil varnish compounded by Arnould, which had for a long time been used by the French military balloon units among others.

The balloon was in Paris not only for purposes of safe-keeping and inspection. It was also going to be enlarged by inserting a new belt, ninety-two centimetres wide, between its two halves.

"All the seams are going to be further strengthened when we get to Spitzbergen," said Machuron. "Lachambre has succeeded in producing a new vulcanized rubber varnish, and with its help we shall be able to make further improvements in the glueing down of the sealing strips."

Machuron evinced an almost boyish pride in the balloon and its construction, and he assured us that it had been manufactured with greater care and precision than any of its predecessors.

The net, for instance, consisted of no less than nineteen thousand meshes, but there was not a single knot. At the points where they met the strings were firmly hanked to each other with strong yarn. Over fifteen thousand metres of twine had been used for this purpose.

"What are the dimensions of the cordage used for the net?" asked Swedenborg.

"Five and a half millimetres," answered Machuron. "Italian hemp."

"Their combined length?"

"Twenty-five thousand metres."

"Weight?"

"A good three hundred and fifty kilos. The weight varies some-what with the humidity of the air."

"The devil knows everything off by heart," Swedenborg said to me.

"The cords are delicate," said Machuron, "but they can take a load of five hundred kilos without breaking. We've made a whole series of load-endurance tests. The worst result was four hundred and twenty kilos, the best five hundred and forty."

7

Our landlady's daughters, Jeanne and Louise, became our guides to the cafés and places of amusement in Paris.

Swedenborg translated and read aloud to them the reports from its Paris correspondent in a London newspaper, *The Daily News*.

"'Mr Fraenkel is a tall, broad-shouldered, jovial giant, the kind of Titan of whom Norway so often gives us examples. He faces the coming dangers and difficulties with quiet optimism.'"

I got up and bowed.

"'It would also be possible to describe Mr Swedenborg as a lean, athletic giant if only he were not in the company of Mr Fraenkel. He too is full of enthusiasm for the enterprise. His eyes flash eagerly when he talks about the expedition, but they become sad at the thought that duty will soon compel him to leave the lovely French girls.'"

"Of course I'm lean and unbelievably agile," he said, "but both during my career as a boxer, and when I won the Royal Swedish fencing championship, I was classed as a lightweight.

"As a matter of fact," he said, "during the time I was acting as page to His Majesty King Oscar II of Sweden and Norway at the Royal Palace in Stockholm, my gilded dress sword was a great nuisance to me. The scabbard often banged on the floor and disturbed the most solemn ceremonies. I was quite simply too short for the Royal Swedish dress sword. The largest of the Royal Swedish dress swords is calculated to suit the jovial giants, of whom such a rich selection is to be found in Norway."

* * *

As far as my limited knowledge of French would allow me to judge Swedenborg's translation of the letter to *The Daily News* was largely correct. On one point however he was guilty of falsification.

What made Mr Swedenborg's 'eagerly flashing eyes' grow 'sad' was not the thought that he would soon have to leave the beautiful French girls, but that he was the reserve man and in all probability would not take part in the balloon voyage to the north.

During our stay in Paris Swedenborg tried systematically to conceal the fact that his value and significance in the expedition was only that of a remotely possible second string.

At all the more or less official gatherings and entertainments, when we visited factories or military balloon establishments, at all the so-called receptions, on all the occasions when we were interviewed by representatives from aeronautical societies, from the daily papers or technical journals he talked about *l'expédition-polaire d'Andrée* as if the only people concerned in it were Andrée, Engineer Fraenkel, and Lieutenant Swedenborg.

I think I understood him.

In Paris his life reached its zenith.

In Paris he embarked upon, accomplished and concluded the only part he actually played in Andrée's journey to the North Pole. At Spitzbergen he was only the reserve man.

8

The day for our first ascent had been fixed, and we arrived in good time at Lachambre's factory.

Between two of the workshops was a fairly large open space, and in it, awaiting us, was a full balloon, anchored or moored by a strong rope. It was swinging gently to and fro in the morning breeze.

"Are you nervous?" I asked.

"Merely impatient," answered Swedenborg, and walked up to the car. I followed him.

"I suggest that you put out your cigar," I said.

"It went out while we were still in the cab," he answered, seizing hold of the mooring-rope, and trying to pull the car down to the ground. He did not succeed.

A few unoccupied workmen were sitting on a bench watching us with curiosity.

"The desire to rise upwards is great," said Swedenborg, "and I'm burning with impatience to try my wings."

Soon after this Lachambre arrived. He greeted us politely, smiled kindly, looked at the occasional wisps of cloud in the sky, shook his head and smiled still more kindly.

"The wind's blowing unnecessarily hard," he said. "Come back tomorrow, my friends."

The next morning Lachambre met us outside the factory.

"The wind will increase in a few hours," he said.

"Tell him," I said to Swedenborg, "that the polar winds always increase hour by hour."

Lachambre answered with a smile and a shrug of his shoulders.

On the third day, 11 March, the sky was cloudless, the sun shone hot early in the morning, the air quivered between the walls of the houses, and the pennant on the factory flagstaff hung limp and motionless.

"Today," said Lachambre, after shaking us warmly by the hand.

The balloon was waiting in the open space. It seemed to be rather larger than before.

Lachambre was wearing a white, collarless shirt. Over one arm he was carrying a thick woollen jersey.

"A lovely day," he said.

The balloon was red. It had a name, and that name was inscribed in large blue letters on a white base: FRAM.*

The bottom, or floor, of the car was less than half a metre above the ground. I helped Lachambre and Swedenborg into the basket and then climbed in myself. The car then sank to the ground.

* Forward.

An engineer came up to us with two woollen jerseys. We had met him before quite briefly. His name was Lair.

"The nearer one gets to the sun the colder it grows," said Lachambre.

Lair also handed us a basket containing a few bottles of wine, white bread and roast chicken.

Lachambre then gave orders that the moorings should be untied.

The car remained on the ground.

I had an odd feeling that the balloon was not struggling to rise, that it was heavier than the air, that the car-lines were not ropes, but steel struts enclosed in rope, upon which the weight of the balloon was resting.

The car was small and square.

"Why is the balloon called the *Fram*?" I asked.

"Being an aeronaut," said Lachambre, "isn't merely a matter of going up into the air in a balloon. Aerial navigation is not only a way of voyaging, it is also something of a fine art.

"That is what I want to demonstrate to you," he said.

The air between the two workshops was entirely motionless.

Our instructor opened one of the sacks of ballast.

"Why is the balloon called the *Fram*?" I asked.

With the help of a little spade, the sort that gardeners use, he emptied out a few kilos of sand.

"You're very heavy, Engineer Fraenkel," he said, "heavier than I thought."

After another couple of spadefuls the car began to tremble. Lachambre dropped the spade and let a few handfuls of sand trickle through his fingers. The car ceased to tremble. We were now a couple of decimetres above the ground.

Engineer Lair guided the balloon close to the most southerly of the buildings that surrounded the open space. He carried out this manoeuvre quite easily by pushing the car before him.

Lachambre sprinkled yet another fistful of sand on to the ground, and we rose four or five metres.

"The art of ballooning is in truth an art," he said.

He cautiously pulled the rope regulating the valve with his left hand. For a second or two we heard the hiss of escaping gas. The

73

balloon sank, and he halted its downward movement by dropping a few tablespoonfuls of sand to the ground with his right hand.

We were once again a couple of decimetres above the open space.

"These lovely calm days are wonderful," said Lachambre, our instructor. "With the valve and two handfuls of dry sand I can rise or sink as I please. I can compel the balloon to come to rest at exactly the point I myself choose. I can balance it as a jeweller balances his scales.

"That mark on the wall of the building over there," he said pointing, "that indicates a height of eight metres above the ground."

He threw out a little sand. The wall of the building sank. He eased open the valve for a fraction of a second. The wall sank more slowly, the car passed the mark indicating eight metres, it stopped, the wall began to rise again—or, the balloon to sink. He let a little sand trickle through his fingers. We again glided past the mark, stopped once more, rose slowly, almost hesitatingly, and finally came to a stop exactly level with the eight metre mark.

"Just like balancing a jeweller's scales," he said with a smile.

About ten people were assembled on the open space beneath us. They were standing in a cluster looking up at us.

"Look out!" called Lachambre.

The little group moved to the northern side of the open space.

"Balloon ascents are the most popular form of public amusement today," said Lachambre, "even for people who work in balloon factories. And people have learnt that they must stand to one side if they don't want to get sand in their eyes."

He filled a plate-like metal dish with sand. It held at a guess a good half litre, and probably weighed something under two kilos.

"We shall rise now," he said. "At first we shall rise at a uniform speed. But, Engineer Fraenkel, please note that our speed will suddenly increase when we reach a height of approximately thirty metres."

Lachambre emptied his plate-like metal dish.

The balloon rose. The ground beneath us sank.

The barograph registered our rise metre by metre.

At just under thirty metres our speed increased noticeably.

"The black roofs," Lachambre informed us, "suck up the heat

74

of the sun and transform it into rising currents of air.

"These thermals are local and short-lived," he said.

The roofs of the houses sank beneath us.

Our aeronautical pedagogue threw out about ten spadefuls of sand with his short-handled gardener's spade.

At the height of three hundred and fifty metres we were caught by a light south-westerly wind and carried towards the north-east.

The Arc de Triomphe and the Eiffel Tower.

Under us an enormous spider's web of streets, light-coloured houses and dark roofs. Also patches of greenery, some large, some small.

The sky was cloudless, the sun was hot.

I helped Lachambre to empty out the whole of the first sack of ballast.

We rose to a height of two thousand five hundred metres.

Lachambre put on his woollen jersey.

"I'm happy," he said. "I don't know how many hundreds of ascents I've made, but each time I experience the same sensation of complete happiness."

I do not think I felt at all afraid during the first phase of the ascent. I was altogether too much occupied by what Lachambre was saying and doing.

I am quite certain that I was neither afraid nor nervous by the time we had risen to the height of a thousand metres above Paris.

Instead I was seized by a feeling that resembled mild intoxication.

The depth beneath us did not worry me at all. It was as if I had been freed from a great weight of whose existence I had previously been totally ignorant.

The red balloon above us was a globe of safety.

There was safety too in Lachambre.

"*Sehr glücklich?*" I asked.

"*Unbedingt,*" he answered.

He was standing close beside me in the cramped car. He was smiling, not only with his mouth, but also with his eyes, brown eyes, half hidden by his heavy eyelids.

Lachambre was the type of human being who, because they themselves are secure and self-confident, inspire feelings of security and self-confidence in the people who are in their company.

Andrée too was this type of human being.

"Paris is the centre of the world," said Lachambre.

He described the city beneath us in short sentences. He spoke slowly, and in a clear voice.

We drifted north-eastwards with the wind. The sky was cloudless and blue, and the sun was hot, in spite of the refreshing coolness of our great height.

Vilhelm Swedenborg?

I had forgotten his existence. As far as I knew, and contrary to his usual custom, he had been perfectly quiet during the preliminary manoeuvres in the balloon. I do not think he had uttered a single word.

It was not until we reached a height of two thousand metres that I remembered that I and Lachambre were not alone in the car.

Swedenborg was standing with his back resting against one of the corners of the car.

His mouth was open, he had red patches on his cheeks, and small beads of perspiration on his forehead.

"Are you afraid?" I asked.

"Only damnably excited," he answered.

"Did you hear," he said, "did you hear the way sounds changed? The voices of the people when we started, clear at first, and then dying away into the hubbub of Paris, a strange hubbub, that turned into a diffuse rumble. And in that rumble you could clearly distinguish the shrill whistle of trains, and the dull hooting of ships' sirens. And also the sharp barking of dogs!

"Out of everything in the world of men—the voices of barking dogs!

"How high?" he asked.

"Something over two thousand five hundred metres," I answered, after glancing at the barograph.

"An amusing detail," he said. "That business with the ballast, sacks filled with sand. I'd imagined that one simply threw them overboard. Now I understand why they are filled with sand and not with scrap-iron, or small stones.

"With the help of a trickle of sand you can balance a balloon as

76

a Dutch jeweller balances his scales, a few carats here, a few there.

"A sack of sand thrown down on Paris from a height of a couple of thousand metres would crack the house it struck. But sand that is emptied out of its sack at a height of a couple of thousand metres, that sand disperses, separates into its almost microscopic particles. The air checks its fall, spreads it about, transforms it into a cloud, so that when it strikes the ground it is like an invisible and quite harmless drizzle."

"As ingenious as Columbus's egg," I said.

"Monsieur Lachambre," said Swedenborg, "please forgive us for conversing in Swedish, this miserable hyperborean language of ours."

He continued:

"This is my first ascent in a balloon. I'm in the grip of a fever. I'm happy for the first time in my life! I wish I were a poet. I should like to thank you, Monsieur Lachambre. But words fail me. I'm no poet. I'm only a Swedish officer. If I'd been wearing uniform I could have saluted you with my gilded dress sword."

We drifted slowly north-eastwards.

Soon after we had passed over the most northerly suburbs of Paris Lachambre opened the valve and we landed gently on a field of short spring grass.

Some peasants came hurrying up. They trampled out the remaining gas from the balloon, rolled it up into a large bundle, and got it ready to be transported back to Paris.

Lachambre, Swedenborg, and I threw ourselves down in the shade of an ancient oak and there, in peace and quiet, laid out the provisions we had brought with us.

"A hundred years ago," said Lachambre, "the peasants would have attacked the balloon with pitchforks and scythes."

"Why is the balloon called the *Fram*?" I asked.

"In honour of your countryman, Nansen," said Lachambre.

9

Lachambre was a cautious man. He would not willingly go aloft except in the most favourable meteorological conditions.

One can understand him. Balloons are expensive things.

It was eleven days before we made our second ascent. It was a beautiful morning, a clear blue sky, and pleasantly warm.

When the wind had carried us clear of the built-up area of Paris Lachambre brought the balloon down to a height of one hundred and fifty metres. He wanted to let us practise sailing with the guide-rope. This rope was about two hundred and thirty metres long.

Anyone who wants to understand the technique of ballooning must know something about the use of guide-ropes.

These ropes are usually thick, and consequently heavy. They drag the balloon down to earth. As the vessel sinks, and an ever increasing part of the weight of the ropes rests on the ground, the load on the balloon is successively diminished. The balloon ceases to sink, it stops in a state of equilibrium.

The idea was that we should practise sailing with the guide-ropes at a height of about one hundred and fifty metres.

The countryside over which we were gliding was hilly and wooded.

The wind suddenly increased in strength and became squally and veering as well. Clouds covered the sky. Showers of hail and rain drummed on the balloon.

The wind carried the balloon along at an increasing speed, but the passage of the trailing rope was hindered by trees and uneven-nesses in the ground. We three in the car were thrown about as if we had been in a rowing boat on a choppy sea. Lachambre ended up in the bottom of the car under us both.

We were approaching a rather large area of open ground.

I ordered Swedenborg to throw out the anchor while I myself opened the valve.

The anchor cut a black furrow in the ground but did not catch firmly in the turf. The gas poured out of the valve. The black furrow grew longer and longer and the balloon slackened and sank.

The car landed with a thud and started to career about. We had the greatest difficulty in remaining in it, for the balloon, which still contained some gas, was dragging us at a tearing speed over stony hillocks and shallow ditches, or through prickly thickets.

Our trip came to a sudden end when the anchor stuck fast between two stones. I was thrown several metres forward and became entangled in the car-lines when I tried to stand up.

We were able to wash, and put plaster on our wounds, in a neighbouring farm. The balloon meanwhile was packed up and put on a wagon drawn by two horses.

"Aeronautics is not only a method of travel," said Swedenborg, "it is also something of a fine art."

He looked at his face in the glass.

"A very fine art," he said, "which has resulted in three lovely bruises, and a long thin scratch on my cheek."

He wiped his wound with a wet linen rag. It had stopped bleeding.

"What a pity that it's only a superficial wound," he said. "It's actually more than two inches long. If it had gone deeper it would have made a handsome scar. Isn't that called a *Renomage-Schmisse*? That business of fencing with sabres, German students, duelling you know."

IO

We had gone to Paris to get practical experience in the art of navigating a balloon. But in his written memorandum Andrée had also urged us to try to learn as much as possible about balloons in general and the theory of aeronautics, etc.

We spent many days in Lachambre's factory. We followed all the processes in the making of balloons and accustomed ourselves to the strange mixture of smells: linseed oil, vulcanized rubber varnish, and slightly impure hydrogen gas.

We visited Gabriel Yon's workshop. He received us kindly but languidly. It was he who had made Andrée's balloon the *Svea* some years previously, and he could not conceal his disappointment at not having been entrusted with the task of manufacturing the North Pole balloon.

"There's only one way of constructing a gas-tight balloon," he said. "You build an inner sphere of several thicknesses of gold-beater's skins glued together. That will be absolutely gastight. But it will be fragile and easily damaged. It must therefore be protected by an outer sphere of varnished silk. This method will produce a balloon that can keep afloat for months. Lachambre's balloon is one gigantic sieve of small holes. It will sink to the ground, or to the ice, in less than a week."

We also studied Maurice Mallet's balloon factory.

Mallet was a very young aeronaut and engineer. He did not use glue for joining together the pieces of silk in a balloon. His method was entirely different. He used a sort of solder, applied with a warm soldering iron, but he would not reveal the secret of it to us.

His manufacture of balloons was on a small scale, and was carried on in an almost ramshackle wooden shed. He clearly had neither private capital nor wealthy patrons.

Per Nordenfelt of the Nordenfelt Company succeeded in obtaining permission for us to visit the French Army's *Aérostation militaire* at Meudon, just south of Paris, a visit which the requirements of military security must have made it difficult to arrange.

Our guide was no less a person than the chief of the establishment, Colonel Renard, assisted by his younger brother, Captain Renard.

Gaston Tissandier was at the meal given afterwards, and also Henri Giffard and the aged Fonvielle, the most distinguished aeronaut of our time.

Gaston Tissandier and Colonel Renard were the experts engaged by Nordenfelt to supervise the making of Andrée's balloon. They had followed all the stages of its manufacture with fastidious care, a care which Machuron, Lachambre's nephew, assured us had been carried on a couple of occasions to the verge of morbid suspicion.

The central topic of our conversation at table was the dirigibility of Andrée's balloon.

More than ten years previously Gaston Tissandier and his brother had experimented with a dirigible balloon equipped with a backward-pointing propeller which could rotate at a speed of one hundred and eighty revolutions per minute. This balloon was not round, it was oblong and resembled a cigar.

The propeller made it possible for the vessel to travel at about three metres per second, and it was therefore only really dirigible when there was a dead calm.

Colonel Renard, with his brother and an engineer called Krebs, had also experimented with dirigible aerial vessels. Their balloon too had been oblong, like a cigar. It had been driven by a pulling propeller, that is to say not a pushing propeller. They had reached a speed of rather more than six metres per second.

"We made seven ascents," said Colonel Renard. "On five occasions we managed to return to the place from which we had started."

"When was this?" asked Swedenborg.

"Our last ascent must have been made eleven years ago. Six metres per second is far too low a speed."

Both Renard and Tissandier had used an electrodynamic machine manufactured by Siemens to drive their propellers.

"The accumulators are heavy," said Renard, "and their store of energy is far too small."

"Ask them what has been happening during the past ten years," I said to Swedenborg.

Their answer was wordy, but in substance brief: Nothing.

A free-sailing balloon is of course wholly dependent on the winds, on the movements of the air.

It is impossible to understand Andrée's plan for reaching the North Pole unless we try to enter into his thoughts on how a balloon can be made at least partially dirigible.

A balloon must be equipped with a number of ropes that drag along the ground, in the water, or over the ice.

The friction of these ropes checks the speed of the balloon. It becomes less than the speed of the wind.

If the balloon is equipped with a sail set at an angle, the wind can be used to make the balloon sail in a direction that deviates from that of the wind itself.

This idea is in essence a simple one.

"Andrée's balloon is not of course completely dirigible," I said. "But it should be possible to steer it well enough to enable us to reach the immediate neighbourhood of the Pole, to get to a point that lies above Nansen and Johansen's famous latitude of 86° 14′ N."

Colonel Renard said:

"If you think, gentlemen, that Andrée's theories about the dirigibility of a balloon are newfangled, you will be making a mistake. Andrée's ideas were worked out in detail long ago by an Englishman called Green. You wonder whether he is still alive? Experimental aeronauts are seldom long-lived. Green sailed in his balloon the *Nassau* from London to the interior of Prussia in less than twenty-four hours.

"Green's ideas," Renard continued, "were adopted by many French balloonists and abandoned. But that is long ago.

"In our time," he said, "there's only one expert on guide-ropes and sails, that is on balloons that can be partially steered, namely your famous engineer."

"Tell him," I said to Swedenborg, "that in practical experiments Andrée managed to steer his balloon the *Svea* on a course that deviated from the direction of the wind by an average of nearly thirty degrees."

Gaston Tissandier said in English:

"Engineer Andrée reckons that his balloon should be able to remain afloat for thirty days or longer. This presupposes a hitherto unknown degree of impermeability in the envelope of the balloon. The gastightness of a balloon increases—or to put it more precisely, the rate at which a balloon loses gas decreases—with the size of the balloon. It does so for the simple reason that the surface of a balloon in relation to its volume grows smaller the larger a balloon is."

"Elementary mathematics," said Swedenborg.

"I don't remember exactly," said Tissandier, "but I know that up to now no balloon of the size of Andrée's polar balloon has remained in the air for longer than seventy-two hours."

"You mean you are sceptical?" I said.

"Yes," answered Tissandier.

"All the same you've accepted the task of acting as the experts controlling the manufacture of the balloon?"

Gaston Tissandier leant over the table and seized my hand.

"I'm an old man though I'm no more than fifty-five," he said. "I'm ill. I shall be dead in less than five years. I know more about the art of ballooning than anyone else now alive—with the possible exception of your remarkable Andrée.

"On the instructions of Engineer Nordenfelt," he said, "I and Commodore Renard have watched over the manufacture of the polar balloon with the most pedantic care.

"I'm an old man," he said, "weighed down by my experiences of great heights. I'm ill, I've flown far too high. Mv lungs are ruptured, I'm going to die. But I like experimenters, pioneers, daring explorers.

"Renard, his brother, and I are of the same mind. You won't reach the North Pole. You'll probably never return.

"Your balloon," he said, "is the best balloon that has so far been made. Of that we can assure you, Renard and I. But your journey will fail. Nevertheless I urge you to set out.

"Experimenters, pioneers, and determined and daring explorers must always be prepared for death," Tissandier continued.

"John Franklin's well equipped polar expedition, a hundred and thirty men, went out to meet a slow and terrible death. More than fifty relief expeditions were sent out. What did they find? Nothing but dead men, of whom a number had been forced to commit the most frightful crime of which a human being is capable. How many hundreds of people have been lost in that world of ice since then?

"And the art of ballooning. Pilâtre de Rozier was the world's first aeronaut. A year and a half later he was the first victim. How many hundreds of balloonists since then have met with sudden death?

"Don't imagine that all of them have crashed and been smashed to bits on the earth or drowned in the sea.

"More than twenty years ago—yes, I'm an old man—I tried to reach a greater height than Coxwell and Glaisher. Crosé-Spinelli and that admirable aeronaut Sivel were with me.

"We took off from the gasworks at La Vilette. We rose very rapidly and in a short time reached a height of seven thousand metres. Billowing drifts of white clouds lay beneath us, the sky above us was a dazzling pale blue. The sun burnt our faces but the cold was frightful. We were well wrapped up. It was of no avail, our fingers and our joints grew stiff. The last notes I wrote are illegible, even to me.

"Sivel asked if we should throw out more ballast. I nodded and he emptied overboard three sacks of sand. The effort required was enormous and after making it he staggered and fell to the floor.

"The car was round and equipped with a bench as round as itself.

"Crosé-Spinelli bent over him and gave him oxygen from the tube.

"It did Sivel no good. He was writhing with violent cramp. Blood was trickling from the corners of his wide-open mouth and his eyes were starting.

"We seemed to have been caught by a rapidly rising current of air.

"Crosé-Spinelli put the tube of oxygen to his own mouth and then handed it to me.

"My hands were powerless, I couldn't open it.

"Sivel flung his arms round my legs. His blue-black face was a terrifying sight. Then the cramp slackened, he slipped slowly over on to his back and lay dead.

"The balloon went on rising. It was as if my friend's death had reduced the weight of the car.

"Crosé-Spinelli succeeded in opening the valve at the apex of the balloon. He had to tug the valve-line time after time. Like the car-lines it was covered with white hoar-frost, and very probably the mechanism of the valve too was covered with frost and ice.

"His exertions were too much for him. I sat as one paralysed. I'd neither the strength nor the will to help him. He fell against me, groped for the tube of oxygen, fell to the floor beside Sivel, dropped the tube and couldn't find it again, or hadn't the strength. He raised his arm and pointed upwards. 'Jésus Marie' he said. His eyes were starting like Sivel's, his face was just as blue-black, his mouth just as wide open. His arm fell heavily across his chest. His head twisted to one side and blood ran from his mouth and nose. Crosé-Spinelli too was dead.

"I myself was half unconscious—more than half unconscious. I heard the gas streaming out of the valve. We began to descend. The car touched down two hundred and fifty kilometres from our starting point.

"How high did we rise? I don't know. Eight thousand metres, or ten thousand metres.

"So far, as you see, I've survived the death that comes at altitudes that are far too great," said Gaston Tissandier.

"Engineer Andrée's polar expedition will fail," he said.

"The question is, will it fail in the air, or on the ice of the Arctic Ocean?"

I I

Tissandier and Renard were pretty well the only pessimists. Nearly all the eminent persons we met, thanks to Lachambre and Engineer Nordenfelt, expressed their confidence in the undertaking and offered us their warmest good wishes. Among these were men like Flammarion, Professor Janssen, the former Foreign Minister, Berthelot, and old de Fonvielle, who lamented the fact that his great age prevented him from coming with us. All the other well-known aeronauts whom we visited, men like Godard, Besançon, Courty and Surcouf, were equally optimistic.

Machuron laughed at Tissandier's statement that our balloon

would not keep afloat for more than seventy-two hours.

"On the other hand," he said, "he's right in the sense that no one, as far as I know, has ever attempted a balloon voyage of that length. Twenty-four hours in a cramped car can seem like forty-eight. No one sails for longer than is absolutely necessary."

Swedenborg asked him if he knew how long a fairly large captive balloon could remain afloat.

"That's quite irrelevant," he answered. "A military *ballon-captif* is simply constructed, made of cheap material, and covered with second-rate varnish. It's not designed to remain afloat for any length of time. It can easily be hauled down and filled with fresh gas."

"How much gas does your own balloon the *Fram* lose in twenty-four hours?" I asked.

"That depends on how high one rises, and how much gas escapes when the air-pressure is reduced."

"But when it's anchored beside your workshop?"

Machuron shook his head and threw up his hands.

"Don't know," he said, "I've no figures handy."

"I never thought I should see that lad at a loss for an answer," said Swedenborg.

Machuron laughed as if he had understood what Swedenborg had said. Then he said: "Graham investigated the matter a couple of years ago. A medium-sized balloon of the best quality. Graham and Poiseuille made the experiment jointly. If I remember rightly the balloon only lost about ten kilos of its lifting capacity in the course of several weeks."

"Do you know who Graham is?" I asked Swedenborg. "Graham and what's his name, the other chap?"

"Let's try to hide our lack of education," he answered.

"When Andrée put forward his plan at the big Geographical Congress in London two years ago," said Machuron, "it was criticized and discussed by all the people in the world who knew what they were talking about, and by those who didn't know as well— you know who I mean, don't you? Of course you must know. That was when Colonel Watson mentioned that tests had been made which proved that a military balloon could retain its gas for three weeks with only a very small leakage."

"Watson," I said to Swedenborg, "he's the head of the British

Army's aeronautical division, or he was at any rate. I don't know if he's still alive. Balloonists often die very suddenly."

"You know," said young Machuron, of the long upward-turned and waxed moustache, "Charles's balloon of 1783 was the first hydrogen balloon in the world.

"Its construction was novel, but even at birth it was in principle perfect.

"The envelope of the balloon was of varnished silk. Round the envelope was a rope net. The net carried the car. The car was made of rattan or willow. The balloon was furnished with a valve that could be manipulated from the car. In the car was ballast in the form of sand, kept in sacks. There was also an anchor attached to a long rope.

"I've described the first hydrogen balloon," said Machuron. "The description applies equally well to Andrée's polar balloon, made one hundred and thirteen years later."

"There are differences," said Swedenborg.

"Only details. The guide-ropes. Andrée's much-talked-of steering sail. Better instruments for measuring height and speed, and for taking bearings."

"What's happened during these hundred and thirteen years?" I asked.

"The strength and impermeability of balloon fabric is many times greater," said Machuron. "That's the most important thing. The rest is merely detail.

"In the course of more than a century a conception that was perfect in principle from its inception has been further improved and become even more perfect.

"Your balloon will keep afloat for at least a month," he said. "If you let the car and the sail fall and cling to the net you'll be able to manage another week in the air."

"What he says alarms me," said Swedenborg. "First a long journey to Spitzbergen, followed by a long stay there waiting to start, and after that forty days in a balloon! This remarkable young man knows everything—well, almost everything—about the soul

of a balloon. But he appears to know nothing at all about the love-
life of a Swedish lieutenant."

I 2

It was doubtless true that Lachambre had a perfect command of
all the niceties of the art of ballooning, and that he could balance his
balloon as a jeweller balances his scales. All the same our ascents
with Machuron were more instructive.

This slim, dapper little Frenchman was not only an eminent
theoretician in the art of ballooning, he was also an able, and above
all a daring aeronaut.

When we made our first ascent with Machuron as our guide
the anemometer on the highest roof-top showed that the velocity
of the wind was oscillating between thirteen and sixteen metres
per second. The balloon was being tossed hither and thither. It was
pulling and jerking at its moorings to such an extent that we had
some difficulty in getting into the car.

He hurried us on. "The old man may come at any minute," he said.

He gave the order for all the mooring-ropes but one to be released,
and the balloon shook and pulled worse than ever. He threw a
whole sack of sand overboard. "It's a question of getting up aloft
quicker than hell's devils," he said.

The reason? So that neither we nor the roofs of the adjacent
houses should be damaged.

Our ascent was indeed rapid. After a few minutes we reached a
height of a thousand metres, and into the bargain were a thousand
metres further east.

The instant we left the roof-tops I had again the same fascinating
experience : the whining and whistling of the ropes and the net died
away, the flapping flag suddenly hung limply on its rope, the buzz-

ing in my ears vanished, the wind ceased to blow, there was absolute calm in spite of the fact that we were moving over Paris at the rate of about fifty kilometres an hour.

"If I lit my cigar," said Swedenborg, "you wouldn't see the slightest flicker from the flame of the match."

In the midst of this calm the sounds of the city beneath us increased. Voices of people talking, laughter, the sound of wheels on the cobbles, the hoofs of horses, the joints in railway lines rattling as wheels passed over them, steam whistles, sounds that rapidly merged into a dull roar, in which only the voices of barking dogs were distinguishable.

"Look at our friend Alexis Machuron," said Swedenborg. "Then look at me! Are my eyes shining as brightly as his?"

The balloon was not the same as the one in which we had made our ascents with Lachambre. It was called the *Nobel* and was rather larger than the *Fram*.

"Why *Nobel*?"

"A slight obeisance to your great countryman, Alfred Nobel," answered Machuron. "I sincerely regret his far too early death."

"Thirty or forty days in a balloon," said Swedenborg. "It's certainly an alarming thought for several reasons. Fancy not even being able to light your cigar!"

"Snuff," I suggested.

"Damn this confoundedly explosive hydrogen!" he said.

13

A small delegation from Madame Tussaud's waxworks in London called upon us.

They worked rapidly, methodically and earnestly. They measured and noted down lengths and widths, made sketches, took us out into the sunshine of the street and photographed us from every conceivable angle. They wanted us to put on the clothes we should wear on our polar journey, but were in no way annoyed when we explained that we had not got them with us, and that we did not even know in detail what our equipment would be like.

14

On 11 April we made our eighth ascent.

This was made in the balloon the *Touring Club* with its owner, the well-known balloonist Besançon and his assistant Engineer Cabalzar.

Besançon demonstrated the variations in the direction of the wind at different altitudes.

We came down near the town of Argent-sur-Sauldre, moored the balloon, and took in at a small hotel. We had an excellent dinner of which Besançon's friend, Count de Mombel, the lord of the manor, also partook. Both our host and Count de Mombel made speeches and drank toasts to the success of the Andrée expedition.

A multitudinous gathering of peasants and other people gathered in the garden of the hotel and gave three cheers for *l'expédition-polaire d'Andrée*.

Swedenborg ordered the landlord of the hotel to take wine out to the crowd, but de Mombel threatened to challenge him to a duel if he was not allowed to settle the bill.

On the following day, 12 April, Swedenborg and I made our ninth and last ascent. It was our first independent voyage.

The *Touring Club* had lost a good deal of her gas and therefore of her lifting capacity, and an ascent with four men in the car would probably have been fairly unsuccessful.

Besançon put me in charge of his valuable balloon.

The idea was that we should practise sailing a balloon with the aid of guide-ropes. We rose slowly to a height of barely one hundred metres, and then drifted northwards with the southerly wind. The balancing effect of the guide-ropes kept us at a fairly constant level.

The warmth of the sun increased the carrying capacity of the balloon, and when we were confronted by a low ridge we rose rapidly to a height of several hundred metres. I wanted to open the valve in order to keep the guide-ropes in contact with the ground, but Swedenborg emptied two of our remaining three sacks of sand, and the *Touring Club* rose to a height of four thousand metres.

We had only dressed for a low-altitude voyage. We had no woollen jerseys or other winter clothing with us, and we shivered with cold.

"The nearer the sun the colder it gets," I said.

"Symbolically enough it's my feet that are coldest," said Swedenborg. "Those old Greeks were wrong, damn them. What did they call the man who flew so high that his wings came unstuck because he'd got too near the sun. He'd glued them on with wax and the wax melted in the hot sunshine. Wasn't he called something that began with 'Dae' and ended with 'us'? Wax just gets colder and harder the higher one flies."

"Daedalus," I answered.

"We should have brought a bottle of brandy with us," said Swedenborg.

"It wasn't Daedalus who flew much too high when he was fleeing through the air from Crete and King Minos. It was his son and fellow fugitive, Icarus. It was his wings that came unstuck. He crashed into the sea. They called that sea the Icarian Sea until they thought of another name."

"Brandy's just as warming as a Norwegian jersey," said Swedenborg.

"Couldn't Icarus swim?" he added. "It's much harder to learn to fly than to learn to swim."

With the help of the valve and the remaining sack of sand we made the *Touring Club* rise and fall time after time between the heights of fifteen hundred and three thousand metres until the sand gave out.

We made notes of the divergencies in the direction and strength of the wind at different levels. Besançon's maps were altogether too general, and we lost track of our position.

We travelled in a mainly easterly direction for the last hour, and then made a perfect landing on a field outside a small town at three o'clock in the afternoon. The landing was perfect in Lachambre's sense of the word.

At the height of a good hundred metres we let down the anchor. The wind was slight. The anchor got a good hold on the turf. I opened the valve cautiously. The balloon sank slowly. When we were about twenty metres above the ground Swedenborg threw out his cap and his coat. The downward movement ceased.

Swedenborg unrolled a large Swedish flag made of silk.

Crowds of people swarmed towards us from all directions.

"Vive la France," said Swedenborg.

"Vive l'expédition-polaire," answered the mob beneath us.

I cautiously touched the rope controlling the valve, as cautiously as a jeweller when he is balancing his scales.

The *Touring Club* sank almost hesitatingly. Swedenborg leant over the side of the car. He was holding two opened bottles of mineral water, one in each hand. He met and parried the downward movement of the balloon by allowing the water to run out of the bottles in carefully calculated quantities.

The crowd of people grew larger.

The car touched the ground without our feeling the least bump.

"Mon Capitaine," said Swedenborg, "your subordinate lieutenant has pleasure in informing you that we now find ourselves on what is in one way *terra firma*, in another *terra incognita*."

*   *   *

A priest or monk in a black habit embraced us.

"My northern brothers," he said in German, the tears running down his cheeks. "Come with me to the cathedral. I shall there bless you in the name of Jesus Christ, and beg the Blessed Virgin to hold a protective hand over you.

"Monsieur Fraenkel, Monsieur Swedenborg," he said falteringly. "Follow me! It was in our cathedral, more than eight centuries ago, that the first archbishop of Sweden was consecrated. The great Stephen, the Right Reverend the Bishop of Upsala, the Holy Stephen."

I released myself from the reverend gentleman's arm.

"*Wo sind wir?*" I asked.

He was not allowed to answer. He was pushed aside by laughing, shouting people.

"*Le stadt Sens,*" said an older man in a uniform like a policeman's.

Swedenborg and I were smothered with flowers and carried shoulder-high into the town of Sens to the accompaniment of cheers and laughter, and ringing cries of '*Vive l'expédition-polaire*'.

15

Two days later, on 14 April, Swedenborg and I left Paris to return to Stockholm and Sweden.

Considerably more than a hundred persons had collected on the platform beside our coach. Foremost among them were Lachambre, Machuron, Engineer Nordenfelt, the sisters Jeanne and Louise, Tissandier, Gabriel Yon, young Mallet, Flammarion, and the Swedish Ambassador in Paris, whose name I have forgotten.

PART THREE

SPITZBERGEN

I

When we returned to Stockholm I, and to a lesser extent Swedenborg, became involved in the urgent work of settling all the hundreds
of details connected with the preparations for our expedition, and
the final choice of equipment.

The days were long, yet all too short.

I fell asleep the moment I went to bed. I slept heavily and dream-
lessly. I woke to a new working-day after all too few hours of rest.

Nils Strindberg was as feverishly active as I was.

We met every day. We often dined together at Runan, Rydberg,
or the Opera Cellar.

We ought to have had a long, confidential talk. But pressure of
work, shrinking time, all the hundreds of details that had to be
settled and sorted, left no room for confidential talks.

Andrée continued his duties at the Royal Patent and Registration
Office right up to the end.

His calm was impressive.

His ability to function as a split personality was even more
impressive. With his right hand, and in his capacity of Civil Servant,
he would draw up memoranda. With his left hand, and virtually
simultaneously, he would, after careful scrutiny, approve the
accounts of the polar expedition, sign documents, applications and
enquiries, answer letters, make notes, and draw up a whole series
of written directives to contractors, to Strindberg, to Swedenborg,
to me, and to other people involved.

His face had aged during my stay in Paris. He complained of
severe headaches several times.

His calm had about it a strange hypnotic power.

I have already pointed out the similarity between Andrée and
old Henri Lachambre, the maker of the balloon.

97

I asked Strindberg if he had noticed how hard it was to catch Andrée's eye, if he had been struck by the knotted wrinkles round his eyes, his tense, downward-drawn eyebrows, and the extremely rapid lateral oscillation of his pupils that occurred periodically.

Swedenborg and I had left a wintry Stockholm and in Paris had met the spring.

We returned to Stockholm. There we met the spring for the second time. Warm winds, hot sunshine, wood-anemones, a hint of green.

2

In the public debate that went on about the balloon and the way it was equipped the things most constantly discussed were the guide-ropes, the three drag-ropes, which would, by their friction on water or ice, check the speed of the balloon and, with the help of the sail, make it dirigible to a fairly high degree.

People expressed the fear that these ropes would get caught in the pack ice.

Andrée had foreseen this possibility and had therefore had the ropes made with a weak point. This would not interfere with the normal action of a rope in passage, but was weak enough to allow it to break if it got stuck.

A large body of sceptics did not trust this weak point.

Andrée had therefore divided the ropes into two halves above the 'weak point'. These two halves were joined by a connecting metal screw. A man in the car who gave the upper half a few twists could separate them.

The cautious sceptics were still not satisfied.

The last remaining parts of the guide-ropes might also get stuck in the jagged walls of pack ice.

Andrée commissioned Törner, a foreman at Wiklund's engineering works, to construct a cunning little device which could be lowered along a rope from the car and then, by means of an electrically ignited charge of explosive and two knives, clip off the rope at the desired point.

"Törner is a genius," said Andrée. "But what we need is not an ingenious clipper to sever our guide-ropes, what we need is simply a strong south wind."

3

Nansen and Lieutenant Johansen arrived in Stockholm to receive the Vega medal on 24 April, Vega day.

At the banquet that followed the ceremony I was placed immediately opposite Fridtjof Nansen. Albert Engström, the gifted young artist and author, was sitting on Nansen's right.

"What do you think of Andrée's idea of flying to the North Pole in a balloon?" he asked.

"Andrée will be putting himself at the mercy of the winds," Nansen answered after thinking for a moment.

"You mean that Andrée's a damned idiot?" said Engström.

"He's the very devil for ignorance and folly," answered Nansen.

Andrée made a speech in honour of Nansen and Johansen.

Then Nansen rose to make a short speech in reply.

"Your expedition," he said, "is the most daring expedition ever planned. But it is dependent on southerly winds. I know that you'll start if you get the right wind. You've the necessary courage and determination. That being so, I wish you good luck.

"I'm convinced that, during the course of a few days in your floating balloon, you'll collect information about the geography of the Arctic—photographic information—which will be more important, more trustworthy and consequently more valuable than all that we've learnt from the hundreds of polar expeditions so far sent out, my own included."

"You're lying, you blackguard," said Albert Engström, in a loud voice.

A painful silence ensued.

Nordenskiöld rose. He sat down again when the Crown Prince burst out laughing.

Fridtjof Nansen continued:

"Last summer, Engineer Andrée, you waited in vain for southerly winds. You'll very soon be setting out again for Spitzbergen and Danes Island, to wait for favourable conditions in which to start.

"It's possible that you may again wait in vain for southerly winds of the desired strength and stability.

"It requires great courage and determination to allow a balloon to rise into the air.

"It will require an even greater measure of courage and determination to give up for a second time because of adverse meteorological conditions. I'm convinced that you possess even that extreme courage and determination."

Nansen's short speech was greeted with long applause.

"What the devil do you mean?" said Engström to Nansen.

"Calm down," said Nansen. "Banquets are banquets. Ceremonious and so on. In any case, why shouldn't one encourage idiots?"

Engström said: "Sometime in the future a monument will be erected to the memory of Andrée. A monument in honour of a man who failed."

"A monument to Andrée only?" I asked, leaning across the table so that Albert Engström should hear what I was saying.

He looked at me questioningly—"Andrée only?"—then a broad smile spread over his face.

"Well I'm damned!" he said. "You must be Knut Fraenkel."

He raised his glass of brandy.

"That's the way things go," he said. "People will forget Knut Fraenkel and Nils Strindberg. But they'll raise a monument to Andrée. The organizer of the daring failure. Your health!"

4

Some days after the Vega festivities Andrée and I had a long consultation with Fridtjof Nansen and Lieutenant Johansen.

Andrée seemed at first to be chiefly interested in the meteorological observations made by the Norwegian expedition. However the conversation rapidly drifted over to their experiences during their long journey across the ice, and their winter sojourn on it, and ended up by turning into a detailed discussion of various sorts of equipment.

Nansen explained that he had found fur clothing unpractical. It might be pleasant wear for someone sitting still in the cold of an arctic winter, but not for a man in action, expending a great deal of energy on pulling a sledge. Such clothes were too impervious. They became saturated with sweat, and the moisture froze to ice, which made it impossible to dry them.

"Porous woollen clothing is best," he said. "But you must supplement it with wind-proof garments made of close-woven cotton material, breeches and a so-called anorak, a tunic equipped with a hood."

"Nordenskiöld pointed out the same thing seventeen or eighteen years ago," said Andrée. "He describes the winter clothing worn by the men of the *Vega* at the end of the first part of his book about his journey through the North-East Passage. Woollen clothing and over that a suit of close-woven canvas."

"I can't remember that Nordenskiöld ever made a journey across pack ice," answered Nansen.

"Albert Engström," said Andrée, "the young man who interrupted Nansen's speech. He's an excellent fellow, even if he doesn't care a tinker's curse for etiquette and correct behaviour. I don't know how we became acquainted.

"He drinks more than he should.

"But that's his business.

"He was with us when we first tried out our boat, the one we shall be taking with us in the balloon. That was out at Djurgården, more than a year ago. He got into the boat with me. It was early in the morning.

"The boat is four metres long and twelve decimetres broad. In spite of its dimensions Engström insisted on calling it a *canoe*.

"After our trial trip Engström invited us to breakfast at the Opera Cellar. He had two tots of schnapps with his herring appetizer.

" 'It *is* a canoe,' Engström said. 'It consists of a fragile spinal keel, and a framework of slender wooden ribs. Round this varnished silk. A boat without wooden planking isn't a boat, it's a canoe.'

"It may be that he had three tots with his herring."

After Nansen's visit to Stockholm the newspapers became more interested in the polar expedition.

Andrée appeared anxious to avoid being interviewed, and often turned the most determined journalists over to me.

With minor variations their questions were always the same.

"When will you be starting?"

"We're leaving Stockholm on 15 May."

"Yes, but when will the balloon take off from Spitzbergen?"

"When the right wind blows."

"How long will it take you to reach the North Pole?"

"About forty-eight hours if conditions are extremely favourable."

"If conditions are extremely unfavourable?"

"In that case we shall never reach the North Pole."

"What will you do then?"

"Make another attempt next year."

"What if you're forced to make an emergency landing?"

"We shall make our way across the ice until we reach Russia, Siberia, Alaska, or the arctic coast of Canada."

"And if you never succeed in reaching dry land?"

"Then we shall be forgotten," I answered. "Forgotten to the benefit of our successors.

"I needn't ask," I said, "if you remember the names Björling and Kallstenius. I know that you've forgotten them. Nevertheless, it's only five years since they set out on their journey to the north."

*　　　*　　　*

The Panopticon in Kungsträdgårdsgatan wanted to make wax figures of me and of Nils Strindberg.

"Don't forget me," said Swedenborg. "It's true that I'm only a reserve, but who knows? I may have to take up my duties at the last moment, at what will be, from your point of view, a singularly unfavourable moment. Moreover, I'm already among Madame Tussaud's waxworks in London.

"What's more," he said, "it's I, and Strindberg, who take first place when it comes to having a really interesting anchorage in history. I'm a descendant five times removed of the great Swedenborg's brother. Nils Strindberg is the son, in the direct line, of a cousin of the great August Strindberg's.

"I'm not," he added, "the right man to decide who was the madder of the two, the great Swedenborg or the great Strindberg."

King Oscar II placed the gunboat the *Svensksund* at the disposal of the expedition.

She was an admirable vessel, not particularly large, about three hundred tons, but she had a powerful engine, and for several winters she had worked as an ice-breaker at the entrance to Gothenburg harbour.

Her Master was Captain Count Carl August Ehrensvärd.

5

"Balloons can sometimes be difficult things to handle," said Swedenborg.

"During the American Civil War," he said, "they often used captive balloons, partly to get a more general view of the enemy dispositions, and partly, in certain sectors, to direct the fire of their own batteries.

"One morning, quite early, they got a big balloon ready to make an ascent. It was kept in position by about forty men who were holding fast to the mooring-rope.

"Forty men must weigh very nearly three thousand kilos.

"The rising sun warmed the balloon and increased its lifting capacity.

"A sudden gust of wind drove it sideways. Ten or fifteen of the soldiers, surprised by the jolt, lost their footing and let go of the rope. The balloon continued to rise. Some men were still hanging on to the rope. I can't say whether it was out of a sense of duty, or because they were paralysed with fear.

"The balloon went right up. Five men were still obstinately hanging on to the rope. At a height of about twenty metres one man lost his hold and fell, carrying one of his comrades with him.

"The balloon rose rapidly to a height of more than a hundred metres. It then drifted northwards across the enemy's lines, and was out of sight in less than a minute.

"Eyewitnesses reported that the three remaining involuntary balloonists bellowed like madmen."

"You must have made a mistake about there being only one rope," I said. "I'm sure there were at least four ropes."

"What a pity that the Southern States lost," said Swedenborg, "in spite of John Ericsson and *Monitor*, and slavery, and all the rest of it."

6

On 13 May Andrée arranged a dinner to welcome home Sven Hedin, who had just returned from the long journey of exploration through Asia, upon which he had set out in 1893.

There were only six of us at table, and neither Strindberg nor Swedenborg was present.

"Doctor Hedin," said Andrée in his speech of welcome, "you're home again after having twice crossed that frightful desert, Takla Makan, after having found forgotten cities, buried under the sand, after having solved the riddle of the Wandering Lake, after having pushed your way through large areas of the Tibetan highlands and mapped them. I congratulate you. You've achieved great things. But your journey is behind you.

"We've never met before," he continued. "We don't know one another. All the same I've taken the liberty of inviting you to a dinner of welcome. I've done so because my great journey lies immediately ahead of me. No one knows whether we shall ever again have the chance of eating at the same table."

"I accepted your invitation with deep gratitude," answered Sven Hedin. "Your plan is magnificent. Your determination is impressive. Your daring is unsurpassed. It would be senseless for me to wish you good luck. Your strength of will is so great that you stand in no need of good wishes."

We did not remain together for long. Andrée was tired and feeling the strain of the hectic pressure of recent weeks.

When we broke up Hedin said to me: "I can understand why you were the man whom Andrée chose from the many applicants. You've a resemblance to one another in a purely physical way. It's not immediately noticeable, but it becomes increasingly plain once one has noticed it. You might be Andrée's younger brother."

7

On 15 May, the very day on which the great Exhibition of Art and Industry opened, Andrée and I left Stockholm for Gothenburg. A few hundred people had assembled on the platform, not really many more than there had been when Swedenborg and I left Paris.

We were decked with flowers and they hurrahed us when the train started to move.

We had a first-class compartment to ourselves.

"On 4 June last year," said Andrée, "the whole of the Central Station was packed with people.

"A mass of people, all *cheering*," he went on. "It sounds absurd—*cheering*—but those people really were cheering. And when at last the train began to move, it did so with the greatest caution, for the platform was filled to overflowing with people. There was almost a panic, and it was a miracle that no one was pushed under the train.

"It was a Thursday evening with a clear but leaden sky, and a damp, thundery atmosphere.

"Many persons who hadn't bought a ticket, several hundreds of them, had boarded the train and they went with us as far as Liljeholmen. There, still hurrahing, they allowed themselves to be driven on to the platform by the personnel of the train and a few policemen who had been summoned to help.

"We were met by fresh crowds of hurrahing people at every station," he went on, "by flowers, and flags, and in some places even by small bands of wind instruments. This went on until far past midnight.

"A fellow passenger, a clergyman, quite unknown to me, came forward. He bent down and picked up a lily of the valley that had fallen out of my bouquet, and asked politely if he might keep it. 'Of course you may,' I answered, and he assured me that he would treasure it for life."

"Lilies of the valley?" I said.

"A big bouquet of lilies of the valley," answered Andrée. "I don't know who gave it me. Masses of white flowers, stripped of their leaves, many thousands of tiny white flowers, strongly scented, surrounded by a circular wall of dark green leaves. It was a heavy bouquet, it weighed several kilos.

"Now," he said, "this year, when we must really do what we set out to do, there are no cheering people waiting at the stations."

"But you've been decked with flowers," I said. "This year too."

"Actually two bouquets."

"Red carnations, one bouquet of thirty or forty red carnations. It must have cost a lot of money."

"The other bouquet: liverwort."

"*Anemone hepatica,*" I said.

"Can be picked for nothing in Djurgården," said Andrée, "or on the heights of Söder, or in Liljans wood, close to the Stockholm gasworks. Plucked liverwort dies after a few hours. The leaves shrivel, the stalks droop, the flowers turn black.

"Moreover, liverwort is a stunted growth. It lacks fragrance."

He settled himself in his seat and shut his eyes.

"I like listening to the thuds from the joints in the lines," he said.

"Tired?" I asked.

"Yes," he answered. "The thuds are soporific."

I have already pointed out that his face had aged during the short time Swedenborg and I had spent in Paris.

Andrée would be forty-three in the coming autumn. He was nearly sixteen years older than I was. He might have been my elder brother.

After a fairly long interval of silence he said:

"A man who is armed with a strong will, an unusually strong will, constantly finds himself in a perilous situation."

"In what sense?" I asked.

"In the sense that he is constantly obliged to subordinate himself to his own will," answered Andrée.

"I don't understand what you mean," I said.

"I don't expect you to understand me," he said. "In fact, I'm thankful in a way that you don't understand me.

"My mother died sixteen days ago," he said, half to himself. "And last autumn Nobel died," he added.

Andrée had closed his eyes, and his chin had sunk on to one shoulder.

"Tired?" I asked.

The lullaby of the rhythmic thud of wheels over joints.

A small crowd was there to meet us when the train stopped at Gothenburg. At least half of it consisted of newspaper-men and photographers. It was raining.

Andrée refused kindly but firmly to say anything.

Half a dozen ladies, of various ages, formed the only reception party of a more official nature. They represented a Liberal and Anti-protectionist Society. Their temporary chairwoman welcomed us to Gothenburg, and dwelt for a considerable time on the necessity for free trade and its importance to Sweden's maritime commerce. She concluded by expressing her belief that our expedition would be successful.

We were each given two gigantic bouquets of white lilac; two each because the delegation had clearly supposed that Strindberg and Swedenborg would arrive by the same train.

"Thank you," said Andrée. "I hope you'll greet me with flowers on yet another occasion. Perhaps in the autumn. That's unlikely. Perhaps next year. Perhaps in two years' time. Perhaps even later. As you know we intend to journey into uncertainty. What can be more uncertain than the time at which those who have journeyed into uncertainty will return from it?"

Alexis Machuron, the balloon manufacturer, Lachambre's nephew, the young man of the rectangular face, and the long, upturned and well-waxed moustache, was waiting for us in the large hall of the station. Beside him stood one of Oscar Dickson's three sons.

8

During the course of the day, and under Machuron's careful direction, the balloon was loaded into one of the forward holds in the *Svensksund*, the driest and best ventilated of them. The car, the scientific instruments, the net of the balloon, the calotte, all the ropes, including the ballast-ropes and the guide-ropes, were also taken on board.

The rest of the equipment was to be freighted to Danes Island and Spitzbergen by the steamship *Virgo*, which had been the only supply ship the previous year.

The capacity of the holds in the *Svensksund* was limited. The *Svensksund* was of course a gunboat and a man-of-war, not a merchant-man.

The next day, 17 May, Strindberg and Swedenborg arrived from Stockholm by the night-train. I met them at the station.

We went straight down to the harbour to inspect the work of loading the *Svensksund*, now almost complete.

Strindberg said that he had visited the great exhibition at Stockholm on the previous day. "A gigantic affair," he said. "We roamed about there for several hours and the only memory I have of it is that everything was gigantic, and that I realized that it would take several days to get any idea of what it comprised, and weeks to study the sections that seemed particularly interesting.

"The entrance fee is pretty large," he added.

"It was opened with great solemnity," said Swedenborg. "The whole of the Royal Family. The Cabinet Ministers of Sweden and Norway. The Diplomatic Corps. The Members of Parliament. The Governors General. The Town Councillors of Stockholm. The Commissioners of the Exhibition, and the Royal Swedish Lifeguards. His Royal Highness the Crown Prince made a short speech and concluded it by requesting His Majesty the King to be kind enough to declare the 1897 Stockholm Exhibition of Art and Industry open."

We then went to the *Virgo*, where the work of stowage was in full swing.

Captain Olsson, the *Virgo*'s Master, was not available. Nils Strindberg made a hasty tour of the ship on his own.

Swedenborg and I waited on the quay. About twenty dockers were at work.

Swedenborg pointed to a foreman with his walking-stick.

"What's your name, young man?" he asked.

"Johansson," answered the surprised foreman.

"Stand to it, Johansson," said Swedenborg.

*   *   *

"Last year," said Strindberg, "the crew of the *Virgo* was an extremely unusual, not to say overqualified body of men.

"But then last year the *Virgo* was our only ship," he said.

"The crew totalled thirty-four men. When it became known through the newspapers that the *Virgo* had been chartered to transport the polar expedition to Spitzbergen, the owners of the ship were inundated with letters from people who wanted to sign on.

"Her Master was Captain Hugo Zachau, an excellent man. Nothing more need be said about him, nor about his two mates.

"Two of the four stokers were ordinary stokers. The other two were engineers.

"Last year the *Virgo* had seventeen ordinary seamen. Six of them were sea-captains, two were qualified mates. Among the rest there was an experienced skipper, a state-employed pilot, an agronomist, a district police superintendent and a civil engineer."

On that same day, 17 May, the members of the expedition were invited to a splendid dinner-party at the house of Oscar Dickson.

Among the guests were the Master of the *Svensksund*, Count Ehrensvärd, and his two officers, likewise the ship's doctor, Lembke, and a civil engineer called Stake, also Alexis Machuron, the man of the long moustaches. Oscar Dickson's three sons were present and two or more other people whose names I did not know.

Baron Dickson wished us welcome in a short speech.

Captain Ehrensvärd was considerably more long-winded.

"Last year," said Andrée in his reply, "our departure from Gothenburg was celebrated by a magnificent banquet for nearly a thousand people at Lorensberg's restaurant. I and my companions were fêted as if we'd already achieved the journey upon which we hadn't even started.

"For twenty arctic days and nights of continuous daylight, for twenty-one times twenty-four hours, we waited in vain for southerly winds. We returned in silence. It's therefore all the better that our second departure from our native land should take place in comparative silence. I won't venture to make any prophecies about our second return.

"During the past year twenty-one times twenty-four weighty criticisms have been levelled against the practicability of my plans.

People think the task is so difficult that it isn't worth attempting. My answer is that is *so* difficult that I can't refrain from attempting it.

"I and my companions," he said in conclusion, "will perhaps be forgotten in a few years' time. The name of our host, Baron Dickson, will forever be associated with the history of arctic exploration, not because of the economic support he has given us, but because practically all the Swedish polar expeditions of the past thirty years have been made possible by his incredible generosity. International maps already bear witness to it. On them you'll find Dickson Bay, Lake Dickson, Dickson Island, Port Dickson, Dickson Land, and so on.

"The first hitherto unknown island that we encounter," said Andrée, raising his glass, "shall be called Dickson's Second Island."

After the dinner we were all invited to a social gathering arranged by the well-known 'Technical Society' of Gothenburg. Andrée however abstained, and went instead to the home of his brother, Ernst Andrée, the sea-captain.

"I won't venture any prophecies," said Swedenborg, "but I suspect that our leader will draw up his will this evening.

"Do you know," he said to me, "I've been doubtful what to do these last few weeks. I've been facing a choice. Should I go to Greece, offer my services to Prince Constantine, put myself under the command of Colonel Metaxas in the European struggle against the Turkish aggressor, or should I stand firm by my undertaking to act as reserve to the polar expedition?

"I chose the balloon and the North Pole," he said. "In spite of the fact that Marshall Edhem Pasha is an Islamic heathen, in spite of my obligations as a Swedenborgian, as a descendant of the founder of the New Church."

"I suspect that the choice wasn't difficult," I said.

The Technical Society's party was lively and a trifle rowdy.

Food and drink was served from a buffet. Many people wanted to make speeches and requested silence, but their remarks were drowned in applause, cries of hurrah, and general uproar.

"If only I'd been in uniform," said Swedenborg.

"Why?"

"I'm a stranger in Gothenburg," he answered. "A lieutenant's uniform breaks down Trojan walls, opens gateways and laps. Particularly in the case of married women. In them expectation is aroused but seldom satisfied.

"Tomorrow evening," he said, "we shall be metamorphosed to ascetics and monks. Not even Emanuel Swedenborg's God knows for how long."

9

At six o'clock on the evening of 18 May the stern moorings of the gunboat *Svensksund* were cast off.

All the vessels in the harbour were dressed overall. Tens of thousands of people had collected to witness our departure.

The clouds had broken up and dispersed, the wind had dropped to a faint breeze, the sun was shining in the west, and Gothenburg was bathed in the moisture-laden warmth of early summer.

Oscar Dickson and Andrée's brother left the *Svensksund*. The forward moorings were cast off. The gunboat left the quay. The propeller whipped the water and the thud of the engine drowned the cheering.

Two small steamers, dressed with flags and pennants, and full to bursting with supporters and newspaper-men, followed us as far as Vinga lighthouse.

The decreasing easterly breeze was suddenly replaced by a rapidly increasing westerly wind.

We parted from our two attendant boats just off Vinga after the Captain of the *Svensksund*, at Andrée's request, had run up the signal 'Long live old Sweden'.

The *Svensksund*—as I have said before—was a powerfully built vessel, but her loading capacity was small, about three hundred tons. She was unusually broad in relation to her length, in fact she was in build like a much enlarged coaster. Her second in command,

Lieutenant Norselius, assured us that the *Svensksund* was also as trustworthy and as seaworthy as a coaster.

Off Vinga we met a westerly wind that rapidly grew stronger, and also increasingly heavy seas.

We sat down to table for a light evening meal. Captain Ehrensvärd embarked upon a circumstantial story about how the gunboat came to be called the *Svensksund*.

"Not the first naval battle at Svensksund," he said, "but the second, the one that took place early in June 1790.

"The Russian armada numbered more than one hundred and fifty ships. The Swedish fleet had nearly two hundred ships. In addition there were about a hundred little vessels armed with small-bore cannons.

"The Russians lost fifty-two vessels, not counting small boats, and more than seven hundred Russian sailors were lost or taken prisoner.

"The greatest naval battle the world has seen up to now," said Count Ehrensvärd.

The *Svensksund* began to pitch more violently.

A short time after we passed Vinga lighthouse the *Svensksund* put over to starboard and held to a northerly course.

Instead of pitching she began to roll.

Machuron was the first to cut short his meal. He rose with a hardly audible excuse, staggered like a drunken man to the door, and would have fallen had he not succeeded at the last moment in grasping the door-handle, which gave him support.

"Yes," said Ehrensvärd, after he had shut the door behind the Frenchman, "I agree that my vessel is what you might call a trifle agile. The shape of her hull has something to do with it. A price you have to pay to get a vessel that is easily manoeuvred in narrow or shallow waters, and which can be used successfully as an ice-breaker, when this is desirable.

"King Philip's much talked of and much admired invincible Spanish Armada," he said, "numbered only one hundred and thirty-four ships."

"Wasn't it an Ehrensvärd who was in command at the battle of Svensksund?" I asked.

"At the first battle," answered our captain, "the one we prefer to forget. He was my great-grandfather. His names were the same as mine, Carl August. He fell out with the King, Gustav III. He was Admiral of the Fleet. He was pushed aside. He wasn't allowed to lead the decisive battle, the second naval battle of Svensksund."

The rolling became more violent.

Andrée retreated to his cabin, followed by Engineer Stake.

Stake was one of the most important members of the expedition. He had been in charge of the generation of the gas at the base on Danes Island the previous year, and he had been entrusted with the same task for this second attempt.

"It was my great grandfather who built Sveaborg," said Ehrensvärd.

Whereupon it was Strindberg's turn to beat a hasty retreat from the table.

Ehrensvärd, Lieutenant Celsing, Doctor Lembke, Swedenborg and I went on sitting there for some hours, while dusk slowly fell.

The gunboat, the *Svensksund*, was a small vessel, and the members of the expedition had to be packed into the few cabins in her stern. I had to share a cabin with Swedenborg, just as Strindberg had to share one with Engineer Stake. Of course Andrée had a cabin to himself, and this was almost large enough to be called a saloon.

Machuron had also been given a cabin to himself, very fortunately, Swedenborg assured us the next day. According to the steward —Machuron himself categorically refused to receive visitors—the Frenchman's seasickness was of a severity hitherto unknown. The stink in his cabin was intolerable, especially as he refused to have the porthole opened, giving as his reason a fear that he might catch cold.

Swedenborg said that this struck him as being very odd, since, in a conversation through the closed door, Machuron had repeatedly declared that he was considering taking his own life.

"A cold is a slow and uncertain way of committing suicide," I said.

We steamed into Bergen at dinner time and took on board two Norwegian pilots who were to guide us up the coast with its thousands of islands and inlets. Our intention was to keep as far as possible inside the belt of skerries, and in calm waters.

A couple of hours after leaving Bergen we ran into a belt of fog, so thick that we were obliged to anchor in a little bay protected by high mountains.

Alexis Machuron appeared on deck again, pale and obviously exhausted, but otherwise in control of himself. He had performed a careful toilet, and his long moustaches were as well waxed and as beautifully turned up as before. He denied that he had ever thought of taking his own life.

The officers of the *Svensksund*, Count Ehrensvärd, Lieutenants Celsing and Norselius, and also Doctor Lembke, took advantage of our enforced halt to arrange a dinner of welcome for the members of the expedition, including Engineer Stake and Machuron.

Ehrensvärd welcomed us on board: "It's an honour for a Swedish man-of-war to be allowed to transport you, the most daring and determined men of our time, to your arctic base, the place from which you will set out upon your great voyage into the unknown."

He then proposed a toast—to be drunk in champagne—to the success of the balloon expedition.

The dinner, unconventionally composed by the *Svensksund*'s purser, Lieutenant Celsing, was excellent. "I hesitated for a long time between champagne and bordeaux," he said, "and settled finally for champagne and bordeaux. There will be punch with your coffee, as much of it as you like."

Doctor Lembke made a speech in honour of Strindberg and Machuron, on the grounds that they had both recently got engaged.

Swedenborg spoke for the only married member of the expedition, namely himself.

"The best of it is," he said, "that I've married a daughter of Nordenskiöld's, the conqueror of the North-East Passage. I tell her that I'm preparing to attempt the North Pole in a balloon. She answers calmly that if that is so I must take a double supply of long woollen pants with me."

Andrée's speech of thanks was very short.

"We've anchored here in this peaceful bay because the fog is impossibly thick, so thick that we can't even see the shores that surround our sheltered bay," he said. "What fogs await us at Spitz-bergen, or over the vast expanse of pack ice in the Polar Basin? Standing by the gunnel and peering out into the dusk and fog is the same as the strange experience of being perhaps a thousand metres over the sea in a thick belt of fog. You don't know where you are. You don't know whether you're moving or not. You don't know whether the balloon is rising or sinking unless you consult the barometer.

"You, Captain Ehrensvärd, spoke of our journey into the un-known. Many people have spoken of our journey into the unknown. It often seems as if people haven't realized that the 'unknown' may also imply great dangers and difficulties. One of the greatest dangers will be periods of fog and dead calm."

At this point Andrée suddenly broke off, shrugged his shoulders, half laughed, and raised his glass. "This is the first time I've sailed under a triple-tongued Swedish naval flag," he said.

During the silence that followed after he had put down his glass I seized the opportunity to give the members of the expedition a present from my mother, some little silver napkin-rings, with the recipient's name, enclosed in a shield, engraved on one side.

"They're small," I said, "not from meanness, but so that their weight shall not hamper the lifting capacity of the balloon."

We continued northwards, sometimes in sheltered waters, some-times out at sea.

On 24 May we crossed the Polar Circle and celebrated the event in champagne, chilled by the snow that had fallen during the night.

We stopped for a couple of days in Tromsö.

Consul Aagaard invited us to a splendid Norwegian banquet at his home: prawns, salmon, smoked reindeer meat, cloudberries and whipped cream, red goat's cheese, and almost runny yellow-white sheep's milk cheese.

A heavy snow shower was just passing over the little town, and our host said he remembered that there had been similar weather when Nansen passed Tromsö in the *Fram* on his way north. "You must take the weather as a good omen," he said, and raised his glass to toast our success.

"What Nansen succeeded in doing," said Swedenborg, "wasn't

to reach the North Pole, but to get himself safely home again."

Machuron, in many lyrical phrases, expressed his wonder at the phenomenon of days that had no nights.

The buds of the birch leaves had not yet begun to burst.

The *Svensksund* refuelled from the Norwegian naval coal bunkers. Our stocks of provisions were completed with the help of Consul Aagaard, rechristened Consul Four A's by Swedenborg.

A pen was nailed together on the foredeck, and four ewes and three lambs were put into it. Beside the pen we had a rough and ready coop containing thirty cackling hens. These animals were part of our stock of provisions, but they too had to be fed, and Lieutenant Celsing had some difficulty in calculating how much corn, hay, and sallow we should need to keep the sheep and the poultry alive, and in good condition, for as long as we allowed them to live.

Captain Ehrensvärd had been brought up on an estate in Skåne, but he had no advice to offer. "My father was first and foremost a politician," he said, "a Member of Parliament, a Lord Lieutenant, a Secretary of State. I'm only a naval officer myself. For that matter," he added, "we never kept any sheep, goats, or hens at my home in Tosterup."

On 26 May we left Tromsö and put in at Buvik, where we had agreed to await the *Virgo*, our supply ship. We arrived at our place of rendezvous in less than two hours. There was no sign of the *Virgo*. We dropped anchor.

Andrée and I did some geologizing on a neighbouring island where we were able to inspect and study an old shore-line which lay about twenty metres higher up the cliff than the existing one.

Machuron, Strindberg, Swedenborg, and Doctor Lembke went on a short hunting expedition, and returned with five dead ptarmigan and several other birds which we thought inedible.

The next day the *Virgo* appeared. She had been delayed by contrary winds and seas. Her Master, Captain Olsson, asked for five hours' grace, so that he could re-trim his coal.

At six o'clock that evening both vessels weighed anchor and headed northwards.

I now began to keep my meteorological journal, and to make regular notes on the velocity and direction of the wind, on the temperature, the thickness and type of cloud-cover, the amount of precipitation, the humidity of the air, and so forth.

For three days and three nights we steamed northwards in the teeth of a stiff northerly wind. The waves were high and athwart. The *Svensksund* pitched, rolled, and lurched with the greatest violence.

Andrée, Machuron and Stake retired to their bunks; most of the crew too suffered severely.

The *Virgo* followed in our wake, and we were anxious not to let the distance between the two vessels become too great to allow of communication by flag-signals.

We passed Bear Island without seeing a sign of pack ice.

A barrel had been rigged up on the forward mast and a look-out stationed in it.

Warm clothing was issued to the crew: woollen jerseys, high boots, fur caps, gloves and scarves.

Soon afterwards we saw the white mountain tops of Spitzbergen rising out of the sea.

All that we saw of the dreaded pack ice were a few isolated floes. The force of the wind abated as we followed the coast-line of the South Cape. We headed north under full steam, and without hindrance.

"Last year the pack ice gave us a lot of trouble," said Andrée. "This year we have open water ahead of us."

He was justified in speaking as he did. The sky was covered at a height of about one thousand metres by compact clouds, and we could not see any sign of 'ice blink' on our course. This is the expression used to describe the flickering light reflected from the pack ice upon the clouds.

When we drew level with the northern tip of Prince Charles Foreland Alexis Machuron appeared on deck wearing a colourful Norwegian jersey. He was pale, you could see that he had lost weight, but his face was one broad grin. The *Svensksund* was pitching and rolling as before.

"An hour ago," he said, "my seasickness suddenly left me. It was like waking up from a frightful nightmare. I got up. Here I am. I'd have brought my bed with me if it hadn't been nailed to the wall."

"We congratulate you," said Swedenborg.

"Is it morning or evening, day or night?" asked Machuron. "I'm hungry," he added.

Then he suddenly discovered the land that lay on our starboard side. He fell silent and his gaze strayed over the steep precipices, flecked with black, the mighty plateaux of inland ice with their shimmer of green, the sharp peaks of the famous Seven Ice Mountains to the north-east.

"Nansen maintains that the North Pole is sea covered by pack ice," he said at last. "I hope he's wrong. The North Pole can't be a spot in an ocean! It must be a great island. Walls of rock, plunging steeply, a garland of mountain tops, several thousand metres high, round a dome of gleaming, blue-green glaciers. The world must have a crown somewhere!"

Swedenborg said: "The creator of the Universe is a great moralist. But there's nothing to suggest that he's applied aesthetic standards to his creation."

10

Some hours later we met our enemy.

The channel between Danes Island and Amsterdam Island which forms the entrance to Virgo Harbour, or Virgo Bay, was blocked with very close pack ice.

At least a dozen binoculars were focused upon this barrier of ice. It really was a barrier. The pack ice had been squeezed into the narrow inlet by the wind and the current. Blocks of ice and floes had been piled one on top of another and frozen together to form a wall of ice about half a metre high. In front of the wall, open water. Behind it, a gently undulating alpine landscape in miniature.

We knew that under the surface of the water the wall went down to a depth of between four and five metres.

"If we'd had open water we should have been there in half an hour," said Andrée. "But this accursed ice may hold us up for weeks!"

"You underestimate the ability of the *Svensksund*," answered Count Ehrensvärd.

The gunboat reduced speed and glided right up to the edge of the pack ice.

The *Virgo* kept in her wake, less than a hundred metres behind her.

The wind abated and the temperature sank sharply as we neared the edge of the ice.

Ehrensvärd gave orders for the stern tanks of the *Svensksund* to be filled with water. Her bow rose, her stern sank.

Captain Olsson on the *Virgo* carried out a similar manoeuvre. The vessel was supplied with peak-tanks that would hold more than a hundred tons of water. When the requisite amount of water was put into them the propeller sank to a depth of four metres below the surface of the water.

The *Svensksund* moved slowly into the barrier of ice.

The blocks of ice were broken up, split in two, pushed aside, or forced up on top of each other.

At times the engine worked cautiously, at times at full power. Lieutenant Norselius, who had gone up to sit in the barrel on the foremast, directed the operation.

The *Virgo* followed in the furrow we had made in the ice. She was often so close behind us that we could have shouted to each other if our voices had not been drowned by the squeaking and groaning of the blocks of ice, and the dull thud of ice against iron.

Andrée was intensely on edge.

"If the balloon-house has been brought down by the winter storms," he said, "everything will be lost."

"Everything lost?"

"Without the balloon-house we can't inflate the balloon," he answered.

"Of course not."

"I can't possibly return from Spitzbergen a second time on board a ship," he said.

A few hours later Andrée caught sight of the flagstaffs on the balloon-house, and of its two upper storeys.

He gave me his binoculars, and at the same time put one of his arms round my shoulders.

The balloon-house had survived the winter storms.

At six o'clock on the evening of 30 May the *Svensksund* dropped anchor in Virgo Harbour. An hour later the *Virgo* too lay at anchor quite near us. In spite of her peak-tanks, the *Virgo*'s propeller had been damaged by the ice, and she had had some difficulty in following us.

We celebrated our arrival at Danes Island and Virgo Harbour with a little dinner-party. Captain Olsson of the *Virgo* was greeted with champagne when he clambered on board the gunboat by her starboard rope-ladder.

30 May fell on a Sunday that year.

I I

Andrée was excited and tense during our late celebration dinner. His conversation was forced, laconic and partially disconnected. I was sitting opposite to him, and I noticed once again the strange horizontal oscillations of his eyes.

During coffee he rose and announced that he intended to go ashore.

In spite of numerous protests one of the *Svensksund*'s boats was lowered into a crack that had formed in the ice. Swedenborg, Strindberg, Machuron, Doctor Lembke, Lieutenant Celsing, Andrée and I got into the boat. Half a dozen sailors under Celsing's command succeeded, more by poling than by rowing, in manoeuvring us forward between the floes and blocks of ice to the shore.

The moment that Andrée set foot on dry land the *Svensksund* discharged a salute of six shots from her guns.

Hundreds of birds rose up and circled round us with shrill cries.

A flurry of large, damp snow-flakes obscured the view.

Only ten metres of the shore was bare and swept clean. After that there was a covering of snow, so loose that we sank into it up to our knees.

Andrée made his way up to Pike's House.

Lembke gave up after less than fifty steps, and turned back to the shore, followed by Celsing.

From Pike's House I led the party up to the balloon-house, I took short steps, dragged my feet, and did what I could to make the going easier for those behind me.

A first inspection indicated that the balloon-house had got through the winter better than we had expected. The structure had been somewhat wrenched round on its vertical axis, one upright beam had been broken, and the walls were leaning towards the north-east, but not very much.

"Bagatelles," said Andrée.

The snow-drifts in the balloon-house were in some places two metres high.

We returned to the shore. This did not take us long as we now had a well-trodden track.

Lembke presented us with a whole bottle of punch, which was passed round the party.

"Cooled in the snows of Spitzbergen," he said.

We boarded the boat and the *Svensksund* simultaneously fired yet another salute of six guns.

12

On Monday, the last day of May, we were roused early by Andrée. He was laughing, keen to be out and doing, full of vitality and energy, dressed in boots, homespun breeches and jacket, and a round peaked cap.

We ate a hasty breakfast. Porridge, herring, spare-rib of reindeer, coffee, served with condensed milk, warmed-up bread, butter, cheese, and English marmalade.

Most of the sailors from the *Svensksund* and the *Virgo* had already been put ashore.

Our boat had on board spades, crowbars, shovels, ropes, axes, and various pieces of timber of different dimensions.

Andrée was welcomed with cheers, to which he responded by waving his cap.

He walked briskly up to the balloon-house along the path we had tramped down the previous day. The men followed close behind him and widened the path to something that resembled a road.

The first four men were told to stop at Pike's House and clear away any snow that was in the way.

The main body was ordered up to the inside of the balloon-house, and there set to work on the hard-packed drifts of snow. Under these drifts was a thick layer of ice.

"It must be removed," said Andrée.

The men broke up the ice with axes, crowbars, and spades.

He took three men along with him to the apparatus for generating gas and set them to work, having given them strict orders to be careful what they were about. The snow-drifts must be removed, but it must be done without damaging any part of the technical equipment.

He returned to the balloon-house and climbed up ladders and rope-ladders. He gave Nilsson and Hansson, the two carpenters, detailed instructions as to how they were to twist the structure back to its proper position with the help of ropes, struts, and wedges.

He ascertained that Pike's House had survived the winter without serious damage.

He inspected the generating apparatus with Engineer Stake, and found that the parts that had been left behind were largely undamaged.

He inspected and discussed the repairs to the balloon-house that Nilsson and Hansson were carrying out.

His energy was impressive.

He also kept a watchful eye on the meteorological observations which Strindberg, Swedenborg, he, and I were entering in a log-book every fourth hour in accordance with a prearranged time-table.

We were bothered by fairly strong north or north-easterly winds. The temperature of the air alternated between minus one and plus two degrees Centigrade.

"I'm not complaining about my insomnia," said Alexis Machuron. "What I'm complaining about is that I no longer need sleep. These incredible days that have no nights!"

On the evening of Thursday, 3 June, Andrée announced that the damage to the balloon-house had been repaired.

I found it difficult to get into close contact with Nils Strindberg. He was cheerful and friendly, but at the same time evasive. He seemed to prefer the company of Machuron and Engineer Stake to mine.

"He's as feverishly active and energetic as Andrée," I said to Swedenborg.

"Photographic experiments with Machuron in their mysterious dark-room in the bowels of the *Svensksund*. Magnetism, that they study in their little tent on the shore—'terrestrial magnetism'—even more mysterious than their exercises in photography.

"His weather-cock on the stony hillside behind the balloon-house, two hundred metres above sea-level, as ingenious in its construction as it's unreliable.

"And then, in the evening he plays the violin, but only after Doctor Lembke and Count Ehrensvärd have urgently requested him to do so."

"We've had a few tête-à-têtes," said Swedenborg.

"Only brief ones, and quite vague. He's undecided though he won't admit it. He's in two minds. Perhaps he'll be the one. Possibly I shall."

13

When the damage to the balloon-house has been repaired, work was started to get it ready in other respects.

The building itself was octagonal; its eight corner-posts were joined together by a system of horizontal planks. Altogether there were eight sections of this timber framework. The walls consisted of shutters, eight centimetres thick and not quite two and a half metres high, which could easily be pushed along grooves in the horizontal planks. There were seven hundred and thirty of these shutters as well as thirty-two windows of the same dimensions.

The windows were not made of glass, but of tectorium, a transparent substance resembling gelatine, which had been rolled out over a metal net.

When Andrée had been forced to leave Danes Island the previous year he had had all the shutters and windows taken down, except those on the second 'floor'.

On the outside of the walls there were four balconies, linked by ladders.

The southern half of the balloon-house was provided with a number of masts, six metres high, by means of which the height of the southern wall could be raised by hoisting a protective piece of canvas when the moment for the start arrived. The northern wall was so constructed that the shutters, the planks and the posts could all be very quickly detached and pulled down, chiefly by means of ropes that hung down to the ground.

The balloon-house, the foundation upon which the whole expedition was based, was an ingenious construction. The shutters that formed the walls, the framework of planks, the windows, the balconies, and the ladders had all been produced in a finished state by the master builder F. O. Pettersson of Gothenburg. They were all made from sound, dry, winter-felled spruce. The bolts that joined the different segments of the building together had been kept to two sizes. They were either twenty-two or twenty-five millimetres in diameter.

The various parts of the balloon-house had been loaded on to the *Virgo* the previous year, transported to Danes Island, unloaded and assembled without difficulty in the space of a couple of weeks.

The man who had designed it was Ivar Svedberg, an engineer at the Billesholm coal mine at Höganäs. His name had been immortalized by Strindberg on his 1896 map of Danes Island, Amsterdam Island and environs. The rocky eminence south of the balloon-house is named Svedberg's Crag.

It was upon this same crag that Strindberg had erected his ingenious weather-cock. (If you had binoculars you could estimate the direction of the wind at the level of Strindberg's weather-cock from the balloon-house, from Pike's House and from the *Svensksund.* These observations were generally considered to be of doubtful value.)

The 6th and 7th of June, Whit Sunday and Whit Monday, were a general holiday.

The humbler members of the crews of the *Svensksund* and the *Virgo* amused themselves chiefly by sliding down the steep, snowy slopes behind the balloon-house on their backsides.

At our celebration dinner on Whit Sunday Alexis Machuron made it plain that he thought our Whitsun celebrations lacked proper solemnity.

"You're a Catholic," answered Andrée. "You therefore have certain expectations and hopes. We Swedes are Lutherans and Protestants.

"Above all," he said, "we're Protestants."

"With all due respect to Luther, to be a Protestant is to be a doubter.

"When we're in the air," he said, "and the temperature sinks by five degrees Centigrade, the balloon will lose ninety kilogrammes of its lifting capacity. If it rains, and half a millimetre of moisture is absorbed by the upper half of the balloon, our lifting capacity will be reduced by a hundred and sixty-five kilogrammes.

"No God can do anything about that," said Andrée.

14

We had great difficulty in unloading the *Virgo*'s cargo. She lay at anchor a couple of hundred metres further out than the *Svensksund*. The obstinate northerly or north-westerly winds had packed the ice harder and harder together.

Andrée suggested that we should try to blast the ice apart by using dynamite.

This blasting operation was partially successful and made it easier to unload the most necessary things that the *Virgo* had brought to Danes Island. Among these—apart from provisions—were the parts of the hydrogen gas apparatus which had been dismantled the previous year, and also eighty tons of sulphuric acid and twenty-three tons of iron filings which were needed for the production of the gas.

On 10 June Engineer Stake was able to commence the work of attaching the apparatus for generating hydrogen to the installation for pumping water.

On 11 June, a Friday, Strindberg spent half the day giving Machuron a lesson in the noble art of skiing. This exercise provoked loud peals of laughter. The Frenchman was as poor a pupil as Strindberg was an inexpert teacher.

"You can see for yourself how unused Strindberg is to managing skis," said Swedenborg. "Try now to imagine Andrée on skis! Then you'll understand why we've Canadian snow-shoes instead of Swedish skis in our equipment."

Swedenborg was an excellent skier, light, swift, and agile. On short runs he got ahead of me. On rather longer runs he could not stand up to my greater strength and the amount of practice I had had when I was growing up.

On this same day Strindberg and I sent off some carrier-pigeons, upon whose wings and tail-feathers the words ANDRÉE AFTON-BLADET STOCKHOLM had been stamped. They were carrying brief communications to that newspaper.

When released the pigeons wheeled round irresolutely a few times, and then returned to our temporary dove-cote in the attic of Pike's House.

We chased them off again, and after circling round in the air over our base for a while they disappeared in a southerly direction.

Machuron and Doctor Lembke were sceptical. Carrier-pigeons had never before been used for such great distances as were now involved. The pigeons came from a dove-cote that belonged to a postmaster on Åland, by name Uno Godenhjelm.

Andrée was not much interested in carrier-pigeons. His many attempts to use them the previous year had produced negative results.

However, all the pigeons were stamped and looked after with the greatest care. They were fed with corn and peas, and small quantities of flax and rape seed.

"They'll either succumb and drown," said Swedenborg, "or they'll turn up in Africa, where devil a one's ever heard of Andrée."

Andrée was still in a state of feverish activity; at the balloon-house, at the hydrogen gas apparatus, at Pike's House, on board the *Svensksund*, on board the *Virgo*, at the unloading of the two vessels, at Strindberg's 'magnetic' tent. He made his presence felt every-where and at all times, instructing, giving orders, directing opera-tions.

He spent many hours in his cabin making notes and writing letters and memoranda.

The unloading of the *Virgo* was finished by 12 June, but the vessel could not leave the harbour that bore her name because of the bad state of the pack ice.

On the same day Machuron succeeded in catching a fox in a trap that he himself had set. It was a young one, with speckled, yellowish-brown fur, a wild, aggressive little creature, with sharp, white teeth. Only with difficulty was it moved from the trap down to a cage close to Pike's House.

Two days later the balloon was brought ashore. This was an extremely difficult operation. It is true that the distance between the *Svensksund* and the shore was only about a hundred metres, but the enormous package weighed over two tons.

Hoisting it out of the forehold of the gunboat, and lowering it into the pinnace was the work of a few minutes. Getting it through a hundred metres of pack ice took a whole working-day.

Lieutenant Norselius led the manoeuvre, and patiently accepted a continuous stream of advice from Andrée, Swedenborg, Machuron, Stake, Ehrensvärd, and Doctor Lembke. For safety's sake the advisers kept to the gangway of three-inch planks that had been laid between the *Svensksund* and the shore.

Ten people worked energetically, but with little success, at trying to cut a channel through the ice with saws, axes and picks.

Two ridges of hummocked ice more than a metre high, what Andrée called 'toroses', had developed during the night as a result of the unfavourable wind. It would be useless to attack them with saws and picks. We should have to resort to the same measures here that we had used when unloading the *Virgo*.

Norselius fitted cartridges of dynamite or bellona to long sticks which were then driven into cracks in the ice and exploded under the toroses. The detonations were not very dramatic. There were no violent blasts, only a dull rumble and a movement of the ice that was hardly visible or perceptible. But the hummocks of pressure ice, the toroses, were broken up in to small pieces which sank slowly into the water and left an opening for the pinnace and the balloon.

Early on the morning of the following day the two-ton package containing the balloon was dragged up to the balloon-house over planks smeared with tallow. Twenty men toiled at the ropes and the rhythmic chant of the previous year broke out again:

That we to the North Pole may go,
To the North Pole may go,
May go, may go, may go,
To the North Pole may go.

Two hours later the balloon had been taken out of its packing and, under Machuron's nervous supervision—his directions were given in agitated and rapid French, quite incomprehensible to most of us—it was got into the balloon-house and spread out on the floor.

No sooner was this done than Engineer Stake began to pump air into it, which he did by using a sort of bellows, designed by Andrée.

On 16 June the ice-pressure between Danes Island and Amsterdam Island suddenly eased and the water became practically free of ice. The *Virgo* put to sea, limping slightly because of her damaged propeller.

The *Svensksund* fired a parting salute and the *Virgo* answered by dipping her flag.

15

Under Machuron's direction the strips of silk that had been glued over the many seams on the inside of the balloon were covered with a coating of the rubber varnish that Lachambre had recently invented. This work was done by nine of the most trustworthy members of the *Svensksund*'s crew.

They began at the very top of the balloon and continued downwards stage by stage as Engineer Stake pumped in more air.

Swedenborg and I crept in on hands and knees through the bottom valve of the balloon. It was an indescribable experience to find oneself in orange daylight under the vast temple-like dome.

A strange silence reigned, apart from the regular panting of the bellows, and the dull thuds that you heard when the wind bounced the balloon lightly against the walls of the balloon-house.

We had to take off our shoes before we crept in by the bottom valve in order not to damage that part of the envelope that still rested on the balloon-house floor.

"*Salaam aleikum*," said Swedenborg, in a rather loud voice.

Neither Machuron nor the nine sailors took any notice. Swedenborg's words were lost in the orange dusk of the balloon.

On 18 June the balloon was emptied and sank slowly to the floor. The manipulating valves were mounted and the net was spread out over the envelope of the balloon.

On the following morning Engineer Stake was missing from our breakfast-table. He had already gone to Pike's House, to the hydrogen gas apparatus.

The generation of the gas and the final filling of the balloon had begun. Theoretically our gas apparatus was able to produce close on two hundred cubic metres of hydrogen per hour. For sound technical reasons Andrée had restricted the production of gas to a maximum of sixty cubic metres per hour. While the balloon was being filled the external seams were coated with the rubber varnish.

The balloon-house had only just been completed, but on this same day Andrée decided to take down the upper quarter of the north wall, as he considered it unnecessary. It took such a long time to get it down—nearly two hours—that he decided to take down yet another quarter of the same wall.

"It will save at least four hours' work when the time comes for us to start," he said.

But as this had made the south wall unstable, it was reinforced with three of the *Svensksund*'s strongest steel cables.

By 22 June, or, to be more precise, by the night between the 22nd and the 23rd, the balloon was fully inflated, five weeks earlier than in the previous year. A few minutes before midnight Engineer Stake had flags run up the two flagstaffs on the balloon-house. All the members of the expedition and the officers of the *Svensksund* were on board the gunboat. A gleam of northern sunshine fell for a while upon Danes Island and Virgo Harbour. Ehrensvärd called for three cheers for the balloon, and Lieutenant Celsing promptly ordered a table to be set out with champagne and all kinds of delicacies.

Strindberg and I, and for that matter Swedenborg too, had some difficulty in holding a glass, as our hands were swollen and our palms flayed. We had spent the whole day rubbing a mixture of tallow and vaseline into the guide-ropes to impregnate them against moisture, and to make them glide over the pack ice with the least possible wear and tear.

Vaseline-tallow had to be massaged into the guide-ropes, the upper parts of which were made of hemp, while the lower parts were wound round with cocoanut fibre. My fingers swelled as I worked, but they were not affected, like Strindberg's and Swedenborg's hands, by a mass of small bleeding sores and blisters.

The combined length of the three guide-ropes was exactly a thousand metres, one kilometre.

"Champagne is a cure for everything," said Swedenborg, "not least for injured and aching hands."

16

The car, the carrying-ring, and the provisions were taken ashore and carried up to the balloon-house.

Our corpulent and good-natured medical adviser, Doctor Lembke, took upon himself the responsibility of stowing our provisions.

The ice disappeared from Virgo Harbour.

Sometimes it rained, but the temperature remained at one or two degrees above zero. The barometer regularly showed a pressure of about seven hundred and seventy millimetres.

The sea to the west was empty and desolate.

The mountain slopes behind the balloon-house were almost free of snow. Between the rising ground and the shore there were patches of bare earth, but also, here and there, deep drifts of snow.

On Midsummer Eve Andrée and I made an expedition on foot to a little freshwater lagoon situated three and a half kilometres west of our base. It was about two metres above the mean level of the sea, and three hundred metres in circumference. It was divided from the sea by a strip of land twenty-five metres wide. One end of the strip of land rose to form a hillock, and on this there were forty old cairns that marked the graves of dead whalers. It was not the graves that interested Andrée, but the origin of the lagoon. He investigated the nature of the strip of land, and examined grains of gravel under his magnifying glass. He regretted that he could not take a sounding of the lagoon. It was to be sure still covered with ice, but this had been so much eroded by sun and rain that it was not safe to walk on it.

He thought he could be sure that the lagoon had not been formed by a rise in the ground level. It was most probable, he thought, that sand, carried down by streams and runnels from the mountains, had started the strip of land, and that it had later been made wider and higher by coarser gravel and stones that the waves had washed up from the shore in stormy weather. He discovered two pieces of driftwood in the ice of the lagoon which had clearly been thrown over the strip of land by the waves.

Before we retraced our steps he filled some small linen bags with various mineral specimens, and also collected algae and larvae from the shores of the lagoon.

I expressed surprise that he should be so much interested in this freshwater lagoon, right in the middle of the preparations for our balloon voyage, when he was neither a geologist nor a biologist.

"We're also taking soundings in Virgo Harbour and Danes Gat," he said in reply.

It was true; ever since the sea had been free of ice comprehensive soundings had been taken whenever the required number of men could be spared from work ashore, on the balloon-house and the gas apparatus.

On our homeward march I kept up a brisk pace. Andrée walked obliquely behind me and only got slightly out of breath.

We celebrated Midsummer Eve in great style. Two of the lambs and one ewe that we had brought from Tromsö were slaughtered and roasted whole over a fire of drift-wood on the shore. This gave great pleasure to our crews.

The officer in charge of the stores had laid out freshly baked rye-bread, butter, smoked sausage and ham, salt herring, and a large caraway-seed cheese on a table firmly nailed to six posts sunk into the ground.

Close at hand ale was being dispensed by the two largest of the foremast men from the *Svensksund*.

Lembke and Swedenborg donated between them a kid of spirits to the men, and entrusted the distribution of it to the storekeeper. The gift was greeted by cries of hurrah.

The members of the expedition and the officers of the *Svensksund* returned to the gunboat, rowed by four impatient sailors who wanted to get back to the shore as quickly as possible.

Lieutenant Celsing had had the usual overpowering meal laid out on the aft deck.

Just as we sat down to table the sun broke through the clouds somewhere in the north-west. Beneath us dark water, above us shining clouds, to the west open sea, to the south and east the steep mountain slopes of Danes Island.

This evening I was struck for the first time by the beauty of Spitzbergen. The sharp peaks, the shimmering green, or greenish-blue glaciers, the tremendous precipices of the craggy walls of rock, the dazzling reflections from the remaining patches of snow, the streams of glacier-water falling down the mountain slopes, pink in the night sunshine, the constantly changing gradations of green in the naked rock, turning from deep red to violet blue.

"Gradations of green from red to violet?" asked Swedenborg.

"I'm lyrically colour-blind," I answered.

The sun was hot and we were obliged to take off some of our clothing. Doctor Lembke consulted one of the thermometers on board and informed us that the temperature was 22 degrees above zero, Centigrade.

Captain Ehrensvärd made a long speech in which he declared that he was sure our expedition would be successful. His speech was not really quite in the right vein. It was probably unprepared,

for he talked chiefly about his great-grandfather, Admiral Ehrensvärd, and about what he had done after he left his profession and
wrote his esoteric and abstruse work, *The Philosophy of the Liberal
Arts*.

The party on shore was a noisy one.

"How much beer?" asked Andrée.

"Sixty-six gallons," answered Celsing, "over and above their
usual ration. It's part of what we were given by the brewery in
Gothenburg."

"It's only Midsummer once a year," said Swedenborg.

"Sixty-six gallons, that equals about three hundred and fifteen
litres."

"A man is posted by the balloon-house," said Ehrensvärd,
"another on the shore by the boats, and two on board the
Svensksund, as well as the steward."

17

On the night after Midsummer Day (if indeed one can speak of
nights in the arctic summer) the little Norwegian steamer, the
Express, arrived. She had been chartered by the German journalist
Lerner and his two companions, Violet and Meisenbach.

Their voyage had been stormy and unpleasant, and they were in a
miserable state when they boarded the *Svensksund* after anchoring
in the relative peace of Virgo Harbour.

She was the first foreign ship we had seen since we left Tromsö.
She had with her a little bag of mail for us, which was naturally
extremely welcome.

Lerner told us that he had chartered the *Express* for one thousand
five hundred crowns a month, and that they had been very much

afraid that they would only arrive at Danes Island after the balloon had started.

On 26 June Engineer Stake began to subject the balloon to additional tests for gas tightness.

For these he used strips of linen which were dipped in acetate of lead and then laid over the seams in the envelope.

The hydrogen gas that we were producing contained some sulphur, and, at the spots where it forced its way out through the seams, the chemical action of sulphur on acetate of lead turned the linen strips black.

The leaks that were discovered were then sealed with a fresh application of our rubber varnish. This had been mixed with lampblack, so that we should know which seams had been treated a second time.

It was odd to see ten or so of the *Svensksund*'s crew clambering about the meshes of the net on the cupola of the balloon with fluttering strips of linen, tins of varnish, and paint brushes.

These tests were discontinued a couple of metres above the equator of the balloon.

"It will be enough if we do the part of the envelope where the gas pressure is greatest," said Machuron.

"A theory," said Swedenborg, "which fits in admirably with the fact that there is no more of the varnish left in our stores."

18

On 27 June the magnificent steamer the *Lofoten* arrived with a fairly large number of tourists and pleasure-seekers of various nationalities. Her Master was no less a person than Captain Otto Sverdrup, who had been in command of Nansen's vessel the *Fram* when she called at Danes Island the previous year.

Among the Swedish passengers were Captain de Champs and Andrée's friend Jonas Stadling, of the newspaper *Aftonbladet*. Stadling was to remain at Danes Island to witness the departure of the balloon. He was a quiet-mannered man of fifty, who had travelled widely. He had spent two years in Russia and was one of Leo Tolstoy's few intimate friends.

The passengers of the *Lofoten* were allowed to see the balloon-house, the balloon, the hydrogen gas apparatus, and the equipment on board the balloon. Andrée was their cicerone.

We were invited afterwards to a late dinner on board the *Lofoten*. The German journalist and editor, Lerner, who represented the *Kölnische Zeitung*, was also one of the party. He had with him a large number of bottles of champagne, a present to the expedition from his employer, he told us.

"I probably know more than anyone else here tonight," said Captain Sverdrup in his speech, "of what it means to be the prisoner of the polar ice and the interminable polar night. Therefore, I'm probably the only person present who realizes the true daring of Engineer Andrée's decision to let the winds carry him in a balloon to the North Pole.

"I dare not say that I think Engineer Andrée will reach his objective," he said. "But I can say that I hope he and his companions will return alive to civilization."

He then proposed a toast to our success to be drunk in the champagne that had been given to us by the *Kölnische Zeitung*.

"Thank you for your good wishes, Captain Sverdrup," said Andrée.

"You're probably right in supposing that you know more than anyone else here present about what it means to find yourself on board a vessel that is frozen fast in the pack ice of the Polar Basin.

"But I'm not going to let myself be frozen fast in the polar ice in a ship," he continued. "I'm no seaman. I'm an aeronaut. I probably know more than anyone else present about the art of travelling over —*over*—the sea. A ship's a ship. A balloon's a balloon. A balloon doesn't allow itself to become the captive and the prisoner of the pack ice of the Arctic Ocean."

At this point Andrée was interrupted by Swedenborg. "Let's

drink a toast," he said rising, and climbing on to his chair. "A toast to the Andréean balloon, to the new daring, the new attempt."

He raised his glass of champagne, the champagne given by the *Kölnische Zeitung*. He repeated his words in German and English, and got everyone to join in giving a somewhat ragged cheer for the success of the polar expedition.

The passengers of the *Lofoten* had hoped to have the experience of seeing the polar balloon take off, but the ship had to weigh anchor and return to the south the very next day.

Immediately after leaving Virgo Harbour she fired a parting salute of four guns, and was answered by twice as many shots from the *Svensksund*'s forward cannon.

From the newspapers and letters that the *Lofoten* had brought with her we learnt, among other things, that Baron Dickson had died.

"First Alfred Nobel," said Andrée, "then my mother, and now Dickson."

19

The balloon was made ready for the start.

The calotte of varnished silk was fixed to the crown of the balloon over the net. The large carrying-ring was then mounted inside the forty-eight ropes that formed the lower and inward-sloping part of the net. Our provisions and other equipment were carefully stowed in thirty canvas sacks, which were divided into a total of about two hundred and fifty smaller pockets or compartments. These sacks were fastened between the carrying-ropes above the carrying-ring. Our three collapsible sledges and our collapsible canvas boat were fastened to the remaining ropes. A sort of floor, made of coarse canvas, was stretched across inside the carrying-ring.

In this way the space above the carrying-ring was made to serve as the hold of the balloon.

The horizontal mast—or more properly the yard—to which the steering-sail would be attached, was also lashed to the carrying-ring. The sail was in three parts and measured altogether nearly eighty square metres.

The three guide-ropes, so indispensable for steering the balloon, were attached to the carrying-ring, and then pulled over the north wall of the balloon-house, and laid out on the ground. The same precaution was taken with the eight ballast-ropes, each of which was about seventy metres long.

The car, already fully equipped, stood at the entrance to the balloon-house. It was made of wicker on a frame of chestnut. It was cylindrical in shape. The conventional car has always been cubic.

It was two metres in diameter. Even a tall man could therefore rest without difficulty on the bunk in the bottom part of it.

The car was provided with a roof, also made of wicker. The distance from the floor to the roof was rather less than one and a half metres.

The car was first and foremost a place in which to rest. When manoeuvring the balloon the crew were to stand on its roof, protected by a railing, the so-called instrument-ring. Andrée had had canvas stretched between the instrument-ring and the car, partly in order to increase the safety of the crew, and partly to prevent any objects or instruments they dropped from falling overboard.

The balloon was kept tethered in the balloon-house, with its carrying ring resting on the floor, by means of mooring-ropes and sacks filled with sand.

When the time for the start arrived the six ropes belonging to the car could quickly be fastened to the carrying-ring.

Andrée's polar balloon could therefore be said to consist of three main parts.

The balloon itself, with its net and its calotte.

The storage-space between the balloon and the carrying-ring, that was itself attached to the net.

The car with its roof and its instrument-ring.

Machuron informed us that during the first five days the balloon had lost approximately thirty to thirty-five cubic metres of gas per twenty-four hours. This corresponded to a loss of lifting capacity of between thirty-three and thirty-eight kilos, still reckoned per twenty-four hours.

"This is a loss of gas that can be tolerated," he said. "It would allow the balloon to remain afloat for considerably longer than a month. And," he added, "by carrying out Engineer Stake's test with acetate of lead we have subsequently discovered and sealed a large number of small leaks."

"In other words," said Swedenborg, "the balloon built by Henri Lachambre and Alexis Machuron is the best balloon in the world so far."

On Thursday, 1 July, a test loading of the balloon was carried out with sacks of sand that were hooked on to the carrying-ring. This showed that in addition to what had already been stowed above the carrying-ring, and taking into account the weight of the car, and the avoirdupois of the members of the expedition, the balloon could lift about seventeen hundred kilos of ballast.

On the same day a number of jobs on the balloon-house were completed. These were intended to make the start as safe and free from risk as possible.

The angular and projecting parts of the building, which might conceivably damage the balloon, were removed, or covered with thick layers of felt.

A number of belts of webbing were put round the equator of the balloon and attached by iron cleats to the inside of the south wall of the balloon-house. They were intended to reduce the lateral movements of the balloon. The cleats were wound round with strips of felt.

The many mooring-ropes were replaced by three strong cables, which could be cut simultaneously at the right moment.

These precautions were necessary.

When they want to make an ascent in a balloon people normally wait for fairly calm weather and favourable, moderate winds. Our ascent was going to be unique in the history of the art of ballooning. It was going to take place when the wind was blowing hard, blowing hard from the south.

20

On Thursday, 1 July, the balloon was definitely ready to start. All that remained to be done now was to wait.

The men did not much like being idle. They were not enthusiastic about the soundings of Danes Gat that were taken. This was done in order to make Strindberg's map of the preceding year more complete.

The winds were light, and in the main obstinately northerly.

The members of the expedition, including Swedenborg, went on methodically with their meteorological observations, which were entered up in a log-book every four hours.

Ehrensvärd and Machuron grew impatient and nervy. They constantly consulted Strindberg's weather-cock on Svedberg's Crag, with the help of a powerful telescope that was mounted on the bridge of the *Svensksund*.

Strindberg was fully occupied with his magnetic observations.

Andrée and I made an expedition to the glacier which lay immediately south of Svedberg's Crag, and which had been named Lachambre's Glacier on Strindberg's map of 1896. We shot a dozen or so birds. Andrée stuffed them into little cloth bags and made careful notes about the time and altitude at which they had been shot. He also collected various samples of the flora, mosses and algae as well as vascular plants. At the elge of the glacier he discovered masses of larvae and pupae, and some already fully developed insects which had stuck to the damp ice.

*   *   *

"Very nearly five weeks of permanently northerly winds," said Machuron.

"All the better," answered Andrée. "The longer the northerly winds last the more likely it is that they'll be replaced by southerly winds."

"A simple and almost obvious way of calculating probability," said Swedenborg.

The little vessel the *Express* with the three Germans on board set out on a trip to the north, but returned a few days later saying they had encountered what they described as consolidated pack ice.

As I mentioned before Lerner had been sent out by the *Kölnische Zeitung*.

It soon became apparent that his companion Violet (or more precisely: Doctor Violet) had also come to Spitzbergen as a journalist. His paper was the *Berliner Lokalanzeiger*. Violet was a very pleasant man; quiet, almost shy, always listening, always making notes.

Lerner's other companion, a very young man called Meisenbach, was probably also a reporter and a journalist.

The fox that Machuron had caught managed to get out of its cage, possibly with the help of some ill-disposed person—ill-disposed, that is, from Machuron's point of view.

On Tuesday, 6 July came the first puffs of southerly wind, followed by clouds and rain. The wind veered from the south-east to the south-west and increased in strength.

A state of the greatest preparedness was ordered. Stake went to the hydrogen gas apparatus to get ready to give the balloon a final fill-up of gas. The men who were to pull down the remaining parts of the north wall of the balloon-house 'took up their stations' as sailors say.

Andrée consulted our meteorological instruments, compared the direction of the wind on the shore with that indicated by Strindberg's weather-cock, and watched the movements of the clouds.

A few hours later he announced that no ascent would be made that day.

"The wind is southerly and the barometer is falling," he said. "Our start will take place when there's a southerly wind and the barometer is falling. But this wind has come too suddenly, and the barometer has fallen far too quickly. This wind will not last long."

He reached this decision without consulting any of us.

The men at the balloon-house and the hydrogen gas apparatus were recalled.

The wind increased during the course of the evening. Just before midnight it reached a force which, on Admiral Beaufort's scale, is indicated by 9. The most violent gusts reached gale force.

All the watch below on board the *Svensksund* were roused, and the whole crew was ordered ashore.

Andrée, Celsing, and I, together with ten sailors, were the first people to arrive at the balloon-house.

The gusts were so strong that at times we found it hard to walk upright.

The southern wall of the balloon house was rocking, and a rising and falling sound was coming from the steel cables.

In spite of the belts of webbing that had been put round its equator the balloon was oscillating violently between the walls of the shed. It was not only moving horizontally but also vertically. The carrying-ring and the net had been loaded with nearly five tons of sand, but this did not prevent the balloon from repeatedly rising at least two metres—all that the mooring-cables allowed—only to be thrown back to the floor a minute later.

Andrée gave orders that the cables should be tightened. His words were lost in the wind and the howling and whistling from all the chinks in the walls.

The three mooring-cables each ran through a pulley placed immediately under the carrying-ring, and were fastened to a sort of bollard close to the walls of the balloon-house.

After ten more men had arrived we succeeded, by utilizing the downward movements of the balloon, in hauling down the carrying-ring so that it finally rested flat on the floor.

Then, by means of belts of webbing and a large number of thin ropes, we managed to stop the balloon from oscillating between the walls, but it took us several hours.

In spite of the wind and the chinks in the walls the house was filled with the peculiar smell of the gas that had been forced out through the bottom valve of the balloon.

"Hydrogen and air produce oxyhydrogen gas," said Swedenborg later. "If some obstinate devil had come in with a pipe in his mouth, or if a charge of static electricity had developed between the balloon and the ground, and been released in a spark, why then the Andréean balloon voyage would have come to a fantastic end of a pyrotechnic nature even before it had started."

On the morning of 7 July the wind rapidly abated and we were able to return to the *Svensksund*. We were tired and drenched through by the pouring rain.

Sandwiches were put out for us. The men got hot coffee, while the rest of us gathered round a bowl of toddy made of brandy, sugar and hot water.

Andrée was very tired and sank in a heap into his basket-chair.

"They must build a larger balloon-house next time," he said. "Not circular but elliptical and orientated north-south. And there must be at least six metres of play between the walls and the balloon."

"Next time?" asked Swedenborg.

"An elliptical and a broader balloon-house," said Andrée.

"Next time?"

"We're only pioneers," answered Andrée. "Behind the pioneers wait their successors, the people who'll complete what they've begun.

"Nansen, for instance," he continued, "is no pioneer. He's had many predecessors whom he's followed. One of them was Franklin. His expedition ended in the most ghastly tragedy. That was fifty years ago. The Jeanette expedition lies nearer to us in time, but that too was a terrible tragedy.

"Nansen was no pioneer when he allowed himself to be frozen into the polar ice on board the *Fram*, he was only an imitator. He succeeded in doing something which many of his predecessors had failed to do, and he used the experience gained through their failures. He was an imitator, not a pioneer."

At four o'clock on the morning of 7 July Strindberg had recorded in our meteorological log-book that the rain had stopped, and the abating south wind had been succeeded by a fairly brisk northerly breeze.

"You were right," Lieutenant Norselius said to Andrée. "The southerly wind was temporary."

"If we'd started yesterday afternoon," said Andrée, "we should have found ourselves back at Spitzbergen by this time, or in two hours' time, after a short trip to the north."

21

The members of the expedition were called to a meeting in Andrée's saloon-like cabin on board the *Svensksund*.

Machuron, Engineer Stake and Captain Ehrensvärd were present as well as Andrée, Strindberg, Swedenborg and myself.

The meeting was conducted by Andrée.

We agreed that only Andrée, Strindberg, Swedenborg and I should have the right to participate in making any decisions. Machuron and Stake were granted the right to have their views recorded in the minutes. Ehrensvärd's function was not clearly defined. Nevertheless he was fully entitled to take part in the discussion and put forward his views.

After much argument and many digressions we arrived at the two following unanimous decisions.

1. Up to 15 July we should insist upon having a very favourable wind before we started.

2. After 15 July—if we were still at Danes Island—we should be satisfied with less favourable meteorological conditions, and get into the air as soon as there was a wind that made an ascent at all possible.

We dined with the three literary gentlemen and newspaper correspondents, Stadling, Lerner, and Violet, and told them of our decision.

"The whole world is waiting," said Doctor Violet.

"That's something to which we needn't pay any attention," said Andrée. "Our start will depend on technical and meteorological considerations.

"On the other hand," he continued. "On the other hand—there's always an 'on the other hand'—after all this waiting and expectation we're strictly speaking obliged to go.

"My comrades," he added, "are entirely at one with me in this matter."

22

While we were waiting we went on two long excursions to that part of the mainland of Spitzbergen known as the Vasa Peninsula, which lies on the far side of Smeerenburg Bay.

Strindberg was told to map the large glacier named after the *Fram* and also to have two large cairns erected, one on each side of the ice, so that future explorers would be able to tell whether the glacier had spread or shrunk.

Andrée and I climbed up the moraine on the north side of the glacier. It was a steep ascent. Andrée paused constantly, dug his hands into the gravel of the moraine and put forward various views as to its composition.

He took what he was doing extremely seriously.

When we had reached a height of perhaps two hundred metres we turned north along the western slope of the ridge called Blessing's Ridge on Strindberg's map of 1896. The ground was stony and the going difficult.

North of Blessing's Ridge there was a deep valley, the far wall of which also formed a ridge, known as Ekman's Ridge. It reached a height of six hundred metres.

Andrée said he thought there might be another glacier in the valley, concealed under gravel that had come down from the rocky ridges.

He asked me to continue round Ekman's Ridge to the Kennedy Glacier to the north of it, and there build two high cairns that no one could miss seeing, one on either side of the ice and close up to it.

When I reached a position immediately west of Ekman's Ridge, I climbed another hundred metres along a pretty steep slope, and threw myself down on a relatively dry shelf.

There was a light northerly wind, and the sun warmed me through a thin veil of cloud. The visibility was good. On the other side of Smeerenburg Bay lay Amsterdam Island, with its strange, colourful rock formations.

The reflection of the veil of cloud made the waters of the bay appear white. The sea far beyond was also white, or at least colourless. Danes Gat, the inlet that separated Amsterdam Island from Danes Island, was a surprisingly dark green. This may possibly have been due to tidal currents and purely local winds.

Through my binoculars I was easily able to distinguish the balloon-house, Pike's House, and the people moving about between the buildings and the shore.

The *Svensksund* and the little steamer the *Express* lay at anchor quite close to each other. From my lofty perch I could see quite clearly that Andrée had chosen the best possible base for his polar expedition, and that Virgo Harbour was a splendid natural harbour, sheltered from the wind on all sides.

The distance between me and the balloon-house was certainly not more than six thousand five hundred metres.

I took out my lunch of bread, butter, cheese, and beer.

Andrée wandered to and fro in the valley between Blessing's Ridge and Ekman's Ridge for nearly an hour. Then he threw himself down on a green bank, having first spread out an oblong piece of canvas. I looked at him through my binoculars. He lay down on his back and put his hands behind his head. He probably fell asleep. He must have been very tired.

The *Svensksund*'s steam-launch was moored in a little bay just north of the point where the Fram Glacier came down to Smeerenburg Bay.

I washed down my sandwiches with beer, and felt contented and at peace. I was sheltered from the light northerly breeze, and the sun shone warm through the thin veil of cloud.

On Dutch Point, the projecting part of Amsterdam Island that pointed in my direction, there were many graves containing the remains of whalermen who, over the years, had met their death in the Polar Regions.

Quite close to the path that had been trampled between Pike's House and the balloon-house on Danes Island there was another of these graves.

A coffin of crumbling boards.

A shallow grave. No one digs deep in ground which is frozen and frost-bound.

The coffin had no lid. The dead whaler was entirely covered with moss from his feet up to just below his shoulders. His cranium was light grey and was lying askew, resting on his left cheek-bone. His lower jaw had fallen away.

"Moss for a shroud," Swedenborg had said. "You can almost imagine that the moss keeps him as warm as a blanket."

The grave had looked the same the previous year. We were surprised that the foxes and the birds had left the skeleton in peace.

From the path to the balloon-house there was a narrow side-track that passed close to the grave.

23

Friday 9 July. Heavy clouds, sailing low, west wind, and pouring rain.

Engineer Stake reported that he had supplied the balloon with a good hundred cubic metres of gas after the stormy night of 7 July.

Nils Strindberg was clearly disturbed.

"Is the balloon damaged?" he asked.

"I don't know," answered Stake. "I haven't had a chance to test the gas tightness of the balloon. I've merely replaced the gas that was lost by fresh gas. I don't know how or why the balloon lost the gas it did."

"You mustn't worry," Swedenborg said to Strindberg. "Only say the word and I'll step into your shoes. You can catch a cold, or have a pain in your stomach, or something of that sort. Temperature thirty-nine Centigrade—easily managed with the help of a match."

Strindberg's uneasiness gave way to a friendly smile.

"My dear fellow," he said, "you misinterpret my worries. They're about the quality of the balloon, not about my participation in the expedition.

"When the *Svensksund* returns to the south you'll have a cabin to yourself. By this time next year you'll certainly have been promoted to captain. If you're lucky you'll be a major in time."

The barometer fell slowly. The westerly winds increased in strength.

A little Norwegian whaler sought shelter in Virgo Harbour and anchored between the *Svensksund* and the *Express*.

The Norwegians had been hunting seals on the edge of the pack ice and had been richly rewarded for their pains. No fewer than seven hundred seals had been shot and salvaged. The crew immediately began to chop up their catch, and the *Svensksund* was permeated by a disgusting stink.

There was a mood of nervousness, impatience and inactivity on board the gunboat. This applied not only to the members of the expedition and the officers, but also to the men.

The dismal and desolate landscape, the wind, the chilly rain, the low, drifting clouds, and the long wait had created an almost unendurable atmosphere.

In the afternoon the wind veered to the north-east, while the barometer still went on falling slowly.

In desperation Swedenborg, Stake, and Stadling, *Aftonbladet*'s man, asked to be allowed to make an excursion in the little Norwegian gig that we had brought with us from Tromsö. They wanted to row round Danes Island, a distance of about thirty kilometres.

Andrée reluctantly gave his consent.

"The time has very nearly come," he said.

Long after the others had withdrawn for the night Doctor Lembke and I went on sitting in the so-called gun-room of the *Svensksund*.

"I've tried to find some sort of philosophy," he said, "a logical, unassailable argument that could provide a justification for this crazy attempt to reach the North Pole in a balloon."

"So you don't believe that we shall succeed?" I said.

"I've no answer to that question," he said. "But it's rightly framed. The whole affair is in some way connected with *belief*.

"There's another thing too," he said, filling up his glass of punch. "In your medical supplies you have, among other things, a considerable quantity of citric acid for use as an antiscorbutic."

"As an anti-what?" I asked.

"Scorbutus, scurvy, as a remedy against scurvy. Professor Almqvist selected your medical supplies," he said. "He was Nordenskiöld's doctor on the *Vega*. Her voyage was accomplished without any outbreak of scurvy. But as a preventive she had on board fresh potatoes bought in Italy."

"Potatoes are too heavy for a balloon," I said.

"Our heathen ancestors ate onions now and then on their Viking voyages," said Lembke. "They never suffered from scurvy. Nordenskiöld recommends a table-spoonful of cloudberries a day as a suitable prophylactic. I don't believe in citric acid."

"Our journey will be short," I said. "We shan't need either potatoes, onions, cloudberries, or citric acid."

"If I'd been twenty years younger," said Jonas Lembke. "I should probably have been as mad as you are.

"A believer, that is."

Early on the morning of 10 July Swedenborg and Engineer Stake returned in the gig having rowed round Danes Island. Stadling arrived on foot soon afterwards. He had gone ashore east of Pike's Point.

They were all three dead tired. They had a light meal, went to bed, and slept for practically the whole day.

24

On Saturday 10 July the steamer *Lofoten* ran into Virgo Harbour for the second time.

She had on board a hundred tourists of many diverse nationalities.

The *Lofoten* fired a salute and was greeted by a salute. The rumble of the salvoes rolled to and fro between Amsterdam Island and Danes Island under the heavy cloud cover.

Myriads of sea-birds rose from their nesting places and wheeled in wide circles above Danes Gat, screeching and complaining.

The wind had abated. The rain was streaming down.

Andrée and I once more showed off the balloon-house and the balloon, the waiting car and the hydrogen gas apparatus, stationed near Pike's House.

The tourists, especially the ladies, were unsuitably dressed for being out-of-doors in the rainy weather of an arctic summer.

There were many journalists among the visitors.

We had dinner on board the *Lofoten*.

Captain Otto Sverdrup made a short speech and, as on the occasion of the *Lofoten*'s first visit, proposed a toast in champagne to our well-being and success.

I sat beside a cheerful gentleman who, in spite of his German name, Obermeyer, was on the staff of *Le Figaro* in Paris.

"Ever since the ascents made by the Montgolfier brothers, by Charles, and the Roberts brothers," said Obermeyer, "champagne has been the drink *par préférence* of all aeronauts.

"Who owns Spitzbergen?" he asked suddenly.

"Sweden and Norway," I answered, "the two realms of the Union."

"A very wide-spread misconception," said Obermeyer. "Spitzbergen is still a no man's land, a *terra nullius.*"

We were fetched less than an hour later by the *Svensksund's* eight-oar cutter. The rain had stopped. The water was almost as smooth as glass.

We climbed on board the boat in which the oarsmen were sitting with upraised oars. When the man in the bows pushed off, and the man in the stern hoisted the flagstaff bearing Ehrensvärd's standard, the passengers on the *Lofoten* broke into ringing cheers and masses of flowers rained down on us. Obermeyer threw down two bottles of champagne. I managed to catch one, but the other crashed on to the floor boards.

The helmsman shouted: "All ready, lie to your oars!" and we moved off from the *Lofoten*, which simultaneously weighed anchor.

"They cleared the dining-saloon of flowers," said Swedenborg. "They're not exactly fresh, but it was a kind thought."

By the time we had again boarded the *Svensksund* the *Lofoten* was gliding into Danes Gat and the usual salutes were being discharged and acknowledged.

The Norwegian flag without the Union device* had been hoisted both on the mainmast and on the aft flagstaff.

"I don't begrudge Sverdrup that little pleasure," said Ehrensvärd.

As it was a Saturday evening the men had been given extra rations. We ourselves usually arranged a festive little meal each

* The combination of the flags of Norway and Sweden carried in the upper square next to the flag-staff in the flags of both countries.

Saturday evening. That matter had now been attended to by the *Lofoten*'s chef so we only assembled to take our coffee and punch in the comfortable easy chairs on the after deck.

The sun almost broke through the clouds, and the temperature rose several degrees.

The conscientious Stake returned from a rapid tour of inspection of the balloon-house and the hydrogen gas apparatus. Everything was quiet, he told us. The men on watch were sober and playing cards for money and what money would buy, in spite of the fact that this was forbidden. The balloon had been given a fill of gas at four o'clock that afternoon.

"About sixty cubic metres," he answered in reply to a question from Strindberg.

The clouds lifted still higher, the air became crystal clear. A relaxed mood pervaded our little party. The sound of an accordion and low peals of laughter reached us from the fore-deck. A party from the watch below went ashore for a short excursion. Our two carpenters were carrying shot-guns, hoping perhaps to bring down some edible wild fowl.

For a short time Andrée and Swedenborg discussed the depot that Doctor Lerner had undertaken to establish as far north on the Seven Islands as possible.

"At this moment," said Doctor Lembke, "I've great difficulty in accepting the fact that we're really in the most godforsaken place in the world. My hunger is satisfied, the coffee is strong, the punch is of the best, those damned birds are quiet for once, the temperature is pleasant, the waiter is wearing a new, well-pressed uniform, we've up-to-date, relatively up-to-date, papers to read. It's just as if we were sitting in a quiet bay among the outer skerries of the Stockholm archipelago on board a Vaxholm boat. The fells around us, the patches of snow and the glaciers are merely a stage set."

Andrée said:

"Do you know, I'm no longer afraid that we shall have to return a second time. I've a feeling that the time is drawing near."

He did indeed give the impression of being completely calm. He was sitting with his eyes shut, and I noticed that he was very tanned by the sun.

* * *

By eleven o'clock everyone had retired to their cabins except Lembke, Swedenborg and I.

We opened the bottle of champagne that Obermeyer of *Le Figaro* had given me.

Ehrensvärd's standard, the long blue and yellow swallow-tailed pennant, was straightened out for a moment from the mast-head by a sudden gust of south wind that rushed past.

"Have you bestowed a thought on Andrée's balloon flag?" asked Swedenborg. "A piece of white silk with a blue anchor on it.

"A flag for a balloon. A blue *anchor* against a white ground! Why an anchor, I wonder?"

"There's something else too," I said. "A balloon is thought of as a vessel, a sort of ship. You sail a balloon, navigate a balloon, it has sails, lines, ropes, pulleys and tackle, even an anchor and a cable. But when Andrée speaks of his balloon he usually calls it 'he' not 'she'.

"What happens in other languages?" I asked. "What gender is a ship? Is a vessel a 'she' as in Swedish? What gender is a balloon?"

Lembke shook his head.

"I fear," he said, "that we shall not again be obliged to return with our mission uncompleted."

He elucidated: "I too have a feeling that the time is drawing near."

PART FOUR

THE BALLOON
VOYAGE

I

Early the following morning, Sunday, 11 July, Swedenborg and I were roused by loud cries: "A south wind, a strong south wind!"

We tumbled out of our bunks, pulled on our clothes in the confined space, and then rushed up to the bridge.

Lieutenant Norselius met us with two mugs of steaming coffee, and rusks spread with butter and marmalade.

"Ever since four o'clock," he said. "A fresh south-westerly breeze. It's gusty and getting stronger."

"Where's Andrée?" I asked.

He had already gone ashore and to the balloon-house with Celsing.

Tattered clouds were being driven rapidly towards the north. At long intervals clusters of blinding sunbeams swept across the *Svensksund*.

Strindberg appeared.

"Now then, you devils!" said Swedenborg.

"Where's Ehrensvärd?" I asked.

"Asleep," answered Norselius. "His second in command's on duty. That's me."

"Lembke?"

"Not often afoot before ten o'clock."

"Stake?"

"Don't know."

Stake wasn't a member of the *Svensksund*'s crew.

There was no boat available to take us ashore.

It was obvious that we were nearing the decisive moment.

"You're afraid," said Swedenborg, turning to me. "There isn't anyone here to make up your mind for you. But Andrée is ashore."

To Strindberg he said: "You were here at Danes Island last year too. You're even more afraid than our friend Fraenkel. Which would be the more hellish? To start, or not to start?"

Norselius went up to Swedenborg. "As one lieutenant to another," he said, "I beg you to hold your tongue."

At this moment two Norwegian whalers suddenly appeared in Danes Gat and sailed into Virgo Harbour. Norselius sent out a signal to stop them from anchoring to the north of the balloon-house. They made one tack northwards, and then steered towards the *Svensksund*, and dropped anchor close to the gunboat.

The skipper of one of the vessels rowed over to the *Svensksund* and explained that they were seeking shelter because they were expecting a strong southerly gale. He was a thickset man with short hair and a forked beard. He came aboard the *Svensksund* on the starboard side and saluted the flag by hastily raising his woollen cap. His manners were free and easy and self-confident, and he was readier to ask questions than to answer them.

His name was Galskjold, at least, that is what my way of spelling it came to.

"I was here last year," he said. "I know Andrée. He knows me. Last year things went their own way.

"They'll go their own way this year too," he added.

At eight o'clock Andrée returned to the *Svensksund*. Celsing, Stake, and one of our two carpenters were with him.

Andrée was very serious and would not say much.

He struck me as being tired, but his activity of the past few weeks was enough to explain that.

"I want an hour to think things over," he said. "Meanwhile you, Fraenkel and Strindberg, should pack your personal belongings and write such letters as you think necessary."

My personal belongings were already packed, and the necessary letters already written.

Between eight and nine o'clock the sky to the north cleared completely, but in the south some heavy, and in places, dark clouds appeared.

On board the *Svensksund* we were registering a wind of between five and ten metres per second in velocity. That is to say, it was decidedly gusty.

"There must be a much stronger wind even as little as a hundred or a hundred and fifty metres up," said Norselius. "Possibly rather less gusty too."

Just before nine o'clock Andrée again appeared on deck and told me to fetch Strindberg, Swedenborg, and Alexis Machuron.

We were taken ashore by the steam-launch.

We walked in silence up to Pike's House where our meteorological instruments had been put, and went on along the path to the balloon-house.

We walked into the balloon-house, came out again immediately, walked round the building, and finally stopped in a cluster on the leeside to the north.

"The balloon is keeping pretty quiet compared with that stormy night four days ago," I said. "Or was it five days? It's damned hard not to mix up days that have no nights."

Andrée turned to Machuron.

"What's your opinion?" he asked. "Shall we try or not?"

He asked the question in French, and of course it was answered in French.

"The wind's gusty. Once the balloon's in the air the gustiness won't matter. If the actual take-off can be achieved without mishap, you ought to try."

Andrée listened with both his hands plunged into the pockets of his breeches. He turned to Swedenborg.

Our reserve said: "A strong wind, a strong southerly wind, is essential if the balloon is to reach its target. You must therefore take the risks involved in getting out of the balloon-house in a strong wind. That's elementary."

It was then Nils Strindberg's turn to speak. He shrugged his shoulders and said: "We can hardly hope for better weather for our voyage. The balloon's a poor thing, we all know that. But nothing that we can do to patch it up will make it any better than it is. I think we ought to start."

Andrée then looked at me.

"I don't like this gusty wind," I said. "Nor do I like the winds that sweep down from the mountains. Things may go infernally wrong. But if we can get out of the balloon-house, and if we can survive those downward draughts, everything should be all right.

"Strindberg is right," I went on. "We can hardly hope for a better wind for our journey. Machuron is right; if we can succeed in getting out of the balloon-house our chances are good. Swedenborg is right; we need a strong southerly wind. Without it a start would be pointless. We must therefore take some risks. I vote that we start."

The gusts of wind were making the walls of the balloon-house bulge in and out. A wailing sound was coming from the woodwork, and the wind was whistling through the many chinks, though not as shrilly as during the recent night of gales.

The two men posted beside the hydrogen gas apparatus were standing side by side on a piece of rising ground, two dark, motionless silhouettes against the patches of snow and the glaciers on the mountains of Amsterdam Island on the other side of Danes Gat.

One of the guards on duty at the balloon-house strolled round the eastern corner of the building (if one can talk of corners on an octagonal building). He had pulled the flaps of his cap down under his chin, and the wind had blown his collar up behind his neck.

He halted a few steps behind Andrée and looked at us expectantly. He was wearing uniform, but was unarmed except for the cutlass at his belt. He was young, clean-shaven, perhaps not yet twenty years of age.

He looked at us expectantly, with an expression of curiosity.

After a silence that lasted for several long minutes Swedenborg said to Andrée. "And you? What do you think about it?"

Our leader did not answer. He cast a hasty glance on the balloon-house, then, screwing up his eyes, he looked at the sky, and across Danes Gat to the sea in the north-west.

After that he walked, still with his hands in his breeches' pockets, along the path down to the shore, at first slowly, then increasingly fast.

Half way back to the *Svensksund* we heard the sound of gruff voices singing a psalm. The sound rose and fell in volume with the gusts of wind.

Lembke, Celsing, and Stake were waiting beside the swing-boom.

A somewhat belated church parade was going on. The crew were standing to attention in their Sunday uniforms. Norselius was reading out of something that might have been a book of homilies for the army. He glanced at us over his shoulder, hurried on with his reading, and brought it to an end with a quick "Amen."

We waited expectantly. The flag in the stern and the pennant on the mainmast flapped in the wind. I met Andrée's eyes and he gave me a fleeting smile.

Ehrensvärd stepped from Norselius's side, saluted and called out: "Long live the King and our Fatherland." To which the crew responded: "Oh Lord, hear our prayer."

Some moments of confusion followed. Norselius used the wrong word of command, the bugler blew the wrong signal. One of the non-commissioned officers burst out laughing, the crew broke ranks and gathered round us in a wide arc.

"Well?" asked Ehrensvärd.

"We've discussed the matter," answered Andrée, calmly and seriously. "Machuron and Swedenborg consider that conditions for a start are favourable. My two companions are of the same opinion.

"Speaking for myself, I'm doubtful," he said. "I find it difficult to account for my hesitancy."

Then in a loud voice so that everyone could hear he added: "We have therefore decided to start."

"It's exactly twenty-two minutes to eleven a.m.," said Swedenborg. "Twenty-two minutes to eleven by Swedish time, and a historic moment."

2

The crew of the *Svensksund* changed into working clothes and by a few minutes after eleven o'clock the first watch put ashore had already begun to pull down the north wall of the balloon-house, directed by Andrée.

The four-metre-high canvas walls, which were to give us extra protection from the wind at the moment of take-off, were hoisted up the masts on the south side.

At twelve o'clock Strindberg and I also went ashore, taking with us our personal belongings.

The wind seemed to be increasing in strength, and was blowing pretty uniformly towards the north-east.

Strindberg took a lot of photographs of the pulling down of the north wall and other preparatory work. In between taking photographs he sent up a number of small meteorological balloons, which showed us that the direction of the wind at a higher altitude was pretty much the same as at ground level.

Then Swedenborg arrived and with him Stadling, the editor from the Stockholm newspaper *Aftonbladet*. Stadling went to the dovecote in Pike's House and put the carrier-pigeons—thirty of them altogether—into the baskets intended for them, and these were then lashed firmly to the carrying-ropes immediately under the balloon.

The crews of the two whalers that had arrived at Virgo Harbour that morning also helped with the work going on at the balloon-house.

When the work of pulling down the north wall was completed the three guide-ropes were stretched out on the ground in an easterly direction.

Norselius and Celsing suggested that the ropes should be laid in coils immediately outside the balloon-house, but Andrée shook his head disapprovingly.

They began to raise the balloon. The sacks of ballast were removed from the net, one by one. The three sailors stationed by the three mooring-cables allowed the balloon to rise little by little until the carrying-ring was rather less than four metres above the floor of the balloon-house.

The car was brought in by six men and placed in a depression, or pit, in the centre of the floor.

In spite of the belts of webbing and the ropes round its equator the balloon was careering about between the walls. It took more than an hour to attach the six ropes of the car to the carrying-ring, partly because it was difficult to reach the ring from the roof of the car, and partly because it was moving all the time, either jerking upwards, or swinging from side to side.

We had reduced the stability of the balloon-house by pulling down its north wall, while at the same time we had made the south wall more sensitive to gusts of wind by adding four metres to its height with the canvas screen.

Andrée gave orders that the wall was to be braced by yet more ropes and steel cables.

Twenty-four sacks of sand, each weighing twenty-three kilos were hanging on the carrying-ring.

Another three bundles of sacks of sand, having a combined weight of at least fifteen hundred kilos, were fastened to the carrying-ring to stabilize the balloon in preparation for the start.

At one o'clock Strindberg and Swedenborg went back to the *Svensksund* to take some final readings of the chronometer and the barometer.

It was an hour before they returned with Ehrensvärd and Doctor Lembke.

"We had a late breakfast," said Swedenborg. "Strindberg was gloomy and dejected. Ehrensvärd opened a bottle of champagne. It didn't help matters."

Lembke had brought with him a little basket of sandwiches and beer which he put into the car.

The wind blew harder and harder.

* * *

Soon after two o'clock in the afternoon Andrée ran up the Union flag and his own flag, the blue anchor on a white ground. The signal halliard ran through a little pulley attached to the net of the balloon.

At the same time the two flags on the flagstaffs of the balloon-house were hoisted.

Andrée announced through a megaphone that his balloon was to be called the *Eagle*. This was greeted by spontaneous cheering.

A last small balloon of goldbeater's skin was released. It rose rapidly and disappeared in a north-easterly direction. The direction of the wind had not changed.

After this the farewell ceremonies began.

Nils Strindberg drew aside for a few minutes with Machuron and Lembke.

"He's gloomy," said Swedenborg, "and his eyes are red and swollen."

"You yourself look happy and relieved," I answered.

"Lembke has brought some medicine with him," said Swedenborg. "A pocket-flask of cognac, the finest quality and the best brand obtainable."

I was seized by a sudden, strong feeling of aversion for him.

"Both Andrée and I are thankful we shan't have you as the third man in the car," I said.

Swedenborg grinned broadly.

"Goodbye, dear friend," he said. "We're about to part, and we shall never meet again."

"Thank goodness for that," I answered.

He held out his hand. I did not take it. I turned aside, stumbled over something, and fell flat on the floor. Swedenborg burst out laughing.

During those last few minutes the atmosphere in the balloon-house was hectic and agitated. The men, the officers, and the crews of the two whalers ran to and fro across the floor, in and out through the door, scrambled up the walls, and stood guard over lines and ropes. Everyone shouted at the top of his voice. Commands were given and then countermanded.

One of the masts carrying the four-metre-high canvas screen was broken by a strong gust of wind. It fell slowly inwards and its point would have penetrated the envelope of the balloon if Engineer Stake had not seen what was going to happen, and sent up four men who succeeded in checking its fall.

Andrée and I said goodbye to the officers and non-commissioned officers of the *Svensksund*.

Andrée handed Captain Ehrensvärd a number of telegrams that he was to despatch as soon as the gunboat reached Tromsö. One of them was to King Oscar: "At the moment of departure the members of the North Pole Expedition beg Your Majesty to accept their humble greetings, and the expression of their most grateful thanks."

Andrée thanked Engineer Stake for the careful and dedicated way in which he had worked.

Stake answered: "Last night it was calm. This morning there was no necessity to pump in more gas. Thirty or forty cubic metres have probably been lost this morning because of the way in which the balloon has been thrown backwards and forwards between the walls. But it's impossible for me to do anything about that now."

"Not only impossible," said Andrée, "but also unnecessary."

Galskjold, the captain of one of the two Norwegian whalers that had sought shelter and safety in Virgo Harbour the night before, was standing a few steps away from the officers of the *Svensksund*.

"You here?" said Andrée.

"Just by chance," answered the fork-bearded skipper. "And you're going up aloft?"

"I must," said Andrée.

"Why?" asked Galskjold.

"A man must do what he's planned to do," answered Andrée.

"I know what you mean," said Galskjold, and seized Andrée's hands between his horny fists.

Andrée then walked up to the car and climbed onto its roof, or deck.

Strindberg and I took our places at his side.

3

Andrée gave orders through his megaphone that the belts of webbing and the ropes round the *Eagle*'s equator should be removed.

The balloon was thrown to and fro spasmodically between the walls of the balloon-house.

The car remained in the pit in the floor.

On Andrée's orders Strindberg and I cut loose the ropes with which the sacks of sand, weighing altogether one and a half tons, were fastened to the carrying-ring.

The *Eagle* rose about half a metre, or as much as the three mooring-cables allowed.

The bustle in the balloon-house, previously so hectic and agitated, suddenly stopped.

Everyone was standing still, silent and expectant.

The mooring-cables as you know ran through pulleys fixed to the floor, and then wound round things like bollards placed close to the walls of the balloon-house. Heavy pieces of wood had been pushed under the cables close to the pulleys. These chopping-blocks, so like the blocks used at executions, held the cables taut.

Everything depended on waiting for the right moment, the ten seconds or so of relative calm between the gale-force gusts.

Beside each of the three mooring-cables stood a sailor from the *Svensksund* armed with a cutlass sharpened on a grindstone. Andrée briefly repeated his instructions to them through his megaphone.

Strindberg and I stood ready to hoist the *Eagle*'s three sails.

The wind whistled through the cracks in the balloon-house. The canvas screen that rose above the top of the south wall flapped and slapped.

Stadling, Lerner, Doctor Violet, Machuron, and several other people took photographs of us from all imaginable angles.

* * *

A strong gust of wind died down and was followed by temporary peace and quiet. The moment had come.

"Attention," called Andrée through his megaphone. "One, two, three, cut!"

The three cutlasses rose and fell practically simultaneously.

For a few seconds the balloon remained motionless, as if its sudden release had taken it by surprise.

"At last," said Strindberg, in a low voice.

There were tears in his eyes.

Andrée's face was pale and set, his mouth tightly shut, his eyes partially closed.

The moment the *Eagle* began to rise I started to hoist our three sails. This was an operation that could be carried out fairly rapidly because of the way in which the rigging was constructed.

The floor of the balloon-house sank beneath us. I heard cries of hurrah. I heard Andrée answer through his megaphone: "Long live old Sweden."

I wanted Strindberg to help me with the sails, but he was bending over the instrument-ring, with one hand outstretched, saying something in French to Machuron.

Everyone, the officers, the men, and the Norwegian whalers rushed to the entrance of the balloon-house, their voices mingling in a cacophony out of which only a few loud oaths emerged clearly.

I was fully occupied with the sails.

The *Eagle* rose slowly and majestically.

As soon as it got above the protective screen on the south wall a fresh gust of wind seized it and hurled it against the east wall

A moment later the car too banged against the wall. The impact was so violent that Andrée lost his megaphone, which fell to the floor of the balloon-house.

A few seconds later I saw that my view to the south was clear. We had succeeded in getting out of the balloon-house and were drifting northwards at a height of about fifty metres.

The wind whistled round us, the two flags flapped, and the sails filled. The car was being dragged aft in relation to the balloon because of the resistance offered by the ballast-ropes and the guide-ropes.

In spite of the wind we could still clearly hear the voices of the people beneath us and the sound of their running feet.

Strindberg seemed to have forgotten his duties as a navigator. He was fully occupied in taking photographs of our departure.

Andrée was still standing where he had stood when we took off.

We drifted across Virgo Harbour.

The *Svensksund* saluted us by dipping her flag.

The guide-ropes and the ballast-ropes dragged across the surface of the water, making the bubbling and swishing noise that you hear when the prow of a fast-moving boat cuts through the waves.

"At last we're off," said Strindberg. "At last that accursèd waiting is over."

"We haven't enough height," I said to Andrée.

He did not answer.

The *Eagle* began to twist round on its vertical axis. The sail was supposed to be leeward, but the balloon went on turning slowly and the sail suddenly appeared to windward, for no reason at all that we could think of.

At the same time the balloon began to sink rapidly.

The sail was so rigged that, so long as it remained in the right position to leeward, it could press the balloon upwards. But as soon as the balloon made a half turn the effect was the exact opposite; the balloon was pressed downwards.

Strindberg shouted something. Andrée looked now at the guide-ropes, now at the balloon in bewilderment. The sails were easy to hoist, but more difficult to take in. Without waiting for orders I climbed up into the rigging above the carrying-ring.

A few seconds later the car bumped on to the surface of the water.

Andrée and Strindberg seemed to be panic stricken. From my position in the net I could see them cutting loose one sack of sand after another.

I called to them.

They could not hear me because of the wind, though I could still hear the voices of the people on the shore of Danes Island, and the sound of the oars of two boats that had been launched, and were rowing after us across Danes Gat as hard as they could go.

We had foreseen, and frequently discussed, these downward gusts of wind that would press on the balloon, and force it down for a few moments. But we had not expected that the car would touch the water.

When I had taken in the sails I climbed down to the deck of the car. The *Eagle* was again rising, and with increasing speed.

The barometer showed that we had reached a height of four hundred metres and were still moving upwards.

"What's happened?" I asked.

Andrée answered: "Two-thirds of each guide-rope is lost. They came unscrewed at their upper joints, all three of them."

We were over Dutch Point with all its dead whalers.

The *Eagle* was a free-sailing balloon, deprived of all navigational aids. The three guide-ropes, that would have made it dirigible, were lost.

We drifted across Dutch Point.

Our speed was the speed of the wind.

We ourselves were in an air-chamber of complete calm. Our flags hung limp. We no longer felt the wind since we were now travelling with it. There was absolute silence except for the shrill cries of birds, and the distant rumble of waves breaking against the rocky shores.

"Ten minutes since we started," said Strindberg.

Those ten minutes had seemed like hours to me.

"How much ballast, how many sacks of sand did you throw out?" I asked.

Andrée counted the severed ropes with his eyes.

"Nine times twenty-three kilos makes rather more than two hundred kilos," said Strindberg.

"That, plus the parts of the guide-ropes we've lost comes to almost eight hundred kilos of ballast."

Of course I fully realize that the layman will find it hard to grasp the meaning of these figures about the ballast the balloon had lost, or their importance.

The *Eagle* rose to a height of six hundred metres.

We travelled with the wind across Smeerenburg Bay and drew near to the island which bears the poetic name Birdsong.

To Andrée I said:

"We can open the valves, pull the rip-panel, and land on Birdsong. We're still within eyeshot of the people on Danes Island."

"Why?" he asked.

"You know very well why," I answered. "The *Eagle*'s been transformed into a free-sailing balloon. We can't steer it any longer."

Andrée said:

"Do you really think we ought to make an emergency landing on Birdsong?"

"No," I answered.

"And you?" asked Andrée, turning to Strindberg.

"I intended to drop a tin containing a letter to my fiancée when we passed over Dutch Point," said Strindberg. "Machuron and I had agreed that I should. I forgot it. There was too much going on. I'll throw it down as we pass over Birdsong."

"So we're of one mind," said Andrée.

"All three of us," I added.

Eighteen minutes later we passed over Birdsong at a height of rather more than six hundred metres.

Strindberg's last letter was thrown from the car in a small cylindrical, aluminium tin. Its fall was slowed down by ten metres of blue and yellow silk ribbon.

Through the binoculars I could see the *Svensksund*'s steam-launch just off the promontory known as Dutch Point in Smeerenburg Bay.

They were clearly coming at full steam in our direction.

"It's useless," said Strindberg, "we're doing more than twenty knots."

Andrée said: "As soon as they see that we don't intend to make an emergency landing on Birdsong they'll turn back."

4

A strange feeling of light-heartedness had taken hold of us. The sun was warm though the thermometer only registered one degree above zero, Centigrade.

We laughed at the absurd little steam-launch that was trying to catch up with a balloon.

We laughed at the inquisitive birds that had gathered round us, some sailing on motionless wings, others circling round the car, their heavy wings flapping clumsily.

Spitzbergen, with its many islands, fjords, gats, glaciers, and sharp peaks lay spread out south and east of us. Here and there woolly clouds cast dark shadows on the ice of the glaciers.

We were in the midst of absolute stillness.

Our flag hung limp.

The sea, the islands, and the fjords revolved rapidly southwards, far beneath us, far away from us.

We were in the midst of absolute stillness. We were supreme. The round earth was being forced to move beneath us.

Far to the north we could see the first isolated floes of pack ice.

"At this rate we shall be at the North Pole sooner than anyone dared to hope," said Andrée.

"I'm longing for a smoke," I said, "but I've put my pipe, my tobacco, and my matches down in the car, to stop me from lighting up without thinking what I'm doing."

Because of our great height the gas was streaming out of the bottom valve at regular intervals, making a whistling and hissing noise.

"I've some snuff in reserve," answered Strindberg, and held out a box.

"It would be a good thing if you'd some gas in reserve," I said.

The remaining parts of the guide-ropes varied somewhat in length; one was a hundred and five metres long, one was a hundred, and the third was ninety-five.

To make the balloon dirigible again it would be necessary to lengthen at least one of them, preferably all three.

We hauled up one of the eight ballast-ropes—all seventy metres long—in order to splice it to the longest of the guide-ropes. It was a troublesome job.

As we were doing it we glided into a still thicker cloud of mist or, to put it more exactly, a cloud began to build up immediately in our path, and grew rapidly both in volume and density. The sun disappeared, and we were dazzled by an intensely white light, that fell upon us from all sides. Visibility shrank to nil. The warmth was replaced by the damp chill of a cellar.

Less than five minutes later a violent jerk shook the car. The three guide-ropes straightened out, and we heard the loud bubbling of rushing water.

Nothing could be seen in the whiteness that enveloped us. But beneath the car we caught a glimpse of the dark sea. Our barograph told us that the cooling of the balloon and the gas had so much reduced its lifting capacity that, in the course of a few minutes, we had sunk from a height of close on six hundred metres to one of between eighty-five and ninety metres.

The braking effect of the guide-ropes was noticeable. There was no longer absolute stillness. We could feel the air streaming past us, our flags opened out hesitantly, the balloon swung slowly round on its vertical axis.

Andrée ordered us to hoist the big sail again. The wind filled it and we were driven forwards, we did not know exactly in what direction, as we were moving in a white void of mist, and had no fixed point of reference.

Andrée reckoned that the wind was still blowing towards the north-east. We moved the guide-ropes so that the yard pointed from south-west to north-east, which meant that the balloon would move in a more westerly direction than the wind, and consequently more towards the north.

"*Navigare necesse est,*" I said.

Fifteen minutes later we glided out of the cloud and into the warmth of the sun. The balloon reacted almost instantaneously. The hydrogen expanded, our lifting capacity increased, the guide-ropes left the water and lost their braking-power, we moved faster and faster until our speed became that of the wind. We were back once more in the calm of absolute stillness, with a slack sail and drooping flags.

We rose rapidly to a height of over five hundred metres. I saw the sea, and the clouds, and the islands to the south-east sinking beneath us, but I could not appreciate the fact that we were gaining height except by looking at our altimeter.

We were the centre of the universe. We were stationary. The earth sank beneath us and rotated slowly southwards.

5

I brought out the basket of sandwiches and beer that Doctor Lembke had placed in the car just before we started.

Andrée and Strindberg each took a cheese sandwich. I ate three, one with cheese, the other two with smoked pork. We opened one bottle of beer and passed it round.

When I threw the empty bottle overboard the balloon rose nearly ten metres.

"There's one grave defect in the construction of the car," I said to Andrée.

"There's nowhere to sit up here on the roof. No one likes eating and drinking standing up."

"You mean we've no veranda for our after-dinner punch," said Andrée.

Strindberg and I became involved in a short dispute

"The first half bottle of beer was emptied at twenty minutes past three," he said, entering the time in his log book.

"At a quarter past four," I objected.

Up there, half a kilometre above the Arctic Ocean, we were arguing for fun, but there was a complication.

Strindberg's chronometer registered Greenwich mean time, while I had set my pocket-watch by the true solar time based on the meridian of our base on Danes Island.

"Time, hours, minutes, and seconds," I said, "in a world where the days have no nights, and summer is one long day that lasts for several months."

However, when making my notes in my meteorological journal I used the same time as Strindberg.

We finished splicing the ballast rope to the longest of the guide-ropes and let it down gently. It was a hundred and seventy metres long. But we were rather more than five hundred metres above the sea.

We were travelling rapidly north-eastwards. There seemed a very high probability that we should soon penetrate further north than Nansen and Johansen.

Andrée and Strindberg had climbed up to the carrying-ring and they called down a warning: "Look out, or you'll get a shower!"

They peed, and the stream of urine described an arc that descended at a reassuring distance from the car.

"We rose fifty metres," I called back.

6

Andrée was worried by the loss of the two lower thirds of the guide-ropes.

"Everyone," he said, "everyone, including Nordenskiöld, was

afraid that the guide-ropes would catch on the ice. I was literally forced to devise those confounded screw attachments. I didn't want to. But I was forced to do it. Look at the result! The screws came unscrewed, we lost the ropes, and with them all chance of steering the balloon."

"You mustn't be upset," I said. "Everything happened very quickly after we left the balloon-house. But I remember it all quite clearly.

"You insisted on having the guide-ropes laid out to the east. Both Norselius and Celsing warned you. You wouldn't listen.

"We rose. We pulled the guide-ropes with us. They twisted on their own axes because they were laid out straight and not in coils. It was because they twisted that they came unscrewed."

"Exactly," said Andrée.

"Don't oversimplify," I said. "The balloon sank and the car bounced across the waves of Danes Gat. The guide-ropes worked loose and we rose. If they hadn't come off as they did they'd have dragged the car under the water, and everything would have been over in a matter of seconds.

"Be thankful for those confounded screws, for that confounded piece of bad luck!"

7

At half-past six that evening—by Strindberg's time—we glided in over the more or less unbroken expanse of polar ice

Four carrier-pigeons bearing despatches were released. They circled round the balloon a few times, and then flew off in an easterly direction, not south.

The temperature sank, and the balloon descended to a height of about two hundred and sixty metres.

We had our first meal on board. This consisted of sandwiches and a soup containing bits of macaroni, which had been made on board the *Svensksund*, and then kept in a jar wrapped round with newspaper and Andrée's woollen jersey.

It was still warm. It tasted excellent.

The sun still felt warm though the temperature was now about zero.

The balloon rose while we were eating our meal.

We had once again risen to a height of about six hundred metres, and beneath us there was nothing but an endless sea of white clouds.

The sun was warm. Its warmth seemed to be doubled by being reflected back by the clouds beneath us.

Andrée peed again, and the balloon rose another few metres.

"I'm horribly tired," he said.

His eyes were two narrow slits, and his tongue moved to and fro across his dry lips.

"I've not slept for more than a few hours for days," he said.

"The car awaits you," I answered.

He crept down through the trapdoor in the deck, made himself comfortable on the bunk, and fell asleep instantly.

"He's lying on his right side," I said to Strindberg in a low voice. "He's drawn up his knees and put both hands between them. He's sleeping like a child."

Just before our meal Andrée had written his first short communiqué and given it to Strindberg to put into one of the buoys and then throw overboard.

These buoys—we had twelve of them—were pear-shaped or conical and made of cork. The cone was weighted with metal, and at the other end there was a flag, fixed to a spike.

The message was short.

'So far our journey has gone well.' "Of course it's gone well," I said, "except for that business just after the start."

We had made ourselves comfortable on the deck of the car by bringing down two baskets from the storage-space above the carrying-ring.

The sun blazed down, and I put on my dark glasses.

The birds had disappeared. It was perfectly quiet except for a faint roar in the east, and an occasional, slight, hissing noise from the bottom valve, announcing that there was too much pressure inside the balloon.

Now and then we caught glimpses of the ice beneath us through the clouds, but these were never long enough to allow us to estimate our speed, nor the direction in which we were travelling.

"Everything suggests that our speed is the same as before," said Strindberg.

We shared another bottle of beer between us. "The famous balloonist's thirst," I said.

Strindberg threw the bottle over the side.

"Unnecessary," I said. "We must be careful with our ballast."

"Every time we breathe we lose a few milligrammes of gas and ballast," said Strindberg. "And what about the cuds of snuff we spat out before our beer? How much do you suppose a good-sized quid weighs?

" 'Weather splendid, morale excellent,' " he said, reading from Andrée's despatch.

"There's one sound you hardly notice unless you make an effort," I said. "The woodwork of the car creaks and squeaks every time we move."

We guessed that we were sailing towards the north-east at a good pace, but also in absolute stillness. The sun was warm. The air was light and dry.

"It's a sheer delight to breathe in," I said, "even if we lose ballast when we breathe out."

"Andrée has spelt your name 'Fränkel,' with an 'ä', that is," said Strindberg.

"I don't care a damn if he has," I said. "I'm feeling pleasantly drowsy, and I'm longing for a cigar, or a pipe."

Strindberg took our bearings at eight o'clock, and again at half-past nine.

These showed us that we were on a still more easterly course.

This was confirmed by observations we were able to make with the help of the pack ice, which was now and then visible through rifts in the clouds beneath us.

"If this goes on," said Strindberg, "we shall find ourselves over the Taymyr Peninsula in Siberia in less than forty-eight hours."

Another thing that we noticed was that the clouds beneath us were travelling in a still more easterly direction than the balloon. This meant that the wind at our altitude was more northerly.

"The *Eagle*," I said. "The balloon is called the *Eagle*. In Paris they called it the *North Pole*. Andrée always says 'he' when he's speaking of the balloon, never 'it' or 'she'. I couldn't think why. A balloon's a sailing vessel, isn't it, a sort of ship? Now I understand Andrée. The name *Eagle* was at the back of his mind. And an eagle must of course be masculine."

"Quite illogical," answered Strindberg. "Half of all the eagles are female."

"Of course it's illogical," I said. "I'm illogical by nature. If I hadn't been I shouldn't be here on board the *Eagle*'s car."

The sun was shining in the north-west. It still had some warmth, but the temperature of the air had sunk by half a degree in less than twenty minutes, possibly because we had now glided in over more compact ice.

A little before ten o'clock—Greenwich mean time according to Strindberg's chronometer—on the evening of that first day, we found that we were only just above the cloud cover.

We emptied our bladders to what you might call the last drop, as we were anxious to avoid the more easterly winds of the lower altitude. The balloon rose slightly, but then sank again.

Each fall of half a degree in temperature seemed to cause us to lose about two hundred metres of height.

Urged on by me Strindberg put Andrée's despatch into the water-tight metal capsule in the buoy, but only after he had made a brief addition to the text.

We threw out the buoy. The balloon rose about ten metres.

I emptied out a third of the contents of a sack of ballast, that is about eight kilos of sand.

The *Eagle* rose fifty metres.

"Our life is full of variety," I said. "One hour we're so careful of our ballast that we regret having spat out a cud of snuff. The next we're busily engaged in both baling out sand and peeing."

With the aid of the pack ice, which we saw through a broad rift in the clouds, we discovered that we had got into the lower air-stream, and were now travelling in a more easterly direction.

I cut off the lowest rungs of the rope ladder that hung between the carrying-ring and the car and threw them overboard. A few minutes later I sent another six rings after them. "They're really just in the way," I said, "and we don't need them."

I reduced the weight of the sack of ballast I'd been emptying by roughly another nine kilos, and threw another buoy overboard.

After that we rose to a height of rather more than six hundred metres.

We were once again in the region of sunshine, stillness, and silence.

Strindberg had put a written communication into the second buoy.

"What?" I asked.

"Only the time and our position," he answered. "And our height above sea-level."

We were once again high above the clouds. Our altimeter registered six hundred and thirty metres.

But we found that the upper winds had now changed direction. As far as we could make out we were no longer on our way to the Taymyr Peninsula, but on a more easterly course to the mountains of Novaya Zemlya.

"Or to the burnt-up valleys of Ceylon," I said.

We moved about softly on the deck of the car and spoke in whispers to avoid disturbing Andrée.

"Stillness," said Strindberg. "Silence and warm sunshine."

"Drivel," I said.

We had twelve buoys on board the *Eagle*. They were numbered one to twelve. We also had a thirteenth buoy, considerably larger than the others. It was to be thrown on to the North Pole and carried the Swedish flag.

The first buoy we threw out was number four.

The second was number seven.

8

Soon after midnight on the night between the 11th and 12th July (if one can really use the word 'night' during summertime north of the Polar Circle) we glided into the shadow of a gigantic cloud to the north of us.

The temperature sank, and as it fell the balloon dropped through the clouds and the mist until the guide-rope that we had lengthened touched the ice.

Our forward movement was checked, and we once more became aware of the wind. The end of the long guide-rope was now resting on the ice, and we reached equilibrium at a height of about a hundred metres.

The *Eagle* turned slowly, the sails filled, our drift as a free-sailing balloon was over, and it was again possible to navigate. The pack ice beneath us was very open. It was really no more than a collection of floes, separated by wide leads. The noises the guide-rope made were distinctive: a limpid ripple when it was cutting through open water, a scratching and rustling when it was gliding across ice.

By using the blocks of ice as a guide it was easy to determine our speed and direction. We were travelling at a hundred metres per thirty seconds, that is at a little over ten kilometres an hour. Our course was dead east.

We were surprised at there being so little wind.

The sail was at right angles to the direction in which we were travelling. "There's no point in moving the guide-rope to bring the sail round to another angle," I said. "The wind's so light that it won't make our course more northerly."

However, the sail did help to give the balloon some lift, and to stabilize it.

The mist prevented us from seeing further than about two thousand metres. The sun was quite invisible. We did not even know where it was without consulting our chronometer and the compass. We guessed that the mist and cloud extended upwards to a height of at least five hundred metres. An astonishing amount of moisture had settled on the balloon. Everything was wet. Water dripped from the opening in the canvas that was stretched across inside the carrying-ring.

Strindberg and I tried to calculate how much carrying capacity the balloon had lost since we started eleven hours previously. We arrived at a figure that was just under half a ton.

"The devil of a lot too much," said Strindberg.

Soon after this the balloon sank so much that the ballast-ropes too trailed in the water or over the ice. This caused the *Eagle* to make another half turn which brought the sail round to leeward.

We threw eleven kilos of sand overboard, and rose again to a height of a hundred metres.

We discussed whether to throw out yet more ballast and thus get above the mist and escape the damp and moisture. At first Strindberg thought that we should, but he later accepted my view that if we did we should risk losing altogether too much ballast and gas.

A few minutes later we began to sink again.

A big black bird circled round the car at a considerable distance from it. It reminded us of a raven. "I don't care much for ravens at this moment," I said. "If only it comes a bit nearer I'll give it a dose of shot."

Our double-barrelled gun was hanging on the carrying-ropes of the car. Its right-hand barrel was smooth-bored, and intended for small shot. Our other two weapons, single-barrelled Remington rifles, were kept in our storage space above the carrying-ring.

"There are no ravens north of Hammerfest," said Strindberg.

The wind decreased. We were still moving east, but at a slower pace.

The ice beneath us was still ragged and open, and the big leads, which were linked together, seemed to lie in a more easterly than northerly direction.

The balloon sank lower and lower, slowly.

"The gas is cooling," I said. "It's losing in volume and carrying power, while at the same time moisture and damp are making the calotte, the net, the carrying-ropes, and the car heavier and heavier."

An hour and a half after midnight—Greenwich mean time—we were only twenty metres above the ice, according to a measurement we took with a lead-line, suspended from the instrument-ring above the roof of the car.

We dropped another twelve kilos of sand, and threw out yet another buoy. This last weighed a good two kilos, not counting moisture.

We rose to a height of eighty metres, measured as before with the lead-line that hung over the instrument-ring.

All three guide-ropes were resting on the ice beneath us.

We occasionally moved five or ten metres eastwards, but apart from that we remained stationary.

Nils Strindberg climbed over the instrument ring and pulled down his breeches and long underpants. He held fast to two of the car-ropes, and at the same time leant back against the two belts of webbing put there for the purpose.

"I'll do what I can," he said.

His excrement plopped on to the ice beneath us.

"A metre and sixty centimetres to the good, according to the lead-line," I said. "A rise, that is. Have we a laxative in our medicine chest?"

"What about you?" asked Strindberg, as he pulled up his breeches.

"Alas, I attend to my business in the morning," I answered.

From half-past one on the night between the 11th and 12th July, the balloon remained at a standstill. Now and then we felt faint puffs of wind from the south-south-west, but these were never strong enough to have any effect upon the *Eagle*.

Our clothes grew as damp as if we had been in a Turkish bath. We were cold.

"Ugh!" I said, "lying still like this is revolting."

"Of course," answered Strindberg. *"Navigare necesse est."*

9

At exactly two o'clock in the morning of 12 July—by Strindberg's time—we roused Andrée.

He scrambled up through the trapdoor in the deck of the car, drunk with sleep, red-eyed, and confused.

"Where's my trunk?" he asked.

"There are no trunks here," answered Strindberg.

"And your dressing-gown is still on board His Majesty's gunboat the *Svensksund*," I said.

Andrée leant against the instrument-ring.

"A glass of water?"

"There isn't much water on board this balloon," I said. "Perhaps that was a mistake. There isn't even a glass. All we can offer you is dry sand, or one of our remaining bottles of beer. And all the moisture that's dripping from the net, the rigging and the carrying-ropes."

I opened a bottle. Andrée drank. Strindberg took a small pull, and I a still smaller one. Then I gave what remained to our leader.

Andrée took a few turns round the restricted space of the roof, or deck of the car.

He looked down at the pack ice and the leads beneath us, gazed at the mist and clouds all round us, and tried to locate the sun in the haze above us.

"We're here," said Strindberg, handing him a scrap of paper with an estimation of our position, as exact as circumstances allowed.

"The wind is slight and westerly. We're at a standstill," he added.

Andrée ordered us down into the car, and shut the trapdoor in the roof. We made ourselves as comfortable as we could. Strindberg put covers over the two small windows so that it was almost completely dark. It was pretty chilly. He spread a blanket over us.

"Where did that come from?" I asked. "It wasn't on the list of our equipment."

"The considerate Doctor Lembke threw it in when the car was being mounted in the balloon-house," he answered.

"What do you make of this calm?" I asked. "Are we at the centre of a cyclone, a cyclone that's moving eastwards? What's your opinion? Will there be north-westerly winds on the other side of the centre of the cyclone?"

"Not easy to say," answered Strindberg, with a yawn.

"Even with light south-westerly or westerly winds we ought to be able to sail in over the Arctic Ocean coast of Siberia in less than a week."

The vast tundra in northern Siberia had always fascinated me. The great rivers. I knew their names by heart. Ob, Pur, Taz, Yenisey, Pyasina, and so on. Much like a children's jingle.

The calm might also be succeeded by another strong, southerly wind—or was that impossible?—that would take us to the Pole, and then on to the plains of arctic Canada, or to the rocks of Alaska.

"If we get southerly winds," I said, "we must also lengthen the other two guide-ropes. It will be essential. We need three guide-ropes, and the braking effect of their friction against the ice and the water in order to be able to steer with the sail, and really navigate ourselves over the North Pole.

"With favourable winds and sunshine, instead of clouds and mist, we could then reach the mainland of America, perhaps in a matter of ten days.

"Let's suppose," I said, "that we get these strong, favourable, southerly winds. We shall sail northwards. We shall cross the Pole, and throw down the polar buoy with its Swedish flag. We shall continue our journey in the same direction as before, but in a trice the southerly winds will have become northerly, and our northward course will have become a southward one. The thought makes me dizzy."

Strindberg did not answer.

He was asleep.

There was absolute silence, except for an occasional creak from the car when Andrée moved about on its deck, and except for Strindberg's deep, calm breathing at my side.

I did not like the mist and the clouds and the heavy, dripping moisture. Whenever Andrée had discussed our polar journey he had always talked of sunshine and daylight all round the clock, of a fairly constant temperature, and of the important part these factors would play in prolonging the time the balloon could keep afloat.

I could not remember that he had ever brought up the subject of mist and damp.

I had a lively recollection that these things had been frequently discussed by Andrée's critics, both in Sweden and abroad.

Soon afterwards I heard the sound of the guide-ropes, and maybe of the ballast-ropes too, passing through water and over ice.

The *Eagle* was moving again.

The car rocked slowly.

I emptied my bladder through one of the apertures in the floor of the car, made myself comfortable again, and slept.

10

Just after seven o'clock on the morning of 12 July—by Strindberg's chronometer—we awoke, and climbed up through the hole, or trapdoor in the roof of the car.

"At this moment we're stationary," said Andrée, "but at any rate we've sailed at least one nautical mile."

"At what height?" asked Strindberg.

"Twenty or thirty metres," answered Andrée.

"Direction?" I asked.

"Mostly dead west," he answered.

The mist and cloud had thickened. We could see the blocks of ice beneath us quite clearly, but horizontally the visibility was hardly more than a thousand metres.

The ballast-ropes were resting on the ice and the water, and the balloon had again made a half turn, so that the sail was to leeward.

During the short time that Strindberg and I had been asleep

the balloon had slowly drifted not to the east, but to the west.

Strindberg and I performed our natural functions and the balloon rose to a height of about sixty metres. It was helped too by the warmth from the sun that was increasing in those morning hours, notwithstanding the cloud cover.

We put water and coffee into the cooking apparatus that Engineer Göransson had invented, and sank it eight metres down its rope through one of the holes in the floor. It was now a safe distance from the bottom valve of the balloon. We lit its flame by means of a mechanism that was as simple as it was reliable.

Just over five minutes later the coffee boiled, and we extinguished the flame by blowing down the rubber tube that was fastened to the rope that held the apparatus.

Meanwhile a slight north-easterly wind had seized the balloon and was blowing it westwards at a speed that we ascertained to be rather more than a hundred and fifty metres a minute.

We ate cheese and sardine sandwiches with our coffee.

We spent a fairly long time over our breakfast.

Our speed sometimes increased to three hundred and fifty metres a minute. We felt at a loss for something to do. All the ballast-ropes were dragging across the ice; consequently the sail was still to lee-ward and there could be no question of navigating the balloon horizontally.

Now and then the sun peeped through the cloud and mist which was obviously less dense than it had been.

With the aid of Gleerup's admirable theodolite Strindberg and I succeeded in taking some rapid readings of our bearings.

"We're clearly following the same route as we were during the hours before midnight," said Andrée, "but in the opposite direction. We're going west, or south-west."

There was an insignificant rise in temperature, but the rays of sunshine that penetrated the mist were noticeably warming.

The coffee was good and hot, and we let the balloon drift where it would. There was certainly not much room for three people to sit on the deck of the car. Our six legs got muddled up, especially when the sun became visible through the clouds, and Strindberg and I jumped up to take our bearings.

"The balloon has been wrongly designed," I said, "or, to be more precise, the way in which the guide-ropes and the ballast-ropes are arranged is wrong. The guide-ropes have been placed far too near the centre of the balloon, not far enough behind the sail. And the ballast-ropes have been fastened to the carrying-ring right under the sail, instead of to the stern part of the ring.

"For," I said, "in spite of its circular shape, the balloon has a stem and a stern.

"The result of this is obvious. Whenever the ballast-ropes drag across ice or water the balloon turns through ninety degrees, and the sail, the steering sail, ceases to function."

"You're right," answered Andrée, "though you mean one hundred and eighty degrees.

"We're pioneers," he said. "This is the first time in history that a long voyage has been made in a dirigible balloon. Our experience will be of the greatest importance when it comes to designing certain details of balloon number two."

"What do you judge our situation to be at the moment?" asked Strindberg.

Andrée smiled, as far as it is possible for a man to smile with half a cheese sandwich in his mouth.

"It would be absurd to judge," he said, "we're in an exceptional situation. It's not our judgments, but our observations that are important.

"We're on our way," he said, "I always feel calm when I'm on a journey, on my way to something."

He rubbed his chin. "I hadn't time to shave yesterday morning," he said, "and my bristles are tickling."

He smiled calmly as he looked at us.

His thin hair had turned grey, so had the vigorous moustache on his upper lip.

His presence, his friendly, untroubled smile created an atmosphere of calm and security.

"Strong coffee and good sandwiches," he said. "And moreover, we three are the first people who have ever floated over the Arctic Ocean in a balloon. Either we're madmen, or we're men whom many will seek to follow."

We glided over a stretch of consolidated pack ice that was at least a thousand metres wide. The ropes drew lines across its covering of snow and the many small puddles of melt water that lay upon its surface.

Our passage across it occupied a good four and a half minutes.

We were still surrounded by mist, but the visibility had improved and was now at least two thousand metres.

Soon after this we reached a small floe on which there was an almost circular bright red patch. This set us arguing enthusiastically. We finally agreed that it must have been the scene of a violent struggle between a polar bear and a walrus, or a large seal.

A few minutes before midday on 12 July we released a number of carrier-pigeons with brief despatches.

They circled round the balloon for several minutes. Two of them alighted on the ice, and one perched on the long guide-rope, but obviously did not enjoy the way it vibrated.

For the moment the *Eagle* was travelling at a speed of about five hundred metres per minute.

I I

At three o'clock on 12 July the car twice bumped on the ice.

Our course at the time was slightly more northerly than it had been during the preceding hours.

We calculated that our speed was two hundred metres a minute.

In order to gain height we threw overboard the much-discussed device—invented by Törner—for cutting our guide-ropes, a small anchor, a number of thin ropes, and twenty-five kilos of sand.

The sand spread out everywhere, and seemed better able to float than the balloon. It drifted in over the car and stuck to lips and eyes, with painful consequences for the three aeronauts

An hour later we cut off one of the ballast-ropes; weight about fifty kilos, not counting moisture.

The *Eagle* then travelled at a speed of about one hundred and fifty metres a minute, mostly in a westerly direction, but with a slight inclination to the north.

In spite of the ballast we had thrown out the car had time after time bounced on the ice.

Everything, the envelope of the balloon, the net, the calotte, the carrying-ropes, the car, and the guide-ropes, was dripping with moisture that must have weighed at least a ton.

Our average height above the pack ice, that became increasingly consolidated, was at the most fifty metres.

Andrée climbed up to the storage-space above the carrying-ring and returned with the big, cork, polar buoy, the buoy that was intended to mark the Pole when we passed over it.

"Shall we throw it away?" he asked.

"We still have sand in our sacks," I said.

"Even if our supply of it is dangerously reduced.

"Is it necessary?" I asked.

Strindberg said: "For God's sake let it go."

12

Soon after that the *Eagle* came to a standstill. One of the ballast-ropes had got caught under a towering hummock of pack ice.

The balloon swung to and fro slowly, but the rope did not work loose. We were involuntarily at anchor.

We measured the force of the wind and found it to be between four and five metres a second; its direction being mainly dead west.

"The force of the wind, say at a height of two hundred metres, is probably at least ten metres per second," said Andrée.

"That equals about thirty-five kilometres an hour."

"Say what you really mean," I said.

"If we threw away another hundred kilos of ballast," answered Andrée, "we could free ourselves. We could do it by cutting away the ballast-rope that has caught in the ice, and several more as well."

"And then?"

"We should be able to land in Greenland towards morning," he said.

"Have you any views about Greenland?" I asked Nils Strindberg.

"I've never been there," he answered. "I've never wanted to set foot in Greenland."

"You've thrown away the polar buoy," I said. "All right, it was heavy. Perhaps it was also unnecessary. We could just as well fasten the Swedish flag to a boat-hook and throw that down on to the Pole.

"All the same it was an act of resignation. You've lost hope of ever reaching the Pole, Andrée. Already.

"Now you're saying," I said, "that if only we cut away a few ballast-ropes we should be able to land in Greenland early to-morrow morning."

Greenland!

Had Andrée's polar expedition really been degraded to a balloon trip between Spitzbergen and Greenland.

You travel to Greenland by steamer, not by balloon.

"Do you really mean you want us to give up?" I asked.

During the past nine or ten hours our voyage had been especially trying and exhausting because of the way in which the car had constantly bounced on the ice. Then there had been the mist, the dripping moisture, the cold, and the discouragement of travelling in the wrong direction, not towards the north, but towards the west. Now we were at a standstill, involuntarily at anchor.

"The *Eagle*'s carrying capacity is low just now," I said. "This isn't primarily due to our loss of gas. It's a result of the meteorological conditions, of the clouds, the mist, the damp, and the constant drizzle.

"Suppose," I said, "that the clouds and the mist disperse, that we get clear skies and radiant sunshine. In the course of an hour or two a ton of water will evaporate from the calotte, the envelope, the carrying-ropes and the car."

"And then?" asked Andrée.

"The *Eagle* will again be a free-sailing balloon, or a balloon that we can steer, to some extent at least."

"Where to, in which direction?" asked Andrée.

"That will of course depend on the wind," I answered. "To the North Pole, to Siberia, to Canada or Alaska."

For our main meal that day I brought out a cooked fowl. We shared it between us as fairly as possible.

"For present purposes," said Strindberg, "this hen should really have had three legs, three wings, and three breasts."

We shared a bottle of beer and a bottle of mineral water.

The car was about forty metres above the ice, swinging to and fro slowly, but not disagreeably.

We did not throw the remains of our meal or the two empty bottles overboard, but put them into a paper bag. They were no longer refuse but valuable ballast.

The hen had been prepared in the galley of the *Svensksund* on the morning before our departure by Lieutenant Celsing himself.

Visibility was poor. It varied between five hundred metres and perhaps one and a half kilometres.

For a while we discussed which of us had slept least since we started from Danes Island. We could not agree about it.

The balloon and the carrying-ring were dripping.

If you put your hand round one of the six ropes by which the car was suspended and ran it rapidly upwards, water spurted from between your thumb and your forefinger.

"It's a pity we haven't got a calliper among our scientific instruments," I said.

"A calliper?" asked Strindberg.

"I should like to measure the thickness of the ropes," I said.

"They must have swelled from their original ten millimetres to at least thirteen or fourteen, in spite of being impregnated.

"Well?" I asked. "We've already been anchored here for hours."

Andrée answered: "We'll stay where we are for the present."

He then told us to creep into the car, and have a few hours' sleep and rest. It was twelve o'clock of the night before 13 July.

"How long?" I asked.

"Six hours or so," he answered. "As long as I can manage to stay awake, or as long as nothing special happens."

I first took a sounding of our distance from the ice. The wind was making the *Eagle* rise and fall gently, so it varied between forty-five and fifty metres.

Strindberg had got our bunk ready. He was sitting hunched up with Doctor Lembke's blanket round him, holding an open bottle of mineral water in his hand.

"This confounded thirst," he said.

He held out the bottle and I took a few pulls, after first spitting out a quid of snuff through one of the holes in the floor.

"It's not more than forty-five hours since we left Danes Island," I said, after I had looked at my watch in the light from one of the two small windows.

"Thirty-three hours," said Strindberg. "Your reckoning is out by twelve hours."

He was right. In this arctic summer of perpetual daylight it was ridiculously difficult to be always sure when it was twelve o'clock midday, and when it was twelve o'clock midnight.

"Thirty-three hours! So much the worse."

"Keep your voice down," said Strindberg.

Fair enough. But the woodwork of the car was creaking and groaning, the sail was flapping, the guide-ropes were brushing against the snow and ice, and the wind was blowing at a rate of at least four or five metres a second. "He can't hear what we're saying," I said.

"And all that feeble rubbish about our being able to get free," I said, "and drift to Greenland, and land there sometime early tomorrow morning."

"He simply mentioned it as a theoretical possibility," said Strindberg.

I took another pull at the bottle and then stretched out on the bunk.

"No," I said. "He mentioned it in the hope that we two would propose a fresh start, a second one, in the direction of Greenland.

"He was trying to delegate, to free himself of responsibility. He's afraid. Or uneasy. He hadn't reckoned with mist and humidity. He wanted us to make a stand. A stand which he would later be able to communicate to reporters from all over the world: 'In view of the unfavourable conditions we encountered my two companions insisted that we should abandon our original plans, and try to reach dry land on the north coast of Greenland.'"

"You're probably both right and wrong," said Strindberg.

"Am I?"

"If only we get some sunshine the carrying capacity of the balloon will increase enormously."

"Have you noticed the strange expression in Andrée's eyes?" I asked. "The way in which he screws up his eyelids, and the way in which his eyeballs vibrate laterally now and then?"

I don't know whether Strindberg answered.

"All the same being near him gives me a sense of security," I said.

The car was rocking like a cradle, but the movement was soothing, not disturbing.

13

I was roused by Strindberg at half-past ten on Tuesday 13 July.

He was throwing small balls of hoar-frost in my face from the hole in the roof of the car.

"Slept well?" asked Andrée.

"Some people find it easy to sleep," said Strindberg. "I've been awake for more than four hours."

I climbed up on the deck of the car.

"Good morning," said Andrée.

His lips were dry and cracked. His chin and his cheeks were

covered with grey stubble, and there were heavy folds under his eyes.

"The wind's changed," he said. "At half-past two it was blowing from the north at nearly three metres a second. It increased to four or five metres a second. Now it's blowing from the west.

"It was blowing mainly from the north until Strindberg climbed out of the car. From the north, but not strongly enough to loosen that confounded ballast-rope, firmly clenched as it is in the pack ice.

"If we'd got free," he said, "if we'd risen two or three hundred metres, and by doing so got into a belt of considerably stronger northerly winds, we should have been back over Spitzbergen by this time."

Then he added:

"Otherwise the night has been uneventful, no birds, no seals, no polar bears, no walruses.

"Mist, whiteness, silence, complete solitude."

Now and then the sun peeped through the clouds and Strindberg and I hastily took our bearings by using Gleerup's azimuth compass. Our measurements, taken independently, and immediately after each other, produced the same result. We were in latitude 82°2′ N., and 15°5′ east of the Greenwich meridian.

The wind veered more and more to the west. It was gusty, and not to be trusted.

Just before twelve o'clock noon on 13 July a series of violent blasts of wind struck the balloon so fiercely that the car was thrown on to the ice.

Andrée and I lost our footing and fell over on the deck. It is possible that we should both have been flung overboard had we not seized hold of one another, almost convulsively, and each managed to get a grip on one of the six car-ropes.

Strindberg was in a position of relative quiet, as he had climbed up above the carrying-ring a few minutes earlier.

The balloon then rose to a height of rather more than fifty metres and began to drift eastwards at a speed of about three metres per second. The ballast-ropes rustled over the snow, and for a couple of hours they functioned perfectly. That is, they kept the car at a fairly constant level above the ice.

As these ballast-ropes, now as before, offered more resistance to the ice than the guide-ropes, the *Eagle* floated 'backwards', with the sails to leeward. The wind was slight, so we did not take them in.

We prepared a nice dinner.

Göransson's cooking apparatus, well loaded with the contents of a large tin of hotchpotch soup, was lowered eight metres under the car. While we were having our soup the apparatus, filled this time with best quality fillet of beef, was lowered again and relighted.

We allowed ourselves plenty to drink with the meal; a bottle of beer per person. It is well known that a balloonist's thirst is not easily quenched. The cooking apparatus was sent down a third time, filled this time with water, cocoa-powder and sugar.

Now and then the sun broke through the clouds for a few minutes. With our cocoa, two large mugs each, we ate biscuits.

Strong raspberry juice was served as an extra dessert. We drank it slowly, and finished off the last of the packet of biscuits as we did so.

"How to heat food was one of my greatest problems," said Andrée. "One can manage very well for a few days with James Dewar's so-called 'thermos' flasks.

"But our journey was to last longer.

"It would be foolish to have an open flame in the car. The distance to the bottom valve of the balloon and the dangerous, explosive gas is far too small.

"Cooking by electricity proved to be impossible. The lead accumulators were far too heavy," he said.

"I tested various chemical methods of generating heat, tested them for months. I managed to obtain a heat of more than eighty-two degrees with caustic lime and water, but alas, that method was unsuitable for many reasons.

"My old friend Engineer Göransson, Ernst Göransson, solved the problem. His solution is before us on the deck of the car.

"A cooking apparatus that is heated by a spirit-lamp, but which can be lowered eight metres below the car, and which, at this distance, can be lit by a mechanism which is nothing less than an invention of genius. A spirit-lamp which can be rapidly extinguished by blowing down a rubber tube."

"He could have made the apparatus even more perfect," I said. "How?"

"He could have supplied it with a tobacco pipe," I said, "lit by the same ingenious mechanism, and enjoyed through another rubber tube."

Our appetites were appeased, our spirits noticeably good. The visibility was still miserable. We reckoned that our average speed was still three metres per second, or rather more than ten kilometres an hour.

Our course was easterly, but rather more northerly than before.

The pack ice beneath us was more consolidated, more welded together, smoother than it had been the previous day.

Strindberg discovered the tracks of a polar bear going northwards. His pads on the snow were very clear.

"Let's drink a toast in raspberry juice to our four-footed brother," I said.

There we were, the three of us, squashed together on the cramped deck of a balloon car, a good bit further north than any aerial vessel had ever been before, and we were drinking a toast to the tracks of a polar bear in raspberry juice!

"Raspberry juice," I said, "out of all the noble beverages there are in the world!

"John Franklin led a considerably less spartan life on board his two vessels, the *Terror* and the *Erebus*. Crystal glasses, spoons and forks of solid silver. A library of two thousand four hundred volumes. Two mechanical organs—one on each ship—on which you could wind out at least fifty different pieces of music.

"They'd probably have toasted the first polar bear tracks they saw in something other than raspberry juice," I said. "And not in mugs, but in crystal glasses."

"But everything went diabolically wrong for Franklin and his two vessels," said Strindberg.

After our dinner we attached brief despatches to four carrier-pigeons and let them loose.

They flew round the balloon a few times, and then settled on the instrument ring of the car, one and all with their heads facing inwards, towards us.

"Be off with you," said Strindberg kindly. "Fly home to Åland! Or at least fly south!"

"They look as if they wanted something to eat," I said. "Corn, peas, or raspberry juice."

We tried to frighten them.

They rose, flapping their wings, flew round the *Eagle* a few times more, and then settled on the long guide-rope. It was obvious that they did not care for the way it vibrated and shook, for they climbed slowly higher and higher, with the stable instrument-ring as their goal.

It was half an hour before they flew off, in a southerly direction as far as we could judge.

14

At two o'clock on the afternoon of 13 July, after the pigeons had gone, Andrée crept into the car for a period of rest and sleep.

Soon afterwards the mist grew thicker, the showers of light rain more frequent.

The temperature sank to something under zero, and the drizzle froze to ice when it met the car, the ropes, the net, and the calotte.

The mist, or cloud, grew denser, and this further reduced the carrying capacity of the balloon.

After a brief consultation Strindberg and I decided to throw out another buoy, a reserve medicine chest—a pretty heavy one—and two kilos of sand.

The *Eagle* was still travelling in an easterly direction at an average speed of three metres per second.

Lateral visibility was reduced to a thousand metres at best.

Strindberg again climbed up into the rigging over the carrying-ring.

"This is the quietest place," he said.

"The whole thing is meaningless," I said. "First we lost the guide-ropes—the two lower thirds of them. Then came our free-sailing voyage to the north, which turned into a voyage to the east. After that a long voyage to the west. Then we remained stationary for thirteen hours. Now we're sailing towards the east again. Not to the north, but back towards the east.

"I don't know what Andrée's thinking of."

"I'm surprised by his lack of determination," I said.

15

Less than half an hour after Andrée had crept into the car we sank so much that it bounced on the ice, first once, and then a few minutes later once again.

I threw out a quantity of sand, and the car rose to a height of forty metres. My one thought was to try if possible to give Andrée the rest he needed.

At half-past five on the afternoon of 13 July the wind suddenly veered somewhat to the south, and our course became east-north-easterly.

Half an hour earlier one of the carrier-pigeons had returned to us. It had circled round the balloon a few times, and then settled on the long guide-rope, rather more than two metres under the car.

It put its head under its wing, sat like that for a short time, and then fell down, and disappeared into the snow and the ice beneath us.

16

Andrée reappeared on deck just before six o'clock on the evening
of 13 July. His eyes were small and swollen, his cheeks sunken. He
had dark circles and pouches under his eyes, and a mask of grey
stubble on his chin and his cheeks.

"Good morning," I said, handing him a half-empty bottle of beer.

"Direction?" he asked.

"East-north-east."

"Speed?"

"Rather more than ten kilometres an hour," I answered.

"Temp?"

"Rather lower than it ought to be, than it ought to have been. Our
speed too is less than it ought to have been."

Andrée emptied the bottle of beer and I managed to catch it
before he threw it overboard. Ballast was as precious as gold.

He studied the balloon, and the degree of 'hollowness' of the
envelope.

"Considering the circumstances," he said, "the loss of gas is small.
Four hundred and eighty cubic metres at the most."

He turned right round and gazed out into the fog and the whiteness, where there was nothing to see.

"No birds," he said. "We must be far from land."

I told him about the carrier pigeon that had returned to us and
then fallen down dead on the ice.

Strindberg climbed down from his perch over the carrying-ring.
In doing so he bumped into one of the remaining buoys, which fell
so unluckily that its metal-shod point hit Andrée on the head.

He sank in a heap, lay still for a few seconds, and then got up.
For a short time he lost control of himself.

"It was a pure accident," said Strindberg. "All the same I'm very
sorry."

Andrée soon calmed down. He was silent for several minutes.
Then he said: "It's I who should apologize," and added: "This
damnable fog! This damnable wetness that makes everything drip."

Between six and eight o'clock that evening the wind veered slightly and our course became more northerly.

The car bumped on the ice and snow a couple of times, but after that we glided into a rift in the mist, or rather, a rift caught us up, as we were moving more slowly than the wind. The sun peeped through for a few minutes, and the *Eagle* rose to a height of thirty or forty metres. Strindberg seized the opportunity and crept down into the car for a short rest.

Soon afterwards we were once more enveloped in mist and drizzle and again the car bumped on the ice. It bounced in long leaps, at intervals of at least fifty metres.

Strindberg became sea-sick and struggled up on deck. He bent over the instrument-ring and vomited violently.

He then climbed up to the carrying-ring. I wanted to help him, but he seemed to be feeling like death, and asked to be left alone.

It was decidedly quieter up in the carrying-ring, and he soon recovered.

The car went on bouncing, but the intervals between its leaps grew shorter and shorter.

"Are we going to let this go on until the car is smashed to bits and all it contains is scattered over the pack ice?" I asked.

"The balloon is holding the gas well," answered Andrée. "It's this infernal moisture, and this infernal layer of ice."

"It's very likely that the damp and the ice are making the seams of the balloon tighter," I said. "But that doesn't help the car."

"You're right," said Andrée. "We must throw out more ballast, and get some peace and quiet in which to discuss the situation."

At exactly eight o'clock that evening we threw out the remaining buoys, six of them, weighing altogether a good twelve kilos. After them went the windlass, sixteen kilos. Then various objects we had saved as ballast, such as empty bottles and the like, amounting perhaps to three kilos.

The only noticeable result was that the car took longer leaps, but as these were also higher, the bumps on the pack ice were more violent.

Andrée and I parried these bumps by gripping hold of the car-ropes, and pulling ourselves up by them. These ropes were now not only wet, they were also caked with soggy ice, and slipped through our hands like eels.

A barrel, five kilos, went overboard, and we heard the crash quite clearly when it hit the ice. We cut loose four sacks of sand, one almost empty and three untouched, about seventy-five kilos.

After that the car stopped bumping, and we settled at a height of forty metres above sea-level, above ice-level.

We again swung further towards the north, so that our course was now dead east-north-east. Our speed remained about three metres per second, or a good ten kilometres an hour. The pack ice beneath us was consolidated and looked smooth and easy to cross.

17

One thing was absolutely clear: we must come to a decision.

"My first question is this," I said. "Do you think we have any chance of getting to the North Pole?"

Andrée smiled his usual calm, friendly, narrow-eyed smile.

"Or," I said, "at least get further north than that confounded Nansen's 86° 13½′ N. lat.?"

"Before our departure," said Andrée, "I worried about the tightness of the balloon. Later on I worried about the loss of the greater part of the guide-ropes. But my—our—troubles now are meteorological. Fog, mist, drizzle, clouds, and temperature. The *Eagle* is carrying a load of upwards of a ton of moisture and ice."

"We know that," I said.

"If we get out into sunshine and clear weather the situation will change radically," he said.

Of course it would change radically, our carrying capacity would greatly increase.

"But," I said, "we're clearly in a very extensive and wide-spread bank of cloud. We're drifting in it at approximately the same speed as the clouds. We're moving in the direction of the eastern part of Siberia. Our speed is low. A limitless sea lies ahead of us. More and more ice is forming. The balloon is being increasingly weighed down all the time.

"It's a question of elementary logic," I said. "Either we go on, and come down on the ice in a few hours' time. Or we throw out still more ballast, so that we can rise high enough to get the ballast-ropes off the ice, and give our guide-ropes the chance to help us to steer a course out of the bank of cloud, either in a northerly, or a southerly direction. We must make up our minds."

"I'm devilishly in need of a smoke," I said to Strindberg, who had been listening to the conversation through the hole in the canvas floor of the carrying-ring. He gave me his snuff-box.

"You're over-simplifying," said Andrée.

"How?"

"The very moment that we get out into sunshine," he answered, "and the ice melts, and the moisture evaporates, we shall feel the lack of every gramme of the ballast you think you ought to throw out."

'Ballooning isn't merely a method of travelling,' Lachambre had said when we were in Paris. 'Aeronautics is also something of a fine art.'

Aeronautics is also an esoteric form of mathematics.

Andrée lowered the lead-line over the side of the instrument-ring. The lead bounced and swung when it touched 'bottom'. Ten minutes later it was obvious that it was trailing through the snow, that the *Eagle* had in fact sunk.

On Andrée's orders I climbed up into the carrying-ring, into our storage space.

It is necessary to elaborate a little here.

The ballast our balloon carried in the form of sand was small compared with what was normally carried by a balloon of its size. Instead, Andrée had devoted more space than was usual to our stock of provisions. This was so packed that parts of it could be heaved overboard to increase the *Eagle*'s carrying capacity.

You may think that provisions are an expensive form of ballast compared with sand, but the major part of our food supplies had been given to us by a number of firms, in such quantity that we had left the bulk of it behind at Pike's House on Danes Island.

The numbered sacks of food were now thrown overboard as Andrée directed. First a hundred kilos, then fifty.

The *Eagle* rose.

The ballast-ropes, which were seventy metres long, left the ice. The three guide-ropes, two being about a hundred metres long, and the third the same plus the length of a ballast-rope, forced the *Eagle* to turn, so that the steering-sail came round to its proper place to windward. The sail filled and our speed increased noticeably. We threw another fifty kilos of food overboard.

I climbed down to Andrée.

He pointed to the full sails. "This is how I meant everything to function," he said.

"We're still drifting with the wind," I said. "Towards the main-land of eastern Siberia, which we shall never reach."

"We've risen to a height of ninety metres," he answered.

"Strindberg is happier up in the carrying-ring," I said. "I'm hungry, but I'm more tired than hungry. I shall creep down into the car and try to sleep for a few hours."

It was then eight o'clock in the evening by my chronometer, five minutes to nine by Strindberg's. We agreed however on the date: Tuesday, 13 July, 1897.

I wrapped Doctor Lembke's blanket round me. I was dead tired, but I did not find it easy to sleep.

'This is how I meant everything to function,' Andrée had said, and pointed to the steering sails.

But the sails were set athwart the direction of the wind. They were increasing the speed of the balloon, but this was simultaneously being reduced by the guide-ropes. They were not being used to *steer* the balloon.

The idea that Andrée should simply be letting the *Eagle* drift with the wind, that he was not trying to put his theories about the dirigibility of a balloon into practice, was absurd.

I heard him giving an order to Strindberg, but I could not catch what he said. His words were lost in the creaking and squeaking of the car.

From our movement, and the way we were shaking, I realized that the guide-ropes were being fixed in another position, one that would bring the sail round to another angle in relation to the wind, an angle at which the sail would steer the *Eagle*, either more towards the north, or more towards the south.

Towards the north, or towards the south.

I sat up. I debated whether I should climb up to the deck of the car, but I was altogether too weary.

My legs and my arms were as heavy as lead.

I tried to count up how many hours I had slept since we left Danes Island. I could not do it.

I found a bottle of beer in one of the many pockets in the car. I opened it and drank, but I could not quench the balloonist's eternal thirst.

I removed one of the two shutters in the floor and gazed at the ice beneath us. Our speed seemed to be about four metres per second. With the aid of my pocket compass I came to the conclusion that we were travelling in a direction which was at least ten degrees more northerly than when I left the deck.

So Andrée had decided to steer north, not south, in so far as the slight wind allowed him to steer at all.

I lay down on the bunk.

I felt a jerk and immediately after it the sound of yet more ballast being thrown out, fifty kilos of it at least.

Then I probably fell asleep for a couple of hours.

Of course a miracle might happen. Sunshine, a cloudless sky, a journey at a high altitude, the *Eagle* driven by a strong wind, at a speed of twenty or thirty knots, either towards the south-east, or towards the north, over the pole to Alaska.

But I had never believed in miracles.

I was convinced that we should land on the ice.

It would have been better for us if Andrée had tried to sail towards the south-east, towards Franz Josef Land.

All the same I thought I understood him.

In the course of a few hours, if the wind increased and the cloud-cover thinned, we should get further north than Nansen.

18

At one o'clock on the morning of Wednesday, 14 July, after the car had bounced on the ice several times, I climbed up on deck.

"Good morning," said Andrée.

"I'm sorry if our rough passage has disturbed your sleep."

"Course?" I asked.

"N. 60° E."

"Speed?"

"One point two kilometres an hour."

"Temp?"

"See for yourself, or ask Strindberg," answered Andrée.

"Height above sea-level?"

"Forty metres at the moment," he answered.

Thanks to the friction on the ice of our much-discussed ballast-ropes the *Eagle* had once again made a half turn, and the sail was now to leeward.

"Two hours ago," said Andrée, "we saw a polar bear. He rushed backwards and forwards trying to get out of the way of the guide-ropes."

The ice beneath us consisted of large, smooth floes, separated by leads that did not look so very wide.

There was no visibility to speak of, and the fog was dense.

"The layer of ice on the balloon and the ropes has increased," said Andrée.

A solitary bird circled round the balloon. It came closer and closer, and we discovered that it was a pigeon. It must have been another of the four pigeons we had sent off nearly twelve hours earlier.

It finally settled on the carrying-ring. Strindberg tried to catch it, but it flew off, flapping its wings half-wittedly, and went on circling round the balloon and the car.

"What are you hoping for?" I asked.

Andrée shrugged his shoulders.

"What are you hoping for yourself?" he answered.

"That we shall be allowed to begin our journey across the ice as near to Franz Josef Land, or to Spitzbergen as possible," I answered.

"You're afraid?" said Andrée.

I thought for a minute.

"No," I said. "I don't think I'm afraid. But I've come to recognize the hopelessness of what we're trying to do."

"The devil you have," answered Andrée, and ordered us to throw out enough ballast to make the *Eagle* rise high enough to give the guide-ropes the chance to bring the sail round to the right position again.

We moved the guide-ropes so that they brought the balloon about as much to the south as possible.

Between one thirty and three o'clock that morning we sailed dead east.

At three o'clock the wind became more southerly, and our course north-easterly.

The balloon sank, weighed down by moisture and ice. The car again bounced on the ice like a ball.

Strindberg's sea-sickness returned and he vomited, coughing violently all the time.

Soon after five o'clock the clouds parted, the sky became blue, and the sunshine from the east hit us like a ray of intense heat.

The *Eagle* rose slowly.

Andrée looked at me questioningly.

"It's for you to decide," I answered.

Andrée hesitated for quite a while. He cautiously opened the valves and closed them again after we had sunk so low that the ballast-ropes reached the ice. He then lowered the anchor and our voyage came to a halt. This was at half-past six on the morning of 14 July.

The *Eagle* swayed slowly backwards and forwards in the slight wind.

"The loss of gas is small," he said. "Only the very lowest part of the balloon is slack."

"Soon," I said, "in a quarter of an hour or so, the balloon will be quite full because of the heat from the sun.

"It's you who must decide," I said. "Shall we continue our journey? Or shall we not?"

I added: "Whichever you decide you can depend on my absolute loyalty."

Andrée scanned the invisible horizon through his binoculars.

I repeated: "You can depend on my absolute loyalty."

"That goes without saying," he answered. "Otherwise you wouldn't be here."

The melting ice was dripping from the balloon, the calotte, and the net.

The ice on the carrying-ropes began to loosen, likewise the coating of ice on the canvas of the car, on the guide-ropes and the ballast-ropes.

"Many kilos of ballast," I said.

Andrée and Strindberg each took our bearings with a fair amount of precision, Andrée in the car, Strindberg sitting on the canvas floor of the carrying-ring.

Their results were the same.

We were in latitude 82°56′ N., and 20° east of the Greenwich meridian.

Now that its lifting capacity had increased the balloon tugged and pulled still more violently at the ropes and the anchor-tow, so that we moved a hundred metres. Then the anchor buried itself in the snow and got a firmer hold on the ice.

The wind had shifted and was now another few degrees more northerly.

Andrée sat down on one of the baskets on the deck of the car. The water dripping down from the melting ice had made his jacket wet, and he slapped his cap against one of his knees.

Strindberg had climbed down from his perch above the carrying-ring. A faint odour of vomit hung about him.

"You must make up your mind," I said. "Cast off and continue, or land."

"I'm not the only man on board the *Eagle*," said Andrée.

He turned to Strindberg: "What about you?"

"The wind is chiefly from the north-east," he said, with a hesitant smile. "We haven't much chance of getting anywhere near the North Pole.

"That is if the wind doesn't suddenly get stronger and more southerly," he added. "I don't think that's likely. It might also veer suddenly, and become a strong south or south-westerly wind that would carry us in over Russia or Siberia in a few hours' time. That doesn't seem likely either."

"Differentiating between the name of a wind and its direction is always tricky," I said. "People sometimes talk of a southerly wind and mean a wind that is blowing towards the south. But southerly winds blow towards the north."

Strindberg said: "If we go on we shall drift across the vast Arctic Ocean in the direction of the New Siberian Islands. The wind is slight, we shall move slowly. And we've already thrown out great quantities of ballast. We're unlikely to be lucky enough to reach the Siberian coast or the islands to the north of it."

"Do you think we ought to land?" asked Andrée. His lips were swollen and cracked, and he was speaking from a dry mouth.

I fished out a bottle of the best 'Crown Ale' from inside the car, and gave it to him after I had drawn the cork.

Andrée repeated his question.

Strindberg smiled again. His forehead was furrowed, his eyebrows sunken, the stubble on his cheeks and chin was dark and uneven, almost blotchy. He kept moistening his lips with his tongue. His eyes were red and swollen, and little yellow lumps were sticking to his eyelashes. I noticed that he found it hard to keep his hands still.

"It's difficult to weigh up the various possibilities," he said at last. "I don't know. But if we're to carry on it must be at a height great enough to allow us to rest and sleep."

"And you?" asked Andrée.

"You already know my views," I said.

"You believed that the *Eagle* would be able to sail for at least thirty days at a height of between a hundred and fifty and two hundred metres above the ice," I said. "Our French friend, Machuron, believed that we should be able to keep afloat for almost another month if we established ourselves above the carrying-ring, and cut off the car and some of the ballast ropes.

"But," I said, "only forty-eight hours after we started, we had lost so much lift that the car bumped on the ice."

"The fog, the damp, the icing," said Strindberg. "And the loss of the guide-ropes."

"Everyone warned me that the balloon wasn't tight enough," I said. "No one mentioned rain and icing. No one, that is, except a few foreign authorities."

"Go on," said Andrée.

"I think we must accept the fact that the balloon voyage as such is a technical failure," I said. "If we continue our journey we shall probably simply be carried further from any islands or mainland. We ought therefore to land. Our journey across the ice will be considerably shorter than Nansen's and Johansen's."

Andrée buried his head in his hands.

"Do you need time for thought?" I inquired.

How many hours' sleep had we had since we left Danes Island?

"Our weariness is the decisive factor," said Andrée at last.

He got up and cautiously opened the valves. The escaping gas hissed. The *Eagle* sank, slowly.

He ordered us to check the speed of our fall with the help of what little sand we had left, and thus make our landing as soft as possible.

A carrier-pigeon was still circling round the balloon and the car. We all three saw it suddenly fold its wings, drop like a stone, and disappear into the snow.

19

The balloon touched down just before eight o'clock.

We remained on its deck. If we had jumped down to the ice the *Eagle* would have risen aloft again for a few minutes.

The car was pulled over and dragged through the snow for a few metres like a plough, while we clung to the instrument-ring and the car ropes.

The valves were small and it was ten minutes past eight before the *Eagle* came to rest like a vast dome on the polar ice.

We left the car and stepped out on to the ice. It was covered by a layer of heavy, wet snow, less than five centimetres deep.

"I feel almost giddy," said Strindberg, "and as if the ice was billowing like the sea."

He obviously did not go on feeling giddy for long. He managed to extricate one of his cameras from the muddle in the car, mounted it on a tripod and walked a few steps to the south, in order to get some overall pictures of our landing.

"First a bit of leg-stretching," I said, "and then for the other great moment.

"I've had a pipe and tobacco in a pocket in the car ever since we set off. Tiedemann's, bought in Tromsö; several cartons of it, and two large red tins." I stopped my pipe, lit it, and took several deep puffs.

"I'm feeling almost giddy myself," I said.

"It was a beautiful landing," said Andrée, "soft, not bumpy. We couldn't have avoided the car being dragged along."

He added: "Nothing has been damaged or destroyed."

He walked slowly round the balloon.

"He's resting with one valve against the snow," he said. "That's why he's emptying so slowly."

'He'—the *Eagle*.

Our first task was to pitch the tent; no need to consult Andrée about that.

I methodically tramped down a firm 'floor' of the required size close beside the car.

Our equipment in the space above the carrying-ring was difficult to get at, to say the least of it. It had been packed into a balloon that was floating upright. Now it had to be unloaded from a balloon that was lying on its side, entangled in a jumble of carrying-ropes and its own net.

I got the tent up with Strindberg's help. We were so tired that we continually slipped and fell. We laughed at one another with a sort of long-drawn-out, vehement, inconsequent laughter, that made the pits of our stomachs ache, and helped to drain the last ounce of strength from our muscles.

We unloaded a number of bags of provisions and carried them to the tent.

Ten metres north of the balloon I found a puddle of sweet water where the snow had melted, and we could drink away our thirst until we shivered with cold.

I found the big, three-man sleeping-bag and dragged it to the tent.

Strindberg set to work on the paraffin stove, the primus, and got it to light immediately.

The clouds had joined up again and it was drizzling hard. This had made the temperature fall. The thin layer of snow had become hard-packed and was easier to walk on.

"Dead tired," said Strindberg. "Absolutely dead tired. I'm staggering about as if I were drunk."

Soon afterwards the sun again peeped through the clouds for a short time.

"Pull yourself together," I said.

"Be damned to you," he answered.

We took our bearings independently.

They confirmed the one taken earlier. We were in latitude 82°56′ N., longitude 20°52′ E.

Strindberg opened two tins of meat, chosen at random, emptied them into the saucepan, and added half a litre of water.

"Meat and water make soup," he said, "and soup's always easy to eat. Even if one's dead tired."

We called to Andrée.

He had taken no part in the work. He had been slowly wandering round and round the balloon.

We called and he came, reluctantly. He helped himself to the hot soup.

"Our voyage through the air is over," I said. "We are now at a turning point."

He answered: "The whole of the envelope, the calotte, the net and the carrying-ropes are all of them coated with a thick layer of ice. At least a ton of ice."

"This is the first time," I said, "that I've had to eat soup with a knife and fork as well as a spoon."

After the meal Strindberg and I went up to the car. We undid the ropes and succeeded by our joint efforts in getting it on to an even keel, though not without a struggle.

Andrée fastened the Union flag to a pole two and a half metres long, the lower part of which he fixed firmly to the wall of the car.

"You two can sleep in the car," he said. "There's not room for three. I'll sleep in the sleeping-bag in the tent."

We had neither the energy nor the wish to discuss the matter.

"I'm dead tired," said Strindberg, "and it's good to be dead tired when you know you can happily curl up and sleep when you want to. You try to put off falling asleep in order to get the last ounce of pleasure out of it."

He knelt down in the car and looked out of one of its two windows.

"Andrée's trying to climb up on to the balloon," he said after a little while.

"Perhaps he hasn't accepted the fact that we're now in an entirely new situation," I answered.

"There's still a lot of gas in the balloon," said Strindberg. "Do you know what I think?"

"Yes," I answered, "you think that Andrée has closed the valves."

We went to bed sometime between two and three o'clock on the afternoon of 14 July.

PART FIVE

THE ICE

I

On Thursday, 15 July, I awoke slowly, with pains in my back, my hips, and my legs, the sort of pains that come from lying for a long time on a couch that is not particularly soft. I got up and opened the trapdoor of the car with my head. All my joints felt heavy and stiff, as they always do when a very exhausted man has had a long sleep.

I imagine that a man who is dead tired sleeps deeply and heavily, and that he lies practically motionless all the time, as if he were unconscious. Hence the pains in his back and his hips, and the stiffness of his joints.

I sat down on the deck with my legs dangling through the trapdoor, and wrote my notes in the new meteorological journal that I had started the previous day. Temperature nearly zero, Centigrade. Sky overcast, but clouds high. Air remarkably clear in spite of fine drizzle. Slight puffs of wind from the north-west. I did not bother about the humidity of the air. Our psychrometer was tucked away in one of the pockets of the car.

Then I lit my pipe.

The *Eagle* had shrunk to half the size he had been the previous day.

I had an absurd feeling that this was a quiet, peaceful Sunday morning.

We were on a large snow-covered ice-floe.

It was impossible to see the line of the horizon.

The whiteness of the snow merged into the whiteness of the mist, and the mist itself turned into white clouds that had closed together over our heads.

It was like sitting under a dome of whiteness of whose size I could form no conception.

The balloon, the carrying-ring, the carrying-ropes, our equipment was outlined clearly against the snow. The three guide-ropes, the anchor-cable, and one solitary ballast-rope lay stretched out behind the car. I could not remember when the other ballast-ropes had been chopped off during those last hours of our balloon voyage.

I walked once round the balloon, returned to the car, and gave the remaining carrier-pigeons a few handfuls of peas after lifting up the canvas flap that covered their baskets.

The flag moved gently on its flagstaff.

I roused Strindberg by rocking the car backwards and forwards until he poked his head through the trapdoor in the deck. A face drenched with sleep, hair on end, a strong growth of stubble.

"Good morning, after more than twenty hours sleep," I said.

He looked at his watch and did not believe me.

"Eight hours, you mean, you're out by twelve hours."

He jumped down on to the ice, opened his fly, and emptied his bladder, trying at the same time by screwing up his eyes to discover the whereabouts of the sun behind the clouds.

"You must be right," he said at last. "I'm damned if I can find out where the sun is, but I've never in my life peed for so long, or been so yellow. Besides, I'm confoundedly hungry."

Andrée had been awakened by our conversation.

He stood in the opening of the tent and regarded us with a smile.

"A fine arctic morning," he said. "No wind, a reasonable temperature, and pleasant drizzle."

"The sleeping-bag was comfortable, but too warm," he added. "I lay on top of it wrapped in a blanket. It was quite enough."

"There's no hurry," he said. "We've plenty of time. What we need now is coffee, lots of coffee, and strong coffee."

Andrée lit the primus stove, I fetched water from the puddle of fresh water, and Strindberg managed to find sugar, condensed milk, biscuits, butter, marmalade, and a couple of tins of sardines.

We made ourselves comfortable on the big sleeping-bag under the tent.

To Andrée I said:

"Now we're on the pack ice. And there lies the proud balloon, the *Eagle*, with the car, the guide-ropes, and all the other equipment. You might say that we've landed. You might equally well say that we're stranded. We never got to the North Pole. We didn't even get further north than Nansen's confounded eighty-sixth parallel.

"All the same we've broken a record," I said. "According to Gaston Tissandier—and who would dare question his aeronautical knowledge—no balloon of the *Eagle*'s size has managed to remain afloat for as long as sixty-five hours. And besides, other balloons have always been anchored at night, which has greatly reduced their loss of gas."

"What are you trying to say?" asked Strindberg.

"That the *Eagle*, with his sixty-five hours and thirty-three minutes has probably kept afloat longer than any other balloon in the history of aeronautics," I answered. "Any other balloon, that is, of a corresponding size."

"I'm grateful to you for the acknowledgement your words imply," said Andrée, and raised his cap. "But if we'd been intending to beat the record for staying power we should still have been afloat. This isn't a competition, it's a scientific expedition."

He spread a thick layer of butter on a biscuit, took a bite, chewed, and drank a deep draught of coffee as he swallowed.

"My young friend," he added with a laugh.

Without a doubt there was a feeling of Sunday in the air, no tension, no haste, no uneasiness, no anxiety.

Strindberg and I each lit a cigar. We all three drank mug after mug of coffee, to quench the balloonist's thirst that still possessed us.

2

"We must take stock of our situation," said Andrée.

"We must make up our minds what to do."

"Of course," I said.

"We've three alternatives," said Andrée.

"What are they?" asked Strindberg.

"Let's take them one by one."

"We can stay on this floe.

"We know that it will drift slowly south. (Just before breakfast, when the sun had been visible through the clouds for a few minutes, Strindberg had taken our bearings, which had clearly shown that we had drifted a good way south-west since the day before.)

"We're drifting south, or at any rate in a southerly direction.

"The drift may change direction. That's not impossible. No one knows anything for certain about the currents in the Polar Basin, or what direction they may take.

"The advantages are obvious. We should not need to exert ourselves.

"The disadvantages are also obvious. Sooner or later we shall reach the limits of the pack ice—no one can say where—after which we shall have to take to our boat, a fragile craft to say the least of it, with its timber frame and skin of silk.

"Our second alternative.

"We can load our sledges and march towards North-East Land in Spitzbergen, or more precisely to the Seven Islands immediately to the north of it."

With the help of the *Express*, the vessel he had chartered, Doctor Lerner of the *Kölnische Zeitung* had undertaken to establish a depot as far north as possible in this little group of islands, in a well-marked place that would be easily seen. There was no reason to suppose that Lerner would bungle this commission, especially as his rival and

Portrait of Knut Fraenkel, S. A. Andrée and Nils
Strindberg. Stockholm, May 3, 1897.

ОБЪЯВЛЕНІЕ.

Flyers with pictures of the balloon and information about the expedition were distributed in many languages in the northern parts of America, Europe and Asia. In accord with a decision of the Russian minister of the interior, a "Proclamation" was sent out to northern Russian folk groups with the decree that the learned foreigners be treated well, as they were under the protection of the Czar. One picture shows a balloon landing, and the text points out that small children are running up to it: thus, it was apparent that the balloon was completely harmless.

Checking to see if the seams of the balloon were airtight, with the help of white linen strips soaked in lead acetate.

Fraenkel poses for the photographer. The sledges were drawn only by means of haul-ropes; they had no guide-poles. This was later to mean great difficulties when the men made their way down the large embankments of pack ice.

In the car of the *Eagle* a minute or so before the start.

The *Eagle* shortly after landing on the ice. From the embankment of snow it appears that the car has been dragged over the ice. Some fifty exposed photographs were found on White Island, and of these, twenty pictures were successfully developed.

Shortly after the start. The car has brushed the water, ballast has been thrown overboard, and the balloon has gained altitude again. Because the ballast-ropes were mounted incorrectly, the *Eagle* has rotated a half turn. Fraenkel is about to take in the sails.

The first polar bear was shot at the landing site by Andrée.

Strindberg has illustrated the arduous trek over the ice with this
clearly composed picture. The camera had a self-timer. To the left,
Fraenkel, to the right, Andrée. Nearest to the camera, Strindberg.

In the summer of 1930 the last campsite of the Andrée party was discovered on White Island by a Norwegian expedition, led by Dr. Gunnar Horn.

Nils Strindberg's grave. Strindberg died first, probably only a few days after the party had gone ashore on White Island.

The remains of the three men were transported from Tromsö to Stockholm on board the gunboat *Svensksund,* the same warship that was put at Andrée's disposal in 1897. This triumphal journey lasted two weeks, during which time both Norwegians and Danes paid overwhelming homage to the heroes.

The cortege was welcomed to Sweden by the navy, the air force, the archbishop, the governor, the king, the diplomatic corps and tens of thousands of Stockholmers.

colleague, Doctor Violet of the *Berliner Lokalanzeiger*, was also on board the *Express*.

As a further safeguard Swedenborg had been told that once the balloon had started he was to make sure that the depot really was established.

"Our third alternative.

"We can trudge across the ice to the south-east, towards the large group of islands known as Franz Josef Land, which consists of at least fifty islands and islets, and is to a great extent unexplored and inadequately mapped.

"That was the route chosen by Nansen and Johansen when they left the *Fram* in 1895. It was there they went into winter quarters. And it was there, in the spring of 1896, that they met that strange sportsman and arctic explorer, Frederick Jackson, quite near to his well-equipped base, Elmwood, on Cape Flora. We've a large depot there too."

"Not really when they left the *Fram*," I said. "They left the *Fram* to try to reach the North Pole. It was only after they'd given that up that they made for Cape Flora."

"That blasted eighty-sixth parallel," said Strindberg. "A little less than four hundred and twenty kilometres from the Pole."

"These then are our three alternatives," said Andrée.

"Stop where we landed. Drift where we drift.

"Go towards the Seven Islands and Spitzbergen.

"Go towards Franz Josef Land and Cape Flora."

"What do you yourself think we should do?" I asked.

"I can't imagine staying put and drifting with the ice," answered Andrée.

"Nor can I," said Strindberg.

"I hate passivity more than anything," I said. "We're all agreed on that. We're not going to drift with the ice. We're going to trudge across it."

We sat on our three-man sleeping-bag, in our tent, drinking hot coffee and discussing our predicament.

"It's about three hundred and twenty kilometres to the Seven Islands," I said. "It's at least three hundred and fifty kilometres to the most northerly islands of Franz Josef Land, and some tens of kilometres further to Jackson's Cape Flora.

"That's right, isn't it?" I asked Strindberg, our navigator. He flicked through his notes and spread out the 'Physical Chart of the North Polar Regions, 1897'.

"You've got your distances pretty well right," he said.

"The simplest commonsense, horse-sense, argues that we should try to reach the Seven Islands," I said.

"But isn't it in the nature of things that horse-sense is just what arctic explorers lack?

"The *Fram*, Nansen's ship, drifted from east to west when she was frozen into the ice. If we trudge across the ice towards Franz Josef Land, won't that probably mean that as we trudge east the ice will drift west?

"How fast can a man travel when he is dragging a heavy sledge?

"How fast does the ice drift in the wrong direction?"

There was plenty of coffee in the pan.

The wind was light, the drizzle particularly fine and hardly troublesome at all.

"We must make up our minds," said Andrée.

"You've already made it plain what you want to do," I said

I turned to Strindberg. "What about you?" I asked.

"Cape Flora," he answered, and threw the stump of his cigar out on to the snow.

"That settles it," I said.

"By Greenwich mean time it's ten minutes to eleven o'clock of the morning of 15 July, 1897," said Strindberg.

3

Strindberg and I went on unloading our equipment from our 'store-room' above the carrying-ring. As we expected the valve on the side that was uppermost was closed.

Strindberg pulled the ropes to no avail. The valve must have frozen fast.

"We'll open the rip-panel," I said.

The device for bursting the balloon consisted of a hole in the envelope which measured at least four square metres. It was triangular in shape, with the pointed end at the top. This hole was covered by a somewhat larger 'lid', consisting of a lower part with three layers of varnished silk, and an upper part with four. This lid was glued and sewn fast to the envelope of the balloon, but on the inside, so that the pressure of the gas would seal the lid and the wall tightly together.

This large bursting device was intended to make a rapid landing possible, if this should prove necessary.

The two small circular valves, twenty centimetres in diameter, were only for manoeuvring. You opened them cautiously, the balloon sank. You threw out a handful of sand, the balloon rose. You opened the valves rather more, the balloon sank more rapidly, but not fast enough to prevent you from annulling or moderating its downward movement by throwing out another two handfuls of sand.

"Lachambre, Henri Lachambre, demonstrated this art to us, to Swedenborg and me in Paris in the spring," I said.

"Valve and sand, valve against sand. Like balancing the scales on which a jeweller weighs his gold."

I had to search for quite a time among the carrying-ropes, the net, and the odds and ends of rope before I found the rip-panel rope.

I need not have searched. The rip-panel rope was red, to distinguish it from all the other lines, ropes, and cables, and make it easy to find.

"We must ask Andrée," said Strindberg.

"I'll be damned if I will," I answered, and tugged at the rope. Nothing happened.

Of course! A bursting device is an emergency device. You must not be able to open it too easily, by accident.

(In the air it was opened by attaching a heavy lead weight to the rope and throwing it over the side of the car.)

I took a firm grip on the rope with both hands, walked up to the balloon, and then ran past the car. When the rope went taut I threw myself forward.

I fell, and as I did so I heard the screech of fabric being torn from fabric.

I fell on my back. It was perhaps a minute before the *Eagle* collapsed.

The layer of ice that covered the envelope, the calotte, and the net creaked and crackled.

I sat up.

The balloon was spreading out over the ice.

For a minute or two I was aware of the strange smell that I had noticed in Lachambre's workshop in Paris, and the balloon-house on Danes Island.

"Well, it's done," said Andrée, from the opening of the tent.

Then he added: "An empty balloon looks like a corpse."

Strindberg and I unloaded some more of our equipment and arranged it as systematically as possible round the car and the tent.

The fine drizzle did not worry us at all, rather the reverse. It made the snow and ice smooth and flat to walk on, like the paving-stones of a market-place.

Andrée wrote a series of despatches, which we put into sheaths and attached to our carrier-pigeons.

The birds were then released, one by one. They circled round, disappeared for a few minutes into the white mist to the south of us, returned and flew round and round our camp. Six of them went back to their cages.

Some of them were attacked and driven off by large birds, whose name I did not know. They disappeared into the dense whiteness to the south and west.

Strindberg and I placed the individual parts of each of the three collapsible sledges in separate heaps, well away from each other for safety's sake.

We laid the framework of the boat, its longitudinal ribs, and its sheath of three layers of varnished silk on the snow between the car and the tent.

Andrée investigated the thickness of the pack ice.

"One hundred and seven centimetres," he said.

"Interesting?" I asked.

"More than you'd think," he answered with a smile.

He also carefully examined the envelope of the balloon.

"It's covered with ice," he said. "Crystal-clear ice, on an average four or five millimetres thick.

"The drizzle," he said. "It rains, but the rain is undercooled. It consists of drops of water, but as soon as these drops meet a solid object they turn into ice."

The sky was heavily overcast, and it was impossible to take any bearings.

In the distance we saw yet another polar bear. It stopped, sniffed the air, and lumbered off towards the south-west.

We ate a substantial supper prepared by Strindberg on the primus stove.

We were still under a globe of opaque whiteness.

"It makes you feel safe," I said, and opened a half bottle of portwine from my private stock of provisions.

We drank to each other.

"A false feeling," I said.

The temperature was something over zero, Centigrade.

The wind was blowing from the south-west at a speed of just over four metres per second.

Andrée slept in the tent wrapped in Doctor Lembke's blanket. Strindberg and I slept in the car.

"Do you understand the situation we're in?" I asked.

"Yes," he answered.

"Really understand it? Take it seriously?"

"The devil only knows," he answered. "By this time, sailing in our balloon, we should really have crossed the North Pole and been on our way to Alaska or northern Siberia."

"Every scrap of sense," I said, "argues in favour of our making for the Seven Islands. Have you any idea why Andrée is determined to set off for Franz Josef Land and Cape Flora instead?"

"Yes," answered Strindberg.

"In Gothenburg, at the farewell party at Dickson's, Andrée promised that the first new island we discovered should be called Dickson's Second Island.

"But the sea between the point at which we now are and the Seven Islands has already been traversed by hundreds, perhaps by thousands of whaling vessels and other voyagers. There are no unknown islands in it."

"Parry," I said, "don't forget him, Edward Parry. It's exactly seventy years since he set off from almost the same spot as ourselves, not in a balloon, but in two ship's boats. They passed the Seven Islands, and when they reached the pack ice they pushed on further north. The boats were dragged on runners of a sort, while the greater part of their equipment was loaded on to four sledges."

"I know," said Strindberg.

"We must have crossed their route at least six times," I said, "while we were sailing to and fro in the balloon. Parry only reached latitude 82°45′N. We got 10′ further north."

"The sea between us and Franz Josef Land is unexplored," said Strindberg. "Even Franz Josef Land itself is unexplored and incompletely mapped.

"We should be able to find Dickson's Second Island."

"Dickson Island Number Two."

"And why not Andrée Island, and Strindberg Bay, and even Fraenkel Cliff?"

It felt chilly, I pulled on a woollen jersey and took off my boots. I lit a tallow candle in order to raise the temperature in the car a little.

While unloading we had found yet another blanket. A coarse, grey one, stamped with three crowns, and thus probably belonging to the *Svensksund*.

I got myself into a comfortable position for sleep. The blanket was larger than Doctor Lembke's, and more than covered us both.

The wind seemed to be increasing. The flag was flying, and a rope, probably the anchor-cable, was banging rhythmically against the canvas covering of the car.

Strindberg was sitting hunched up making some notes in one of his 'observation' books.

"If we'd had skis with us," I said, "I should have been able to race that polar bear and shoot him."

Strindberg did not answer.

I was tired and sleepy, but I wanted to smoke a pipe first.

"What are you doing?" I asked.

"Writing a letter," he answered.

"To Anna.

"My fiancée," he added.

"Where are you going to post it?" I asked after a few minutes.

"No idea," he answered.

The Arctic Ocean was no place for women.

I let my pipe go out and then put it into one of the many pockets of the car.

"I took six tallow candles with me when we left the *Svensksund*," I said. "I ought to have taken more. Two dozen at least. And they don't weigh much."

Then I fell asleep.

4

We were roused by an impatient and laughing Andrée.

Coffee and bouillon were waiting for us in the tent.

I wrote my meteorological notes. Very much the same weather as on the previous day. Rather denser clouds, rather stronger wind.

Our breakfast was warming and stimulating.

Leaving Andrée and Strindberg still sitting in the tent I went out into the wind and began to assemble the first sledge.

The sledges were made of selected ash that was free from knots. They were simple to put together. When assembled they did not weigh as much as thirteen kilos.

We had practised assembling them on Danes Island and the job did not take me long. I had finished the first sledge in less than an hour. It was three metres long and rather more than thirty centimetres high.

I kicked it over the snow, and it slid like a pat of butter on a hot potato.

"Write a note to Granlund's Wagon-works in Gränna," I shouted to Strindberg, "and thank them for a good piece of work!"

I lit my pipe. Everything was the same as on the previous day; white snow, no horizon, mist that merged into cloud, cloud that formed a dome above us.

"The world seems small and finite," I said.

"We know, worse luck, that it's incredibly large.

"Or is it thank goodness?"

I wanted to start on the other two sledges.

Andrée thought otherwise.

"The boat first," he said.

"Why?"

"It's more difficult," he said. "It will be harder work, and need more care than the sledges.

"It's always best," he said, "to do the difficult job first."

"Just as you like," I answered.

"But if that's the case, we should have started our journey across the ice before we left Danes Island."

The design of our boat was remarkable. The most important part was the keel, the overall length of which was four metres from stem to stern-post.

It consisted of three parts which had to be lashed together.

The keel formed a sort of spine.

To it we had to attach a large number of ribs or stays, not with nails or screws, but by lashing them to it.

The upper parts of the ribs were joined together by a pair of slender longitudinal bars, and the uppermost parts of all by a fairly thick coaming that ran from stem to stern.

When we had finished the keel it was time for dinner. Mutton cooked with cabbage, butter, bread, and beer. Strindberg had ceremoniously been appointed cook.

We had no complaints to make about the primus stove.

Our dinner-break lasted for several hours.

It is nice to feel well fed, it is nice to stretch out on a thick, three-man sleeping-bag, to smoke a pipe and gaze up at the dome of whiteness that makes the world small.

"It was the icing," said Andrée, "it was the damp and the ice that forced us to land.

"The ice was five millimetres thick on some parts of the calotte," he said. "If we'd had clear weather, sun and dry air, we should have been a hundred miles from where we are now. Several hundred miles."

"And the right wind," I said.

"Someone ought to think of a way of warming the gas in a balloon," said Strindberg.

"If we'd had skis with us," I said, "I should have followed the bear we saw yesterday and shot him."

I returned to the boat, followed by Strindberg.

Andrée began to make an inventory of our equipment.

Strindberg and I had a lot of trouble getting the ribs into their right places.

In the afternoon it began to snow, small flakes that melted as soon as they touched the wood.

It would have been stupid to go on working in the wet. We carefully dragged the keel and the few ribs already mounted into the tent.

"Write a letter to Plym's boat-yard," I said to Strindberg. "Thank them for the way the boat's designed, but at the same time complain, as nicely as you can, that they've been altogether too ingenious."

By degrees it began to snow harder.

The flakes were still small.

We lit the paraffin stove, made some cocoa, and ate biscuits with butter and marmalade.

The wind slowly increased. The temperature was still above zero. We sat in the shelter of the tent.

We talked to each other quietly, in low voices.

Strindberg wrote in his book.

"A letter to Anna?" I asked.

"Yes," he answered.

"There's no hurry," said Andrée. "We can take things quietly. A day more or less will make no difference."

"Are you so sure of that?" I asked.

Strindberg said: "I've been making a rough estimate of the distance we ought to cover each day if we're to reach Franz Josef Land before winter sets in. Three hundred and fifty kilometres is perhaps further than you'd think."

"You mean?" asked Andrée.

"That we ought to start our journey as soon as possible," answered Strindberg.

"But," he added, "I'm extremely uncertain how our journey will be affected by the drift of the ice."

He did not attempt to be more explicit, and we did not bother him with any more questions. We still knew nothing about the movement of the ice.

*   *   *

As we had pulled the boat into the tent we all three had to squash into the car with the blankets from Doctor Lembke and the *Svensksund* to keep us warm.

The wind increased in strength. We heard the dull and distant crunch of ice being pressed against ice.

Soon after midnight we were awakened by a terrific crash, and the car heeled over on one side.

"An earthquake?" I asked.

"Something of the sort," answered Andrée.

Our large floe had broken right down the middle just fifty metres south of where we had landed. By the morning the lead in the ice was three metres wide in some places.

For our breakfast Strindberg had prepared hot cocoa made with cocoa-powder, condensed milk and water. To go with it he gave us Albert biscuits, butter and some thick slices of cheese.

It had stopped snowing and the wind was less strong. Visibility was poor. Round us, from every quarter, from every direction, we could hear the crunch of ice against ice, floes that pressed against each other, that pushed each other under, that were up-ended, that fell.

It was true that our floe had broken in two during the night, but the part we were on still felt reassuringly large.

Strindberg and I continued our work on the boat. Rib after rib was lashed firmly into position. In spite of the fact that the temperature was above zero Centigrade our fingers grew stiff, and it was hard work handling the twine and pulling the lashing and the knots tight enough.

"It's called to 'lash' not to 'seize'," I said. "You 'seize' two ropes together, but by God you don't 'seize' a rib to a keel."

"To hell with terminology," he answered. "The main thing is that we put together a good boat, and that each piece of wood gets into its right place."

The ribs and the bars were wrongly numbered and marked, and we really had great difficulty in assembling the skeleton of the boat properly.

We ought to have practised during the time we had spent waiting at Spitzbergen.

That was what we ought to have done.

Instead of studying fresh-water lagoons, and glaciers, and taking soundings in Danes Gat, and Virgo Harbour.

Andrée succeeded in detaching the sail from the balloon. He spread it out over our equipment and provisions, after shaking off the snow that had fallen on it during the night and the previous day.

He went on making a fairly thorough tour of inspection round our floe and the ridges of pressure ice that surrounded us.

It was Saturday and we stopped work quite early in the afternoon.

We discussed our menu for dinner in great detail. This discussion was very protracted, and conducted for its own sake. In the end we agreed on the following:

A little tin of pickled herring. Soup made from Rousseaus' meat-powder. Fried corned beef. Cranberry jam with diluted condensed milk. Cheese and hard bread.

We sat on the sleeping-bag just inside the opening of the tent. The wind had abated still more, but the visibility was worse than it had been that morning.

"We're wrapped in grey wool," I said.

The primus functioned perfectly. We boiled the soup first, and put the saucepan aside, wrapped in a woollen jersey. We had organized our meal well.

While the corned beef was being fried we opened the tin of herring, and divided its contents into three equal portions.

I had brought out a little bottle of schnapps from my private hoard.

"I don't normally take it," said Andrée, "but as it's Saturday."

The herring was salt. "Here's to Saturday," I said for lack of a better idea.

The herring was so salt that we drank yet another dram all round.

The Rousseaus' meat-powder soup was just the right heat.

"With all due deference to old Rousseau," said Strindberg, "one can't call this a French delicacy."

"We ought to have tried it out at Spitzbergen," I said. "We've at least fifty kilos of it."

"A certain famous spice will certainly improve its flavour before long," said Andrée.

We rinsed our plates with snow and proceeded to the fried slices of corned beef.

Strindberg put out the primus and the silence was complete. It was a few minutes before we heard the wind again, and the rumbling of the pressure ice.

We shared out two bottles of beer as fairly as we could.

"A few potatoes wouldn't have come amiss," said Strindberg. "But I accept the situation as it is."

To finish up with, a little dab of cranberry jam each.

Cranberries are said to be a good protection against scurvy, just as good as cloudberries.

It was a solid meal. We ate our dessert and our hard bread and cheese lying on the sleeping-bag; replete, tired.

"Coffee?" asked Andrée.

"Unfortunately," answered Strindberg, "we've brought far too little of it."

And added: "It isn't my fault."

"Our floe is smaller than it was," said Andrée, from his reclining position on the sleeping-bag. "A lead has opened up to the south of us, but at the same time we've frozen fast to the pack ice in the north and north-east. That is to say that in the north and north-east a circular ridge of toroses has built up. It's several metres high. The ice has been squeezed together, broken into blocks and frozen solid. Some of the floes that have been up-ended are as tall as a two-storey house.

"What tremendous forces!" he said.

"Think," he said, "floes of ice, that must weigh more than a hundred tons, have been forced dead upright! More than a hundred tons, maybe several hundred tons."

"Yes," I said.

"The ice is partially stratified," he said, "rather like hills of slate. You can see clay and gravel between the different strata.

"And then there's another, quite different thing. The water that's melted on top of the ice freezes and turns into ice when it gets into

231

the sea. A trifle, but an amusing one. Melted water is fresh water. Its temperature is 0° Centigrade. The sea is salt, and its temperature approximately − 1°5′ Centigrade. Fresh water freezes in salt water. It forms strange little collections of spicules, as sharp as needles. Not a film of ice, but a collection of downward pointing spicules, no more than two centimetres long."

"Putting the boat together is pure hell," said Strindberg.

"It's strange watching the ropes and netting of the balloon sinking into the snow and ice," said Andrée.

"They're sucking up warmth from the sun in spite of the fact that no sun is visible."

We went to bed in the cramped car.

I wrote up my notes in the meteorological journal after having consulted Strindberg's chronometer.

"The gravel, the sand, and the clay in the blocks of ice must come from the silt that the great Siberian rivers bring down to Nordenskiöld's sea," said Andrée.

"Nansen said much the same thing," said Strindberg. "The ice of the Polar Basin drifts mainly from east to west, or, to put it better, with the sun."

"But we," I said, "we're not Norwegians, we're Swedes, and therefore we're going to defy the pack ice and march south-east."

Andrée did not answer.

We were very tired. It was warm in the car.

"One simple question," I said, "a mere trifle. You call the ridges of ice 'toroses'. It's a good word, toros. But where did you get it from?

"Toros?"*

"It's a nice short word," he answered, half laughing.

"Where did I get it from? I don't know. Perhaps from the Eskimos? I don't know."

* Toros is the Russian word for an ice hummock. Andrée seems to have used it to describe a ridge of pressure ice.

5

During the course of the following day Strindberg and I succeeded in completing the skeleton of the boat made up of ribs and longitudinal bars.

All the carrier-pigeons had left our landing place. We had failed to notice whether they had done so of their own free will, or because they had been chased off by fulmars.

The rumblings from the pressure ice had decreased.

Visibility was better than on any day since we landed.

From the roof of the car Andrée scanned the horizon to the south time after time through his binoculars.

He was looking for Gilles Land which, according to our 'Physical Chart of the North Polar Regions', should theoretically have been within our range of vision.

He found nothing but fog.

During the afternoon the lead that had opened up through our floe closed. But the following morning we found that it had opened again.

"Panta rei!" said Strindberg.

"Even north of the Arctic Circle," I added.

The weather was good. The sky was cloudy it is true, but there was no precipitation of any kind. Strindberg and I carried the skeleton of the boat out of the tent. It weighed forty kilos at the most.

We were impressed both by its rigidity and its flexibility. We placed it upside-down on two baskets. It took us two hours to cover it with the tailored sheath, or shell, made of three thicknesses of varnished balloon-silk.

We looked upon our work and found it good.

After a hasty dinner we set to work upon sledge number two.

During our meal Andrée told us that the meshes of the net had sunk a good hundred and thirty millimetres into the snow and ice.

We discussed how heavy a load we should be able to pull on our sledges.

"We ought to have made some trial trips while we were waiting at Danes Island," I said to Strindberg.

At six o'clock that afternoon a great event took place.

The silence—our ears no longer heard the rumblings of the pressure ice—was broken by a shot.

Andrée had shot a polar bear with one of our Remingtons.

The bullet had entered its neck just under the spine.

"He simply tumbled over," said Andrée.

I took his rifle, put a new cartridge into the breech, and walked cautiously up to the bear. It was lying on its left side with its legs slightly drawn up. Its neck was red with blood. I let him have a bullet between the eyes for safety's sake.

"You ought to have reloaded immediately," I said to Andrée.

Strindberg came running up with his camera, and Andrée posed willingly beside his prize. Then it was Andrée's turn to take a photograph of Strindberg and me.

We lifted up the bear's head, but Andrée thought that looked absurd. He gave Strindberg his Remington and I fetched our other two weapons. It took some time to set the scene for that picture. Andrée got his own rifle back, and Strindberg held our double-barrelled gun instead. My Remington, unlike Andrée's, had no strap. At last Andrée was satisfied and squeezed the rubber bulb of the camera.

No use denying it: that dead bear caused a great deal of excitement. The first edible victim of our hunting. A moment of pomp and soaring blood-pressure.

It was not a large bear, probably a yearling or a two-year-old. Its fur was very thick, and gleaming white except for a few places where it was streaked with yellow. Its paws were long, its pads disproportionately large and armed with remarkably hard, sharp claws. The shape of its heavy skull was quite beautiful, and perfectly formed for cleaving a way through water. Its smooth lines were like those of a shuttle: a sharp pointed nose, steadily widening jaw-bones, a flat forehead, and an arching cranium. Only the black nose was hairless. Every other part was covered with thick white fur.

234

Its ears were small and the orifices were quite hidden in fur. Its eyes were small, mere slits, these too quite hidden in fur.

Even my last shot in its forehead was invisible. No blood had flowed from it, and the layers of fur had closed up over the hole made by the bullet.

According to Nansen the polar bear is the mobile larder of the Arctic Ocean.

"A splendid larder from many points of view," said Strindberg.

At the moment of death the bear had emptied his rectum.

Andrée examined the excrement.

"Masses of fish-scales," he said.

Strindberg and I skinned the bear mostly for the sake of practice, as we did not need the fur.

This situation might conceivably change a little later on.

We only kept the best parts of the meat. We were not short of provisions, rather the reverse. We had more food than we could take with us on our sledges.

We went back to the tent with our weapons and our cameras.

At least fifty screeching birds were circling over the carcase of the bear.

It was ten o'clock on the evening of Monday, 19 July, according to Strindberg's chronometer.

Back in the tent we made some coffee and ate a few slices of pumpernickel with butter and cheese.

"I had my rifle with me quite by chance," said Andrée. "Suddenly, quite close to me I saw the bear. I fired. I hit him."

"A perfect shot in the neck," I said.

"I'm not really a crack shot," he said. "A passable one perhaps. I've practised a lot these last few years. I find it hard to see the back sight, the fore sight, and the target simultaneously."

"You should have reloaded immediately," I said.

"I'm not a hunting man," he answered. "Or I'm a poor sort of hunting man. Hunting was the favourite pastime on the expedition to Spitzbergen in 1882-83. I didn't care a damn for it. I left it to the others.

"I've never cared for hunting," he said. "To tell you the truth the sight of spurting, pulsating blood gives me an unpleasant feeling. Or rather it did.

"Things are different today.

"In the winter of '82-83 we killed for pleasure. Not I, but the others."

"And now?" I asked.

"We shall have to kill to survive," said Andrée. "Consequently I find myself in an entirely new situation."

"It was a perfect shot," I repeated. "You hit him in the neck, just under his spine, or his cervical vertebrae. His big arteries were torn to bits. Very probably you gave his spinal column a numbing blow at the same time."

"I fired on the spur of the moment," said Andrée. "I can't remember taking aim. The bear collapsed as if he'd been struck by lightning.

"Blood spurted from his neck and ran down on to the snow.

"It was damnably red in the midst of all that whiteness.

"But I felt a kind of joy," said Andrée.

"It was a perfect shot," I said. "But next time, next time you must remember to put a fresh cartridge into the breech immediately."

We were lying on the three-man sleeping-bag in the tent, drinking our ration of coffee from our too scanty supply as slowly as possible.

The clouds rose, the visibility improved somewhat. The air felt drier and easier to breathe.

Just before midnight the sun came out in the north. It looked like a pale full moon.

Strindberg and I each took our bearings, one fifteen minutes after the other.

A rapid calculation revealed, with all the clarity we could wish, that since our landing we had drifted more than thirty kilometres towards the south-west, towards Spitzbergen.

"Towards the south-west," I said to Andrée.

"The ice is moving in the direction of Spitzbergen and the Seven Islands."

"What do you mean?" he asked.

236

"Do you stand by your decision that we're not to go south-west, but south-east, towards Franz Josef Land and Cape Flora?"

"It wasn't *my* decision," he said. "It was *our* decision."

6

Tuesday, 20 July was a pleasant day, with a light south-westerly wind and a clear sky.

All our damp, foul-smelling things were hung up to dry on a line suspended between the car and the yard from the sail, which we rammed into the snow and braced with some bits of rope.

Strindberg and I finished putting together both sledge number two and sledge number three, which was designed to carry the boat. It was to be pulled by me.

Andrée explored our surroundings in a number of brief excursions, and made a variety of observations.

Among other things he estimated that the guide-ropes and the net of the balloon had sunk one hundred and thirty-two millimetres into the snow and ice since we landed.

On several occasions he climbed on to the roof of the car and scanned the horizon to the south through his binoculars.

By five o'clock in the afternoon Strindberg and I were able to report that all three sledges and the boat were ready to be loaded.

"Splendid," he said, "splendid."

"The boat is damned good," I said, "if only it floats. The sledges are damned good too. Their buoyancy is of secondary importance."

We were ready to start, apart from the fact that the sledges were not loaded.

According to our thermometers the temperature was barely plus one, but the sky was cloudless, and the sun gave off a heat that warmed us. The snow that had settled on the envelope of the balloon, and other relatively dark objects, melted and disappeared.

We overloaded our stomachs with a hearty meal of pancakes and diced pork.

We lay in the opening of the tent and let the sun warm us.

"Our last day," I said. "Tomorrow . . ."

We were replete.

We had to keep our eyes shut, or half shut, to protect them from the sunshine.

"When you shut your eyes," I said, "you can almost fancy that you are lying on the grass of a Swedish meadow in summertime."

"I try," said Strindberg, "but I can't, however much I shut my eyes. The rumble from the ridges of pressure ice might be distant thunder, but the smell is wrong, and those confounded white vultures certainly don't twitter like bullfinches."

"Talking of birds. The carrier-pigeons?" (I had not seen them all day.)

"There was one left this morning," answered Andrée.

"She was hopping about on the cages. I gave her a handful of peas. She ate some, but brought them all up again. She flew round me a few times and then perched on my shoulder."

"And then?"

"After a few minutes she rose, flapping her wings. It was as if she'd made up her mind. Then she flew off with steady, rapid wing-beats, and disappeared."

"In which direction?"

"I didn't look at the compass," said Andrée, "but judging by the time of day and the position of the sun, her course must have been in the main due north."

After only six or seven hours' sleep we began a new working day.

The wind was light and south-westerly. The sun still shed some warmth, but through a thin veil of haze.

Strindberg and I carried the boat to the lead and put it in the water. It floated like a swan. We both climbed on board. It still floated like a swan. The varnished silk seemed to be absolutely water-tight.

"The balloon was christened when we started," I said to Andrée, who was still standing on the ice. "Have you a name up your sleeve for the boat? And is it a he, a she, or an it?"

"Our champagne is in such short supply that the boat will have to remain nameless," he answered.

Andrée had made an inventory of our equipment and sorted it into heaps; food in one, then implements, instruments, medical supplies, ropes, tarpaulins, boat-hooks, ammunition and so on, each in separate heaps.

The loading of the sledges provoked a series of discussions. We all had different views about how much we should be able to pull, what was most valuable out of our provisions, which of our implements, ropes, and other items of equipment were most indispensable.

At first these arguments had an almost jocular tone, but after Strindberg and Andrée had expressed conflicting opinions on what foods we should take with us they became rather more acrimonious.

We could not take all the provisions we had at our landing-place. We were quite simply obliged to select and discard.

Strindberg thought that tinned meats and butter and other fatty and albuminous substances should predominate.

Andrée held that it was more important to take as much bread, sugar, and other carbohydrates as we could.

Strindberg pointed out that all arctic peoples, from the Eskimos to the Chukches, lived almost entirely on fat, meat, and other albuminoids or proteins, that they had done so for thousands of years. Everyone agreed, he said, that they were strong, and enjoyed the best of health. We ought to draw the obvious conclusions.

To this Andrée objected that the arctic peoples mentioned had been prevented from practising agriculture by geographical and climatic circumstances. Hunting and fishing were their only means of gaining a livelihood. This affected their eating habits. We were not in a position to say what their health and strength would have been if they had also had access to bread, sugar, and similar forms of food.

Moreover, he added, there was an indisputable connection between man's ability to accomplish work demanding great physical effort and his consumption of carbohydrates.

"It's only a theory," said Strindberg. "An English theory, based on the performance of English athletes. It may possibly be acceptable and right when applied to brief physical exertions. We've no idea how well it applies to prolonged exertion in an arctic climate."

"During our journey south," said Andrée, "we shall be able to shoot both bears and seals, and this will complement our stores of meat and fat. On the other hand our chances of shooting loaves and packets of hard bread are strictly limited."

While this discussion was going on I pulled the boat out of the lead, turned it upside down, crept under it, and carried it on outstretched arms up to my sledge.

Carrying it on my outstretched arms presented no problem. It weighed at the most sixty kilos, moisture included. It was rather more difficult to lower it slowly, and get it into the right position between the curved supports, covered with felt, upon which it was to rest.

"What's your view?" asked Andrée.

"About what?"

"Our provisions."

"I haven't any," I said. "I'm an engineer, not a nutritionist.

"Yesterday, or the day before, we had soup made from Rousseaus' meat-powder. Warm. Probably nourishing. It tasted disgusting. The fact that it's also called Mellin's Food doesn't make it any nicer.

"I'm not lacking in imagination," I said. "I can see myself longing for soup made of Rousseaus' meat-powder as if it were the greatest of all delicacies.

"But I hate passivity," I said. "I don't want to stay put any longer. I want to set off. Southwards. Or northwards. Or towards Franz Josef Land and Cape Flora. Or in any direction you please.

"Your balloon was going to keep afloat for at least thirty days. Our journey in the air lasted just over sixty hours.

"Now we're on a floe.

"It's breaking up.

"Round us an infinitude of squeezing, pressing, rumbling pack ice.

"I've only one wish: I want to start as soon as possible. Preferably with both meat and bread among our provisions."

Andrée and Strindberg stopped arguing, but we did not succeed in getting the sledges, or toboggans, loaded during the course of that day.

Just before five o'clock we stopped work and all went into the tent.

Strindberg got the primus going and fried thick slices of fillet of polar bear, the Châteaubriand of the Arctic, which he served up without potatoes, it is true, but with a dab of butter.

We ate it underdone, a trifle on the bloody side. We were short of paraffin. The meat was tender and easy to chew. It tasted delicious. We each ate three or four substantial slices.

We finished off our meal with bread, butter, and the contents of two tins of sardines.

Our cooking-apparatus, the primus, was so constructed that any surplus heat could be utilized for melting snow or heating water to make something over a litre of liquid.

We shared out this warm water, added some fresh water from the small 'lakes' on the floe, and washed our hands and faces for the first time since leaving Danes Island.

"How nice it feels," said Strindberg, "we've changed from negroes into mulattoes."

We had not been out of our clothes since we started.

"You don't get dirty when you're in the air, or in the Polar Regions," I said, "that is, not in the way you do in Stockholm, for instance, or in Paris."

Strindberg suddenly discovered our incipient beards and burst out laughing. He had also discovered a deficiency in our equipment. We had forgotten to bring a mirror. Those on the sextant were far too small, likewise the control mirrors on Göransson's cooking-apparatus. We had to be content with looking at one another and with stroking our own chins and cheeks.

How quickly does one's hair and beard grow?

Strindberg measured my stubble. "Round about four millimetres," he said, "that makes a centimetre a month. It won't be long enough for you to see with your own eyes until about Christmas."

"You're in luck with your moustaches," I said to Andrée. "If you take care of them you'll certainly be able to see the tips in a month's time. In due course you'll get into Machuron's class. Then you'll have to tie them behind your ears if you want to eat in comfort."

Before we went to bed we took our bearings and found that the drift had swung from south to south-east.

"Eight kilometres in twenty-four hours," said Strindberg.

"In the direction of Franz Josef Land, without our having taken a single step."

7

Thursday, 22 July.

It was about ten o'clock before I awoke. Light wind, fog, visibility a couple of hundred metres. Temp., zero.

I roused Strindberg and almost had to drag him out of the car by force.

"Take a look round our landing-place," I said. "This will be our last morning here."

Andrée was asleep in the tent, wrapped in the blanket from the *Svensksund*. He was lying on his back and snoring gently.

"Is a polar explorer allowed to snore?" I asked.

"That's up to him," answered Strindberg.

"Even asleep," I said, "even when he's snoring, he gives an impression of vigour, will-power, and determination."

"That prominent nose and chin, those slightly frowning eyebrows, that broad receding, and not particularly high forehead."

"I've never before seen a person frown when they were asleep," said Strindberg.

Andrée awoke when we lit the primus to make coffee.

We went on loading our sledges. This provoked a new, but fortunately brief discussion between Andrée and Strindberg on the value of and necessity for food supplies, in which either albuminoids or carbohydrates predominated.

"Your discussion," I said, "not mine."

"There are only two things I want in the culinary line," I said. "The first is that we should take all our ammunition with us. I think it will prove twice as nourishing as the corresponding quantity of hard bread or fat pork. The second is that we take all the coffee we have with us.

"I've noticed with anxiety," I said, "that it's in decidedly short supply. I'm rather afraid that a number of tins of coffee got thrown overboard during the last few hours of our balloon voyage."

We also had to make sure that the loads on our sledges were of approximately equal weight.

Both Andrée and Strindberg made careful notes of how much various objects weighed.

What made these carefully recorded figures fascinating was that some were so exact, while others were no more than rough estimates.

On Andrée's sledge we put, among other things, a boat-hook, weight fifteen hectos; a snow-shovel, weight eighteen hectos; three bamboo poles, weight thirty hectos. Each of these was carefully entered, as nearly as possible to the last gramme. After that came a basket containing a number of different objects which weighed approximately sixty-five kilos, and another basket which was estimated to weigh about sixty-six kilos.

Pedantic exactitude about small items, gross guessing about things that were really heavy.

We were using what was probably a fairly unreliable spring-balance, which could only weigh up to thirty kilos at the most. The weight had been stamped on some portions of our equipment by the people who had supplied it. When we had finished loading the sledges we discovered that we had not remembered the tent and the sleeping-bag.

We stowed both of them away on my sledge. It was easy to put them into the boat.

243

"Tent, nine kilos," said Andrée. "Sleeping-bag about the same. Both together less than twenty kilos."

"Damp and moisture not included?"

"A kilo more or less makes no difference."

At the bottom of the sleeping-bag we found another blanket of the type and material supplied by the Swedish Government.

"Half a kilo at the most," he said, "damp and moisture included."

Late that afternoon we ate a substantial meal of tinned meat.

"The more we eat the less we shall leave behind," said Strindberg.

The fog had grown denser. Everything round us was white.

Strindberg broke open some packets of bread and biscuits and scattered the contents over the ice. The screeching birds left the carcase of the bear for a while.

We were sitting on one of the sails, close to the car and sheltered by it from the light south, south-westerly wind.

"'Give us this day our daily bread'," said Andrée.

"The Sermon on the Mount? Isn't it? Between us heathens."

Strindberg took a final series of photographs of our landing-place.

"Artistic?" asked Andrée, as Strindberg arranged the camera for a close-up of the big carrying-ring that was resting against what remained of the pile of snow the car had ploughed up when we landed.

"Yes," answered Strindberg, "and the empty balloon is more like a corpse than anything I've ever seen.

"As a matter of fact," he said, "we're no longer in the spot where we landed, but thirty or thirty-five kilometres further south.

"Or perhaps somewhat to the south-east."

I was standing ready to start, with the harness over my shoulders, impatient.

At last Strindberg packed his camera.

With a joint effort he and Andrée turned the car upside down.

"Why?" I asked.

"Why not?" answered Andrée with a smile.

The load on Andrée's sledge amounted to about two hundred and twenty kilos, that on Strindberg's to something under two hundred. My own burden was over two hundred and thirty kilos, perhaps rather nearer two hundred and forty.

At fifteen minutes to seven on the evening of 22 July we began our journey across the ice.

Andrée went first. I had to give several tugs before I could get my sledge to move.

Behind me I heard Strindberg's happy shouts.

8

During the day the lead that had opened when our floe broke in two had closed. That suited us admirably. It lay in the direction in which we intended to travel. In all other directions, for as far as we could see, there were ridges of pressure ice.

"Hurry up, boys," said Strindberg, half sprinting past both me and Andrée. "Compass in hand, straight ahead for Cape Flora!"

The thin layer of wet snow made both a firm foothold for us and good gliding for our sledges.

Strindberg's recklessly rapid tempo was singularly short-lived. When he had gone fifty metres his sledge slid sideways into a puddle of fresh water. To stop it upsetting he leapt into the puddle and held it upright, standing knee-deep in water, until Andrée and I came up.

The bag containing his private possessions had got wet, and he did not calm down until he had made sure that his notebooks and his letters to Anna were undamaged.

We wanted him to change into dry breeches.

"What, five minutes after we've started! I'll be damned if I do," he said.

He unlaced and emptied his boots, wrung the water out of his knee-length socks, and squeezed as much wet as he could out of his breeches. That done he was ready to march.

"My clothes will be dried by the warmth from within," he said.

"I didn't manage to pull my sledge very far, but far enough to discover that it's an occupation that generates heat."

"It wouldn't really take very long to change into dry clothes. What about catching cold, developing pneumonia?"

"Caused by bacteria and bacilli," said Strindberg. "Doctor Kock proved that long ago, and many other scientific men have confirmed what he said.

"Bacteria don't care for the climate in the Arctic," he said. "Infectious complaints never occur north of the seventy-fifth parallel, not even a runny nose, a cough, or a sore throat."

He fastened the harness over his shoulders.

"Many authorities have said the same thing," he said. "Bering, Franklin, Ross, Parry, Peary, Nordenskiöld, Nansen, Sverdrup, Ekholm, and Nordenskiöld junior. And S. A. Andrée. To mention only a few among many.

"Get going," he said to Andrée with a laugh. "You'd best take the lead. Compass in hand, as straight a course as you can for Cape Flora!"

Andrée shook his head, bent forward in his harness, and trudged on.

I followed him. I had again to take a run at it before I could get my sledge to move.

Behind me I heard Strindberg's happy shouts.

After a few hundred metres we were obliged to turn westwards to avoid a high ridge of pressure ice, a toros. After that we were able to resume our south-easterly course.

We crossed a fairly large floe. The foothold was good, but there were small, almost invisible undulations which made the sledges slip sideways, and wasted a lot of energy.

After half an hour we were brought to a halt by a lead of open water about thirty metres wide.

Small floes were drifting about in the lead.

Andrée and Strindberg went towards the west, I towards the east.

It was a relief to be rid of the heavy drag of the harness on one's shoulders for a while.

With the aid of our two boat-hooks and a little grapnel on ropes we succeeded in collecting together a number of small floes which made a bridge over the lead.

Floes brought into contact with each other have a tendency to suck on to each other, as it were, to form a single if fragile unit.

We first pulled Strindberg's sledge across our bridge. It was easier than we had expected.

After that Andrée's sledge, and last mine, the heaviest.

We rested for a short while.

It was impossible to see the slightest sign of our landing-place even through our binoculars.

"We've burnt our boat behind us," said Strindberg.

"An uninflammable boat," I answered, "at least when it lay on the ice like a gigantic piece of wet silk. A corpse."

"But extremely inflammable as long as he was floating through the air," said Andrée.

The *Eagle*, 'he'.

We pushed on into the fog that slowly grew lighter and lifted.

When we had gone another hundred metres we were confronted by another lead, not as wide as the previous one.

There were plenty of small floes, and Strindberg and I were easily able to push them together with our two boat-hooks, so that they formed a bridge.

What we had observed previously was confirmed. Floes or blocks of ice which are drawn close together freeze on to each other, or become in some way fairly firmly attached.

We pulled our three sledges over our new bridge without any serious warning of disaster.

Soon afterwards we reached our third lead.

At first glance it appeared impassable.

It lay in a north-easterly—or, if you prefer it—a south-westerly direction.

We left our sledges by the 'bank'.

I walked north-east, and very soon found a fairly large floe, which I succeeded in capturing with the grapnel and rope. By exerting myself to the utmost I pulled it along the lead. It must have weighed at least fifty tons.

I never got as far as the spot at which we had left our sledges.

The lead slowly narrowed. The edges of the ice got closer and closer, and suddenly my floe was too wide, or rather, exactly the right width. It formed a bridge across the open water.

I summoned Andrée and Strindberg by shouting and blowing my whistle.

I pulled my sledge, the heaviest, over the bridge without difficulty.

But when the other two arrived the lead had narrowed so much that my floe—I'd come to regard it almost as my personal property—had been pushed up over the north bank.

By all lending a helping hand we succeeded in lifting Strindberg's sledge up on to the ice bridge and dragging it across to the south side.

The operation only took a few minutes, but by the time we got back to the north side the difference between the level of the floe and the bank had increased by more than a metre.

There was obviously no time for consultation.

We attacked that bank of ice with an axe, a harpoon, and a shovel, and managed to make a sort of smooth slope, with a sufficiently gentle rise to allow us to pull Andrée's sledge on to the bridge, and let it glide 'ashore' on the south side of the lead.

We rested again. We were hungry, but too tired to eat.

The visibility had improved noticeably. We could see the sun in the north-west. It looked like a golden disc through the clouds, but it cast no shadows in our landscape of ice and snow and water.

We crossed two fairly insignificant ridges of pressure ice.

Then came a large field of flat ice thinly covered with snow. Andrée went first, then I, and last Strindberg.

Ten white birds circled about in the air above us.

After an hour or two Andrée stopped.

"The sledges aren't gliding as well as they were," he said. "It's hard work pulling them."

"Both Fraenkel and I entirely agree with you on that point," said Strindberg.

"We must try a new technique," said Andrée.

We all three pulled Andrée's sledge a distance of four or five hundred metres.

It was an easy way of getting along which gave us a chance to converse.

"No, I'm not cold," said Strindberg. "My breeches and my under-pants are already dry."

We went back to fetch his sledge.

"It's far too light," I said.

We went back to fetch my sledge.

"It's far too heavy," said Strindberg. "One always tends to over-estimate the strength of heavily built people."

It was a great field of flat ice without any toroses.

We all pulled Andrée's sledge for perhaps another five hundred metres. Went back to fetch Strindberg's.

Went back again to tackle mine. Strindberg and I pulled. Andrée walked behind and pushed.

The veil of cloud lifted bit by bit.

We pitched our camp at eleven o'clock that evening in dazzling sunshine.

9

The tent and the sleeping-bag, both in the boat on my sledge, were easy to get at.

Before we set off Strindberg had prepared some cheese sandwiches and a tin of cold tea.

"The sledges are too heavy," I said.

Andrée answered:

"We're in the same position that Nansen was in when he started his journey across the Greenland Ice Sheet nine years ago.

"All earlier expeditions to the interior of Greenland had started from the west coast, from the inhabited places on the west coast of Greenland. They not only had with them provisions and equipment for their journey eastwards, but also for a return journey to the west.

"Nansen started from the east coast, he travelled westwards. He only needed food and equipment for one journey."

"And we?" I asked.

"Our situation is the same.

"We're where we are, and we're on our way south. We only need food and equipment for our return journey.

"In that lies our strength."

"The loads on Nansen's sledges didn't weigh more than a hundred kilos," I said, "apart from the fifth sledge, which carried a load of nearly two hundred kilos, but two men pulled that one. Even so they complained that their sledges were too heavy."

"Nansen's journey across Greenland was undertaken in circumstances quite unlike ours," said Andrée.

"We're travelling at sea level. Nansen had to climb to a height of two thousand eight hundred metres, higher than the top of the highest mountain in Sweden. He was going uphill all the time for the first half of his march.

"He was on dry land, we're on the sea. We have to have a boat. He didn't need one.

"They were six, we're only three. Much of what we have to pull are things we use in common. They have to be distributed between three sledges. Nansen was able to divide the same kind of equipment between five sledges, one of them pulled by two men."

He added: "Nansen and Johansen's long sledge journey across the pack ice from the *Fram* to Franz Josef Land and Cape Flora was quite another matter. On it they used dogs to pull the sledges."

"Any one can see," I said, "that our journey resembles Nansen's Greenland expedition in two respects. First: he travelled from east to west, while we are travelling from north to south-east. Second: the loads on our sledges are twice as heavy as the loads on his."

Andrée laughed long and heartily.

*   *   *

Our shoulders were badly chafed by the harness of our haul-ropes. We greased the affected spots thoroughly with vaseline.

We took off our boots and stockings, and for the first time all crept into our big three-man sleeping-bag made of reindeer skin.

"Clever dimensions," I said. "A tight enough fit to enable each of us to enjoy the heat generated by the others, yet wide enough to let us turn over in our sleep without waking them. N.B. they're dead tired and sleeping heavily."

Andrée lay in the middle.

Strindberg on his left, I on his right.

It was not a question of any sort of understanding. Andrée simply crept into the sleeping-bag first, and I happened to be sitting on his right.

Andrée fell asleep—or appeared to do so—immediately.

I wrote my notes in our meteorological journal.

Strindberg wrote in his little observation book.

"A letter to Anna?" I asked.

I curled up in the sleeping-bag.

It was midnight before Strindberg put his book and pen into his 'private' bag and lay down to sleep.

Gentle, intermittent gusts of wind made the canvas of the tent billow in and out. I became aware of the dull rumble of the pressure ice. Now and then there was a louder noise, like a cannonade. I guessed that it arose when a large floe broke in pieces, or when a small one, that had been upended, was pushed up so high that it finally fell down on to the surrounding ice.

I was tired, but not sleepy.

It was rather hot in the sleeping-bag.

"Good night, Nils Strindberg," I said.

"Good night, Knut Fraenkel," he answered.

10

I fell asleep last and woke first.

Both Andrée and Strindberg were fast asleep when I crawled out of the sleeping-bag. The sun was in the south, and it was almost hot in the tent.

"You're hard to wake," I said, "though you've slept for eleven or twelve hours."

We ate a hearty breakfast. Excellent thick, hot, meat soup, made from the contents of two tins from Beauvais' factory in Copenhagen, and some slices of rye bread with butter and cheese to go with it.

By two o'clock in the afternoon we were ready to start. The sun was still intensely hot, but clouds were gathering far away in the south-west.

We did as we had done on the previous day: all pulled one sledge about five hundred metres until we were halted by a lead, turned back and fetched the other two sledges, one at a time.

It was slow work, but our shoulders were so badly chafed by our efforts of the previous day that, though the ice was good, it would have been quite senseless to suppose that one man could pull a sledge by himself.

The lead was not more than fifteen metres across.

It was almost entirely free of floes. It ran in a north-east, south-west direction. It was obvious that we had to cross it.

Andrée and Strindberg engaged in a lengthy argument as to how best to force a passage. They then went off in different directions to look for suitable floes for a bridge, each armed with a boat-hook.

I unloaded the boat, took it from my sledge, and put it into the water, securely moored to the edge of the ice.

Then, not without an effort, I managed to shoot the sledge along the boat at right angles to its length.

The boat floated perfectly, like a swan.

I paddled across the lead with an oar, landed, and pulled the sledge down on to the ice.

I returned and ferried across the tent, the sleeping-bag, and the rest of my load.

It did not take long, and I managed yet another journey before Andrée and Strindberg got back, the one from the south, the other from the north.

I had just loaded another hundred kilos or so on to the boat, including my two companions' 'private' bags.

Before anyone had time to utter a word I had jumped on board, and the impetus of my leap was strong enough to carry the boat to the other side. The lead was only fifteen metres broad.

Unloading my cargo took only a few seconds. I then gave the boat a shove that sent it slowly across to the northern side of the lead where it was caught by Strindberg.

"I've done my bit now," I said, "and by Jove I'm ready for a smoke."

I sat down on the rolled up sleeping-bag and lit my pipe.

"I won't give you any advice," I said. "But if I were you, I should get the heaviest and largest things from the sledges and ferry them across first. Take the ones that it's easiest to unload.

"After that," I said, "I should put the sledges, one at a time, at right angles across the boat, and ferry them across to this side of the lead."

It was easy to talk across the water. The lead was of course only fifteen metres wide.

I lay on my back on the bundle of sleeping-bag, looked at the sky that grew more and more cloudy, and continued to make remarks about what Andrée and Strindberg were doing.

"I really believe," I said, "that we could ferry the sledges across as they are, fully loaded. All at one go. But of course it's best to begin rather carefully, to feel one's way."

After about an hour, the whole expedition, men and all, was assembled on the right side of the lead.

The sledges were reloaded.

"You would do well to learn the art of holding your tongue," said Andrée, when for a moment he happened to be standing beside me.

He uttered the twelve words in a low, quiet and friendly voice.

"Yes," I said.

"Or no, why should I hold my tongue?"

The boat was waiting at the edge of the ice. I got no answer.

I drew up the boat, turned it upside down, crept under it, rose, carried it on my outstretched arms to my sledge, and placed it in its right position on the felt.

I I

We set off again towards the south-east, all three pulling Andrée's sledge.

Went back to fetch Strindberg's sledge. It took us about fifteen minutes to get back to where we had left the first sledge, by which time we had covered about a kilometre, according to Andrée's pedometer.

It took us five minutes longer to pull my sledge.

After we had gone another kilometre or so we reached a new lead.

The sky was now quite overcast. The wind was a little stronger. At times we were exposed to short-lived showers of wet snow, or equally brief showers of fine drizzle.

This new lead too was open water, in which there was no floating ice suitable for making a bridge.

Andrée was hesitant and undecided. He did not trust the boat he himself had designed, or helped to design.

I unloaded the boat, lifted it from my sledge and put it in the water. I then shoved my fully loaded sledge across it at right angles to its length.

"Its carrying capacity is greater than you think," I said. "And my sledge is the heaviest."

We were all three across the lead in less than half an hour, and five minutes later had resumed our journey towards the south-east.

Half an hour later we encountered a new lead, the broadest so far.

This time the ferrying was done, not without difficulty, but entirely without doubt.

We came upon the absolutely fresh track of a bear in the thin layer of snow.

Strindberg and I followed it for a few kilometres, but in vain, and we returned to the sledges.

Andrée had wrapped himself in a blanket and was asleep under the lee of my sledge.

On the blanket lay a light sprinkling of snow, hardly more than a symbol.

He was deeply, heavily asleep. I put my hand on his shoulder and shook him gently. He woke with a start and sat up.

"We lost the bear," said Strindberg.

"If only we'd brought at least one pair of skis," I said.

We ate a spartan meal and then pushed on, mainly in a south south-easterly direction.

We adopted the same tactics as before: all three pulled one sledge a short way, returned and fetched the other two, one by one.

The fog grew denser. The velocity of the wind slowly increased.

We pitched camp at ten o'clock in the evening, according to Strindberg's time.

Putting up the tent did not take many minutes.

Strindberg made a peculiar soup of Rousseaus' powder, butter, condensed milk, peas, and two cubes of chicken stock.

Andrée believed that, with the assistance of his pedometer, he could say that we had covered a distance of nearly two kilometres since Strindberg and I had gone off on our unsuccessful bear-hunt.

A southerly wind and light snow-fall when we woke. Temp. minus ½.

"Not very tempting," said Strindberg, when he put his head through the opening of the tent. "But we've got to loosen up our arms and legs in any case, so we may as well continue our stroll towards Franz Josef Land."

We did not actually get off until towards afternoon. We still pursued the same time-consuming method of pulling the sledges one by one.

We constantly encountered leads and cracks which made the stages of our journey short. By degrees the ridges of pressure ice grew higher and more and more difficult to cross.

We followed a broad channel in the ice, a sort of stagnant, arctic river, constantly joined by little tributaries of stagnant streams and brooks, separated by ridges of piled-up ice, and isolated marsh-like patches of slushy snow.

The ridges of pressure ice were more troublesome than the ferrying or 'bridge-building'. The largest of them were certainly seven or eight metres high, and hauling the sledges up between the blocks required enormous exertions, especially as we constantly slipped into cracks and crevices that were concealed by the fresh snow.

The sledges were being strained to breaking point. At times they swung about like loosely bound rafts of logs in a choppy sea. On several occasions when we encountered a particularly steep ridge of ice, we had to lift the boat off my sledge, pull the sledge over first, and then fetch the boat. Sometimes we were even obliged to carry out the same manoeuvre with Andrée's and Strindberg's sledges: lift off the heaviest baskets of provisions, drag the sledge over, and then go back for the baskets.

We rested on a floe.

"How far have we gone?" I asked Andrée. "What does the pedometer say?"

"Difficult mathematics," said Strindberg. "We walk each stretch at least three times.

"No, five times. There are two sledges to fetch, remember, and extra trips to fetch the boat and the baskets in addition to that."

On one occasion we had covered altogether eleven hundred metres in order to transport our equipment over an area of pressure ice only a hundred metres wide.

"The question is whether we ought not to reduce our loads," said Andrée. "The question is whether either we or the toboggans can stand the strain."

There were many arguments in favour of this measure.

"The first things to go will have to be some of our provisions," said Andrée.

"What was it you said about Nansen's journey across Greenland?" I asked. "His sledges only weighed a hundred kilos. They wouldn't have been able to manage more because they were travelling uphill, towards a height of two thousand eight hundred metres above sea-level.

"We, on the other hand, were going to remain at sea-level. Isn't that so?

"How many toroses have we forced so far today? Twenty of them? Is that enough? Average height about five metres. Twenty times five makes a rise of a hundred metres.

"What distance have we covered? Say one kilometre. So, in principle we remain at sea-level, but when we've covered a kilometre we have in practice hauled our sledges up to a height of a hundred metres."

Andrée burst out laughing. "You exaggerate so confoundedly," he said. "The toroses aren't usually five metres high. Four hundred and seventy-five centimetres at the most."

At our midday break we ate bread, butter, and cheese.

Strindberg and I were content to chew snow as a mealtime drink, but Andrée went to a puddle in the floe and fetched water in an empty aluminium bread-tin.

Half-way back he took a sip from the tin, stopped dead and spat it out, coughing hard.

"Down the wrong lane?" I asked.

Andrée turned, took a few steps towards the puddle, cautiously tasted the water again, and spat.

"Salty as sin," he answered.

He walked round the sheet of water once—it was more than a hundred metres broad. In some places he sank quite deep into the slushy snow.

He walked away towards the far edge of the floe, nearly up to the ridges of pressure ice that surrounded it. He walked along beside these ridges, and thus described another circle, but now in the opposite direction. He stopped several times. Twice he stumbled and fell down.

We followed his doings with rising interest.

"He must have walked a good hundred metres in going round the sheet of water," I said, "and at least another eight hundred metres when he went round the outer edge of the floe. Add to that the radial distances and, to put it briefly, before he gets back he'll have covered a greater distance than the whole expedition has so far covered today."

"I've not got the slide-rule handy," said Strindberg, "but I think you've arrived at figures of about the right order of magnitude."

We lit our pipes and waited for Andrée to return.

"Well?"

"The water in the puddle is sea water," he said, "not melt water, not fresh water, but the saltiest of salty sea water."

"Wash down the salt with snow," I said. "It's guaranteed salt-less."

"The puddle is only a couple of decimetres deep," he said. "The floe is floating nearly half a metre above sea-level. There must be some reasonable explanation of why the water is salt."

"Cracks," suggested Strindberg.

But Andrée had not found any cracks. He had walked once round the puddle, and once round the outer edge of the floe, and besides, even salt water could not run uphill.

Andrée had an open sore under his left armpit, made by the webbing of his harness. It was difficult to bandage. I covered it with lanolin ointment and a compress. I wanted to keep this in place, if I could, with a triangular bandage which we managed, with some difficulty, to put across his chest and back, and fasten on his right shoulder.

For reasons which it is not difficult to understand he refused to undress in the wind and snow.

"What about reducing our loads?"

"A serious matter," he answered.

"Perhaps it would be better to wait a little longer before coming to a decision," he said. "Who knows what the ice will be like a few kilometres further south-east? And who knows how the currents and the winds affect the movements of the ice?"

"It was you who brought the matter up," I said, "not we."

"I can't understand it," he said. "On a compact floe, a puddle of sea water, a puddle the bottom of which lies at least three decimetres above sea level. A puddle of sea water, bitingly salt."

Running immediately along the edge of the river-like channel was a flat 'bank' of ice. Its width varied between two and five metres.

We tried to walk along this bank.

It had a light covering of snow over which the runners of the sledges glided very easily. For an hour each of us even managed to pull his own sledge.

The 'tributaries' of open water were so narrow that we were able to cross them without too much difficulty.

The ice edges of the bank were however by no means reliable. The falling snow concealed cracks. Thin, newly-formed crusts of ice also looked safe when they were covered by snow.

Strindberg was far too incautious.

Andrée and I suddenly heard his urgent cry for help. His sledge was still on the bank, but he himself was a couple of metres out in the channel.

It did not take us more than two minutes to pull him out by his haul-rope and his harness.

At first he laughed, but then fell in a heap on the ice.

He was breathing extremely rapidly, and he was deathly pale. The expression on his face was one of bewilderment, there is no other word for it. He could not speak.

We undressed him, wrapped him in Doctor Lembke's blanket, and massaged his arms and legs.

I fetched a little reinforced schnapps, and gave him two good drams of it. Then I made coffee which we all drank.

"Damned cold water," was the first thing he said when he had regained control of his breathing, his tongue, and his lips.

I wrung out his wet clothes, rolled them into a bundle, and took dry clothes out of his private bag. He pulled them on lying under the blanket to keep off the falling snow.

He swayed when he got to his feet and moved unsteadily.

"My muscles are aching," he said. "How long was I in the water?"

"Three minutes," I said, "possibly four. And then it must have been about as long before we got your wet clothes off."

"The temperature of the water is minus 1.9 Centigrade," said Andrée, holding a thermometer in his hand. "Half a metre under the surface," he added.

An hour later we were again trudging along the bank, but now showing greater respect for the outer edge. Each man was pulling his own sledge.

Andrée first, then I, last Strindberg.

The intense whiteness of the falling snow, and the fog, and the diffuse light irritated my eyes.

Andrée walked slowly.

I twice shed my harness and helped to bring Strindberg close up to Andrée, then went back to fetch my own sledge. Andrée did not even look over his shoulder.

After an hour, or an hour and a half, Andrée stopped. We pulled up beside him.

He took out a half bottle of sherry—obviously put in an easily accessible place in his luggage—and opened it with a corkscrew.

He looked at his chronometer. Some minutes passed.

"Now," he said, "now it's twelve o'clock midnight at home in dear old Sweden. We've crossed the boundary to Sunday, 25 July.

"It's your fiancée's birthday," he said to Strindberg. "I don't know how old she is. One ought never to know a lady's age, however young she is."

He then called for three cheers for Anna Charlier.

"Here's to Anna," he said, and gave the bottle he'd opened to Strindberg.

Strindberg drank, and passed it to me. I drank and handed the bottle back to Andrée.

"Of course it would have been more like a celebration if we could have drunk simultaneously," said Andrée. "But our mugs are far too well packed away in some other toboggan than mine."

Andrée sank on to his sledge and gently stroked the sore place under his left armpit with his right hand.

Strindberg sat beside him, close to him, and leaned his forehead against his shoulder.

They talked to each other for a little while, in voices so low that I neither could nor would hear what they were saying.

I had—I have—difficulty in analysing my attitude to Andrée.

To begin with an excess of confidence and trust.

Then a sprinkling of doubt, uncertainty and mistrust.

But this halt at twelve o'clock midnight on the night of 24th-25th July, to celebrate the birthday of Strindberg's fiancée?

Deliberate?

Spontaneous?

Soon after this Andrée rose, shouldered his harness, and continued his march towards the south-east.

In less than half an hour we reached a large floe, more than a kilometre wide. We pitched our camp in the middle of it.

Strindberg had been stumbling along in the rear. I went to meet him and helped him over the last lap.

I 2

We ate a substantial evening meal—night meal if you prefer.

Afterwards we drank strong coffee.

We found it hard to settle down to sleep, possibly because of the coffee.

We felt thirsty, and opened a little bottle of fruit juice, which we diluted with melt water.

We discussed our situation in detail.

"All my calculations indicate that we shall have to winter on Franz Josef Land," said Strindberg. "If we're lucky, with Jackson at Cape Flora. If we're unlucky, in Nansen's hovel. There's no point in hoping that we shall get home before next summer."

"I'm sure you're right," said Andrée. "I pointed it out time after time to I don't know how many journalists. But it seemed to me that they all counted on our being on dry land by this time."

"You led all those journalists astray," I said. "You told them that the *Eagle* would remain afloat for at least a month. Everyone thinks that we're now in Alaska, or Siberia. But the *Eagle* didn't keep afloat for a month. Only for sixty-five hours.

"Now we're on the pack ice.

"Sledges that are too heavily laden.

"Not even one pair of skis.

"Not on our way to the North Pole, but on our way south. Sail north through the air in a balloon; struggle south across pressure ice and leads."

"I warned you the first time we met," said Andrée.

"Don't misunderstand me," I said. "I'm not grumbling. But a month is a month, and sixty-five hours are only sixty-five hours. It's a question of facts.

"Into the bargain," I said, "there's this confounded whiteness! Fog, falling snow, ice covered by snow, no shadows, no visibility, impossible to reckon the distance from one ridge of pressure ice to the next—fifty metres or two hundred metres.

"Even the open water in the channels and leads is white. The tent and the sledges are white with snow. The only things that are not white are you two. And myself, the little I can see of myself.

"A man can't see much of himself without a mirror. His chest, his stomach, his feet, his legs, no, not even the whole of his legs. The back sides of his thighs are partially inaccessible. His arms, almost the whole of his shoulders, certain bits of his back. Come to think of it, quite a lot really."

We went to bed in the sleeping-bag.

Andrée had a rubber pillow that he inflated with a mouthpiece.

"It's comfortable," he said. "I've thought of chucking it away several times, simply because I'm the only one who has one, because you haven't any pillows."

"We don't begrudge you your pillow," said Strindberg.

"It's a moral problem," said Andrée. "We're all three in the same situation, the same predicament. We're all three dependent upon one another. Our way of life is pure socialism.

"I always sleep with my head high," he said. "I sometimes have migraine. That's why I want to sleep with my head high. It's doctor's orders."

"I'm a smoker," I said, and lit my pipe, stopped with Tiedemann's tobacco. "We're all three in the same situation. We're dependent upon one another. Our way of life is pure socialism. You don't smoke, Andrée. But it would never occur to me to chuck my pipe away because of that."

He chuckled.

After a while he said:

"I'm conscious of my weaknesses. They're part and parcel of my strong will, my obstinacy. I'd made up my mind to carry out this voyage to the north in a balloon. And when I've once made up my mind to a thing, then I *must* carry it through. And now we're here, not balloonists in the air, but wanderers on the ice."

The falling snow was settling more thickly on the outside of the tent, and as it did so the inside grew progressively darker.

"And you, Nisse," I said. "What are your weaknesses? I'm not asking out of idle curiosity, I'm really interested."

"I've many," he answered.

"Any predominant ones?"

"Don't know."

"Try to think."

At last he said:

"Possibly that I'm much too great an optimist."

His answer was followed by the obvious question: "And you, Knut, what are your weaknesses?"

"My body consists of about ninety-five kilos of bone and well-trained muscle," I said, "plus a certain quantity of perfectly functioning bowels. In my clothes I weigh what Nansen would have thought too heavy a load to put on any of his sledges when he was marching across the Greenland Ice Sheet."

"But your weaknesses?"

"I wanted to be one of the first three men to reach the North Pole," I said.

Eight or nine hours later I was awakened by the splash of rain.

It is possible that it was not the rain that woke me but the way the ice was trembling and quaking.

This quaking surprised me. The floe, in the middle of which we had pitched our camp, was at least a kilometre square.

The rumblings of the pressure ice were louder than on the previous day. All the same the trembling and quaking of our floe surprised me. I was sure that it must represent a weight and mass of three or four million tons.

The wind was slight and changeable. The rain was pouring down. The temperature was just above zero. The visibility at best two hundred metres.

I finished making my observations. Felt the rain running down the back of my neck while I relieved nature.

Andrée was lying on his back with his mouth open.

Strindberg had crept lower in the sleeping-bag, and was lying curled up like a bundle.

After a fairly prolonged hesitation, for which I cannot account, I woke them.

It was at least half an hour before they were fully awake.

"Rain?" asked Andrée.

"Rain," I answered.

I fetched water from a puddle. "Guaranteed fresh," I said.

Strindberg made cocoa after he had mixed the water with a tin of condensed milk. We ate biscuits and butter.

It was four hours before we were on the move again.

The rain had eased off to drizzle, but as the fog had simultaneously thickened, the visibility had diminished still further.

"A desert of whiteness," I said.

It was impossible to locate the sun or take our bearings. We trudged on under a huge, limitless dome of whiteness.

As on the previous day we kept to the bank that ran beside the large channel.

According to our compasses it ran in a south-easterly direction.

The geographical North Pole is one thing, the magnetic pole is another.

Ross, not the great Captain Ross, but his nephew, had established the position of the magnetic pole seventy years ago. That was all very well, but we knew nothing about what local magnetic declinations there might be in the spot in which we found ourselves.

"But by and large," said Andrée.

The runners of our sledges glided well over the rain-drenched snow. It also offered a firm foothold, and we were each able to pull our own sledge.

In spite of the misfortune of the previous day Strindberg was careless, and once more ended up in the water.

Fortunately we got him out quickly, and he did not show any signs of having been severely chilled.

He stripped down to the skin and I supplied him with clothes out of my private bag.

"A bit on the large side," he said, "but better too large than too small."

On a number of occasions we saw seals, not herds of them but single individuals.

Strindberg and Andrée engaged in a silly discussion as to whether they were Greenland seals or ringed seals.

Strindberg fired a shot, but missed.

"No point," I said. "If you kill a seal in the water he will simply sink. Wait," I said, "until you can fire a shot that will kill, at a seal that is lying on the ice."

The going got worse after a few hours, and we had to revert to our method of all three pulling one sledge at a time, and then returning to fetch the others.

"You said something about reducing our loads," I said to Andrée. "Was it yesterday, or the day before, or even longer ago?"

"We must discuss the matter," he said.

"When?"

"As soon as possible."

We had to ferry ourselves over channels and leads a number of times. They were all very troublesome and exhausting.

Once, when we were resting, Andrée asked me to help him

with the sore place under his armpit. It had got bigger, and his shirt and his chest were caked with blood.

I cleaned it as best as I could and covered it again with ointment and a gauze compress.

"It must hurt like hell," I said.

"No," he replied.

We came to a broad lead, so broad that we decided to pitch camp for the night.

The tent was wet, and heavy to put up.

We opened a tin of Beauvais' meat from Copenhagen and shared it between us. We were too tired to light the primus stove.

Strindberg fell asleep, and did not wake up when I pulled the chronometer out of his coat pocket—Greenwich mean time—for the notes I wanted to make in our meteorological journal.

Slight northerly wind. A few degrees below zero. The rain had stopped and in its place snow was falling lightly. Thick fog or mist. Visibility, one hundred to two hundred metres. Humidity low.

I walked a good hundred steps in a southerly direction. The tent and the sledges were barely visible. Visibility must be nearer a hundred to a hundred and fifty metres.

The tent and the sledges were hidden under snow.

I was in a little world of whiteness which I knew was a vast desert of ice and snow and whiteness.

I spread out Strindberg's wet clothes on the sleeping-bag. I lit the primus stove and left it burning on a low light for thirty minutes, having first closed the opening of the tent.

The temperature rose rapidly.

"Who's that?" asked Andrée.

"Only me."

He was asleep.

"Good," he said.

"A desert of whiteness," I answered. "And above us a dome of whiteness that isn't quite white, absurdly enough, either a small one or a very large one. The dome I mean."

13

We awoke, and I could record the same weather as on the previous day, or really, when we went to bed, for that had been on this same day, though only just after midnight.

Light snowfall, small dry flakes. Half a degree of frost, Centigrade. Fog, visibility at the most one hundred and fifty to two hundred metres. Wind slight, direction variable.

Two bears, one large and one small, had prowled round the tent during the night. One of them—the small one—had clawed at the baggage on Andrée's sledge.

Strindberg made our breakfast soup out of Rousseaus' meat-powder, having first ascertained that his clothes were nearly dry, the clothes I had spread out over the sleeping-bag.

"What are we going to do about the loads on our sledges?" I asked.

"There are many arguments in favour," said Andrée. "There are many arguments against."

"You don't know."

"No," he answered.

"By the sound of your no," I said, "you've quite made up your mind."

Strindberg and I took down the tent while Andrée ferried my sledge across the wide lead on the boat.

He returned and we helped him to place his own sledge athwart the boat.

I carried the tent and the sleeping-bag down to the lead.

Suddenly a shot rang out.

A whip cracking, a detonation, in the midst of all that opaque whiteness.

Strindberg had shot a polar bear hardly fifteen metres from the spot where our tent had been.

I ran up to him with my Remington at the ready. Strindberg's bullet had hit the bear between an ear and an eye. No further shot to finish him off was needed.

Andrée was soon beside us.

Strindberg sank to his knees beside the bear, stroked its head, and lifted up one of its heavy paws.

He looked at us with shining eyes. His mouth was half open. "By Jove," he said. "The first polar bear of my life."

We ferried all our equipment, including Strindberg's bear, over the lead.

We spread out our belongings on a small floe.

It took us two or three hours to ferry the things across.

The slight, variable wind veered north, and increased to breeze force. It stopped snowing. The fog dispersed a little. The air grew both colder and drier.

We had a long and thorough discussion of the necessity that might arise of reducing the weight of the loads on our sledges.

The cloud-cover thinned for about half an hour, and the disc of the sun became visible. Strindberg and I both took our bearings independently.

The result in both cases was the same.

For five days we had marched towards the south-east. During these same days the ice had drifted towards the east, or north-east.

After five days of the most strenuous exertions we had not in fact reduced the distance between ourselves and Franz Josef Land by more than something between two thousand five hundred metres and three thousand metres.

"Five or six hundred metres a day," I said.

These figures were decisive.

We pitched the tent once more on the far side of the lead, less than a hundred metres from our camp of the previous night.

We ate a hearty meal of fillet of polar bear, unhung it is true, but tender, and with an excellent flavour.

After that we unloaded all the sledges, repaired them where necessary, and shoed the runners with metal.

"Working methodically like this is delightful," said Strindberg.

We all agreed that we must reduce the loads on our sledges enough to make unnecessary the time-consuming labour of all three pulling one at a time.

Each of us must in future be able to cope with his own sledge.

Our stock of provisions was the first thing to be hit by this decision.

This step was easy to take after we had filled our stomachs with Strindberg's fillet of polar bear.

The reloading and repair work took up the whole day, or, to be exact, the rest of that day and the whole of the following night. We did not get to bed until between six and seven o'clock in the morning.

We had reduced the load on our sledges to between a hundred and thirty and a hundred and forty kilos.

Before we went to bed we indulged in a fantastic celebration dinner composed of the provisions we had thrown out.

We concluded the meal with a bottle of champagne.

"Intended for the North Pole?" I asked.

"Intended to be drunk," replied Andrée.

What did we eat?

Pickled pigs' trotters. A large tin of liver paste. Two tins of ham. Corned beef. Pressed tongue. Salt meat. Stewed beef. Half a dozen tins of sardines in tomato sauce. Herring. Peaches. Pineapple, and pears in syrup.

The argument between Andrée and Strindberg on the necessity for foods rich either in albuminoids or carbohydrates broke out anew.

We calculated that our provisions, not including what we got by hunting, should last for forty-five days.

14

We slept our eight or nine hours.

Light northerly wind, overcast sky, two degrees below zero.

Strindberg fried some bear steaks. "Rather unusual for breakfast," he said, "but then it's rather unusual to be eating breakfast at four o'clock in the afternoon."

During our meal we heard a gentle splash, and saw a bear come swimming across the lead near our camp. It glided with supple movements up on to the ice on our side, came to a halt a hundred metres away, and gazed at us, describing small circular movements with its head.

"He's not even shaking the water off himself," said Andrée.

"He," I said. "Are you sure it's not a bitch?"

"It's the smell from the newly-fried steaks," said Strindberg.

"The wind isn't blowing that way," I said.

"Our larder's full at the moment, altogether too full," said Strindberg.

We looked at the bear, and the bear looked at us, quite motionless except for its rotating head.

We blew our whistles. The bear did not budge.

After a couple of minutes I got up and picked up my Remington.

"It's my turn now," I said.

I walked towards the bear. Strindberg followed close on my heels, armed with his double-barrelled gun, coarse shot in one barrel, a sharp-nosed explosive bullet in the other, the grooved barrel. Andrée stayed at the opening of the tent.

"You needn't go so damned near," said Strindberg, when we were about fifty steps from the bear.

I pulled up for a moment. "I want to see what he'll do," I said. "He's a big brute."

At the sound of my voice the bear lowered the forepart of his body, stretched out his neck, and stiffened.

I advanced slowly with the gun raised. When I could hear his breathing—he was breathing, not panting—I stopped, took aim, and fired. The bear sank in a heap, his legs did not so much as twitch.

"Good," I said. "Now there's a corpse. I aimed between his eyes, black fore-sight, black back-sight against white head."

Our third bear was the cause of a fresh argument between Andrée and Strindberg about our need of carbohydrates versus albuminoids.

We arranged our provisions again. Tins of meat and meat-powders were discarded in favour of tins of bread that we had thrown out the day before.

Of course we could only take with us the best bits of the two bears.

My bear had a splendidly close, soft pelt, and Andrée thought it would be a good idea to keep some parts of it for the time when we had to repair our sleeping-bag.

All this further delayed us, and we did not leave our camping-place until after midnight.

The temperature had sunk again and the leads were covered by a thin film of ice.

In order to save the balloon-silk of the boat from being cut to bits when we ferried our sledges across, we had to take great care to break the ice up into small pieces.

The leads were separated by ridges of pressure ice which were high, but not very broad. Time after time, though we had reduced the load on our sledges, we all three had to drag them one at a time over the blocks of ice.

When we pitched camp Andrée and Strindberg sat watching silently while I put up the tent and dragged in the sleeping-bag.

"You'll have to do the dinner, Strindberg," I said. "It's your job. I'm sure Andrée will help you to get out the food if you ask him nicely.

"I'm devilishly tired too," I added.

"In a bad temper?" asked Andrée.

"No," I answered. "I'm well known for the sweetness and even-ness of my disposition."

Strindberg boiled up two litres of meat soup. "Best to keep to what's easily swallowed," he said.

We stretched ourselves out on the sleeping-bag and allowed our muscles to relax.

"Not a good day," I said. "We've been on the march for nine hours. We've forced fourteen channels and leads, and each of them has cost us half an hour. That leaves two hours of effective marching time, over ridges of piled up ice. Include in them a few short rests. How far have we got today, do you think?"

"We've had a pretty strong north-west wind," said Andrée, "and we can reckon that the drift of the ice has been in the right direction."

"Do you still trust the winds?" I said.

"As one aeronaut to another? As one balloonist to another?"

I suddenly had to go out of the tent.

"Now I've got rid of my debauch of the day before yesterday," I said when I returned. "It took time. But it was a relief, my breeches aren't as tight as they were."

Andrée and Strindberg followed my example.

"A certain amount of effort was required," said Andrée, "but it was finally crowned with success."

We crawled into the sleeping-bag.

"This absence of day and night," I said.

"You're right," said Andrée. "There's no rhythm in our existence. We sleep when it's convenient, we go to bed in the morning, sometimes begin our working-day at midnight, eat our breakfast in the afternoon, or in the middle of the night."

We discussed this lack of rhythm for a while.

Strindberg wrote in his notebook.

Just before I fell asleep I heard heavy drops of rain falling on the canvas of the tent.

The following day the wind was still north-westerly, two metres per second, half a degree of frost, fog, and snowing. The canvas of the tent was covered by a substantial crust of ice.

After doing some unavoidable repair-work on our sledges, and having a simple breakfast, we broke camp just before nine o'clock in the evening.

In the main we were still following the broad channel in the ice.

We got out on to a large floe, how large the thick fog made it impossible to say.

Our sledges slid easily over the crust of ice.

I expected to see a large toros, or a troublesome lead appear in our path at any moment. But we went on and on over smooth ice minute after minute, quarter hour after quarter hour, half hour after half hour.

The temperature again rose to above zero, and it began to rain slightly, but we still had the same smooth, flat ice.

The slushy snow and grease ice on the fresh-water puddles still bore the sledges, but we trod through them.

We paused for a short rest.

"This is what it ought to look like," said Strindberg.

Andrée was rather annoyed at getting his feet wet. At his special request we took out our Canadian snow-shoes. We had tried them out at Danes Island, but now, for the first time, we were going to make practical use of them.

Yes, they carried us, even in the slushiest places, but it was impossible to use them when pulling our sledges. Andrée walked about a hundred metres, but he sank to his knees time after time, and finally fell over.

Strindberg and I practised with them by making our way slowly and carefully up to him.

"You've got to straddle like a camel to walk with snow-shoes," I said.

Andrée replied that he had never heard that the Canadian Indian straddled like a camel.

Strindberg wondered if in fact camels straddled.

I asked them if they had never read Nansen's description of his crossing of Greenland. In it he had told of their unsuccessful attempt to use Canadian snow-shoes. The only result had been a series of somersaults.

"Snow-shoes are useful things to have," I said, "when you have to walk or run in loose snow after a toboggan drawn by dogs."

"What we need," I said, "is skis. Not ordinary skis, but the ones we have in Jämtland that are shod with elk-hide with the hairs running backwards."

* * *

We continued our journey across the floe without snow-shoes.

The wind became more northerly, and at times veered about ten degrees east of north. It increased in velocity.

There was no visibility to speak of.

We rested again, but did not allow ourselves long enough to cook food. Instead we contented ourselves with sandwiches and sweetened fruit juice.

"Your carbohydrates," Strindberg said to Andrée.

I measured the force of the wind—six metres per second. The temperature was one degree above zero.

Up to now Andrée had walked in front. I took his place after he had shown me our course by the compass.

The fog grew denser. My sledge slid easily over the snow. The whiteness was complete. If I looked to my left I sometimes caught a glimpse of the wide channel in the ice, a strip of something that was not quite white. Ahead there was nothing but limitless whiteness.

I kept expecting that we should be halted by a ridge of pressure ice, or a lead. But we were able to proceed across our flat desert of whiteness for hour after hour.

Now and then we crossed small rises in the snow and ice, probably the places where two gigantic floes had frozen together. They were invisible in the shadowless light, but I could feel them beneath my feet and by the way the resistance of the sledge increased for a few seconds.

There was nothing upon which to fix your gaze, nothing to catch your eye, and I consulted the compass every few minutes. I did not dare to rely on the wind as an indication of direction. And it was impossible even to guess the whereabouts of the sun behind the heavy clouds.

The only things that were not white were my companions behind me. I had to stop and wait for them several times.

"Tired?" I asked.

Of course they were tired.

"But we must take advantage of the conditions," I said. "Smooth ice, good going, and a favourable wind."

We did not dare to take any long rests. Our feet were soaking wet, we were damp with perspiration, and we began to shiver in the cold wind if we stopped, even for a few minutes.

"A straight course for Franz Josef Land," I said. "We're doing at least two kilometres an hour, possibly two and a half. Add to that the effect of the wind on the drift of the ice."

The intense whiteness bothered me, the absolute lack of anything upon which I could fix my gaze.

My eyes ran.

I put on my sun-glasses.

The ice was still flat, no toroses, no leads.

Andrée and Strindberg lagged behind. I slackened speed somewhat, but not enough to enable them to catch me up. I had to force them to exert themselves to the utmost. We must take advantage of the exceptionally favourable conditions.

I know that when one is dead tired one has at least half one's strength left.

I was dead tired myself. But then I was pulling the heaviest sledge. When we had rearranged our loads before starting off Andrée, to suit his calculations of the weight of the various items, had transferred the tent from my sledge to his. After the last rearrangement—occasioned by the bear I had shot—the tent was again on my sledge, and in addition the bear's pelt, and the portions of its flesh that we had kept.

We crossed at least half a dozen bear-tracks, most of them fresh, and all of them following a line at right angles to our route.

At one point Andrée and Strindberg stopped. I did not notice that they had done so until I was three or four hundred metres ahead of them.

I stopped too.

After about ten minutes they began to move again. I waited until they were about seventy-five metres away from me; then I too continued the march towards the south-east, towards Franz Josef Land.

It was a relief to be brought to a halt after another couple of hours by a very wide lead.

I had time to put up the tent and spread out the sleeping-bag and the blankets before Andrée and Strindberg arrived.

The wind was still strong, and from the north. Showers of drizzle, at times quite heavy.

"Our best day so far," I said.

Strindberg sat down on my sledge. "Listen, old boy," he said. "Don't just rush on ahead tomorrow, wait for us. It's so pleasant when we all keep together."

Andrée looked at his chronometer. "Sixteen hours," he said. "A good day's work.

"Or a good twenty-four hours' work."

"The hotel awaits you," I said.

"The kitchen staff suggests meat soup," said Strindberg.

"To hell with meat soup," I said. "We need something more substantial than meat soup. Even if it's strongly sugared with carbohydrates."

"Always ready to oblige," said Strindberg. He lit the primus stove, cut a piece of bear's meat, a kilo of it at least, into small bits, boiled it, put in some condensed milk and a couple of handfuls of flour, salt and pepper. Spread nine pieces of hard bread with butter, and put a thin slice of cheese on each.

We took off our breeches, stockings and boots, and hung them up to dry under the roof of the tent.

Strindberg pulled the primus inside the tent, and I let the flap fall into place.

The temperature rose rapidly to about twenty-five degrees.

Strindberg served our evening meal just before eleven o'clock in the morning.

"Absolutely excellent," said Andrée. "What do you call this dish?"

"Ragout Strindberg *ursus maritimus*," answered our chef.

"It's devilishly hot in here," I said.

"Let the stove burn for a little longer," said Andrée. "We must dry our clothes."

We scraped the bottom of the pan containing Strindberg's polar bear ragout and we each drank a little drop of fruit juice with our sandwiches.

276

I was very weary. My arms, my thighs, and my shoulders were tingling and tickling with weariness.

"You were wearing your sun-glasses," said Andrée.

"My eyes don't like this confounded whiteness," I answered.

I went outside to pee. Standing in my bare feet in the snow was not unpleasant.

Strindberg wrote in his notebook. "A letter to Anna?" I asked.

Andrée made some notes in his diary.

"A letter to whom?" I asked.

"To posterity," he answered.

"Oh indeed," I said, crept into the sleeping-bag on his right-hand side, and fell asleep instantly.

15

Ten millimetres of rain had fallen while we slept. The wind was still northerly, the temperature some tenths of a degree above zero. Thick mist.

We struck camp quickly—practice makes perfect.

We had to cross many leads, and it seemed quite natural that I should go first as the boat was on my sledge.

Between the leads, great stretches of floe, over which the sledges glided easily.

There was no visibility to speak of, and we had to rely entirely on our compasses.

I pursued the same tactics as on the previous day. I pushed on as hard as I could in order to entice the others to follow me.

The ice-fields between the many leads were broad enough to enable us to put behind us a considerable distance in the direction of Franz Josef Land.

We were helped by the northerly wind, which however decreased to a force of between three and four metres a second.

After a march of twelve hours, and just as we had made up our minds to pitch camp, Andrée slipped into a freshwater puddle.

We hauled him out snorting like a hippopotamus.

"Walrus," said Strindberg. "A snorting walrus without tusks."

My eyes bothered me. I could not stand the diffuse but intense light. I had to wear sun-glasses all the time though no sun was visible.

We were so weary when we bivouacked that we almost had to force ourselves to eat the food we knew we needed so badly.

We left the primus burning for quite a long time in order to dry our clothes.

16

On the evening of the following day the sun broke through the clouds, and we had a chance to take our bearings.

It was 31 July, the twenty-first day after our departure from Danes Island.

Strindberg and I each took a bearing, one immediately after the other. The result was the same for both of us.

During the past forty-eight hours we had travelled south-east, towards Franz Josef Land, under the most favourable conditions. We had put kilometre after kilometre behind us. But these two bearings proved indisputably that the ice had drifted further towards the west than we had succeeded in marching towards the south-east.

"And we've been having northerly winds too," I said.

Andrée went through our figures once again.

"The wind blows in one direction," I said, "but the ice drifts in another. We march in one direction, but we travel in another.

"How much nearer to our goal have we got after these forty-eight hours of forced march across smooth ice? Five hundred metres?"

"Approximately a kilometre," answered Andrée.

"But you've got the days mixed," he added. "It was yesterday and the day before that we had good ice. Today has been a fiendish day."

"Navigare necesse est," I said, and put the theodolite back in its case. *"Vivere non est necesse.*

"Or what, dear friends?"

"It's essential to navigate, but it's not so damned essential to survive."

It was a pleasant evening, temperature some degrees above zero, a light north wind, and sunshine.

We hung up our clothes and our blankets to dry on a rope stretched between the stem of the boat and an oar we had driven into the ice. Both Andrée and Strindberg had fallen into the water during the day. So far I had managed to avoid doing so, but my breeches had got very wet plodding through the slushy snow.

I followed the absolutely fresh tracks of a bear for a few kilometres west, but was forced to turn back at a lead four or five metres wide. If I had had skis I might have caught up with him.

His tracks went dead straight towards the west except for a few bends round projecting blocks of ice.

Fried bear's meat, sandwiches, and biscuits were awaiting me when I got back to the tent.

The humidity was low and our clothes dried quickly. Strindberg turned his private bag inside out to find if anything else was wet or damp.

At the bottom he found a mirror and gave a loud shout of joy: "At last I'll be able to see another face! Something a bit more human than your ugly mugs."

He leaned his head out of the tent to get a better view, rubbed the stubble on his face, studied his eyes and the cracks in his lips. "Not too bad in spite of everything," he said. "Cheeks a bit thinner. A full beard will probably be most becoming. Decidedly darker skin, half dirt no doubt, but half good honest sunburn.

"I'll let you hire my mirror," he said, "if you pay me well. I won't insist on cash. A written IOU will do quite well."

Andrée threatened violence. Strindberg tried to escape from the tent, but I caught hold of one of his feet, and Andrée sat on him and rubbed his head with snow until he voluntarily relinquished the mirror and solemnly agreed that in future it should be regarded as common property.

"You first," I said to Andrée, "by right of seniority."

He held the mirror in front of him. "Not particularly encouraging," he said at last. "My seniority seems to have increased by three or four years these past few weeks."

After that it was my turn.

The stubble on my face was thicker and stronger than I had imagined.

"Well?" asked Strindberg.

"Looking in a mirror is like standing face to face with yourself," I answered. "But you see yourself as it were darkly.

"I'm quoting Paul," I explained. "When one is a child one goes about with the mind of a child, thinking and hoping as a child. But when one is a grown man, then one sees oneself as in a glass, face to face, but one doesn't know what it is one's seeing. I can't remember the exact words," I said, "but it comes from that man Paul, you know, the fellow who wrote the letters in the Bible.

"Addressed to posterity."

Strindberg made us some cocoa, not much, two decilitres each. We did not drink our meagre ration until we had crept into the sleeping-bag.

Andrée made some quite extensive notes in his diary.

Strindberg wrote a letter to Anna.

I lit my pipe.

"That fuss over the mirror," I said.

Strindberg stopped writing.

"Yes," he said. "Egocentricity? Or just ordinary curiosity?"

The wind bloweth where it listeth. The ice drifteth where it listeth.

We march in one direction. We travel in another.

17

We continued our march towards the south-east, towards Franz Josef Land. In places the ice was good, in others it was intersected by leads and ridges of pressure ice.

We were again enveloped in dense fog.

At times we were able to cover six or seven kilometres in less than five hours. At others we had to toil for ten hours to cover two kilometres.

Our supply of bear's meat came to an end.

On the following day, to our surprise, we stumbled upon a bear just after striking camp. In our excitement Strindberg and I both missed him, but Andrée brought him down with a shot from his Remington.

It was our largest bear so far, but thin and dilapidated in spite of its weight and size.

Its teeth were severely affected by caries. We discussed this for hours. None of us had ever heard it spoken of except as a degenerative disease that only attacked man.

"It's probably an old bear from a menagerie who's succeeded in escaping from captivity," I said.

"How old can a bear, a polar bear live to be?"

Soon after twelve o'clock on the night between 3 and 4 August we had clear weather and good visibility.

After making thorough observations we were able to establish that, though we had obstinately marched south-east, we had in fact reached a position which was practically ten kilometres dead west of our camping-site of 31 July.

"We must consider whether to continue to press on towards Franz Josef Land, or to divert our steps towards the Seven Islands," said Andrée.

"Important decisions should not be taken on an empty stomach," I said.

We camped on a fairly large floe covered by snow with a hard crust of ice. The temperature had crept down to a couple of degrees below zero, as it usually did in clear weather.

Strindberg fried a number of slices from the pieces of meat we had brought with us from Andrée's bear of the decayed teeth.

It was as tough and hard to masticate as if it had been impregnated with rubber.

To complete our meal we had a sort of stodgy gruel made of meat-powder, Mellin's Food.

Hunger is the best sauce.

"We must make up our minds," said Andrée.

"You don't say so," I said.

"For two weeks we've made for Franz Josef Land," he said. "We've dragged our toboggans at least a hundred and fifty, possibly two hundred kilometres. But the drift of the ice has thwarted us. We've drifted towards the north, towards the north-west, towards the west. Perhaps in actual fact we've only got forty kilometres nearer our goal."

"Are the figures you quote exact or only apparently exact?" I asked.

"Apparently exact," he replied.

"You've got to know the exact time before you can determine your position in an east-west direction.

"A difference of more than two minutes has developed between our three chronometers, Strindberg's two and mine, since we left Danes Island," he said. "One of them is telling the wrong time, probably all three are. We can't trust any of them. Therefore we can't establish our longitude with certainty."

"Go on," I said, "as between mathematicians, engineers and aeronauts."

"We're drifting westwards, that's indisputable. The ice is drifting westwards."

"That can't be news to you," I said. "Nansen's *Fram* also drifted from east to west. Frozen into the polar ice. For two or three years, or thereabouts."

"Do let us discuss the matter calmly," he said.

"We are discussing it calmly," I answered.

"You simply want us to make up your mind for you," I said.

"What do you mean?" he asked.

"You want us to consign Franz Josef Land, Cape Flora and Frederick Jackson to the devil, and to march towards the Seven Islands instead."

"The drift of the ice argues in favour of that alternative," he said.

"Nils Strindberg," I said, half lifting myself up, "what do you think? Franz Josef Land or the Seven Islands?"

Strindberg had crept down into the sleeping-bag.

"The Seven Islands," he said sleepily, and with a dry tongue. "Seven's a good number."

Andrée and I also settled down to sleep and rest.

"Two capitulations," I said.

"The first: give up our plans to reach the North Pole. The second: give up our plans to reach Franz Josef Land.

"If you think about it," I said, "there have really been three capitulations."

"What do you mean by that?" asked Andrée.

"The start," I answered. "Our start from Danes Island, when the downward currents of air forced the *Eagle* on to the water and you and Strindberg lost your heads completely, and cut away bag after bag of sand.

"If you hadn't done that," I said, "the *Eagle* wouldn't have been converted into a free-sailing balloon, and suffered the unnecessary loss of gas those words imply. If you hadn't done that the ballast-ropes would have functioned properly, and we might have found ourselves in Alaska or Siberia by this time."

I added: "If we'd even lengthened all three guide-ropes we might have made it to some extent dirigible."

Strindberg said sleepily: "What's the good of talking about the balloon that sailed last year."

I helped Andrée with the sore place under his armpit. It had healed well and would certainly not trouble him at all in a few days' time.

18

On the afternoon of 4 August we ate a hearty breakfast of the meat from Andrée's tough bear.

While we were packing up Andrée made a rapid inventory, and came to the conclusion that we must be careful, especially with all our farinacious food.

"Why so?" I asked. "Why should we be careful about our carbohydrates? They're surely the things we need most."

"Don't worry," said Strindberg. "I'm sure we shall find enough bears and seals and other concentrations of proteins."

The bearings we took when the sun peeped through were reasonably satisfactory, and guided by the sun we fixed our course towards our new objective, the Seven Islands.

One hour after breakfast we were all three standing harnessed to our sledges in marching order. I first, then Andrée and last Strindberg.

"Is the caravan ready to leave the serai?" I asked. "The blessed fog has returned, there's no visibility to speak of, the signs from the heavens would seem to favour departure."

"The bells of the snow-shoeless camels are ringing impatiently," answered Strindberg.

"There's only one God," I said. "May He hold His warmly gloved hand over us! Onwards to the seven-branched group of islands. The Seven Islands of Arctic Wisdom! Where Parry started and finished his journey to the north seventy years ago.

"Course S. 40° W.," I said, and jerked my sledge into motion.

Days and nights of monotony.

Heavy clouds, fog, mist, snow, rain, a few moments when the sun broke through, often so brief that we had not time to get out the instruments necessary for determining our position.

The arctic topography too was monotonous. Ridges of pressure ice, which it cost us the maximum of physical effort to surmount and cross. Leads and channels of open water, across which we could only force our way by building bridges of floating floes, or by ferrying ourselves across in the boat.

The flat floes, across which we could travel at a fairly brisk pace, were also monotonous.

Equally monotonous were the alternations between crusty snow, glazed ice, loose snow, and shallow puddles of fresh water with fragile ice on top.

Our clothes were always wet; because of rain, because we had fallen into leads, or stumbled and fallen when the ice on the fresh-water puddles broke under us.

We pitched camp, put up the tent. We ate a fairly decent evening meal, we slept, we woke, we ate a relatively hearty breakfast, struck camp, pushed on S.40°W., pitched camp, ate a fairly decent evening meal, and so on.

It was not all monotony.

The wind veered for a few days and nights and became southerly. Andrée was afraid we should drift northwards.

"Do you still believe in the winds?" I asked. "As between aeronauts?"

We began to be troubled by runny noses, a sort of catarrh, a sort of cold in the head. But colds do not occur in these northern latitudes. "A medical impossibility," said Strindberg.

By degrees the temperature sank, but it grew hotter and hotter in the tent. Andrée and I took to sleeping not in, but on top of the sleeping-bag, each wrapped in a blanket. Andrée complained that his jacket was much too warm. But if he took it off he immediately started to shiver.

I was attacked by sudden, violent pains in my stomach, stopped, bent forward, and only succeeded in getting my breeches and long pants down just in time. My faeces came bursting out of me in a spray, and spattered all over the ice.

There I crouched. On my right Andrée, on my left Strindberg, both regarding me and the plight I was in with interest, and not without a certain uneasy amusement.

When I had done, I straightened up, after first washing my crotch with snow.

"I'm not shy by nature," I said.

"No, no," answered Andrée. "Forgive us."

"Aren't you going to keep a sample of my excrement," I said, "in the interests of science? And measure the thickness of the pack ice, one metre or two point four metres? Make a note of the direction and force of the wind, the temperature and the humidity?"

Andrée's tough bear of the decaying teeth grew more and more tender as the days passed.

"All meat should be hung," said Strindberg.

"Or be taken for a bumpy journey through the world," I answered. "Be ridden tender as it was under the saddles of the Huns."

19

I had a second violent attack of diarrhoea.

Immediately after it we saw a polar bear looming out of the fog. Strindberg and I tried to creep up to him, I with my Remington, Strindberg with his double-barrelled gun.

The bear turned aside, at first hesitantly and slowly, but he finally made off with tremendous bounds towards the east.

This happened on a large floe covered with fairly dry, powdery snow.

"If only we'd had skis," I said.

"We haven't any skis," answered Strindberg.

When we returned Andrée was putting up the tent.

"Well?" he asked.

"We couldn't catch him up," I said. "We could have done if we'd had a pair of skis instead of just camel's snow-shoes."

Strindberg weighed out seven hundred and fifty grammes of the meat of our tough old bear, cut it into very small cubes, fried it quite quickly, and then made a strong sauce.

The stew was divided between us in three strictly equal portions.

For dessert we ate an almond cake, produced by magic from a small tin.

The sun was visible through the clouds for a few moments and Strindberg and I took our bearings.

We consumed our almond cake, slowly.

An almond cake eaten on the Arctic Ocean should be eaten slowly.

Strindberg was occupied with all his figures.

"The sledges are wrongly designed," I said to Andrée.

"They've two faults."

"I'm listening," he said.

"To begin with," I said, "when we've surmounted a ridge of ice and are happily on our way down on the far side, our sledges come after us like Jehus, and it's a wonder that none of us has been crushed by his own sledge.

"Nansen," I said, "had not only a haul-rope on his sledges, he also had a strong pole, a pole by means of which the man hauling could keep his sledge at a proper distance. That was on his crossing of Greenland, of course."

"And the second fault?" asked Andrée.

"Nansen's sledges," I said, "had a raised rail at the back, which provided the person pushing with a handhold. Much the same as on a kick-sledge. Our sledges ought to have been designed in the same way."

"Nansen's a clever fellow," said Andrée.

"I've checked and rechecked," said Strindberg.

"Well?"

"For six days we've travelled south-west," he said, "but we've undoubtedly drifted south-east, straight for Franz Josef Land."

Andrée studied his figures. He was unable to raise any objections.

"It's fascinating," I said. "First of all we trudge day after day, shrouded in fog, mist, rain, and snow towards the south-west. But we drift westwards.

"After that we trudge through the same white shroud towards the south-west, only to find that we've drifted south-east."

Diarrhoea and pains in my stomach forced me to go outside again. I was exceedingly exhausted when I crept back into the tent. Andrée gave me a gelatine capsule of opium and a drop of fruit juice and water.

"Now go to sleep," he said. "It's eighteen hours since we set off this morning."

I drank and swallowed. I had violent pains like cramp just below my ribs.

I crept into the sleeping-bag. It felt far too hot, but I slowly subsided into a doze. The pains relinquished their grip.

Andrée and Strindberg discussed the design of the double-barrelled gun. They were peevish and cross.

"Just one question before I go to sleep," I said. "Why did you never have the balloon filled with hydrogen in Paris, either last year or this year? Why didn't you make a test voyage before we set off from Spitzbergen? It's odd if one comes to think of it."

I fell asleep.

I don't know whether Andrée answered.

20

We celebrated the fact that we had indisputably got south of the eighty-second parallel by opening three of our remaining nine tins of sardines.

"I'm childishly fond of sardines," said Andrée.

"Also of lobster, crab, and sweet things," I said.

"Not to mention eggs," he said. "Once, a long time ago, I ate forty lightly boiled eggs at one sitting. Two score. Mind you, it was a bet."

"We had a bottle of champagne with us in which to celebrate our arrival at the North Pole. Now we're emptying three tins of sardines to celebrate our crossing of the eighty-second parallel on our flight towards the south.

"For the first time in my life: Let's drink a toast in sardines!"

"We drank a toast in raspberry juice once," said Andrée.

"When?"

"Our first polar bear."

"No," said Strindberg, "not our first polar bear, but when we first saw the tracks of a polar bear. They were easy to see. The bear had been going north."

"Of course, I remember now. You surely remember, Andrée. It was a few hours after the car bumped on the ice for the first time. That same car, which in a week at the most, was going to carry us right across the Arctic Ocean, that was going to remain in the air for at least thirty days.

"Thirty days, one month. It's exactly a month since we took off from the balloon-house on Danes Island. Has it struck either of you? A month to the day since we left Spitzbergen."

2 I

Mist, fog, cloud, now rain, now snow, brief moments of middling visibility.

Because of the drift towards the east we changed our course to S.50°W.

I led, behind me came Andrée, last Strindberg.

It was naturally not possible to keep strictly to a compass course. Ridges of pressure ice, freshwater puddles, channels and leads constantly forced us to turn south, turn north, turn west, or turn east for longer or shorter periods. I did what I could to keep to the direction in which we had decided to march. If we were forced to bend towards the west, I tried as soon as possible to bend towards the east. When circumstances had compelled us to travel south, I did what I could to counteract the effect by striking a more northerly course.

Andrée and Strindberg followed without raising any objections.

Once again days and nights of monotony and strenuous exertions.

Fog, rain or snow, brief periods of better visibility, even briefer glimpses of the sun through the clouds.

Difficult crossings of open channels of water. Sometimes we managed to make bridges of floes by pulling them together. More often we had to ferry our sledges across on the boat.

At first we ferried one sledge across at a time. Then we tried two at a time, but finally we made journeys with all three sledges laid athwart the boat at the same time.

This showed us that it could carry all our equipment, including our own bodies, with more than thirty centimetres of freeboard to spare. "The boat is a work of genius," I said. "The *boat*, you understand."

We constantly stumbled into freshwater puddles and saltwater leads. We no longer paid any attention to such trifles, never changed our clothes, but simply wrung them out and continued our march along a line S.50°W.

The exertion of dragging the sledges over the toroses dried our clothes, dried them, that is, as far as anything can be dried in this region of almost perpetual damp and mist.

How many calories of heat per unit of time does a man's body generate when he is working hard?

The division of labour when pitching and striking camp became more and more systematic.

I put up the tent, spread out the sleeping-bag and the blankets and, when the weather allowed, put up a line on which to dry our wet clothes. I then busied myself with making notes in our meteorological journal.

Strindberg attended to the catering, lit the primus, carried our weapons into the tent, and saw to it that they were in the best possible order.

The following morning I took down the tent, stowed it away with the sleeping-bag and the blankets, handed out any clothes that might have dried during the night, and wrote my meteorological notes. Strindberg got breakfast, made an inventory of our stores, stowed away the saucepan and the primus, and took our bearings, weather permitting. He also prepared a meagre midday meal for us to eat on the march that lay ahead.

And Andrée.
First and foremost he devoted himself to making scientific observations. He investigated the thickness of the ice. Compared the ice of frozen sea water with that of frozen fresh water. Discovered and noted down layers of gravel, sand, and clay in the blocks of ice. Tried to sound the depth of the Arctic Ocean, but never reached the bottom and complained that our lines were not long enough. He put forward views on the connection between the direction of the wind and the width and orientation of the large channels of water. He constantly referred to the hydrographic observations made by Nansen and Sverdrup about the currents of the Arctic Ocean, and never failed to point out that they had not taken sufficient account of the movements of the tides.

He collected plankton and algae in numbered test-tubes, and was overjoyed when he found the odd insect. He announced on several occasions that we should have brought a microscope with us.

Strindberg found a piece of drift-wood embedded in the ice. Andrée chopped it free. It took him an hour.

"Siberian timber," he said. "From one of the many rivers, one of the rivers that run from south to north."

I hung this piece of wood—it appeared to be part of a branch, without bark, of some species of tree which we could not identify—under the roof of the tent to get it as dry as possible.

I realized that it would be put in the boat on my sledge. After it had dried for forty-eight hours its weight fell to two kilos.

Once, when we had good visibility under thick clouds, I thought I could see land far west-south-west of west. For a few hours we altered course and trudged in an even more westerly direction.

Then Andrée discovered, with the aid of his binoculars, that it was not land, that it was not Gilles Land, only an unusually high ridge of pressure ice.

We changed back to our course of S.50°W.

My eyes troubled me and I always had to wear sun-glasses. So did Strindberg, but his eyes neither hurt nor smarted, and he only wore them because he believed that the slightly coloured glass made him able to see better.

Andrée assured us that he did not need sun-glasses.

"I screw up my eyes," he said one evening in the tent.

"Why?"

"It suffices," he answered.

"Forgive me," I said, "but I've noticed your eyes and your expression. You always screw up your eyes, you frown."

"The light," he said.

"No, even last autumn in Stockholm," I said. "Your knitted brows, your screwed-up eyes, your difficulty in meeting the eyes of the person you were talking to. And all your photographs—there are hundreds of them—show the same narrowed gaze, the same taut muscles round your eyes."

"Drivel," he said.

"No, I've often noticed the way your eyes vibrate laterally, oscillate at lightning speed from right to left, from left to right, from right to left, from left to right, at lightning speed. Not always," I said, "not regularly. Sometimes. Quite often."

"Damned drivel," he said, and crept into the sleeping-bag.

"Perhaps," I answered.

I added: "I've read the reports of the ascents you made in your balloon, the *Svea*. Not once. Not twice. But time after time. I know them almost by heart. I've noticed one thing in particular. Your reports are dry, interestingly dry. It's only once in a way that you mention visual phenomena. On the other hand you constantly dwell upon acoustic experiences. The sound of a hammer, or of a ship's siren. The singing of birds, the echo of your own shouts from the earth, or from lakes you were passing over.

"You listen," I said, "but you don't see."

Andrée did not answer.

"And now," I said, "in this damnable whiteness of a light that has no direction, and no shadows! We, Strindberg and I have to wear sun-glasses. But you, Andrée, you say you only need to screw up your eyes.

"I don't think you're speaking the truth," I said. "You're lying.

"You're half blind, or more than half blind."

"You're very tired," he said at last.

"Your diarrhoea indicates that you're also ill."

"Perhaps I'm ill," I said. "It's possible. But the load on my sledge weighs a hundred and fifty kilos. The load on your sledge weighs a hundred and thirty-five kilos, and that on Strindberg's sledge a hundred and forty kilos.

"For that matter the attacks of diarrhoea and cramp are over.

"I'm not as ill as all that. But what about your sight, Andrée?

"And who is it who leads our caravan through this desert of mist and whiteness, channels and ridges of pressure ice? You or I?"

"We must sleep," he said.

Of course, we had to sleep and rest.

22

Three horrible days. Or two.

No connected stretches of floe, only a terrible terrain of blocks of ice that were pressed against each other, on top of each other. Many weighed hundreds of tons, most were so small that we could have loaded them on to our sledges and taken them with us.

The first day began with rain that turned to snow.

The surface was good, the runners of the sledges glided well over the shiny wet blocks of ice, or the thin covering of snow that came later. We had not the strength to keep on the march for more than seven hours. The last hour was wrung out of us because we were trying to find a spot in which it would be at all possible to pitch our camp.

The second day: two degrees below zero and a fresh northerly wind; fog, the same detestable terrain of blocks of ice, large and small, pressed together.

We had breakfast at half-past ten in the morning. Bear's meat, Schumacker's bread without butter, a drop of coffee, biscuits.

Immediately after we set off I made a detour round a puddle of melt water. It was covered with thin ice and snow, but I had learnt to recognize these treacherous accumulations of water.

Andrée did not appear to appreciate the wisdom of my circuitous route, but walked out on to the puddle. Of course the ice gave way under him, he fell over, and the whole sledge disappeared under water. Strindberg and I rescued the equipage with some difficulty.

Andrée was worried about the sledge, but laughed at himself while he changed into dry outer garments.

"I ought to have taken the opportunity to have a good wash with soap and a scrubbing-brush," he said.

Soon afterwards, as we were on our way down from an unusually high toros, Strindberg's sledge came ploughing into mine with the speed of an express train. It dragged Strindberg with it like a bit of rag in the harness.

Our boat, our balloon-silk boat, was damaged, fortunately not seriously.

"There you see," I said to Andrée, "A haul-rope alone isn't enough. You've got to have a pole as well, so that you can hold the sledge back on a downward slope."

"Like the poles on Nansen's sledges," he said.

"Yes, not just a guide-pole," I said. "Something more effective than that."

We came to an entirely new type of lead. It was the same width as most of the others. It emerged out of the fog to the north-west, and it disappeared into the fog to the south-east, just as most of the others did.

But it had a floor of ice, about thirty or forty centimetres below the surface of the water, too deep for us to cross it without more ado, too shallow to allow us to ferry ourselves across in the boat.

I was standing on the edge contemplating the situation, when suddenly, a piece of the floe came adrift under me, and I landed full length in the water.

"A more than usually damnable day," I said, as I squeezed the water from my breeches and jacket. I put on a dry jersey, but for the rest contented myself with pulling on my wind-proof trousers on top of my wet ones. "A heat-producing wet compress," I said.

The piece of floe that had broken off was large enough to be used for ferrying ourselves across.

"A peculiar raft," said Andrée.

"Damned peculiar," I answered.

I poled myself across with a boat-hook, shoved the floe back to the other side, and pulled the three sledges over, one at a time, by using the grapnel and rope.

Andrée wanted to investigate the thickness of the ice on the floor of the lead.

"With pleasure," I said. "But I don't intend to freeze to death, not yet anyhow."

I set off with my sledge. Course S.50°W. The Seven Islands.

Andrée shrugged his shoulders, harnessed himself to his sledge, and we proceeded on our way.

The terrain was as horrible as ever; a few large blocks of ice and a multitude of small ones, pressed together so that they formed a landscape of low, steep ridges, up which we climbed with the greatest difficulty, and from which we often descended sledge first.

Our sledges capsized time after time and we were always having to load and reload them.

The toroses, the ever recurring puddles of melt water, with their thin covering of ice, constantly forced me to swing to the west or to the east.

"Are you keeping to the right course?" asked Andréc.

"As well as I can," I answered. "You've got your own compass, you've got a pedometer. You can keep a check. If you don't trust me you're welcome to go first.

"You don't need sun-glasses either," I added.

"Perhaps you can see better than I can."

We ate our dinner at eight o'clock in the evening, rather more than nine hours after we had set off.

A spartan dinner. Schumacker's bread, butter, a few thin slices of cheese, and a handful of biscuits.

"There are carbohydrates both in bread and in biscuits," said Strindberg.

A solitary sea-gull circled over the spot where we were resting. We stayed there for about an hour.

I levelled my Remington at the gull.

"Use my double-barrelled gun," said Strindberg. "The right-hand barrel, loaded with fine shot."

"More amusing to pick him off," I answered, and fired when the gull was perhaps twenty-five metres above us.

When the bullet hit him the bird was thrown another ten metres or so upwards, and then fell dead on the ice close to us.

"Our first bird," I said.

Andrée studied it, and then made some notes in his diary. "Quite white," he said. "Black legs and feet, webs between his claws. Yellow beak, small flecks of grey on the tips of his wings."

The bullet from the Remington had hit him in the middle of his breast.

"Did you notice how he was thrown upwards?" I asked.

Andrée cut off the bird's head and carefully packed it away.

"Why?" I asked.

"For the sake of its eyes," he answered.

"Its eyes?"

"To find out how they are formed, how the pupils shield the retina from the intense light."

Strindberg and I rested on my sledge after our simple meal.

Andrée ascertained that the ice was one hundred and forty-five metres thick.

He found a block of ice that contained five well separated layers of clay and fine sand. He discovered three withered leaves. He collected a whole series of examples of algae, green, or greyish green.

He made another attempt to sound the depth of the sea, but our ropes were too short.

He compared the thickness of the ice that had recently formed on the saltwater and on the freshwater puddles.

He pointed to a couple of large blocks of ice and assured us that they were not made of frozen sea-water, but had broken off a glacier somewhere or other.

"Perhaps in New Siberia, or in Severnaya Zemlya, if we're to trust Nansen and Sverdrup's theories," he said.

"Taste the ice," he said. "It's sweet, it's not salt."

"It's time we were moving," I said.

"The ice on the freshwater puddles is two centimetres thick," he said.

We shouldered our harness and marched on S.50°W., I first, then Strindberg, last Andrée. We had a fresh northerly wind at our backs.

The sky was covered by thick clouds. The visibility was bad, but improved as the temperature fell.

The terrain was as repulsive as it had been the previous day. Some large blocks of ice, but mostly small blocks pressed tightly together.

The runners of the sledges glided easily.

I pursued the same tactics as before. I tried to keep a certain distance between me and my companions, in order to spur them on to more strenuous efforts and exertions.

For at least four hours I was so far ahead that we could not talk to each other.

Soon after midnight I found a pretty large floe, the first stretch of connected floe that we had seen for a long time. We had then put behind us a day's work of more than fourteen hours.

I had time to put up the tent and spread out the sleeping-bag and blankets in the usual order before Andrée and Strindberg arrived.

We ate a late, or perhaps one should say an early, evening meal at two o'clock in the morning. It consisted of a quarter of a kilo of bear's meat per man, and a couple of mugfuls of cocoa.

The temperature had sunk rapidly and was now eight degrees below zero, but the primus stove produced a pleasant room-temperature in the tent after we had almost entirely closed the opening.

"The trouble with our sledges," I said to Andrée, "is that they only have a haul-rope. I don't know that we should have been much better off if we'd had Nansen's braking-poles.

"Sledges that are to be pulled across pack ice should have shafts," I said, "they shouldn't be pulled by ropes at all."

The following day: still an overcast sky, poor visibility, a temperature eight degrees below zero and, on top of this, a north-westerly wind with a force of eight metres per second.

Andrée woke us just before twelve o'clock, and immediately afterwards set off on a tour of reconnaissance.

"If he'd been able to use them he'd have felt the lack of skis," I said.

"Very likely," answered Strindberg.

"May I ask you a straight question?" I asked.

He looked at me with a smile, his open, almost childlike smile.

"Perhaps," he answered, "but I won't promise to give you a straight answer."

"What do you really think about this whole business?"

"What business?"

"This voyage to the North Pole in a balloon?"

He was still smiling as he lit his pipe.

"Two things," he said.

"What are they?"

"It's a bit difficult to get them into their proper relationship to one another."

"Try, now that we're able to talk undisturbed."

"Firstly," he said, "I knew just as well as Doctor Ekholm that the balloon leaked far too much. I knew that it would never be able to keep afloat for a month, or even long enough to make it possible for us to count on being able to reach the mainland of Siberia or North America. Those thirty days of Andrée's and Lachambre's were only a day-dream."

"And?"

"Secondly, I knew that we were not properly equipped for a journey across the ice after the balloon came down."

"Anything else?"

"That's all," he said.

"Ekholm backed out. You didn't?"

"I'm young. Ekholm's old. Forty-nine."

"Andrée's forty-three, only six years younger, and from a physical point of view in very middling condition."

"He has a fiendishly strong will."

"Has he? Has he really got a strong will? Or, is he merely possessed by a fixed idea?"

Strindberg sucked his pipe. "A fiendishly strong will," he repeated.

"Your forecast?" I asked. "Shall we reach the Seven Islands, or shan't we?"

"I'm an optimist," he answered. "I've always been one."

Andrée returned from his tour of reconnaissance wet to the waist.

"Have you been in?" I asked.

"Not to speak of," he answered.

"Oh yes," I said. "It's cold, the air temperature is eight degrees below zero, and there's a strong wind too. Your breeches are frozen, you're wearing a sort of armour of ice, a lower section and an upper section, with the hinges where your knees are. But it's not proper armour with the iron hinges that armour has. You must change into dry breeches. If you don't they'll break apart at the knees and fall to bits, irreparably."

Strindberg had begun to get breakfast ready. Our paraffin stove was hissing and making the tent intensely hot.

Andrée pulled off his armour-plated breeches, hung them up to dry just to one side of the primus, and got into dry breeches, but he kept on his long underpants, his stockings and his knee-warmers which were still wet.

"Put on your wind-proof overall trousers," I suggested. "It's not a bad idea. I've tried it myself. It's based on the warm, wet, compress treatment."

"Wretchedly bad ice in every southerly direction," said Andrée.

"Do you remember," he asked, "when we were first sailing in over the ice, we noticed that it was very ragged and broken up, and full of leads and accumulations of open water?

"That's the sort of ice we're in the middle of now," he said, "and it can only mean one thing, namely that we're getting near to the outer edge of the pack ice, and that any day now we shall meet with open water, and a sea comparatively free of ice.

"I climbed up a toros that was almost five metres high," he said. "Add to that my own height and the horizon would be about three kilometres away. The visibility to the south was reasonable. I could see the line of the horizon through my binoculars, but I couldn't see Gilles Land. According to our chart I ought to have been able to see the island, even if it was ten kilometres away. It must rise at least some few metres above sea-level."

"Bad visibility?" asked Strindberg.

"For quite a while the view to the south was open and clear," answered Andrée. "I could see the horizon quite well through the binoculars. It's reasonable to suppose that I should have been able to see land, even at a distance of twenty kilometres."

"You only saw the horizon?"

"Yes."

"Did the horizon consist of ice or open sea?" I asked.

"Impossible to say," replied Andrée.

"We can only draw one indisputable conclusion from this."

"And that is?"

"That though Gilles Land is certainly to be found on our 'Physical Map of the North Polar Regions', it doesn't exist in the world of the senses.

"You'd rather we made for Cape Flora," I said, "than for the Seven Islands, because the sea down towards the Seven Islands has been thoroughly explored, and there's no land, nor island to discover and name.

"But now at least we've made a discovery, a contribution to geography. We've discovered that Gilles Land doesn't exist. We can therefore erase the name from our maps, and call the area 'The Andrée Sea'."

Andrée's face went rigid. "I've never uttered a word about the

300

existence of unknown islands between Cape Flora and the North Pole."

23

A sudden change in temperature. A swing from eight degrees below zero, Centigrade, to above zero and light rain.

I found it difficult to keep the days apart, though it was my job to write up our meteorological journal, and to keep precise records of time in Greenwich mean time.

We employed four different times: Greenwich mean time, astronomical time, true solar time (at our base on Danes Island), and finally homely Swedish time.

Our measurement of time was complicated by the fact that Strindberg consistently tried to reckon a day and a night as one stretch of twenty-four hours, while Andrée divided them into twice twelve hours. Neither Andrée nor I kept strictly to what you might call our 'everyday' way of thinking of time. We would make a note about—or remember—something that happened at eleven o'clock, meaning by that eleven o'clock p.m., and immediately after —after midnight that is—make a note referring to 13 o'clock, when the proper way of expressing it would have been 1 o'clock a.m. on the following day.

"This indicates that we're moving towards a change for the better," I said.

"I hope you've both noticed it.

"At midnight the light grows fainter, dims the whiteness of the clouds and the fog.

"The long polar day is nearing its evening.

"More rapidly than anyone would imagine after two months of days without nights. The arctic summer is short. The arctic autumn is no less short. After it come months of days that consist only of night.

"Very soon we shall not be able to struggle on with our sledges without regard for the rhythm of light and darkness.

"I think it will be good for us," I said. "A rhythm in our activity, in our alternations between work and rest, will be forced upon us. A periodicity."

"Of course you're right," said Andrée. "But your choice of words is hardly scientific."

In what way was it unscientific?

Before we struck camp we ate a late afternoon breakfast consisting of fried cubes of bear's meat, two pieces of hard bread without butter, and a meagre portion of coffee.

Two hundred grammes of meat each.

"The last of your bear of the bad teeth," said Strindberg.

"Old to start with, nevertheless decidedly more tender when we'd only had him a few days.

"Coffee?"

"Sorry," said Strindberg. "One third ground coffee, two thirds old dregs."

"But it was a warm drink," I said.

24

Our joints were stiff, and our limbs heavy when we struck camp. We loaded our sledges. Damp and unmelted ice made our loads considerably heavier than on the previous day.

Strindberg fired a shot at a seal that was much too far away. He may have hit it, but the animal disappeared down a hole.

The temperature remained at about zero, and the sledges glided well over the snow and ice.

The everlasting fog, the thick drizzle made the visibility poor.

I went first. Main direction S.50°W. Immediately behind me Strindberg, last Andrée.

We forced a fairly broad lead without much difficulty. There were plenty of floes—which we were able to draw together with the boat-hook and grapnel—to make a bridge that would take our weight.

Just as we had crossed the lead, and before we had had time to shoulder our harness, Strindberg said in a low voice: "Three bears! Holy Moses, three bears!"

He pointed.

On a toros to our left stood an exceedingly large polar bear, most likely a she-bear, and just behind her two cubs, probably yearlings.

The she-bear was moving uneasily, stretching out her nose, and sniffing.

The wind was blowing from us to her.

She looked yellow in the white fog.

We split up. I went to the right, Strindberg slowly to the left, Andrée straight ahead.

"She's hungry," I said. "She's got two cubs. She must weigh at least four hundred kilos. She's not curious, she can scent a quarry, she's ready to attack."

"Are you both ready?" asked Andrée.

"Yes."

He moved slowly towards the she-bear, partly crawling, a sort of decoy.

She heard him, she smelt him, she took about ten hesitant, taut strides in his direction.

She was as big as a horse, but her movements were smooth and supple. She might have been a gigantic marten or weasel.

Needless to say I had a cartridge in the breech of my Remington, and three more in my left hand.

Andrée crawled, or half crawled, towards the bear.

She moved slowly towards him.

Suddenly he shouted something, got up, ran forward and fired a shot that would obviously miss. She took several tremendous leaps forward. I fired, she pulled up, and reeled about long enough to give Andrée time to reload and fire a shot that killed her.

Seconds later Strindberg brought down one of the cubs. The shot
—a charge of small shot—hit its neck, and the bleeding creature
writhed to and fro over the snow and ice for a long time before it
died. Andrée and I shot the other cub practically simultaneously.
Both our bullets hit it in the chest, but it succeeded in crawling up to
its mother before it finally sank in a heap, its head and legs limp and
lifeless.

"It's over now," said Andrée.
Three yellowish white polar bears lay on the snow that was stained
with great patches of red blood.
"Something of a blood-bath," said Strindberg.
"There's no colour that contrasts so vividly with white as red," I
said.
"Try to imagine blue blood," I said. "There are animals that
have blue blood—though they're not to be found in the *Almanach
de Gotha*. No indeed, little animals, invertebrates.
"You're upset by the sight of red on white," I said. "How would
you have reacted to a great mass of blue liquid on a white that is
not only white, but also somewhat greenish?"

Strindberg made some rough measurements of the bloodstained
area, and discovered that it extended over almost a hundred square
metres.
"Any comments?" I asked. "Any reflections?"
"I can't put it into words," he answered.

Our march that day was very short, only the three or four hundred
metres we had covered before we met the bears.
We pitched the tent.
We dragged the three bears down to our camp. The two cubs
did not give us much trouble.
The she-bear, the mother, was another matter. She probably
weighed more than four hundred kilos rather than less.
To slaughter and cut up the animal in one spell of work was
almost more than we could manage.
The bits we wanted to keep were primarily the heart, the brain,
the liver, the kidneys and the tongue, the meat from the back down

the ribs and some parts of the hind-leg thighs.

Andrée was anxious that we should flay and take with us the fur from the forelegs, in order to have these pieces in reserve when we came to repair our increasingly worn sleeping-bag.

It was half-past six the following morning before we were able to go to bed, after first eating a hefty meal of fresh bear's meat from one of the two cubs.

There was something disagreeable, in a way frightening, about the she-bear, the mother. At the moment of death she had chewed up her lips, her tongue, and her cheeks into ragged bits of meat interspersed with lumps of coagulated blood, slimy and partially flecked with yellow.

We each ate more than half a kilo of lightly fried meat, without bread or biscuits.

"Albuminous matter," said Strindberg.

"Blood contains more carbohydrates than you'd think," answered Andrée.

We crept into the sleeping-bag, sated and tired.

The gentle rain pattered on the canvas of the tent.

One degree above zero Centigrade, light, variable wind.

"At this moment," I said, "everything feels good.

"This night and morning after the blood-bath of the polar bears."

"You'll be a fool if you try to moralize," said Andrée.

"That's the last thing I want to do," I answered.

"But there's one thing that's worrying me. A mere trifle. Really only a trifle.

"Nansen always writes about his *sledges*. You, on the other hand, always talk about a *toboggan*.

"My simple, trifling question: what's the difference between a sledge and a toboggan?"

Andrée burst out laughing.

"I'm an engineer," he said. "A technician. I'm not a philologist. How the devil should I know the difference between a sledge and a toboggan!"

We were full of food, tired, drowsy.

"The wind has veered, just now it's coming from the north-east," I said. "It's slight, only a few metres per second, but north-easterly. It's not impossible that we may be drifting in the right direction. Towards the south-west."

"I'm not being sentimental," said Strindberg, "but seven hundred kilos of meat is lying outside our tent. There may be even more, three quarters of a ton of meat perhaps. We shall have to leave most of it behind. A hundred square metres of snow is dyed red with blood."

"You are being sentimental," said Andrée.

"The she-bear," said Strindberg, "she was going to attack. She would have killed you if Fraenkel hadn't hit her after you missed.

"A human being is a pitiful creature compared with a hungry polar bear. A polar bear is five or six times heavier, and four or five times more agile. A polar bear could kill an ox with a single blow of its paw, or grind the neck of a walrus to pieces with a single bite of its jaws."

"Yes," we said.

"I find it difficult to say what I mean," he said.

"We all do."

"The she-bear," Strindberg went on, "there was no other choice. We needed the meat. We also had to fire in self-defence.

"But the cubs. We've got three dead bears here, many hundreds of kilos of meat.

"We can only take a little of it with us. We shall have to leave most of it to the foxes and the birds," he said.

"What are you trying to say?" I asked.

"I don't really know," he said doubtfully.

"Who was it who shot the first of the cubs?" asked Andrée.

"I did," answered Strindberg. "I don't know why. I just fired. I didn't think. I pulled the wrong trigger, not the high velocity bullet, but the load of small shot in the right hand barrel. At close range. Just as the cub was turning to run away."

"Well? Go on!"

"I can't find the words," he said.

"You're fooling yourself," I said.

"We're in a warm sleeping-bag in a warm tent, and we've seven hundred kilos of food just outside the entrance.

"Everything feels fine, safe, satisfactory.

"You're forgetting that our tent is pitched on a damp little floe somewhere in the middle of the arctic pack ice.

"You've forgotten that we're somewhere in the neighbourhood of the eighty-second parallel, hundreds of kilometres from the nearest known island or other dry land.

"Of course the ice and snow outside our tent is stained red with the blood of polar bears.

"But tomorrow we shall pull our sledges further south, if the ice doesn't drift west, or east, or north.

"It isn't summer any longer.

"You've surely noticed the gathering dusk of the midnight hours?

"And the mist, the haze, the fog, the clouds, the rain, the squalls of snow. That confounded dome of whiteness above us. That confounded white dome, that is either a snug little hive, or a damnable great globe, half a sphere, of damp and cold.

"Of course the snow round us is red with the blood of the polar bears.

"The red may be hidden tomorrow by a thick covering of hoarfrost.

"In any circumstances, two hours after we set off the red of the polar bear's blood will lie far behind us. To the joy of the polar foxes, and those white vultures whose name I cannot and will not learn.

"At this moment you're feeling warm, and tired, and safe.

"Tomorrow we shall set off for the south, regardless of where the ice drifts.

"Don't think about the dead cubs, or the red ice!"

25

We were not allowed to sleep for more than a few hours. Andrée suddenly scrambled out of the sleeping-bag and rushed out of the tent.

He did not get far before we heard something spurting out of him. Strindberg sat down on top of the sleeping-bag.

"I've a pain in the pit of my stomach," he said. "Just here, between my navel and my breast-bone."

"It'll be your turn next," I said.

He took off his woollen breeches.

"It's raining," I said.

"Then it'll be all the better to have a pair of dry breeches to put on over my underpants if it's a long business," he replied. He was bent double, breathing heavily, and his face was pale under the dirt and tan.

Some minutes passed before Andrée crept back into the tent. "I took a turn or two," he said, sat down, pulled off his stockings and wrung them out.

"Strange," he said. "The big bear, the she-bear, grew stiff and rigid in four or five hours, you remember? It was easy to cut through her muscles and sinews.

"She's lying as we left her. A split and empty head, her forelegs sticking up just as they were when we flayed them. Rigor mortis, you understand.

"But the cubs," he said, "they're still supple. You can lift up a paw as if the animal was still alive, but unconscious, and when you let it fall, the paw hits the ice with a slight thud.

"When did we shoot them?" he asked.

"At least twelve hours ago," I said.

"And not stiff yet," he said. "It's very strange. It's the same with both cubs," he elucidated. "But not with the she-bear."

Strindberg walked out of the tent unsteadily after first removing his socks. He went further than Andrée, but we heard the same unpleasant sound, and how he also began to cough, and his coughs turned to vomiting.

I made a move to get up, but Andrée seized hold of my shoulder. "For God's sake let him be," he said. "There are times when a man prefers to be alone, and when he should be left alone."

It was fifteen minutes before Strindberg raised the flap of the tent.

"Feeling better?" I asked.

He nodded.

His naked feet were frozen stiff. I massaged them for quite a while before I pulled on his woollen stockings.

He lay down on his back. His underpants were dripping wet. I pulled them off and helped him to creep into his dry breeches. His jersey was wetter still, and the front of it was splashed all over with evil smelling vomit. I threw it out through the opening of the tent, and lent him one of my own, fairly dry jerseys. I did not want to dig into the bag that held his private possessions.

"Dead tired," he said.

"No wonder," I replied. "It takes it out of you when you have it spurting out of you at both ends simultaneously."

"Andrée was right," he said. "The bodies of the cubs are still supple. If you lift a paw it falls to the ice. As if they were still alive. As if we'd never shot them."

"Strange," said Andrée.

"You might almost think their bodies were still warm," said Strindberg.

"Fraenkel's disease," said Andrée.

"What do you mean by that?

"I feel as sound as a bell," I added.

"But it began with you. You had diarrhoea and stomach-ache first."

"So you've caught it from me," I said. "It's an illness with an incubation period of about a week?"

"Why not?"

"An infection presupposes bacteria," I said. "And any number of authorities have pointed out that there are no bacteria as far north as this.

"Moreover," I said, "you yourself have often said the same thing."

It was raining heavily. The wind had veered from north to south-east; slight breeze. Half a degree above zero. Visibility practically nil.

There was no point in striking camp. We stayed put in our tent.

"Those bacteria I mentioned," said Andrée. "I was thinking primarily of the ones that spread infections of the respiratory organs; influenza, colds in the head, coughs, etc."

"But not the bacteria that make you shit the bowels out of your body?" I asked.

"You've always got to be cautious and sceptical," he answered. "The obvious is often only apparently obvious. What has been definitely proved must be constantly re-examined and proved afresh."

We were lying on the sleeping-bag, and I lit my pipe.

"Do smoke," he said. "I don't like the smell of tobacco, but there are other smells that are even more annoying.

"Take for instance my bear with his rotten teeth," he went on after a while. "The toughest bear in the world. I know a great many doctors who are convinced that caries is caused by bacteria. If they're right, there must be caries bacteria in the North Arctic Ocean too.

"We threw the skull into a lead," he said. "Damnably stupid of us. We ought to have taken it with us, the jaws and teeth at least.

"Then there's that nasal catarrh we're all suffering from," he said. "We snuffle and sniffle, sometimes only a little, but there have been days when we've brought down great quantities of mucus. Is it caused by a cold in the head? Is it an ordinary cold, or a special arctic variety that no one has heard of before? Is it caused by bacteria or not?"

"We'll have to collect some specimens of it," I said. "Of the mucus, I mean."

Strindberg was given a dose of opium and went to sleep after we had wrapped him up in the blankets and put him up against the back gable of the tent.

Andrée and I set to work on the sleeping-bag which was badly in need of repair.

"A reindeer-skin sleeping-bag," I said. "If you'd asked my advice we shouldn't have had to put up with that misery.

"Reindeer skin is warm, the warmest thing you can think of. The hair on the skin is coarse, enduring, and filled with air. Reindeer skin insulates you against cold better than anything else. But it doesn't stand up to moisture and humidity. The Lapps wet their reindeer skins when they want to remove the hairs and only use the skin itself.

"Our sleeping-bag has been damp ever since we left the place where we landed," I said. "We've carried out a de-hairing process. What a pity that you never asked my advice. After all I'm the one who knows what it's like to live above the tree-line."

The top of the under half of the sleeping-bag was the part that was most worn. We cut it away and replaced it by fur from my first bear, and the bears we had just killed.

"It looks nice and white, it feels thick, and warm, and soft," I said. "But it's only raw hide, and it will go as stiff as sheet-metal. It ought to be tanned. But have we a bottle of tannin in our stores? $C_{14} H_{10} O_9$, if you want the correct chemical formula."

"Sometimes you talk a confounded lot of shit," said Andrée.

"You can cure the skin in a more primitive way," I said. "You can chew it. Carefully, and with as much saliva as you can muster. You chew the backside, the hairless side that is. But you have to do it energetically, purposefully, with no slacking. If we go in for curing by chewing, and begin at opposite ends, it will be at least twenty-four hours before we meet. One advantage of the chewing method is that you don't need to eat while you're at it.

"Have you ever been in the mountains of Lappland, Andrée?

"Been devilishly cold?

"Been out on skis in a snow-storm?

"Spent the night in a hollow in the snow?

"Travelled day after day across the white uplands, far above the tree-line?

"Have you ever studied the way in which the Swedish Lapps cope with their sub-arctic winter? Or have you merely sat in your room at the Royal Patent Office?

"You say I talk a lot of shit.

"You're a scientist. Wouldn't you like to collect some samples

311

of excrement from all the shit I talk?

"But this is Sunday. We've a right to take things easily today, whether we chew, or whether we don't.

" 'For in six days the Lord made heaven and earth, the sea, and all that in them is'—polar bears among other things—but he rested on the seventh day."

Strindberg woke at four o'clock in the afternoon. He sat up and gazed at us with vacant eyes.

His mouth was dry, and he found it hard to talk. Andrée gave him a mug of melt water.

"What's the time?" he asked. "Have I been asleep? For a long time? Are you both hungry? Is it time to strike camp and push off? The weather? The wind? The pressure ice? The visibility? Where the deuce are my underpants?"

"The wind is south-westerly," I said, "but slight. The temperature's over zero, but not much. It's raining quite hard, and it's been raining for quite a long time. The tent is admirable. It's keeping it out. It's very nearly four thirty in the afternoon, and it feels as if it were about time for breakfast. The long pants are soaking wet, they're hanging on the ridge-pole, your long pants, that is. How are you? How does your tummy feel?"

He didn't answer. Pulled on his boots, brought in the primus and lit it.

The tent, which had been slightly chilly, grew hot.

Both Andrée and I had views about what we should like for our afternoon breakfast. Strindberg would not listen. He was suddenly wide awake and had decided views of his own.

"Who's chef?" he asked. "I or you?"

He boiled up a fairly clear chicken broth and added two spoonfuls of Mellin's Food, alias Rousseaus' meat-powder.

He cut the heart of one of the cubs into small pieces and put them into the broth.

Half of the mother bear's brains—granulated, reddish, greyish white stuff—went the same way.

Then some meat from the ribs of one of the cubs was cut into slices and popped into the saucepan.

While the decoction was cooking—it was giving off a most promising aroma—Strindberg spread six biscuits with butter and put a thin slice of cheese on each.

Polar bear's brains, polar bear's heart—it all tasted delicious. We ate more than we could really manage.

We lay on the sleeping-bag. The paraffin stove hummed, the temperature rose to above twenty-five degrees.

On the canvas of the tent the rain pattered soporifically.

We spent the rest of the day inspecting our clothes and mending them as well as we could. We left the primus burning on the lowest flame possible in order to dry all our wet things—or really—to get everything that was soaking wet as dry as circumstances allowed. Our stock of paraffin—'Snowflake' brand—was not very large.

Strindberg felt better after his opium-drugged sleep, but he discovered that he had rather a deep cut in one hand. He had no idea where he had got it.

"My guess is that you got it mingling blood with one of the cubs," I said.

He also had a nasty boil on his upper lip. I bandaged the cut and treated the boil with a solution of mercuric chloride.

"The wound is quite clean," I said, "but the boil looks like an infection. Andrée, aren't you going to make an incision in it and collect the contents in a test tube?"

The temperature sank slowly, and the rain turned to wet snow-flakes that gradually grew drier.

We got the sledges ready for departure. In our loads we included forty-two kilos of meat from the three bears, giving precedence to the hearts, the brains, the kidneys, the tongues, and the fillet. The greater part of the meat landed on my sledge. It was so easy to throw oddments into the boat.

The only things left in the tent were the sleeping-bag, the blankets, our private bags, a little food, the cooking stove, and the instruments.

The wind was still blowing from the south-east, and the visibility was practically nil.

"Don't worry about the wind," I said to Andrée. "By this time you must have seen that the wind blows in one direction and the ice drifts in another, while we obstinately march in a third. And all the time you're thinking of a fourth."

We let the hours glide past. Sometimes we slept, sometimes we lay half awake.

Andrée told us about his youth. About the time he had spent in America, and of how he had worked as a caretaker and cleaner at the Swedish-Norwegian section of the Philadelphia Exhibition twenty years ago. He told us of how he had become acquainted with the legendary American balloonist, John Wise, and the whole of his family, all balloonists. He had intended to make an ascent with him, but it came to nothing because the balloon exploded, or at least split up. He said he had also met another balloonist, almost as well known, a man called Boltrey, who had turned him down as a passenger because he, Andrée, only had fifty dollars, and Boltrey charged seventy-five dollars for an ascent.

"I was young," he said, "younger than you are now. But I knew all there was to know about balloons and aeronautics, apart from the fact that I myself had never had the chance to practise ballooning.

"No disrespect to the French," he said, "for it's they who have left the greatest mark on the history of ballooning, they who have been in the van, apart from a handful of Englishmen, and an even smaller handful of Germans.

"But they lack the energy of the Americans," he said, "and their determination to test novelties by methodical, practical experiments. If the northern tradewinds did not unfortunately always blow from east to west, American balloons would have sailed across the Atlantic long ago."

I said: "I'm sure that American—did you say his name was Boltrey?—must regret that he didn't let the Swede, S. A. Andrée, make his first ascent at a reduced fee. If he's alive and well, that is."

Andrée laughed. "Regret, what the devil is regret?"

We drank coffee made from dregs and let the hours glide past.

Now and then we put out the primus, but relit it again when the temperature became uncomfortably low.

We had to do what we could to get our clothes dry. We also had to do what we could to save our stock of paraffin.

Andrée told us how he had got the post of chief engineer at the

Patent Office, where his boss was that much talked-of man, Count Hugo Hamilton. He told us of his involvement with social problems, of his membership of the Stockholm Municipal Council, and of how the Stockholm Gasworks had refused to deliver gas to his balloon, the *Svea*, because he had criticized the long hours worked by its employees. He talked of his views on the subject of Patent legislation, and his contributions to that eternal subject of discussion, the 'Woman Question'.

"Now we've reached the vital subject," I said.

" 'The Woman Question', Women. Woman. The Sexes.

"You're forty-three," I said. "You're unmarried."

"Yes."

"Will you be annoyed?"

"No," he answered.

"You belong," I said, "to the little group of Stockholmers who, with Nordenskiöld, Fröding, King Oscar, and Strindberg at their head, are the people best known, most often mentioned, and most frequently the objects of rumour and gossip. I suppose if I tried I could think of another ten, twenty, or thirty names."

"That's what has happened," he said. "People have noticed me. Written to the papers about me. And so on."

"But," I said, "I've never heard so much as a single word whispered about you and any woman."

"Well, what about it?" he said.

"You are annoyed, aren't you?"

Strindberg half sat up and lit his pipe.

"You've never married," I said, "but it would be nonsensical to suppose that you've lived a celibate life. It's impossible to imagine August Salomon Andrée as a monk, or a eunuch. Saloman August Andrée, I mean, age forty-three. It's a bit difficult at times to get your christian names in the right order."

"What do you mean?" he asked, very kindly.

"Your question is bad rhetoric," I said. "You know very well what I mean.

"Put bluntly: how have you managed your sexual life? You, chief engineer at the Royal Patent Office, City Councillor in Stockholm, the most discussed and written about balloonist in the world?"

Andrée was lying on his back on the sleeping-bag. He was smiling, and his smile widened until it became a silent laugh.

"You're right," he said. "I'm forty, and I'm unmarried. I've never had a permanent mistress. But of course I've had more women than you and Strindberg put together. Discreetly, secretly. How many I've had, whom, why, and under what circumstances is my private affair. It's of no consequence. It doesn't concern you, or Strindberg, or posterity."

"Doesn't it?"

"No."

"I think the North Pole is a bad mistress," I said.

26

Just before one o'clock on 16 August we struck camp after a simple breakfast of coffee, bread, biscuits, and butter.

Strong south-west wind, heavy snow-fall, high degree of humidity.

I led, keeping a course S.50°W.

The terrain was appalling. I cannot describe it without being guilty of repetition. Blocks of ice, large and small, squeezed into ridges of pressure ice that were constantly in movement. Channels of open water, wide and narrow, that we could only traverse by floating ourselves across or by ferrying ourselves in the boat.

Most of the toroses were so steep and sheer, that we could only force them by cutting a way through with an axe and an ice-chisel.

We were on our way south-west.

Our great problem was not to keep on course, but to cross the ridges of pressure ice and the open leads without damaging the boat too severely.

"We're near the open sea," Andrée said several times. "I recognize the ice. This was what it looked like when we drifted in over it in our balloon.

"Listen," he said.

We stopped and listened.

"Far away," he said, "far away, can't you hear the roar of the open sea?"

We tried to hear the roar of the open sea, but we did not succeed.

We had pitched our camp after a day's march in which we had covered at the most one kilometre. The tent had been put up. We had eaten an evening meal at ten o'clock in the morning.

The wind had veered north. It was snowing.

We were all utterly exhausted.

Andrée heard a disturbing noise just outside the tent. He lifted the flap a fraction.

"A bear," he said in a low voice, "a devilishly large bear, rummaging in the load on my sledge."

I had just finished cleaning through the barrel of my Remington, and greasing its moving parts.

I put a cartridge in the breech and gathered up four more in my left hand.

"A Remington," I said. "A single-shot rifle. What do you know about firearms, Andrée? When we were on board the *Svensksund* did you by any chance study the weapons used by the crew—automatics, with a repeater mechanism?"

"A devilishly large bear," said Andrée as I left the tent.

I was dazzled by the intense whiteness of the light.

For a few seconds I knew what it was to be blind.

The polar bear was scratching and tearing at the load on Andrée's sledge.

"Old boy," I said, and walked close up to him.

He stopped, sniffed, and turned towards me.

He paused for half a minute, examined me, and suddenly leapt towards me.

I fired at a range of less than ten steps.

The bullet hit his under-jaw, penetrated his neck, cut through his windpipe, and smashed his cervical vertebrae.

The bear tumbled about as if he were playing at turning somersaults.

I had not time to jump clear, but ended up with the weight of the dead bear on top of me, pressing me so hard against the ice that I was unable to move.

I could just see Andrée and Strindberg at the opening of the tent.

"Brothers," I said, "be not afraid. He's more dead than you think."

This was our eighth bear, a gigantic male, who weighed at least five hundred kilos, meat enough to provide dinner for a whole company. We contented ourselves by cutting out his heart, his kidneys, his tongue, and some of the best bits along his backbone. We also cleft his skull and took out his brains. Total weight, about ten kilos.

"These damnable Remingtons," I said to Andrée. "You're no hunting man, you've said so yourself. Why have we got Remingtons? They're all right in themselves. On a shooting-range, for instance. But how long does it take to extract the cartridge, put in a new one, cock the rifle, and fire again?

"Ten seconds.

"If my first shot hadn't killed him," I said, "I should have been dead myself.

"And yet," I said, "there are heaps of modern sporting rifles, developed along the lines of a Mauser, a Mannlicher, or a Lee-Metford. And American or Russian repeaters. Or Danish. Have you never heard of a Krag-Jörgensen rifle?

"What have we got? Two smooth-bore guns of the Remington type, presented to us by Husqvarn, the munitions manufacturers. Cartridges with round bullets. *Round bullets!* We might just as well have been equipped with muzzle-loaders.

"With powder-horns, ram-rods, wadding, bullets."

Andrée did not answer. He only smiled.

"Strindberg's double-barrelled gun, one barrel for small shot, one for a sharp-nosed bullet, that's another matter. What I'm talking about are the weapons we're supposed to use for hunting one of the most dangerous beasts of prey in the world."

"There's something wrong with the mechanism of the double-barrelled gun," said Strindberg.

27

It grew both colder and clearer. The fog turned to crystals when it settled on the ice, the clouds thinned.

The moon was fully visible, and Strindberg carried out a series of observations and measurements according to the rules of advanced navigation.

"The chronometers," he said, "we can't trust them any longer. They're getting more and more out of step. We shall have to work out the astronomical time if we're to put them right and determine our longitude."

He sat wrestling with his figures for a long time.

The wind had veered east and increased in strength.

"Excellent," said Andrée.

"Do you still put your trust in the winds?" I asked.

The visibility from the south-west to the south-east was good, and he scanned the horizon through his binoculars from a toros that was at least four metres high.

"Could you see anything?" I asked.

He shook his head.

Our great geographical discovery had not been disproved. Gilles Land only existed on the map, not in the world of the senses.

"You still put your trust in the winds and the currents, Andrée," I said. "I'm beginning to lose faith in the compass!"

That damnable and incalculable drift! We walked towards the south-west, but we drifted east, or south-east.

Fog again, thick clouds and light snow-fall.

We dragged our sledges up and over ridges of pressure ice. Often we had to chop a passage with our one axe.

Not a single flat floe more than fifty metres wide. Between the toroses open leads of salt water which we only crossed with difficulty.

The puddles of melt water gave us even greater trouble. They were frozen over and covered with snow, but the crust of ice was not strong enough to take our weight, or that of our sledges.

It gave way and we slid into the water—seldom deeper than half a metre—the sledges capsized, everything got soaking wet, we ourselves, our clothes, and our loads.

We learnt the art of not caring a damn about being wet, and trudged on, soaked through as we were.

We learnt that the heat generated by a toiling human body has a remarkable power of drying soaking wet clothes.

We ate a great deal of meat, about one and a half kilos per man per day.

Andrée thought that bear's heart had a rancid taste, almost bitter. Strindberg and I did not agree with him.

The muscular flesh was hard to chew, but it tasted sweet rather than bitter.

I marched at the head of our caravan.

Sometimes I had to have help from Andrée or Strindberg when we came to a ridge of pressure ice that was altogether too steep.

I tried, by using my compass, to keep on course as well as I could. S.50°W., that is, a course more westerly than southerly.

I often had to make big detours to the east to avoid the treacherous snow-covered ice of the freshwater puddles.

On the night between 18th and 19th August the covering of clouds lifted enough for us to see both the sun and the moon.

We had pitched camp, and Andrée had at once crept into the sleeping-bag, and fallen asleep immediately.

Strindberg and I spent more than an hour on astronomical observations, and on taking our bearings. We worked slowly and methodically, and strove to make our calculations as exact as possible.

We did not believe our figures. We began again from the beginning, calculated slowly and methodically, with the greatest possible care.

"Facts are facts," said Strindberg.

For twelve days, or eleven, or thirteen, we had trudged towards the south-west, more west than south. During those same days the drift of the ice had carried us about fifty kilometres towards the east.

"In spite of the winds," said Strindberg.

"In spite of Nansen's Polar Drift," I said. "We walk south-west, towards the Seven Islands, and the ice doesn't even carry us towards Franz Josef Land, but north of it, roughly speaking towards the Taymyr Peninsula.

"It's all very strange," I said. "You take a step towards the south-west. The ice moves so rapidly towards the east, that when you've finished taking your south-westerly step it has become south-easterly."

Strindberg replaced the instruments in their cases.

"What do you make of it?" I asked.

"Nothing," he answered. "We're on our way south-west. We're sitting on your sledge. During the minute that has just passed we have probably drifted fifty metres towards the east."

Andrée studied our calculations and our figures.

"Worried?" I asked.

"It wouldn't be reasonable to expect an arctic expedition to have no worries," he answered.

"We must adjust our course," he said.

"By all means," I answered.

He thought for a while, then he said: "S.60°W."

"In other words," I said, "W.30°S."

28

The ice became more broken, more tightly squeezed together, more ragged, harder to force.

The sore under Andrée's armpit had healed.

The cut on Strindberg's hand had knit. The boil on his lip had disappeared.

The terrain was excessively difficult.

The pressure of ice on ice was more violent than ever before. Huge floes were upended, fell, and were covered by other floes or blocks of ice.

The wind was moderate.

The sky was covered by thick clouds. Short showers of snow. A degree, or a few degrees below zero.

We toiled on, forward, in a white world of white cliffs of ice and a rumble like thunder.

We did not know exactly where we were. I led, and followed a course S.60°W., or W.30°S.

Every time we encountered a new lead of open water a long and futile discussion took place as to how we should best get across it.

On two occasions I lost control of myself and fell into what my companions must have thought to be a violent fit of temper.

"I can't make any sense of this misery," I said to Strindberg. "Ridges of pressure ice, puddles of fresh water that neither bear nor break, leads, being in wet clothes all the time, this hellish fog, one hour rain, the next snow, struggling west, pulling insanely heavy sledges, and drifting east all the time."

One afternoon—or morning—just as we had put up the tent, we were set upon by three polar bears, a she-bear and two cubs.

It really was a full-scale attack.

They came rushing towards us as if we were not human beings but seals, who had to be killed before they had time to disappear down a crack in the ice.

Strindberg brought the she-bear down with a shot in her shoulder.

I killed one of the cubs—if you can call a polar bear weighing a hundred kilos a cub—with two shots.

Andrée missed the other cub though he fired a whole series of shots, but hit, and streaked red with blood, it dived into a lead and disappeared.

This meant that we were in no way short of meat, but we had to severely ration our stock of Schumacher's bread and biscuits.

At Andrée's suggestion I made a sort of batter, by mixing oat-meal with the blood of the bears we had just shot, and fried some pancakes. To our surprise they tasted excellent.

"Just a bit sweet," said Strindberg.

"It can't be because of the oatmeal," I said. "What about it, Andrée? Are there carbohydrates in blood?"

A little later Strindberg collected quite a quantity of algae, large clumps of which drifted about in the leads. He stirred in a few handfuls of Mellin's Food and boiled up a greyish green soup. It certainly did not look very appetizing, but it too tasted good as a change from our meat diet.

"You should be glad, Andrée," said Strindberg. "I can guarantee that this is pure carbohydrate."

The ice was still rough and broken, very difficult to cross, and constantly in motion. Ridges of pressure ice were forced up, and then sank. Leads opened only to close again immediately.

I had violent cramp in one calf, and the other two took it in turns to massage me. This cramp sapped my strength severely.

Strindberg had developed a boil on the big toe of his left foot, rather like the one he had had on his lip. The latter was now reduced in size, but his boot galled the one on his toe and he limped badly.

I still went first, course S.60°W.

There were days when we had to make twenty crossings in the boat, all of them time-consuming and troublesome.

On other days we succeeded in reducing the number of our boat trips, and were thus able to cover six or perhaps seven kilometres.

The temperature gradually sank to about six degrees below zero. This was an advantage, as the ice on the puddles of fresh water grew strong enough to support us, and we were spared many unnecessary bends and detours.

We constantly saw the tracks of bears, but were not lucky enough to shoot any. After making an inventory of our stocks of food we agreed to ration ourselves to four hectos of meat at breakfast, and a good hecto at supper. In addition we were to have seventy-five

grammes of bread, and one and a half hectos of biscuits—per man,
of course.

29

I had several more bouts of diarrhoea and pains in my stomach,
followed by cramp, particularly in my calf muscles. Andrée too
was attacked by 'Fraenkel's Disease', though to all appearances less
violently, and without cramp.

Andrée announced that he did not require any medicine.

Soon afterwards I saw him secretly take a dose of opium. There
was no doubt about it. I saw him conceal a capsule of opium in his
hand. I saw him smuggle it into his mouth a moment or two later,
and I saw him swallow it, not without difficulty.

It seemed like an act of treachery. I felt surprised and annoyed.
I had a spiteful question on the tip of my tongue, and was still
more annoyed when I found I could not bring myself to utter it.

The word 'capsule' requires some explanation. Most of our
medicines were divided up into doses, and each dose was enclosed
in a small square of gelatin, which was to be swallowed whole. The
gelatin dissolved in the stomach, of course. The rest of our medicines were packed in glass bottles or tubes, which in their turn
were packed in wooden containers.

After the cramp had released its grip, and the opium had deadened
the worst of the pain in my stomach, I went out to make the usual
meteorological observations.

Wind between five and six metres per second, north-westerly.
Temperature near six degrees below zero.

"The wind's in the right direction," said Andrée.

"Do you still put your trust in the winds?" I asked.

"We've done a good day's march, today," he said, "one of the best for a long time."

The sky had cleared, particularly to the north. The sun was lying close to the horizon, and was encircled by an enormous, shining ring, a halo, on which there were another two suns, both pink.

The sky above the three suns was dark blue, the nearer the zenith, the darker it was. The wild landscape of ice was now a gleaming red, and its colour varied all the time in depth and intensity.

The highest of the hummocks cast sharply defined red shadows. It was the first time in my life that I had seen a red shadow.

These ever-changing hues of red faded away in the east and west, and became first pink, then orange, then greenish-yellow, and finally ice-cold bluish-green.

Strindberg and I each took our bearings which he afterwards completed by lunar observations according to the rules of advanced navigation, which I had not mastered at all.

We calculated and recalculated.

Andrée busied himself with his samples. The head of another gull we had shot was put into the proper chemical solution. He was still most interested in the eyes, and in how their structure had preserved them from snow-blindness.

He sorted, packed, and numbered a series of different samples of mud, of algae, of leaves—probably originating from the forests of Siberia—of things like long threads, clearly vegetable in origin, of more mud and gravel.

He also made a great many notes and sketches of the thickness of the layers of ice and the hummocks, and of their stratification and probable age.

By ten o'clock in the evening, though Strindberg and I had calculated and recalculated, we had almost always reached the same result.

He had of course carried out the major part of the mathematical operation.

"Come," I said to Andrée, "let's creep into our tent and light our primus stove, and prepare our evening meal, our meagre ration of one hecto of well-whisked bear's brains per person, diluted with water, and seasoned with a few pinches of salt and some Mellin's food, our Rousseaus' meat powder."

This was on the evening of Saturday, 28 August.

"Well?" he asked, after Strindberg had got the primus going.

"A lovely evening," I said. "Clear, dry air. A fantastic phenomenon, that halo, and the most incredible colours. The wind is perhaps a trifle strong, considering the lowness of the temperature, but we can still work without gloves, for short periods at least."

"What are you driving at?" he asked.

"This," I said. "For the past five days and nights the condition of the ice has been reasonably good, and we've covered some not inconsiderable distances."

"You sound damnably arrogant," he said.

"How far south do you think we've got since we took our bearings at twelve o'clock noon on 23 August?" I asked. "That is, in five days and nights plus twelve hours."

"Difficult to say," he answered.

"Yes, but guess, give a rough estimate."

His glance wavered unsteadily between me and Strindberg.

"At least twenty, at most thirty kilometres," he said at last.

He added fiercely: "You've no right to put me with my back to the wall, damn you. You and Strindberg are the persons responsible for taking our bearings."

"But you're the leader of the expedition," I answered.

"Let's make a summary of the position," I said, "sum it up calmly and sensibly.

"Don't lose your temper! I'm not putting you up against a wall. I'm not accusing you. I'm only trying to summarize, to take a very rough summary.

"First we decided to make for Franz Josef Land, course southeast.

"We drifted steadily west.

"On 4 August we decided to turn south-west, towards the Seven

Islands, course S.40°W. But we drifted east. We altered course to S.50°W.

"Each day our marches were hard and exhausting. Can you remember when our clothes were last quite dry?

"The ice drifted east. We had to alter course to S.60°W. or, to be more precise, to W.30°S.

"These past five days the going has been good. It has grown colder, and those accursed puddles of melt water, of fresh water, are now covered with ice that bears, that is five or six centimetres thick.

"You're right, Andrée," I said. "We can boast that we've covered a distance of thirty kilometres in the past five days."

"Is all this necessary?" asked Strindberg.

"I'm just running through everything," I said.

"Thanks to the glowing sun and the somewhat paler moon Strindberg and I have been able to take our bearings with unusual precision.

"We've counted and calculated, we've recounted and recalculated. Especially Strindberg, who's better at mathematics than I am."

Soup of bears' brains, grey, reddish.

Strindberg served it up in our mugs.

"I'm waiting impatiently for the 'knock-out'," said Andrée, slurping his soup from his mug.

"Those damnable movements of the pack ice," I said. "We've marched south-west, but the movement of the ice has suddenly changed. It's no longer drifting east, nor has it been affected by your north winds, Andrée! I can't understand why you still put your trust in the winds!

"No, it's drifted in the opposite direction, towards the west, and a little towards the north.

"For the past five days we've journeyed across the ice towards the south-west, but we've drifted at least thirty kilometres towards the west, and what's worse, two or three kilometres towards the north.

"All the ground we've won by our exertions, has been lost in the westward and northward drift of the ice."

Andrée did not answer. He spread out the Englishman Bartholomew's 'Physical Chart of the North Polar Regions' on the sleeping-bag.

"You're undoubtedly right," he said. "We've drifted towards the west, and also somewhat towards the north.

"Still the fact remains," he said, "that we're now nearer the Seven Islands than we've been at any time since we left the place where we landed.

"That's indisputable."

I had a fresh attack of diarrhoea and returned to the tent frozen stiff.

"Opium?" asked Andrée.

"I'd rather have morphia," I answered. "I need sleep. It's essential for you too that I should sleep, that I should to some extent be rested."

He gave me a capsule of morphia and I swallowed it with a sip of lukewarm polar bear's brains.

"If you listen," said Andrée, "don't you hear the roar of the open sea? We must be on the outskirts of the pack ice."

We listened, Strindberg and I, but we heard nothing except the flapping of the canvas in the wind, and the dull rumble of ice being squeezed together, of floes being pushed on top of each other.

"We must be on the outer edge of the pack ice," said Andrée. "We shall soon meet with the open sea."

"You talk about the open sea," I said. "Have you forgotten the long discussion we had after we landed on the ice?

"You were afraid of the open sea.

"You were afraid of leaving the ice and the sledges, and of putting our lives at the mercy of our fragile craft of wooden ribs and varnished silk."

"Was I?"

"Yes," said Strindberg, "you certainly were."

"It's obvious that I've changed my mind," answered Andrée. "Our experiences to date have increased my confidence in the boat, in its carrying capacity, and its sea-worthiness. I'm man enough to be able to change my mind."

"You've good reason to," I said, and crept into the sleeping-bag. "What do you mean by that?"

"I can only think of two things that have been thoroughly well thought out in the whole of our expedition, things that are almost works of genius."

"Which two are they?" asked Andrée.

"One is the balloon-house," I said. "An inspired building. The other is the boat. Plym's boat-yard in Stockholm, if I remember rightly. A pity we can't send him a telegram of thanks, send the boat-yard one."

"The sledges?" said Strindberg.

"Good in themselves," I replied, "but you must have seen for yourself that they're too lightly built.

"On top of that: the haul-harness is a mistake. You ought not to pull with your shoulders, but with the whole of the upper part of your body. The webbing belts should rest on your hips, not on your shoulders. As we haven't got skis, we haven't got ski-sticks either. Our pulling-power in exposed places would have been increased by half as much again if we'd had good strong sticks in our hands.

"Nansen had sticks with him on his journey across Greenland, and he and his men used them even when they couldn't use their skis.

"I'd like to repeat what I've said at least once before," I said. "It's madness to pull a sledge weighing more than a hundred kilos by ropes.

"Try to think of a horse pulling a load of timber simply with ropes. The very idea is insane. Timber-sledges have shafts. Our sledges too should have had shafts, made for instance of coarse rattan."

I had taken my gelatin capsule of morphia, and I could feel sleep creeping over me.

"I'm no fool," I said. "I've a whole catalogue of objections to the organization of this expedition, I've taken morphia. I shall be asleep in a few minutes.

"Hang up all our wet clothes on the ridge-pole. Put out the primus. We're short of paraffin. Light Göransson's spirit-lamp instead.

"Air the tent.

"The humidity is low. Our soaking wet clothes may be almost dry tomorrow morning.

"Warm yourselves with the spirit-lamp, and air the tent as often as you can."

I fell asleep.

30

We altered course to S.45°W.: more simply expressed, we went due south-west.

This was the theoretical direction of our march. Our real course, the result of our wanderings plus the drift of the ice, would remain unknown to us until we had another opportunity of taking reliable bearings. It was not impossible that we were dragging our sledges along a line parallel to the 82° of latitude, in the direction of the infinitely distant northernmost coast of Greenland.

The leads and channels had grown wider, and crossing them by the time-wasting method of ferrying became even more repulsive.

We did not get far each day. The wind blew mainly from the north-west and slowly increased in velocity. The temperature rose to four degrees below zero and then sank again.

I shot yet another polar bear, our eleventh.

This bear turned in his tracks and fled. I let him go for I was certain he would soon drop dead. I had fired a lucky shot and hit him in the neck, and we had to be careful with our ammunition.

All the same when he threw himself into a lead I fired another shot that killed him instantly.

By using the grapnel and a boat-hook we got him up on to the ice.

"Enough meat for ten days," said Strindberg, delightedly.

"But it has cost us four bullets," said Andrée.

"You've got your figures wrong, damn you," I said. "I only fired two shots! You boast that you don't need sun-glasses, but it strikes me that you hear double."

"And you?" asked Andrée, turning to Strindberg.

"I didn't count," he said, "I don't know how many shots were fired."

"Meat for fourteen days," I said. "We can put it on my sledge, in the boat."

A short day's march with a falling temperature and a strengthening wind. We did not get under way until ten o'clock in the evening.

The ice was under violent pressure, and it seemed to us that it was also being affected by the waves of an invisible sea.

It was an unforgettable landscape, a drawing, or rather a lithograph by Doré. Massive blocks of ice with perpendicular sides four or five metres high, often hooded with newly fallen snow. Some were worn away by water so that their sides were not perpendicular, but overhanging. These blocks must have gone down to a depth of thirty or forty metres, and weighed four, five, six, or ten thousand tons. Between these gigantic blocks were floes, large and small, all more or less broken up and ground to pieces. Lastly there was the newly formed ice that covered the leads and channels, crystal-clear, a few inches thick, sometimes split and then rafted, so that up to ten layers might be lying one on top of the other, frozen together, or not yet frozen together.

This landscape was full of a continuous rumble punctuated by frequent roars that sounded like peals of thunder.

Did Doré ever make any lithographs, I wonder?

The following day we managed for the first time to cross a broad lead without either having to ferry ourselves across or build a bridge of floating floes.

The lead was about twenty-five metres broad and covered by a single layer of newly formed blue ice. The temperature was seven degrees below zero, the wind mainly north and strong.

This lead ran almost due north-south, and we were therefore obliged to cross it in order to continue our west-south-west course in our wanderings towards the south-west.

We stopped to discuss the situation. Andrée had a slight attack of diarrhoea, and withdrew behind a small toros.

When he returned he fastened the rope of the grapnel round his waist and crept out on to the frozen lead, after having first tested the thickness of the ice with an axe. He crept prostrate, almost as if he were swimming. Halfway across he drove his knife into the ice and found that it was five centimetres thick. He got cautiously to his feet and went on, walking, to the other side.

He then pulled across his sledge and Strindberg's. We kept mine to the last as it was the heaviest.

Strindberg and I arranged an improvised race across the springy ice.

He won, but collapsed on the other side coughing violently. He spat out great quantities of phlegm, but was not sick.

At midnight between the last day of August and the first day of September the sun touched the horizon for the first time.

There were only a few clouds in the sky.

Almost at the very second that the lower rim of the sun brushed the northern horizon the white-hot light was extinguished, and in its place came red flames that set the whole landscape on fire.

We stood still for a long time turned towards the north.

"Ice like a sea of flame," said Andrée.

"Fantastic spectacle," said Strindberg.

"Hard to decide," I said, "which of you is being most lyrical. The temperature is four degrees below zero, the force of the wind seven point seven metres per second, from the north-north-west. Our course is still S.45°W. Or W.45°S."

We travelled at a good pace across stretches of ice almost a kilometre long, formed by floes that had frozen together.

I forced as rapid a tempo as I was able and Andrée and Strindberg had hard work to keep up with me.

The fantastic spectacle, the flaming landscape of ice, meant that we had passed a chronological boundary.

We had left the arctic summer behind us.

Night had returned.

We were on our way into the short arctic autumn, and the arctic winter that would follow it.

We pushed on for a few hours after midnight, into a new day, a new month.

I pulled my sledge up a toros that was not particularly high. Its western slope was unexpectedly steep. I slithered into a crack between two blocks of ice and fell over. The sledge came rushing after me like a steam-roller. The haul-ropes acted as a brake; it swung round abruptly and rolled over several times.

The boat escaped without injury, but the sledge itself was badly damaged.

I lost consciousness for a few seconds, but had time to warn Andrée and Strindberg to halt on top of the hummock of ice.

It was difficult to judge distances and the steepness of the descents in the rosy dusk of those midnight hours.

We pitched camp at the foot of the toros, put up the tent and spread out the sleeping-bag and the blankets.

Strindberg boiled up a soup of bear's brains and Mellin's Food, and added some diced polar bear's kidney.

We were all hit almost simultaneously by attacks of diarrhoea.

Strindberg returned to the tent as fast as he could to attend to the soup.

Andrée started to chop holes in the ice, partly with the axe, partly with our harpoon.

I sat down on a sledge. The wind made me shiver with cold, but I felt I must watch his futile investigations.

He managed to make three holes in the ice.

"How thick is it?" I asked. "The ice? The ice, of course?"

He turned slowly towards me. "You here?" he said.

"Where else should I be?" I asked.

"Between seventy and a hundred and thirty-five centimetres," he answered.

He then bent forwards over the ice and supported himself on his elbows.

I ran up to him and threw my arms round his waist to stop him from falling over.

"What's wrong?" I asked.

"Nothing," he answered.

"Cramp?" I asked.

"Not on your life," he answered.

After about half a minute he extricated himself from my grasp, walked up to the tent and crept in.

The tent was warm. It sheltered us from the piercing northerly wind. We ate our soup of polar bear's brains and tiny dice of polar bear's kidney.

Strindberg had to interrupt his meal to pay a hasty visit outside the tent.

"We must rest, we must sleep," said Andrée.

He dealt out three doses of opium between us. "For our diarrhoea," he said. We also had a capsule of morphia each. "For our stomach cramp," he said. "And to promote a night's sleep. It's good for arctic explorers to sleep."

Strindberg fell asleep first.

He went on coughing in his sleep, a long, rasping cough.

"What do you make of that?" I asked. "There are not supposed to be any coughs and colds in the Arctic Ocean. Nor any bacteria that produce colds. But our noses are always running, and Strindberg there looks like a very ordinary case of influenza."

Under the stubble on his face, now two centimetres long, his cheeks were hollow, his hair was tangled and damp.

A temperature?

Andrée took his pulse cautiously, with an unpractised hand. "Between eighty and ninety," he said.

"What's normal?"

"Really impossible to say what's normal under circumstances like ours," he said, and turned Strindberg gently on to his side. Soon afterwards he stopped coughing.

I wrote my meteorological notes.

"Do you know," I said, "it's almost exactly fifty days and nights to the hour since we took off from Danes Island."

But Andrée was already asleep. Even in his sleep he kept his eyes screwed up. His beard had grown unevenly. It was grey, and he gave the impression of being an old man. He was perspiring, and his forehead felt hot to my touch.

He too was sleeping on his back. I turned him gently on his side, not because he was coughing, but to avoid having to hear him snore.

3 1

I awoke to renewed attacks of cramp, very painful ones in the calf muscles of both my legs. I massaged them as well as I could until my companions awoke and came to my rescue. We had found that the best way of loosening the cramp was to shake the muscles sideways and then rub them energetically from the lower part upwards.

When the worst of my pain had eased it was Andrée's turn to writhe in agony. His cramp was in the thick muscles at the back of his right thigh. They were knotted so hard that they felt as if they had been carved in wood.

"Now it's your turn," I said to Strindberg, when we had got Andrée's thigh back to normal.

"I've an important errand to run first," he answered, and dived rapidly out of the tent.

He came in again with his breeches undone, sank on to the sleeping-bag, and burst out laughing.

"What luck that it spurts out of itself," he said, "for God knows, I've not the strength left to help it on. What's more I can hardly stand on my left foot.

"We're certainly a pitiful sort of caravan," he said, and burst out laughing again.

He then lit the primus stove and began to prepare our usual afternoon breakfast, while I wrote my meteorological notes: still the same north-westerly wind, force about seven metres per second, temperature five or six degrees below zero.

During breakfast we discussed all imaginable reasons for our attacks of cramp and diarrhoea. We arrived at two possible explanations: general over-exertion or, getting the whole body too severely chilled by falling into the water, and by marching in clothes that were damp, or often soaking wet.

"Or a combination of both," said Andrée.

Both explanations were arguments in favour of our taking twenty-four hours' rest.

The humidity was low and, by a combination of warming and airing the tent, we should be able to get our clothes reasonably dry with only a modest consumption of paraffin.

We also had quite a number of things to attend to. We had to repair the sleeping-bag, to mend our clothes and footwear, to repair my sledge, and so on.

The decision to take twenty-four hours' rest made us all feel so relaxed that we did practically nothing. We lay on our backs most of the time, we chatted and dozed.

I did however perform a minor operation on Strindberg's left toe, which was twice its normal size. I sharpened my pocket knife carefully on the whetstone, warmed it over the flame of the primus, and made a small incision close to the nail. The boil literally exploded, and I got a large lump of pus and blood on my palm.

"A big toe with diarrhoea," I said to Andrée, and held out my hand to him. "Don't you want to take charge of this scientific specimen?"

"That's eased it," said Strindberg, and washed the sore with a solution of mercuric chloride.

The following day Strindberg was able to move without difficulty, and we set to work to repair my broken sledge.

Andrée spent most of his time measuring the thickness of the ice. He also attempted to take a sounding, but our lines were not long enough to touch bottom. However, he did ascertain that the line did not sink perpendicularly, but curved eastwards, which indicated the presence of strong currents.

At midday the sun peeped through the haze, and Strindberg succeeded in taking reliable bearings which showed that, during the past five days, we had drifted no less than thirty-one nautical miles, or over fifty-seven kilometres, practically dead south.

We celebrated the event in polar bear's kidneys, biscuits, and strong coffee.

This drift of barely sixty kilometres towards the south excited us to the brink of intoxication.

"Why?" I asked.

"Well, at any rate it's between a fifth and a seventh part of the way from where we landed to the depot on the Seven Islands," said Andrée. "And we've covered most of it lying in our tent.

"Resting, eating, repairing ourselves, and all our goods and chattels."

"But we've drifted south," I said, "not south-west. We've not got more than perhaps five kilometres nearer the Seven Islands."

"We've at any rate got fifty-seven kilometres nearer North East Land, Spitzbergen," said Strindberg.

He was right. Fifty-seven kilometres nearer dry land and a fresh chance.

"All is well," I said. "We must be happy, and thankful for this new and rapid movement of the ice.

"I've a bottle of schnapps in my bag. I should like to take it out and drink to the day.

"But I don't trust the ice.

"I don't trust its rapid movements or their direction.

"They're far too rapid, and they take far too many directions.

"Another five days with another drift of sixty kilometres towards the south, why then we'll open my bottle.

"But not till then."

In the afternoon the northerly wind fell light, veered and became south-westerly, though it did not blow hard. The temperature rose slightly. It grew more cloudy.

Andrée did not approve of the new direction of the wind.

"Don't worry," I said. "Why do you still believe there's a connection between the winds and the drift of the ice and the currents?

"Lying on the pack ice is one thing.

337

"Floating through the air in a crazy balloon that's wrongly designed is another."

We spent yet another night in our camp.

Now we could really talk of nights. During the hours round midnight dusk reigned out of doors, and there was an even deeper dusk in our tent.

We decided that in future we would respect the fact that there were days and nights and adapt the rhythm of our work to it.

On this last night in our rest-camp I awoke to hear Andrée scrambling out of the sleeping-bag and out of the tent. It was just after midnight.

I realized from the sounds I heard that he was suffering torments.

After a few minutes he returned to the tent, crawling on hands and knees.

"Are you asleep?" he asked.

I did not answer. He repeated his question. I did not answer.

He dug into the medicine chest which was just by the opening of the tent and, still sitting, smeared his crotch with—I guess—lanoline ointment. He then pulled up his long pants and breeches. He was breathing heavily. For a couple of minutes he massaged the muscles of his right thigh.

There was about half a cupful of lukewarm water in our cooking apparatus. He poured it into his mug. He took three gelatine capsules from the medicine chest, probably two doses of opium and one of morphia. He swilled them down with the drop of water in the mug.

There was enough light for me to follow everything he was doing.

He took off his stockings, hung them up on the ridge-pole of the tent, and put on a pair of thick, goat's-hair socks.

After that he tied up the flap of the tent and crept into the sleeping-bag.

His movements were heavy, slow, and fumbling, as if he were very drunk.

I lay awake for at least an hour. The light grew stronger.

Strindberg was sleeping deeply and peacefully.

338

Andrée was lying curled up on his right side. His face was turned towards me. It was flaccid, except for the tightly clenched muscles round his eyes. His mouth was half open, and yellow saliva dribbled slowly from its right-hand corner and was caught by his tangled grey beard.

For a few seconds I wondered about my own growth of beard, and my own appearance, but I made no attempt to find the mirror.

For a few minutes I brooded upon the belief and trust I always felt when in Andrée's presence. Or that I had formerly felt in his presence.

I could not make up my mind how much there was left either of belief or trust.

Andrée was an old man.

What are an old man's weaknesses?

How much are an old man's experiences worth?

32

Strindberg roused us and gave us bear's meat and hot cocoa.

The temperature was only a few degrees below zero, and the wind slight and westerly. The sky was cloudy.

We were able to pull on clothes that were less damp than they had been for a long time.

Nevertheless, the inside of the tent—not least its floor—was covered with a thick crust of ice, which must have represented a considerable weight. Our sleeping-bag too had a heavy layer of ice on the under side.

The pack ice had split up to a surprising extent. We were on a floe that was surrounded by open water.

We put the boat into the water, placed the sledges athwart the gunwale, got in ourselves, and found that the boat floated with more than thirty centimetres of freeboard.

Strindberg and I took the oars. Andrée steered.

We rowed for hours through a delta-like landscape, between islands of ice now large, now small, through a network of channels that were sometimes wide, sometimes narrow.

We tried to keep to a south-westerly course, our objective being the Seven Islands.

"Rowing is a heavenly way of travelling," I said to Andrée. "Especially for those who have walked for so long in the wrong direction to no purpose.

"Aren't we on the outer edge of the pack ice?

"The place you've so often talked about?

"Shan't we throw the sledges overboard? Three times at least sixteen kilos makes close on fifty kilos."

"Not on your life," he answered. "The sledges are our life-line."

Soon after this our lead of open water narrowed and became un-navigable. We tried to turn back and look for a passage through another lead, but were halted by a large, immovable block of ice.

We unloaded the sledges and our baggage and pulled the boat on to the ice.

We pitched camp for the night.

During a brief spell, in which we were able to see the disc of the sun, Strindberg took our bearings and found that we had travelled another ten kilometres south.

Morning, 4 September, a Saturday.

I awoke first, assisted by cramp. I gently roused Andrée, and together we woke Strindberg by singing in unison. It was his twenty-fifth birthday.

I fired a salute with my Remington. Andrée handed him two letters; one from Anna Charlier, his fiancée, and one from his parents. I dug out a brief letter from the great Svante Arhennius, which I had been keeping for far too long in one of my back pockets, so long indeed that it was difficult to extract the letter from the envelope.

We ate a grand breakfast consisting of Stauffer's pea soup, bear-steaks, plus bread and coffee—strong, hot coffee.

Our day's march was short.

We had only been going a couple of hours when Strindberg and his sledge landed up in the water. He had been rashly trying to cross a lead covered by new ice.

I got the tent up while Andrée salvaged Strindberg, his sledge, and its load.

Strindberg was all but unconscious with cold by the time we dragged him into the tent, took off his wet clothes, wrapped him in a blanket, and succeeded in persuading him to creep into the sleeping-bag.

Dealing with the load on his sledge was worse. Practically all our bread and biscuits were soaked through with salt water, and had been transformed into a glutinous mass. All our sugar too was wet with salt water.

We had some difficulty in knowing what to do with the theodolite, and Strindberg's two chronometers. We rinsed them carefully in fresh water and then dried them over the paraffin stove.

I was impressed by Andrée's calm and self-control.

That evening we had a celebration dinner consisting of bear's meat, a plentiful number of liver-paste sandwiches, Stauffer cake out of a tin, fruit-juice and water, and finally a mug each of hot coffee.

"You fall into the water far too often," said Andrée. "You must be more careful."

"Have you begun to hope again?" asked Strindberg.

PART SIX

WINTERING ON THE ICE

I

A week of strenuous exertions.

A wind that constantly changed direction, and slowly but steadily increased in strength.

A temperature that oscillated between one degree and seven degrees below zero.

The movements of the ice were visible to the naked eye.

A lead, fifty metres wide, could open up before us, or close, in the space of ten minutes or so.

Short spells of heavy snow-fall.

Even shorter spells of half-freezing drizzle.

Andrée complained of constipation. Strange after his long period of constant diarrhoea.

I shot some gulls, five of them, with two bursts of small shot. They tasted good, but there was not much meat on them.

"Be sure you keep their eyes," I said to Andrée. "They may perhaps teach us something about the mechanism of snow-blindness."

Our supply of polar bear's meat was running out.

My left foot began to give me a great deal of trouble. I had two large boils on it, one just behind the big toe, the other a few inches behind the little toe.

"I know what it feels like," said Strindberg.

"You do?"

"I've had a boil myself," he said.

"You can't measure pain," I said. "You had one boil, I've two. It's naïve to suppose that two boils hurt twice as much as one. It's possible that my two boils hurt more than five times as much as your one.

"What's more, you haven't had the muscular cramp that I've had.

"Pain and torment can't be measured," I repeated.

My foot swelled up, my boot pinched me. I could not get a purchase on the ice, and I could not pull my sledge single-handed.

Andrée and Strindberg had to walk a few hundred metres along our route, turn back, and take over my sledge. All I could do to help them was to push it from behind.

The whole of my left leg ached.

Our progress was further hampered by the fact that Strindberg too was having trouble with one of his feet.

We had altered course to west-south-west.

Our day's marches grew shorter and shorter.

The nights grew longer.

The first stars became visible in the sky when the fog and clouds thinned enough for us to see them.

2

For two days snow-storms and cold forced us to remain stationary.

Let me explain: by 'remain stationary' I mean that we huddled together in the tent and let ourselves drift wherever the ice took us.

The temperature was mostly about eight degrees below zero, and the force of the wind varied between ten and fourteen metres per second.

Eight degrees below zero, Centigrade, is not much in itself. But the wind!

I held a damp stocking outside the opening of the tent, just above the ridge-pole.

In thirty seconds it was frozen stiff.

"Make a note of it in your scientific report," I said to Andrée. "Damp stocking frozen stiff in less than thirty seconds."

*   *   *

We lay still in our tent.

The pressure ice rumbled and roared, sounds that we now had to exert ourselves to hear.

On the first day—12 September—the weather cleared enough at midday to allow Strindberg and me to take our bearings.

"Strong wind from the north-east," I said to Andrée. "Just what we want, isn't it? We're drifting southwards, almost straight for the Seven Islands, aren't we? What's given you your faith in the winds? Do you know where we really are?"

"I should very much like to know," said Andrée, "but drivel doesn't interest me."

"Well," I said, "we're ten kilometres east and somewhat north of the point at which we were ten days ago. We're clearly making good headway at the moment. We're sailing close to the wind. Direction, the North Pole.

"The pack ice is better able to move against the wind than your excellent balloon. What a pity we haven't still got the polar buoy. We may have use for it in a few days' time perhaps."

"You sound a trifle unbalanced," said Andrée.

"No," I said, "I'm a sturdily built jovial giant. I've had that in black and white from the *Daily News* of London. I'm not unbalanced. I'm tired, but I'm not unbalanced.

"I've done a lot of thinking these last weeks," I said. "There are many things I should like to talk to you about, but I'll refrain if you don't feel inclined to listen."

"Talk as much as you like," he replied. "Just go on talking."

He crawled out of the sleeping-bag and lay down on top of it wrapped in Doctor Lembke's blanket. "It's confoundedly hot," he said.

"No, it's not confoundedly hot," I said. "On the contrary, it's very much on the cold side, but you've got a temperature."

The light in the tent was dim in spite of the fact that it was only about one o'clock in the afternoon. The inside of the tent was covered half way up by a crust of ice, and ice and snow had collected on the outside and settled there.

I took out a tallow candle and lit it.

"I've another four," I said. "I'm sorry I haven't fifty or a hundred. A single candle lights the tent," I said, "and if we chuck some snow on the outside it's enough to keep the temperature inside from falling. But there are no candles in our equipment, Andrée. I brought along six in my private bag, I had a feeling we should be glad of them. Why were there no candles in your list of requirements?"

"I had to choose," said Andrée, "to make up my mind for and against, to reject many things you may think were essential."

"I've often mused over the moment of our start," I said, "when we lost two-thirds of the guide-ropes, when the car was pressed down on to the waters of Danes Gat, and you and Strindberg fell into a panic, and cut away sack after sack of ballast and transformed the *Eagle* into a free-sailing balloon."

"Go on," said Andrée.

"I'd always thought of you as an expert balloonist," I said. "I wasn't the only person who did. The whole of Sweden, almost the whole of Europe thought likewise. I've read all the short articles you've written about your ascents in your balloon the *Svea*. I've some of them with me here. I've read them over again when I've not been able to sleep."

"Well?"

"Do you know," I said, "how many ascents Charles Green made? I seem to remember it was five hundred and twenty-six. It may have been five hundred and sixteen, or five hundred and thirty-six. Gaston Tissandier? I don't believe he ever counted all the hundreds of ascents he made.

"And then," I said, "about a week ago, it suddenly struck me that you, Andrée, who'd planned and set off upon the greatest and most daring balloon expedition the world has so far witnessed, that you had no more than nine ascents to your credit, and those in a frail little balloon!

"Nine ascents! That was all.

"In actual fact," I said, "as a balloonist you're really only an amateur, a beginner. Your balloon the *Svea*, with a volume of just over a thousand cubic metres, was a pygmy among manned balloons!

"You're self-taught," I said. "No disrespect intended to the self-taught in general. I too made nine ascents with Swedenborg in Paris. But we made our ascents with singularly knowledgeable people, who gave us methodical instruction. The cautious old Lachambre, for whom aeronautics had become the noble art of the weigh-master. The daring Alexis Machuron, with his long moustaches. That extraordinarily clever man Besançon, to whom ballooning was both a fine art and a sport for professionals.

"I don't want to hurt your feelings," I said.

"They aren't easily hurt," answered Andrée.

"It's not beyond the bounds of possibility," I said, "that I know more about ballooning than you do. I felt I did when you cut loose those sacks of ballast in Danes Gat."

Strindberg lit the primus and prepared a simple midday meal.

The floe had twisted round towards the east, and the north-east wind was blowing snow in through the flap of the tent, though I'd fastened it as tightly as I could.

"Here in my bag," I said, "I've your account of how you tried to steer your balloon the *Svea* by using guide-ropes and a sail.

"The attempt was made on 14 July 1895. The article is dated 12 December of the same year."

"Quite correct," said Andrée.

"An excellent account, with many data, many sketch-maps, and plenty of information about the direction of the wind and the direction in which you sailed.

"According to the text," I said, "you managed to make the balloon deviate from the direction of the wind by up to thirty degrees."

"Quite correct," said Andrée.

"But your whole voyage didn't last longer than three and a half hours," I said.

"If I remember rightly," he said, "my sixth ascent in the *Svea*."

We ate bear's-meat soup and the bread we had dried out, still salty from sea water.

After that we drank weak but hot coffee.

The wind was increasing in strength. The pressure ice was rumbling and roaring. We could not hear these sounds without making an effort.

* * *

"It was on this single experiment—that only lasted three and a half hours—to steer a balloon with a sail and guide-ropes that you based our attempt to sail to the North Pole," I said.

"Not only did you convince King Oscar, Alfred Nobel, Dickson and Retzius—not counting Nordenskiöld—that it would be possible. You convinced the whole world that it was possible, if we exclude the aeronautical experts.

"What's more, the design of your sail, and the way in which the guide-ropes were placed was one huge mistake.

"The three guide-ropes were placed far too close to the centre of the balloon. The ballast-ropes were made fast to the carrying-ring in front of the sail. When the balloon sank so low that the ballast-ropes trailed in the water and over the ice, the balloon made a half turn about and the sail came round to leeward, instead of remaining to windward. Thus the ropes ceased to have any effect on the steering."

"What you say is entirely correct," said Andrée. "If I'm not mistaken you've brought the subject up before."

"Both the guide-ropes and the ballast-ropes should be put to leeward of the carrying-ring, and as far aft as possible."

"You're right," answered Andrée.

"I'm not fond of arguments," said Strindberg. "And I don't much want to start criticizing you at this late date. But the fact is that both Ekholm and I pointed out as long ago as last year that the guide-ropes were far too near the centre of the balloon."

"Did you?" asked Andrée.

"You promised to attend to the matter," said Strindberg. "Nothing was ever done."

We ate warm meat-soup and our salty bread. Afterwards we drank hot, weak coffee, without sugar.

Andrée was lying on top of the sleeping-bag. He pushed off Lembke's blanket.

"Hot as hell," he said.

"You've a fever," I said, "though there are no fevers north of the seventieth parallel, or thereabouts.

"Would you like opium or morphia?" I asked.

"Neither," he answered.

"I don't want to bully you," I said.

"You can't bully me," answered Andrée.

"When Doctor Ekholm resigned," I said, "he asserted among other things that the balloon leaked far too much. That it would not be able to keep afloat a month, as you had promised."

"Among other things," said Andrée.

"Now your views," I said.

"What views?" he asked.

"That the *Eagle* would keep afloat for thirty days, for seven hundred and fifty hours. But after only fifty hours the car began to bounce on the ice and drag across it. Seven hundred and fifty hours against fifty hours."

"The icing," he answered. "The moisture and the icing. When we landed the balloon was weighed down by more than a ton of ice and moisture.

"If it hadn't been for the moisture and the ice we should have been in Siberia or Alaska by this time," he said.

"Ekholm thought that the balloon leaked too much," I said. "Nobel offered to pay for an entirely new balloon. You refused his offer."

"Of course," answered Andrée. "The *Eagle* is the best balloon that has ever been made. Why build a new balloon? At the best it could only have been as good as the *Eagle*."

"The guide-ropes, the sail, the dirigibility of the balloon?"

"Confoundedly complicated details," said Andrée.

"Why didn't you test the balloon beforehand? Test its loss of gas, its lifting power, its dirigibility?"

"Lack of time," answered Andrée. "We simply hadn't the time. We simply hadn't the time, my dear man."

3

What I remember about the second day is a falling temperature and a north-easterly wind, that veered more and more to the north-west.

It was with the greatest reluctance that we left the tent to perform our natural functions.

I had some bad attacks of cramp in the muscles of my calves. The two boils on my left foot were spreading.

Strindberg opened the boils by making two small incisions with my pocket-knife. A jet of pus and blood spurted out of both. The pain subsided. He washed the sores by flushing them with a solution of mercuric chloride.

"Service for service rendered," I said.

Gale and severe cold.

We discussed our situation for hours.

"We must be realistic and cynical," I said.

"Why not?" asked Andrée.

"I'm tired," I said, "damned tired. I've cramp in my legs and two boils on my left foot.

"All the same I'm the strongest of us. You're no longer young, Andrée. And you, Strindberg, are too young and too delicate.

"There's no sense in continuing to toil along like this with our sledges. There's no sense in wandering on any further, wandering blindly, trudging east and drifting west, trudging south and drifting north.

"And no matter in what direction we trudge or drift, one thing is indisputable: we're on our way into winter, into snow-storms, and lower temperatures than any of us can conceive of.

"I'm the strongest of us, and I've the courage to say straight out that I feel I can't go on any longer. The wounds on my foot will prevent me from pulling my own sledge for another two days. And after that it will be my turn to help with your sledges.

"There's only one sensible thing left for us to do. We must build a solid hut of snow and ice in which we have a chance to survive the winter. When spring starts to return we can continue our journey."

"I've been thinking the same for a long time," said Strindberg.

"I bow to the view of the majority," said Andrée.

"As always," I said.

During a brief lull, when the wind decreased somewhat, Strindberg and I made a hasty inventory of our provision.

The result was not encouraging.

We should have to introduce strict rationing: four hectos of meat, two hectos of Mellin's food, seventy-five grammes of soaked biscuits or bread, and two helpings of a warm drink, made either from thirty grammes of coffee, or thirty grammes of cocoa, all reckoned per twenty-four hours between the three of us.

If we adhered to these rations our supplies would last for three weeks.

Andrée was fast asleep, wrapped in Lembke's blanket.

"He's been making an inventory of our medical supplies," I said. "The chest has been moved a few decimetres, and there's no longer any snow on the lid. At a guess, one capsule of opium and one of morphia."

The velocity of the wind increased again.

We had some difficulty in inserting Andrée into the sleeping-bag.

After doing so we fastened the opening of the tent as securely as we could.

4

Light northerly morning breeze, slight snow-fall, fog, visibility no more than a few hundred metres, temperature two degrees below zero.

It was plain that we could not remain on our present floe. It was quite small, and seemed to consist of a toros that had collapsed, and some sheets of ice that were insecurely frozen together.

"What a pity it is, Andrée," I said, "that during the two days we've lain here you didn't take the opportunity of making some of your scientific investigations about the thickness of the ice and its composition."

Andrée suggested that we should do some reconnoitring to try to find a suitable floe on which to build our hut.

"And leave all our equipment here?" I asked.

"Yes, we shall be quicker that way, and be able to explore a larger area."

"Each of us on his own? Each of us in a different direction?"

"Yes, why not?"

"You must be fuddled," I said, "or not yet properly awake."

"This ice is moving all the time. The leads open and then close again, the ridges of pressure ice are pushed upwards and then collapse, it's snowing, it's foggy, the visibility is only a few hundred metres. You're talking like a madman! You want us to go off reconnoitring, you east, Strindberg south, and I west!"

"Perhaps not," he said.

"In less than fifteen minutes we should each be the loneliest of living creatures in this damnable white swamp. We should never find either our camp or each other again."

"By tomorrow," added Strindberg, "we should all be dead."

We struck camp. Our tent, covered as it was with a crust of ice both inside and out, gave us a great deal of trouble. We pulled off as much ice as we could, but even then did not dare to fold it and thus risk splitting the canvas. We spread it out in the boat.

"It once weighed nine kilos," I said. "Now it must weigh at least twenty."

The underside of the sleeping-bag was also reinforced with a thick layer of ice which was even more difficult to break up and remove. We put it on top of the tent.

"There was a time when the sleeping-bag also weighed nine kilos," said Strindberg.

While we were packing a broad lead opened immediately south of our camp. So we continued our journey, our search for a suitable floe, with a short boat trip.

"It's strange," I said, "how obstinately, and as a matter of course, we go south, though at this moment the ice may be drifting west, and we should get further south by walking south-east."

And on we pushed, southwards.

It was impossible for me to manage my sledge alone. When I made the effort to do so I could feel blood and pus filling my left boot. Andrée and Strindberg helped me a few hundred metres forward, and then went back for their own sledges. Thus we proceeded on our way.

Our progress was exceedingly slow. Because of the frequent ridges of pressure ice, because of the new snow that did not give a firm foothold, that covered over cracks and crevices, and had in places piled into drifts a metre high. These last were invisible in the diffuse shadowless light, and you did not know they were there until you stumbled and fell headlong.

In the afternoon we found a fairly large floe that inspired confidence. It was unusually flat, and had no open puddles of fresh water.

We stopped in the middle of it, close to a large, square hummock, which shot up about two metres above its surroundings.

I noticed that Andrée was limping too.

"A boil?" I asked.

He shook his head.

"Cramp?"

"Nothing to worry about," he said.

"Are you in pain?"

"Not worse than I can bear," he answered.

Strindberg and I sat down on a sledge in the lee of the big hummock of ice.

Andrée wandered round the floe. It was bounded to the north, the east, and the south by rather low ridges of pressure ice. To the west a lead of open water was forming and being covered as it grew with a thin film of new ice.

It had stopped snowing, the visibility was still negligible. The temperature was falling, and the wind slowly increasing and blowing mainly from the north.

Strindberg and I lit our pipes. We were sweaty after our march and we were cold. But we were so used to being cold that we no longer thought much about it.

"Like the rumbling of the pressure ice," said Strindberg, "you have to make an effort to hear it."

Andrée was wandering round the floe in ever-decreasing circles. He had our harpoon with him, and at every other step he drove it into the ice.

The snow covering was about two decimetres thick, except to windward of the projecting blocks of ice where there were deep drifts.

"Well?" I said, when he came back to us.

"The floe seems stable," he said, "but it's covered with snow, and in this light it's difficult to see how it's been formed."

"In spite of the fact that you don't need sun-glasses," I said.

After a short discussion we decided to pitch camp. Discussion was indeed superfluous, as we were all too tired to go any further.

Getting the tent up was difficult because it was so encrusted with ice.

The sleeping-bag creaked and squeaked like a ridge of pressure ice when we spread it out on the floor.

Strindberg lit the paraffin stove and prepared our meagre supper. Warmth spread through the tent, and when the ice and frost stopped dripping off the inside of the canvas, it became quite pleasant.

Strindberg curled up and went to sleep immediately.

I let the paraffin stove burn on a low light for half an hour to reduce the humidity in the tent.

Some hours after midnight—it was beginning to get light—I awoke to find Andrée kneeling by the flap of the tent, which he had half opened. He had taken off his jacket, and was pulling his thick woollen jersey over his head.

"Can't you sleep?" I asked.

"It's so damnably hot," he answered, over his shoulder. "Why aren't you asleep yourself?"

"It's not hot," I said. "You've got a temperature. And you woke me."

He was silent.

"Do you think I've been too aggressive?" I asked.

"Everyone's the right to be himself," he answered.

We spoke in low voices in order not to wake Strindberg.

"Are you ready to admit how crazy the whole balloon expedition was?" I asked. "Wrongly planned. Stupidly organized. Badly equipped. Doomed to failure from the outset. Even apart from the guide-ropes, and the fact that you fell into a panic at the start?"

"No," he said.

"You won't admit it?" I asked.

"No," he answered.

"That's where we meet, that's where we resemble each other," I said. "I wouldn't see the craziness of the whole expedition either."

He lay down on top of the sleeping-bag and rolled himself in a blanket. "It's confoundedly warm in the tent," he said.

"You've got a temperature," I said, and crawled out of the bag to close the flap of the tent.

After a few minutes he said: "Nobel, Alfred Nobel, was one of the biggest madmen I've ever met."

5

Five degrees below zero, strong north-north-westerly wind, heavy cloud-cover, visibility still poor.

We began to build our winter quarters up against the big projecting hummock of ice, so that we could make this one of the four walls of our hut.

Strindberg and I worked out a plan of the building. It was to be three and a half metres wide, and nearly six metres long, and was to have three rooms, or compartments: a store-room, a kitchen cum living-room, and, furthest in, a bedroom, not much larger in area than the sleeping-bag.

We agreed that it should have double outer-walls, separated by a cavity about a decimetre wide. This would naturally give us better insulation against the cold that awaited us.

We started building as soon as Strindberg had been appointed master builder.

Our building material—ice—was all round us in any quantity we needed, but we lacked the proper tools. We had only an axe (brass with a steel edge), and a little saw, an absurdly short little hand-saw.

What we needed were a couple of ordinary timber-saws, three feet long, the sort that foresters use.

"We ought to have had an ice-drill too," I said to Andrée. "Now that we're on the subject of things we haven't got. You'd have found it much easier to carry out your scientific investigations into the thickness of the ice if you'd had one.

"For that matter," I added, "for the first time since we started our wanderings I'm really and truly interested in how thick the ice is, the ice on which we're standing, I mean. I'd like to know how it's been formed, how homogeneous it is, and so forth."

By the afternoon Strindberg and I had succeeded in building the foundations up to a height of a few decimetres. This did at any rate enable us to see what the hut would look like, and gave us the chance of finding out if we had calculated the size of the various compartments correctly.

At this point our work was interrupted by a shot. Andrée had succeeded in surprising a seal and killing it with one shot, a high velocity bullet fired from the grooved barrel of Strindberg's double-barrelled gun. This had gone through its head just below and behind its eyes.

We rushed up to Andrée and dragged the seal in triumph to our camp.

It was no longer the case now, as it had been with the bears, of only taking the heart, the kidneys, and a few small pieces from the back, and of leaving the rest, the greater part, to the polar foxes, and the white vultures. The weight of our sledges was no longer a problem.

"Provisions for the coming three weeks," said Andrée.

We ate a hearty meal of seal steak fried in blubber. We ate more than we could manage, and the fat dribbled down the beards on our chins.

"Eight more seals," said Andrée, "and we shall have all the food we need to get through the winter."

"Meat, and fat, and albumin," I said. "But what about your carbohydrates? How do you think we shall manage without them?"

"The blood," he said. "Blood has a sweet taste. It must contain carbohydrates."

Strindberg and I went on with our house-building in a strong north-westerly wind and a falling temperature.

I found a frozen fresh-water puddle only thirty paces from our hut. I chopped a hole in the ice. This made our work easier as we were able to use small pieces of ice and snow, over which we poured water which rapidly froze, and produced a wall as hard and stable as if it had been built of bricks.

My foot improved, but Strindberg developed new boils on both his feet.

Andrée made several unsuccessful attempts to investigate the thickness of the ice. He collected a number of samples of clay and gravel which he dug out from the snow that covered the toroses. He even found a piece of rotten wood.

He put out a long-line in the open lead to the west of our floe, an absurd long-line, with bent pins for hooks and speck for bait. Of course he did not catch anything.

Once he fell over on the ice near the lead and remained lying on his back with his legs drawn up. We ran up to him, but he raised an arm to fend us off. "Only cramp," he said. "Don't touch me. It will soon pass off."

After a few minutes he was able to stretch out his legs, but he could not get up. We carried him up to the tent in spite of his protests.

"Will you have a dose of opium?" I asked.

He shook his head.

17 September was a great day. The sun was visible through the clouds for a while, and the bearings we took, which were pretty reliable, showed that, during the past six days and nights, we had drifted southwards at an average speed of not less than two kilometres an hour.

The visibility was not particularly good, but two hours later Andrée was able to report that he could see land a few degrees west of south.

It was not a hallucination.

An ice-clad island was clearly visible to the naked eye.

Strindberg and I had built up the walls of our hut to a height of half a metre and we stopped work for that day.

There was no doubt about it. For the first time for two months we were looking at dry land. We reckoned that it must be about two kilometres away.

The day had to be celebrated. I shot some gulls with a couple of bursts of shot.

The gulls were plucked, and fried in seal-oil. We allowed ourselves a little bread with butter and each had a mugful of sweet raspberry juice to drink.

"It must be New Iceland, between Spitzbergen and Franz Josef Land," said Andrée.

There was no possible alternative.

"We've drifted more than one degree of latitude," he said.

"Since when? How long has it taken us?"

Andrée burst out laughing. "We've drifted one degree of latitude," he said. "I don't care a damn how long it's taken us. But we've moved quickly, towards the south."

He woke me that night too. I must have become a light sleeper.

He had crawled out of the sleeping-bag, and was rubbing and massaging his thigh muscles, stretching out his legs, drawing them up again, and writhing about.

At last he relaxed, got to his knees, dug into the medicine chest, and swallowed something with a mug of melted water from the cooking-stove.

He then lay down on top of the sleeping-bag.

After a while I asked: "What's the matter?"

"It's warm."

"No, it's not warm. Have you a pain anywhere?"

"No," he answered.

"Perhaps you ought to take a little morphia or opium," I said.

"I can manage without medicine," he replied.

I lit my pipe.

"Listen," I said, "that business with the long-line and the bent pins. When I was a little boy I fished for river trout in Jämtland with a rod, sewing-cotton and bent pins for a line. But we three, we're grown men in the middle of the Arctic Ocean. We're not three children, we're three grown men.

"We've two old-fashioned smooth-bore Remingtons instead of two modern grooved repeaters. We've no fishing tackle, only one useless jig. We haven't even a net. We've only a home-made long-line, with bent pins for hooks, to put down in the richest fishing-ground in the world! Not even a net."

Andrée did not answer.

He was asleep. He was breathing far too rapidly, and through his mouth.

I spread one of the blankets over him.

6

18 September.

We slept late, and were woken by a somewhat unmusical blast on my hunting-horn, executed by Strindberg.

Andrée and I tumbled out of the tent.

Strindberg had fastened the Union Flag to the boat-hook and thrust it firmly into the ice. The flag was flapping in the light northerly breeze.

His call for three cheers for King Oscar was answered by hoarse hip hip hurrahs.

It was a solemn occasion, the twenty-fifth anniversary of the coronation of King Oscar.

Good weather, dry air, two degrees below zero, cloud cover pretty thin, and unusually high.

"I'm better on the violin than on the hunting-horn," said Strindberg.

We ate a solid breakfast of seal meat and weak coffee, so solid that we subsequently lay on the sleeping-bag for a couple of hours, drowsy, half asleep, incapable of doing anything.

Strindberg and I did not continue our work on the hut until the afternoon.

Andrée strolled round the floe, scratched up the snow, and tried in vain to measure the thickness of the ice by the open lead, which now lay north-east of our camp instead of to the west.

We finished the day with a meal that was a veritable feast.

Gulls and seal steaks. A strange soup made of Mellin's Food, Albert biscuits, and raspberry juice. "Nourishing and tasty," said Strindberg.

A bottle of port wine, Antonio de Ferrara, vintage 1834, given to the expedition by His Majesty King Oscar himself.

Andrée made a speech in the King's honour which we followed up by drinking his health. We then sang the National Anthem in unison, after which we each consumed two biscuits topped with a thick slice of cheese.

Just before midday Andrée had managed to shoot another seal. Food for yet another three or four weeks was his estimate.

The following day. Four degrees below zero, light northerly wind.

We drifted past the north-east tip of New Iceland at a distance of two kilometres at the most.

Strindberg and I went on energetically with our work on the hut.

Its walls rose. We laid blocks of ice one on top of the other, and used snow that we scratched together as mortar. Then we drenched the whole step by step with fresh water from the puddle I mentioned before.

The walls were firm and solid.

In the afternoon that prowling scientific investigator Andrée succeeded in shooting three more seals, one of them a big male.

Simple mathematics: we now had enough food to last us until the end of February.

We collected the seals' blood, some of it in a couple of empty tins, some of it in two linen bags. The blood oozed through the material at first, but rapidly froze into solid lumps.

"Not only meat, fat, and albumin," said Andrée. "We must also have carbohydrate, and that is to be found in blood."

After passing the north-east tip of New Iceland we drifted slowly westwards. We discussed several times whether we should try to land on the island but could not come to a unanimous decision.

It was quite obvious that we were moving south-westwards, and that we ought to have a good chance of reaching North East Land, Spitzbergen.

New Iceland was only a low, glacier-covered island in the Arctic Ocean.

Besides, our splendid erection on the floe was nearing completion. We were tired of our tent, covered as it was by a thick crust of ice both inside and out, big enough to lie in, but much too small to move about in.

7

Andrée managed to measure the thickness of our floe, and found that, disregarding the isolated large blocks, it was on an average something under one and a half metres thick.

"Are you satisfied?" I asked.

"Don't know," he answered.

In the afternoon something exceedingly worrying happened. Our primus stove went on strike, our primus stove, that had functioned perfectly and uncomplainingly ever since we had landed on the ice nine weeks earlier.

The flame spluttered and went out, was relighted, burnt for a few seconds, died down with a wheeze, went out, was relighted, only to go out again. We were unable to make our soup more than lukewarm.

I tried to make a train-oil lamp. We had plenty of seal-fat.

It is not altogether easy to make an effective train-oil lamp when you have neither materials nor tools, and when you know nothing about train-oil lamps. I failed.

Strindberg and I went on with the hut. The walls grew, froze as hard as stone, became as solid—I repeat—as if they had been built of brick. We were able to drag our seals into the entrance-room, still without its roof.

In the evening we had more trouble with the primus. The flame fluttered, shuddered, and went out, was relighted, went out again.

A polar bear suddenly appeared. He was discovered outside the opening of the tent by Strindberg. He and Andrée rushed out, stumbled over each other, and both scored a miss.

I brought the bear down with a nice shot in his chest and heart.

This was our twelfth bear since our landing, a plump, heavily-built male, with a fine thick coat.

We dragged him to our camp with shouts of joy. He weighed at least four hundred kilos, perhaps nearer a ton.

"We've made sure of the winter now," said Andrée.

Work on the hut was abandoned, and we devoted ourselves to flaying the polar bear. We removed his guts and put his heart, his kidneys, his liver, and his brains into our store-room, after we had thrown his lungs and his intestines to the birds.

8

We ought to have been pleased, almost happy, after the additions we had made to our larder during the past two days.

That evening we got involved in a violent discussion. It was heated and unreasonable.

The cause, our primus stove.

It failed us again when we tried to boil up our evening soup.

I directed the operation, Andrée fiddled with the cleansing needle, and Strindberg held out lighted matches. The flame burnt for a few seconds and then went out.

Strindberg said: "This is nonsense. We must change the burner."

Andrée answered: "Unfortunately all the spare parts were left behind on Danes Island."

Strindberg gave way to a surprisingly violent outburst of rage and fury.

I sat still, looked at him, and listened.

Andrée said nothing, bowed before the torrent of words and gave me a helpless, appealing look.

The situation was both simple and complicated.

We had no spare parts for the primus stove. They had been left behind on Danes Island.

Who the devil was to lay the blame, or take the blame?

9

The next day Strindberg shot yet another seal. I brought down six gulls with three bursts of shot.

Strindberg and I went on working at the hut. Andrée occupied himself by studying and analysing what he found in the stomach of Strindberg's seal.

He also carried out a new series of investigations into the thickness of our floe, and arrived at figures that varied between something under two metres and rather more than three.

We were now south of New Iceland and the ice was moving very slowly. It seemed as if we had got into a sort of backwater between two southward-moving currents that met below the island, south of the island.

There was a clash between Andrée and Strindberg over the Göransson cooking-apparatus.

"Why not use it?" asked Strindberg.

"It burns methylated spirit."

"Why not use methylated spirit?"

"Because we haven't any," answered Andrée. "Apart from a little tin that we need for warming up the primus."

"Two weeks ago we had a whole can of methylated spirit," said Strindberg.

"We may have had," answered Andrée. "but there's none left now. I don't know who's made away with it."

I had to use force to get Strindberg out of the tent and back to our house-building, our architectural creation of snow and ice. The wind abated, blew fluctuatingly from the south. The temperature rose. A slight drizzle fell on the days during which we finished our hut and laid a domed roof over its three rooms.

The nights grew progressively longer.

It was still not very cold, but we knew that the cold was drawing nearer.

We were all three very tired, in spite of the fact that we had recently been able to wear reasonably dry clothes, and had escaped any violent attacks of diarrhoea.

At night the clouds often lifted and a starry sky was fully visible.

"At night we can manage without sun-glasses," I said, "both Strindberg and I."

Andrée and I succeeded in getting the primus to work. We emptied it, poured in a drop of paraffin, shook it, emptied it, and filled it again. After that it gave no trouble. Some dirt had probably got into the tank, perhaps just a drop of water.

On 28 September, the eightieth day after our start from Danes Island, we moved into our magnificent ice-hut.

On the following morning Strindberg shot our thirteenth bear.

It was a splendid male, and we only dragged it back to our camp with great difficulty.

Andrée discovered that quite a large piece of ice had broken off the southern part of our floe which, according to him, was being squeezed against New Iceland. The fact that the sea between us and the island was covered with large ridges of pressure ice, from which came a constant rumble, punctuated by roars like thunder, seemed to prove that he was right.

The drizzle stopped, and the temperature sank below zero. The visibility improved slightly, but we were unable to take reliable bearings.

The next day we were still nearer the island, unless it was that the better visibility had led us to misjudge the distance. The temperature had fallen to ten degrees below zero. The sky was still covered by thick clouds.

Strindberg and I worked at strengthening the outer wall of our hut which we had christened 'The Home'. The fresh water, with which we sluiced the walls and the roof, rapidly turned to ice.

"A marble palace," said Strindberg.

We worked slowly and languidly, partly because we were tired, and partly because we had no reason to hurry. We had a whole winter before us.

After our midday meal Andrée went out to look at the floe.

Strindberg and I lay on the sleeping-bag, each smoking a pipe.

Under Andrée's inflatable pillow lay some of his personal belongings rolled in a woollen jersey. Among them was his diary. I took it out. It was the first time I had held it in my hand.

I moved nearer to the candle.

Strindberg watched me but said nothing.

I turned the pages of the diary.

"Just listen to this," I said. " '12 July, in the balloon after the start'. Listen. 'It's more than a little strange to be floating along up here above the Arctic Ocean. The first person who has ever floated here in a balloon.'

"Did you hear that, Strindberg. The first! We two obviously didn't count. 'How soon shall I'—he's changed his mind here and crossed out the 'I', put 'we' instead. 'How soon will other people follow our example?'

"And here, listen. 'I can't deny that feelings of pride have overmastered all of us.'

"He's been seized by feelings of pride, and they've overmastered you and me as well, Strindberg.

"And, 'We think that we can well face death having done what we have done.'

"Not bad, that," I said. "As early as the second day he was so proud of our thirty hours in the balloon that we were all three prepared to face death.

"What have you to say to that?" I asked.

Strindberg shook his head. He had nothing to say.

"He was prepared for the whole thing to fail from the very beginning. And after thirty hours—or was it thirty-two?—he thought that all of us, not only he, but all three of us, could die proudly."

"I've already read all that," said Strindberg. "A long time ago. I used to wake up at night, get hold of his diary and read it. That was in the good old days when the nights were light."

"It's a long time since you've stopped writing letters to Anna," I said.

"Yes," he answered.

Then added with a smile: "No point in your trying to read them on the quiet. You won't be able to. They're in shorthand."

After that we went out and got on with our work.

10

The next day, after our evening meal, we again discussed our position.

"We've a good hut," I said. "We've already got enough food to last us through the whole winter, and we shall certainly be able to shoot still more seals and bears.

"There are many things we haven't got," I said. "For instance, the candle we're now burning is my last but one. We shall soon find ourselves in a night that will last for months. I'm sure we shall solve the problem of light. I think we can make an oil-lamp out of the Göransson cooking-apparatus.

"There's a strong possibility that we shall survive the winter.

"But," I said, "we shall no longer have our sledges to pull. We shall no longer have hopeless marches that sap the goodness out of us.

"In our house, and with all our provisions, we shall have practically nothing to occupy us. Not just for a week, or a month, but for almost half a year.

"What are you trying to say?" asked Andrée.

"Bickering," said Strindberg.

"Bickering, yes, that's unavoidable."

"We must try to control ourselves," I said. "Try not to get too irritated, try not to annoy one another, try to avoid violent disputes. We shall have plenty of time to think, and I'm afraid that you in particular, Andrée, will have to hear many harsh truths about your insane plan to sail to the North Pole in a balloon."

"I never asked you to join me," said Andrée.

"There you have it," I said. "The beginning of a dispute that can easily develop into a quarrel.

"But we must control ourselves.

"We have our hut, we have our food, we must try to live through our winter on the ice calmly."

I I

Eight hours later, to the accompaniment of tremendous crashes and roars, our floe began to break up. Water forced its way into our bedroom. We scrambled out of the sleeping-bag, and out through the door.

It was morning. Severe cold, but thank goodness no wind.

We managed to pull the boat across to our floe with the grapnel and its rope. It proved exceedingly useful when we came to collect our equipment together.

What gave us most trouble were the carcasses of the two bears. These were lying close together on a floe so small that it could hardly bear their weight. They were split open but not cut up, and it was impossible to think of transporting them in the boat. Instead we towed them to the floe where our hut was and pulled them up on to it. Both Strindberg and I slipped and fell into the water.

The seals, the two that we had not yet put into our entrance-room, were easier to handle.

Strindberg and I changed into dry clothes. The water in our jackets and trousers had frozen solid, and we were in danger of tearing the cloth.

By evening we had managed to salvage practically all our belongings, and assemble them on what was left of the floe where our hut was.

The paraffin stove lit without a hitch, and we ate a substantial meal of seal-meat soup, an easy delicacy to prepare as, when we boiled it for a few minutes, the meat disintegrated and turned into a sort of gruel.

Both Strindberg and Andrée were troubled by boils on their feet and short attacks of cramp. For once I came off best.

We could not lie in our bedroom, the innermost compartment. The gable end hung in mid air, and water was washing in from a newly formed lead.

We spread out the sleeping-bag in the entrance-room, crept into it, and fell asleep immediately, before we had time to discuss the events of the day.

We woke late the following day, October 3rd. The leads had closed again during the night, but in spite of the cold the ice had not frozen together. What remained of our floe was surrounded by low hummocks of pressure ice, made up of small blocks. These slowly rose and fell, and rose again as the sea water forced its way up the crevices between them.

Our floe was now pear-shaped, and furthest out on the pointed end lay our dwelling. The back gable hung over pressure ice that was much broken up and wet. A few metres from the other gable and the entrance there was another low and slightly undulating toros. The big hummock, previously mentioned, which formed the long wall on the far side, was more than a man's height, and probably went down to a depth of at least fifteen, and possibly eighteen metres.

The rest of the floe was almost circular, and at least thirty steps in diameter.

The temperature had fallen to under ten degrees below zero. The wind was light and south-easterly. The clouds were heavy, but under them the visibility was quite good.

Andrée thought we ought to begin to build another hut in the middle of the floe.

"We can't trust the old one any longer," he said. "Sooner or later the hummock will come adrift from the floe, shoot up into the air, come crashing down, and demolish the hut completely.

"The hummock is large," he said, "but we see only about a tenth of it. The rest is under water. I don't know," he said, "but I guess that it's a tremendous pillar of ice which has been kept permanently upright by being frozen to a large floe. Now that floe has been crushed to pieces. In a couple of hours, or a couple of days, the pillar of ice will come loose. It will heave itself out of the water and topple over with a force of which we can have no conception."

"It probably weighs between a hundred and fifty and two hundred tons," said Strindberg.

"So we must build another hut as near to the centre of the floe as possible," said Andrée.

I put up the tent again, and spread out the sleeping-bag on its ice-covered ground-sheet.

We emptied 'The Home' of all our belongings. Some we put in the tent, the rest we collected in a heap by the entrance, and covered them over with a piece of varnished silk.

Strindberg had a violent attack of diarrhoea. When it was over Andrée and I helped him into the tent, and into the sleeping-bag.

He fell asleep immediately. Exhaustion is sometimes a better tranquillizer than opium and morphia together.

Andrée boiled up some seal-meat soup and a meagre ration of coffee.

I pulled all our sledges close to the tent, and placed our boat in its proper position on mine. The boat was surprisingly heavy. It was covered with a thick crust of ice both inside and out.

I walked round the remnant of our floe and collected up all the oddments that were still scattered about.

I searched 'The Home'. Nothing was left in it, either on the floor or in recesses.

We ate seal-meat soup, and drank coffee, Andrée and I.

Darkness and evening had already fallen. The days were now shorter than the nights. The clouds lifted. We saw the stars, and the faint, flickering of the northern lights.

I lit a candle.

"My last," I said. "We had half a candle left from yesterday evening, but it must have got trampled into the snow and ice."

"Let us discuss the matter sensibly," I said.

"I've always found sensible discussion most tempting," he answered.

"We've two alternatives," I said.

"They are?"

"One is to stay on the ice," I answered.

"The other: to go ashore on New Iceland."

*   *   *

Andrée thought for a while.

"The disadvantages of staying on the ice and building a new hut is that the ice may break up again," he said. "The advantage of staying on the ice is that we shall probably drift even further south, or south-west, and be able to go ashore on Spitzbergen.

"The disadvantage of pitching our camp on New Iceland is that once there we shall have to stay there. For the whole winter. And we don't know if we shall be able to make our way across the pack ice in the spring."

"There's also another disadvantage about staying on the ice," I said.

"What's that?"

"It took us, Strindberg and me, two weeks to build our ice hut. An excellent hut of ice and snow with two rooms and a kitchen. That hut no longer exists, except as a ruin. Two weeks."

"I know."

"What I'm saying is that you mustn't count on our spending another two weeks building a new hut on a floe that's two metres in diameter. A floe that we don't trust, and which may be crushed into small blocks of ice tomorrow or the day after.

"Go to sleep, Andrée. Think it over.

"Tomorrow you'll have to take yet another decision."

12

We had drifted on and were near the south-western tip of New Iceland. We could see a long, dark stretch of shore. So the glacier did not cover the whole island. There was some bare ground.

The morning was cold. A light wind and, as on previous occasions, good visibility under the heavy cloud-cover.

We were woken by Strindberg who had fried some bear steaks

373

and made cocoa, with which we ate some of the once sodden biscuits.

"Andrée wants us to stay on the ice," I said. "Build a new hut which he hopes will drift towards Spitzbergen.

"I, on the other hand, think we should go ashore on the island, and take up winter quarters on dry land."

Strindberg smiled at us.

"Don't you realize that the decision rests with you?" I said. "If you say the ice, the ice it will be. If you say New Iceland, then New Iceland it will be. Plain, straightforward democracy.

"Do you understand?"

"Devil take you, of course I understand," said Strindberg.

He leant against Andrée and put one of his hands on his shoulder.

"I'm not afraid to die," he said. "Some months ago I was—afraid to die. But not now. I would like someone to find my body. Some time in the future, that is. If we stay on the ice no one will ever find what remains of us.

"Forgive me, dear friend," he said, with his hand on Andrée's shoulder. "I vote that we go ashore on New Iceland.

"I'm not afraid to die," he repeated. "A couple of months ago perhaps I was. Not now. But I want to die on dry land, not on a drifting floe."

13

We loaded everything we possessed on to the sledges and began to pull them towards New Iceland. Andrée and Strindberg had very little strength left, and we had to do as we had done before, pull one sledge at a time and go back for the others.

The ridges of pressure ice between us and the shore were the most difficult we had ever had to force. The distance was not great, only a few kilometres. But it was two days before we finally got all three sledges on to the bare gravelly shore of the island.

Andrée and I pitched the tent on dry ground, on coarse gravel, which did not make a good floor.

We ate bread, and seal-meat soup. "Easily prepared," I said.

"What's the time?" asked Andrée. "And the date?"

"I haven't kept my meteorological journal these past few days," I said. "Or the past two days. Judging by the light it must be evening, and it's probably Tuesday, 5 October. It might be Wednesday."

Strindberg ate very little. He curled up in the sleeping-bag with his legs drawn up very high, and fell asleep. He breathed quickly and in gasps.

The next day I was woken because a strong north wind was blowing down the tent.

I roused my companions.

In spite of the fierce wind and whirling snow we had to get out of the tent, re-erect it, and adjust the guy-ropes with the greatest possible care.

Not much snow was falling, but the wind was no less strong for that and frightfully cold. Strindberg was seized by horrible cramp in his legs and stomach. We gave him some hot coffee and a dose of opium.

In the afternoon, after the wind had abated somewhat, Andrée and I went out on a short tour of reconnaissance.

There was plenty of drift-wood along the shore. Apart from that New Iceland had nothing to recommend it as a place in which to spend the winter.

In the gravel along the shore there were hardly any stones bigger than a clenched fist. It was therefore useless as building material.

We decided that we must move our tent higher up the shore, close to a low wall of rock.

This move was accomplished the following day.

We pitched our tent in the shelter of the low rock, and used pieces of drift-wood and walrus bones to hold down the ground-sheet.

The efforts it cost us to drag our sledges up to the neighbourhood of the tent were almost ridiculously great.

"The aurora gives a poor light," said Andrée, "and no warmth whatever."

The nights had grown longer.

We made up our minds that we would build an igloo over our tent as soon as enough snow had fallen to give us something to build with.

On the night of 8 October the wind again became very strong. The ice boomed and thundered. We listened, but it no longer mattered to us. We were on dry land.

"What if we'd still been on your damnable little floe!" said Strindberg.

The primus stove again gave us a certain amount of trouble, and I renewed my efforts to turn the Göransson cooking-apparatus into a train-oil lamp, that would be a source of both light and heat.

When the wind abated a little we made a short expedition up on to the glacier, which was considerably higher than we had supposed.

The sky was covered by heavy, grey clouds, but far away to the west we could see what we thought must be the mountains of Spitzbergen.

"When spring starts," said Andrée, "as soon as spring starts, we'll make our way there. Across the pack ice while it's still in the grip of the winter frost."

We waited for snow with which to build our igloo.

Andrée and I cut up the last bears we had shot, and the seals.

"Food for more than half a year," he said.

Strindberg did not come with us up the glacier. He did not help us to cut up our booty. He stayed where he was in the sleeping-bag. He would not have anything to eat, and he talked a great deal.

"In the spring, while the sea is still frozen, we'll make our way over to Spitzbergen," said Andrée.

14

Strindberg complained of pains in his stomach and of cramp in his arms and legs.

"This cramp," said Andrée. "I don't understand it.

"Why should we suffer from cramp?"

"No previous arctic expedition has had this to contend with," said Strindberg. "Scurvy, but not cramp. And diarrhoea."

And then there were the boils. On both his feet, on one arm, on his neck, his upper lip, close to his eyes and his ears. They were small boils, but troublesome.

One morning—probably of Sunday 10 October—Strindberg called to us. It was quite a pleasant day of moderate cold and little wind. Andrée and I were busy collecting drift-wood for future use.

We crept in through the opening of the tent.

"Are you there?" said Strindberg. "I can hear, but I can't see."

"Both here," I said.

"Snow?" he asked.

"No," I answered, "still not enough to build an igloo with."

"Andrée," he said, "are you there?"

Andrée did not answer.

"What the hell drove you to set out on this journey?" asked Strindberg.

He smiled broadly for a few seconds with his eyes shut, coughed violently, and then ceased to breathe.

His face relaxed, his mouth and his eyes fell half open.

Andrée bent over him, laid his ear to his mouth, while at the same time he tried to find the pulse in one of his wrists.

"He's dead," said Andrée.

Of course Strindberg was dead. That half-open mouth, those half-open eyes.

It was afternoon before we carried him out of the tent, dragged his body up to a cleft in the wall of rock, twenty-five or thirty steps.

Andrée took charge of his chronometers, his purse, and some other small articles. I stuffed his notebook into one of my inside pockets.

"He's the first dead person I've seen," I said. "In the whole of my life."

"I find it hard to realize that it's really he," said Andrée.

"No wonder," I said. "Not an elegant young scholar, but a very thin man with matted hair and a dark beard."

We covered Nils Strindberg's body with stones that we carried up from the shore to his burial place in the rock. We were very weary. We carried, walked backwards and forwards until darkness fell.

"A poor grave," said Andrée.

"Like the graves of the dead whalers on Dutch Point, and Danes Island," I said.

15

A day of snow-fall.

Andrée and I began to build a little wall, the foundations of an igloo, round our tent.

To reinforce the snow with ice I carried up water from the shore in a saucepan. It was a slow business.

"Like the job the cabbies were having building their snow hut beside the pump in Brunkebergstorg, the first time we met," I said.

"We ought to build a cairn by Strindberg's grave," said Andrée. "Put up something to remember him by."

"Of course.

"But we must finish our winter quarters first, our igloo built round and over our tent.

"This isn't cynicism," I said, "just a simple fact. As a result of Strindberg's death our stocks of food have risen by thirty per cent."

"Not a simple fact," said Andrée, "pure cynicism."

Cynicism? Ruthless candour?

"Between you and me," I said, "there's only one cynicism that's worth discussing. You know what I'm referring to?"

"Naturally," he answered.

"That you could bring yourself to let us embark on an undertaking that you knew was doomed to fail."

We ate a late supper; fried bear's meat, raspberry juice, two slices of bread and liver paste, weak coffee.

It was dark in the tent. The clouds had lifted. Piercingly bright stars, faintly fluttering aurora. The arctic winter was already upon us.

I found it hard to remember the warm sunshine of only a few weeks earlier, not merely warm, but warm enough to make you hot.

"I was forced to," said Andrée.

"Forced?"

"I had no choice, we had to start."

"You had no choice. We had to start."

16

Two days of severe cold and clear skies. Our theodolite was outside in the boat, and it never occurred to either of us to try to take more exact bearings.

Most of the time we lay on our backs in the tent. We took a few short walks, collected a little drift-wood.

Andrée wrapped his first diary in shoe-grass, a sort of sedge, and protected it still further by wrapping it in a woollen jersey.

He began a second diary.

A rising temperature, southerly wind, and heavy snow-fall.

We went on building our igloo. Collected snow with our hands,

379

laid it on top of the foundations already there, drenched it with sea water.

Our progress was slow. We had only our hands, no spades or shovels.

Andrée had two violent attacks of diarrhoea.

"Not only cramp," I said, "but also this damnable diarrhoea."

"We all know about scurvy. But what about this cramp? This diarrhoea? And these peculiar boils?"

Andrée stripped to his skin that evening and studied his body carefully. "Three small boils," he said. "One on my instep, one in my groin, and one under my right arm."

"And two little ones on your back," I said.

He dressed again and complained that it was far too hot in the tent.

"It's not hot," I answered. "You're feverish."

"Not only cramp, diarrhoea, and boils, but also fever."

A polar bear suddenly appeared close to our camp, and I shot at him in the dark with my Remington. I did not hit him, but he was frightened and ran away.

Our other Remington and the double-barrelled gun lay in the boat on my sledge.

17

It snowed a little and I went on working at the igloo. Scraped the snow together with my hands, carried it to our low wall, increased its height infinitely slowly, drenched it with sea water.

The temperature had again begun to fall. The snow was dry and powdery.

Andrée lay in the sleeping-bag.

He called to me a couple of times, and I had to massage the muscles of his legs to ease the cramp.

He complained of the heat. The temperature in the tent was two or three degrees below zero.

"We must put up a cairn beside Strindberg's grave," he said.

"When the igloo is finished," I answered.

"He died without pain."

"He even smiled," I said.

I went on with the infinitely slow work of building the wall of the igloo. It had taken Strindberg and me fourteen days to build our big hut on the floe. The new hut would be considerably smaller, but much less snow and ice were available. I thought it was senseless to go down to the shore and chop loose and drag up heavy blocks of ice.

I reckoned that it would take me at least three weeks to finish the work.

"Fortunate that there's plenty of drift-wood," I said to Andrée, during a pause for rest. "It will be useful for making the roof."

"I can't do anything now," he said, "but in a couple of days I shall be able to help you."

"That's all right," I said.

"What day is it today?" he asked. "What's the date?"

"Don't know exactly," I answered. "12th, 13th, 14th October, or thereabouts."

The days grew noticeably shorter.

"Fever, cramp, diarrhoea," said Andrée. "But in a few days, when the fever and the cramp are better, we'll build the igloo together. We'll make the roof of drift-wood and cover it with snow."

At night, clear skies, aurora, deepening cold.

"Weak," said Andrée one morning. "To lie here and feel your weakness running out. Your strength running out, I mean."

He was lying on top of the sleeping-bag wrapped in two blankets, both worn, and stiff with ice.

"That confounded whiteness," he said. "That continuous light without any shadow."

"The nights are longer than the days," I said. "At this moment it is morning."

"Get on with the igloo," he said, "that's what matters."

He added: "I don't want any food, just a scoopful of water."

I gave him water out of an aluminium tin. I had to raise him by his shoulders before he could drink. His back felt thin and bony under his clothes.

"Are you in pain?" I asked.

"Not any longer," he answered.

Then he said, "Aren't you going back to your work?"

"I'll stay a bit longer," I said.

I dozed off for an hour or two. When I woke Andrée was lying quite still. He was not breathing, and he did not answer my questions. One eye was still tightly closed. The other was open. The cornea had already had time to dry.

I looked at him for a long time. He was an old man, a very old man, with his grey beard and his wasted body.

It was several weeks since I had looked at my own face in the mirror.

The temperature had fallen to ten degrees below zero. I took a short walk round our camp. It was good to move my legs a bit. The boat on my sledge was still almost fully loaded.

I thought over my situation, went over it again and again. I had food in plenty, more than enough to last me through the winter. But my plight was not a question of food and sustenance, it was a question of loneliness.

I fastened on a black rosette, and laughed at myself as I did so.

No, not loneliness. Better: no one with whom to share.

The primus stove functioned perfectly. I boiled up a couple of mugfuls of coffee, strong coffee. There was no point in using it sparingly.

After I had put out the primus stove I opened the whole of the gable end of the tent.

I took off my boots and crept into the sleeping-bag. It was thin and worn, and the underside had lost almost all its hair.

Six capsules of opium and eight capsules of morphia. I swallowed

382

them down one by one with a couple of gulps of hot coffee. After that I emptied two glass tubes from our medicine chest, one contained opium, the other morphia. The glass tubes were carefully packed in wooden tubes, and were quite undamaged. I drank a few more gulps of water, no, not water, strong hot coffee.

It was already dusk, evening. Twelve degrees of frost.

The chill from the floor and from the opening of the tent felt refreshing. Sleep began to spread through my body, through my arms and my legs.

I lay on my side near to Andrée. His beard was grey. He was an old man.

I was still young.

Per Olof Sundman was born in Vaxholm, Sweden, in 1922. Formerly a member of Sweden's Parliament and currently a member of the Swedish Academy, he is the author of numerous other works of both fiction and nonfiction. *The Flight of the Eagle* has received several awards, including the Nordic Council's Prize for Literature in 1968.